CONNECDEAD

CONNECDEAD

<a Jake Lydon mystery>

JOHN OWENS

OTTAWA
PRESS AND
PUBLISHING

ottawapressandpublishing.com

ISBN (pbk.) 978-1-988437-10-1
ISBN (EPUB) 978-1-988437-11-8
ISBN (MOBI) 978-1-988437-12-5

Cover design: Glenn Torresan
Page design: Magdalene Carson

WARNING:

The following tale does not include a major character who is physically awesome and God-fearing. Nor will dear readers find a reformed drinker and/or smoker who sometimes flashes back to Korea/Vietnam/ Desert Storm/Iraqi Freedom and so on where he acquired small arms expertise and some ease with killing people. Lots of people.

Sorry.

H ere's a fact: there's nothing like driving for hours through flat, low scrub fuck-allness to make you focus and give you the time and space to reconstruct events that have overtaken you.

Particularly when someone's trying to kill you and you have no idea why.

I say this with complete confidence as I hurtle into desert nothingness along Highway 80, somewhere east of Reno and bound for the Canadian border.

Bound for what? I ask myself.

Having survived one murder attempt, smart money says I'll have to face another.

You play the story backwards and forward, filling in the details, trying to connect the dots that might explain how, in the name of our living lord, sweet bleeding Jesus, you are where you are.

The problem, of course, is that life outside of most movies isn't a string of action sequences. The story isn't propelled; it lurches and meanders, extending back beyond the catalogue of recent events, shading in background and unearthing motivations that eventually collide like those eighty car pile-ups on fog-bound freeways.

But somewhere in the story of my last few weeks is a reason.

I wouldn't mind knowing what it is.

Even if finding out likely won't change a goddamned thing as time runs out on me.

And while I may not have developed a full-on rage against the dying of the light, I'm mightily pissed off by it.

PART ONE

BACK THEN

<**CHAPTER ONE**>

I honestly don't know why Alistair MacNeil's death struck me so hard. But one thing's true: if it hadn't, then none of the shit that followed would have happened.

It was too easy to say that it was only because I'd spent a huge chunk of my alleged career working for him, that he'd made me a goodly amount of money, an amount that these many years later has, more or less, continued to maintain me.

I genuinely liked the guy. But it's not that I was particularly close to him, not that I knew of his death before the media did.

He was famous enough to get a news story, not just a family-financed obit.

Besides just the facts, ma'am—aged 76, born Moncton, New Brunswick, died Toronto; natural causes; two law degrees, owner of numerous technology companies—the online story in the *Globe* covered some of the highlights and most of the lowlights of his business CV.

I was there to witness a bunch of the highlights, almost fifteen years of them, at a time when I and everyone else around him had a real *Bonfire of the Vanities*-type of life. Amongst ourselves, we well-paid minions had a general guideline: the plane you arrived in had to be about the same size or smaller than the car that picked you up on the tarmac.

In the mid- to late-80s, there was a constant series of financial road shows that I had to oversee as the Vice President of Corporate Communications for MacNeil's Montrose Technologies. My title impressed even me during my hubris years but, truth be told, I was more or less a roadie overseeing the A/V equipment and logistics while drenching reporters with pap in San Francisco, New York, Chicago, Boston, London. Raising tens of millions, then hundreds of millions over the decade as the deals got bigger and bigger.

Other than a bad case of road ass, I got rich—in my terms anyway. A million bucks or so on stocks, mostly anything that MacNeil had touched—but always after he touched it. I bought and sold on my own, real tidy profits. All legit. When MacNeil would tell me about the next quarterly results or an upcoming acquisition, he'd finish the terse commentary with "And of course, you can't buy or sell until it's announced." And I never did. I swear.

He was scrupulous about that; insider trading by anyone made him crazy and he wouldn't hesitate to turn in his own people to regulators. Actually, he was scrupulous about a lot of other things that had nothing directly to do with business.

That's one of the reasons I liked him although he was not an instantly likable man. Personally and through the company, he was a huge donor to the United Way and a bunch of other charities but refused publicity of any kind. He hated to see women subjected to any kind of abuse or discrimination. His companies were forbidden to deal with South Africa until apartheid went away. Ditto for Cuba—although I know he was stiffed by Castro over a shipload of recycled paper from one of his many companies—so that may have had some influence on his anti-Communism stance.

MacNeil got real rich partly by thinking of something great and partly by putting money into people who were thinking of something great. Analysts and reporters called him a gambler but I knew he only bet on what, for the moment, were sure things. Variously described as industrialist, tycoon, magnate, he was just, by far, the brightest human being I've ever known, a veritable brain in a bell jar. He was *always* the smartest guy in the room, even if that room were to be Carnegie Hall hosting a MENSA conference.

But that's not why I liked him. It's because he didn't care if I liked him or if anybody else—I bet his family included—liked him. How liberating is that?

As far as I could ever figure, he also didn't much care about the wealth he had. This money-making thing was only his way to keep score with what really mattered to him: cutting a deal.

I once watched him negotiate with a parking lot attendant ten minutes before the cheaper evening rates kicked in. I can still see the exasperated look on the attendant's face, him shaking his head as he accepted the bargained-for price while, no doubt, thinking, "I came all the way from Nigeria to get beat for five bucks by a guy in a huge Mercedes?"

People made and lost piles of money with him—Alistair, not the parking lot attendant—on the stock market. Whatever the outcome, it elicited neither sympathy nor pride from him. As he told me: "Jake, we already have their money. They're big boys and they gambled on making more. Sometimes you lose. We haven't lied to them."

And I have also never lost sight of the fact that he gave careers to thousands of people, me included.

Not a lot of people either survived or wanted to survive working fifteen years for him. I did. Most likely because I am the personification of Newton's very first law of physics: "An object at rest will remain at rest unless acted on by an unbalanced force." I mean, it *is* the Law, for Christ's sakes. Plus, I came to fill a somewhat useful role. In exchange for all the gifts given him, Alistair was missing the humanity gene. He just couldn't understand why people let emotions and petty feuds and all the other things that make us not computers determine what they did when logic clearly dictated they ought to do the opposite.

So Alistair would use me as a sort of human bomb-sniffing dog. For all the gifts I hadn't been given, I usually was able to spot a bullshit artist within about five minutes of conversation. He'd send me in to talk to prospective senior hires. Sometimes he'd take my on-the-spot advice; sometimes he wouldn't. He'd get quite pissed off if I were merciless about a potential vice-president in the making when he had already made up his considerable mind to hire him. After the guy (please, back then, it was *always* a guy) didn't pan out—as invariably happened—I was smart enough to resist saying "I told you so."

I think he liked the fact that I was pretty quick on my feet when it came to reporters and pissed-off investors. And I know I amused him from time to time. For his fiftieth birthday, I had commissioned a limited edition T-shirt which read:

The Two Simple Rules of Life:
1) Don't shower with small appliances.
2) Don't fuck with Alistair MacNeil.

He smiled, but looked instantly embarrassed when I unveiled it at his party. Years later, when he was in the middle of a proxy fight, he marched into my office, ostensibly to discuss our tactics regarding the guy leading the board membership brawl against him.

"Medium. I think he's a medium," he said.

"What?"

"His T-shirt size. Send him one."

Then he marched out.

For reasons known only to God (who doesn't exist) and psychiatrists (whom I won't ever go to), I am compelled to push stuff, to cross the line. And Alistair let me which, looking back, was both pretty unusual and pretty swell of him.

Here's a sterling example of how he indulged my penchant for juvenile behaviour. I'd always let my hair grow to the point that it even bothered me in its unruliness. For no other reason than to watch him slip a ten out of his worn wallet and tell me to get it cut.

The fact that I even got hired in the first place was also proof of Alistair's contrary view of things. I had absolutely no affinity for, or understanding of, what most of his companies did. I am a techno-moron; I say that with neither pride nor disgust. It's just a fact, a state of affairs that I see no reason to change.

I have never owned a cell phone, for example. And I never will. There are estimates that suggest 95% of humanity will have one within the next twenty years. I figure soon after that, if I live that long, I'll have a legitimate shot at being the last person on earth without one. I reckon it'll come down to me and a stubborn teenager living in a yurt in Outer Mongolia. And I like my chances.

Alistair's succinct reasoning behind offering me a job: "You're an idiot about these things. If our people can explain it to you, I'm betting you can explain it to other idiots."

He worked me like crazy. And I let him. The 60- or 70-hour weeks became completely normal to me—although not to my wife. Work hard, make good money, drink. Repeat.

In other words, show me a rut and I'll climb into it. Like I said, it's positively Newtonian.

It was an unlikely rut to climb into. A post-graduate degree in English lit with a couple of years teaching high school in the Bahamas and a couple more with a brand name charity and I wind up doing PR and marketing for a conglomeration of nine relatively small companies doing everything from business software to computerized mapmaking to big custom computer systems. Incongruously, two of his companies made paper and packaging. All these companies became relatively large over the decade and a half I was with him. Three of them were publicly-traded; the other six were 100% MacNeil-owned. Montrose Technologies was his holding company, the one that stroked my progressively larger pay cheques.

But everything has a limit; everything ends, (except *Seinfeld* re-runs). There are only so many shaves in a razor or laughs in a relationship, so many clicks in a garage door-opener or high notes in a public career.

My expiration date with Montrose was reached when the giant telco putting millions into MacNeil's holding company stipulated, among many, many other things, that I be whacked. Everyone could be all grand about the reasoning for me getting two behind the ear—differing visions of PR and public communications, inflexibility over new corporate communications techniques and such—but I'm thinkin' that me calling their PR slut a PR slut didn't help my prospects.

Alistair was pretty shaken up when he had to fire me. He even told me how much doing the deed was upsetting him *while* he was doing it. I pointed out that perhaps it was a little tougher on me.

He wanted to have me escorted out of the building that day, lest all sorts of proprietary knowledge accompany me.

"Aww, for fuck's sake, Al," I said, "do you really think, after fifteen fucking years, I'm going to plunder the company secrets? Give me a month to get my stuff cleaned up, will ya?"

He did and so, for thirty days after the public announcement, I was dead man walking. During that time, I got some job offers and was stalked by a few headhunting firms. As flattering as this was to my zeppelin-sized ego, I determined that, at the ripe old age of 42, I wasn't ever going to work for anybody again.

I set up my own business, mostly thinking and writing for other people. Speeches, ghost-written articles, communication plans, media training and so on. This freelancing let me work where and when I wanted to as long as I had Internet service.

I claim no genius in anything I've ever done—personally or professionally. Here's the sum total of my communications wisdom:

#1: Tell the truth.
#2: When you can't, shut the fuck up.
#3: Answer the questions you *know* the reader has.

That's it.

Oh, and #4: Drink with reporters as often as you can. And I understand that #4 has sadly gone the way of rotary phones.

I also scored a monthly column in a middling technology magazine called *Tech View* in which I got to rant about how companies ought to look and act under the public spotlight. It provided me some notoriety, some new clients and a whole lot of cynicism because every one of these new customers started out insisting they wanted my largely unconventional thinking which, I learned, was a code phrase for no, they didn't.

This column—entitled Jake's Take—lasted almost two years, but never really took off. I liked to think that its trajectory could be traced as starting out a "been there/done that" professional providing some useful tips on PR and such, then descending into a tech version of St. John howling in the desert. In reality, its arc was no doubt closer to Neil Young's priceless introduction of *Don't Let It Bring You Down* on CSNY's *4 Way Street*: "It sorta starts off real slow and then fizzles out altogether."

To their credit, the magazine fired me. Sorry, they "decided to go in a new direction" and my fifteen seconds were up. Gloria's not feeling well but on the move, as the ol' Romans would say.

My ramblings gave me enough to live pretty well, not crack open the family nest egg and they let me slide into a figurative and literal wilderness.

I own a hovel and almost four acres (don't ask me the metric equivalent) on a point jutting into Mississauga Lake about two hours northeast of Toronto. It's a three-season cottage bought for peanuts twenty years ago when the shoreline was devoid of houses and I was making a six-figure salary and eyeing eventual early retirement. Beth, my wife at the time, wanted a year-round place but I resisted. Why three-season? Because it's cheaper and because you couldn't live through a Canadian winter in it unless you were prepared to go all pioneer. I'm not one for roughing it in the bush—roughing it anywhere really—so, in retirement, it would force a months-long southern trip on us, probably to Mexico or the Dominican.

In the meantime, our daughter, Halley, would have a swell place to be a kid until she wasn't a kid anymore, when she reached an age where, I anticipated, the idea of spending weekends and summers with her parents in the forested middle of fucking nowhere would make her skin crawl.

Beth and I split our time between our standard-issue pleasant home in the Toronto 'burbs and the bush. Over the years, we renovated our rustic-as-hell log cottage, built and acquired and planted all sorts of stuff and created a place that was pretty much the ideal we had in my mind. If not perfect, my life—our life—was going to be the next best thing as we slipped into dotage wearing Tilley hats and being able to use the Latin names for all our plants. Real *On Golden Pond* stuff, except Beth called me, "you old shit."

But then, fifteen years ago, my wife went and died. Fast and vicious ovarian cancer.

With our best-laid plans gone way the fuck awry, my life came to a standstill and then started reversing itself. Since then I've been shedding, paring down. Most of my clients went first, replaced by tequila and a general and more-pronounced-than-usual nastiness. Things that broke or wore out weren't replaced; food became little more than fuel.

When we weren't submerged in our own unlit, sense-deprived, altered-state of grief, Halley and I propped each other pretty well, I guess. You can never know for sure. At the age of thirteen, her childhood had come to a screeching halt and wasn't ever coming back, which was hardly fair to the bug's-ear cute and previously smiley kid.

To the best of my knowledge neither of us ever asked "Why me, Lord?" Speaking only for myself, this was due to the fact that I don't believe there is a Lord and because I have always suspected that the uncaring universe's even-handed answer would be: "Why *not* you, asshole?"

I kept the house in Toronto for four years after Beth died, until Halley graduated from high school and went off to university in British Columbia—in criminology no less—and I slunk off to live full-time at the cottage.

Our contact is infrequent, warm and, I guess, fairly odd.

So now both my workload and my inventory of human relations and possessions are pretty slim. A bunch of books, a closetful of Hawaiian shirts—gaudy souvenirs of every Caribbean vacation Beth and I ever took—and a thirteen-year-old Pontiac Vibe that I sometimes talk to.

Aquatically, I've got a fleet consisting of canoe that's spent most of the last fifteen years lying upside down on the shore of the lake and an ancient 14-foot aluminum fishing boat whose unpredictable 5hp motor exists only to drive me crazy.

What else? Well, I do have a ridiculously large television which takes up an inordinate amount of space in my small living room. It's more than ten years old and no one would ever accuse it of being a smart or even a marginally intelligent TV. And I have a shitty seven-year-old laptop.

In one of the several million ironies populating my life, I loathe—truly loathe—the idea of being robbed even though I have nothing anybody wants. Of course the guy breaking and entering won't know that until after he's broken and entered. I have toyed with the idea of putting a sign up over the front door: "There is fuck-all inside this house. Seriously. Go be a thieving fucktard somewhere else."

Most of the break-ins up here happen during the winter when the young lads on snowmobiles (please, they're *always* young lads) raid remote cottages to take anything their obscenely noisy sleds can carry. Usually booze.

So Carl and I have this immensely enjoyable habit of "closing up the cottage" for the winter by drinking every ounce of alcohol in the place before I leave. Sometimes that can take days but we're gamers.

Carl's this maybe 75-year-old guy who has lived on the lake most of his life. He, quite literally, lives *on* the lake, on a small island about a hundred yards from the shore. He's my nearest neighbour. I can see the island but not his house from my picture window. His house is surrounded by huge spruce or pine or whatever the fuck trees that you're not allowed to cut down anymore. Somehow, he and they find a way to exist on what amounts to a big granite rock rising out of the water.

When he wants to come to the "mainland", he paddles his canoe or putt-putts over in his little fishing boat with a 5hp motor and docks at my place where he keeps his old F-150 pick-up. A lot of the time, Carl swims to my shore. I marvel at his muscular strokes slicing the water as I hurl pine cones at him.

I get accused a lot—mostly by me—of being bone lazy. But Carl is so laid back he makes me look like a coked-up Chihuahua. When he has to, Carl can work like a madman doing all sorts of outdoorsy things like trapping and cutting firewood for sale, as well as fixing things for morons like me who have moved to the lake full-time and who can't and won't ever be able to fix things. All these cash-on-the-dash chores keep him self-sufficient and in remarkable shape. He's also quite the physical presence; I'm six feet tall—well, I used to be, before age started compressing me—and I look up to Carl who's at least 6'5." And don't ask me the metric equivalent of that; no one knows the metric equivalent of that.

Most of the time, Carl has a completely chill view of the world and his place in it. His tanned, wrinkled face usually sports the hint of a bemused grin.

Carl and I have a delicately balanced symbiotic relationship: I go fishing with him and he goes drinking with me. The fishing part bores me stiff except we've rigged up a fake gas can to hide a small beer keg that dispenses frothy goodness while we wait around to kill something that's innocently, stupidly swimming below us. We engage in this subterfuge because the provincial government we live under decided years ago that alcohol and boating don't mix which, as any boater or drunk knows, is the exact opposite of the truth.

We never venture away from our little lake. And we never venture past the Angler Arms, an old-time, cottage country bar and restaurant about a half mile from my place. The place has honey-coloured log walls festooned with stuffed trout and bass and novelty signs saying shit like "Keep it reel" or "Fishful Thinking."

The joint—and it is an archetypal joint—also has a great deck overlooking the water and a great waitress named, I swear, Carla overlooking us. Carla smokes with us sometime even though the provincial government we live under has decided that smoking outdoors on an empty restaurant patio on private property represents a plague-like threat somewhat akin to those mustard gas attacks in Double-U, Double-U One.

Carl and I refer to our outings to the Angler Arms as "going to AA." After all this time, I still find that pretty funny.

We are scrupulous in our record-keeping of who bought the last round, so much so that, after ten years and thousands of bottles of beer together, I think I owe him for two pints. He says three, but he can go fuck himself.

Lest anyone get the idea that we're just a couple of aging, alcoholic wastrels, we do exert ourselves occasionally. That's because Carl has a pretty strange idea of a fun time. He likes to get lost in the bush at night. After a bout of AA, we'd slather ourselves in Deep Woods Off!—I love that exclamation point!—and head straight into the dark, thick forest across the road from the houses lining the lake.

The first few times that big bastard would ditch me, just slip away, and abandon me to the forest. I'd be all Hansel-y wandering around, bumping into shit and tripping over shit and genuinely fearful that I'd wind up a candidate for the Darwin Awards, my decomposing body eventually found a few yards from civilization.

After a while—well, some years—I could feel a sense of direction and distance come to me, and a calmness where I wasn't afraid and panicked by killer owls or squirrels and I didn't expect to stumble onto a gingerbread house—although that would've been bonus.

Carl's pretty quiet most of the time, and he's smarter than hell, and funnier than the aforementioned hell. He loves NFL football and NHL hockey and Molson Export Ale which, as it turns out, are also huge interests of mine. He calls me "Son" even though I turned sixty this year and I like that. I tell him he's my role model for my rapidly approaching decrepitude and he likes that.

I don't know much about Carl's story; I've never asked and he's never offered. He's never asked and I've never offered anything about my past either, which is another fair deal in our friendship. I do know, however, that I've never seen a non-related adult treat my daughter with more affection and kindness than Carl showed Halley when she was growing up. That's good enough for me, even though he cheers for the fucking Dallas Cowboys.

Towards the end of every October, after the trees have turned from yellow and orange to leafless grey, I wrestle my ridiculously large TV into my boat and motor over to Carl's and he keeps it for the winter. Carl also keeps quite an array of guns, likely approaching the clinical definition of an arsenal and everyone on the lake knows it or "ought to have known it", as the lawyers would say. So I figure the TV's pretty safe.

And every year for the past four, Carl drives me to Pearson Airport in Toronto for my flight to Samana and then picks me up six months less a day later. I don't pay him for his taxi service but I do put the NFL and NHL cablevision packages on my bill so he can watch football and hockey or shows about football and hockey all winter long. Sometimes, when I'm in Big Dave's American Bar in Las Terrenas watching the *Carneros de San Luis* or the *Atracadores de Oakland*, I think about him hunkered down in front of my ridiculously large television with a goofy smile on his face and a cold "Ex" in his hand and the snow piling up to his windows and I am somehow comforted.

<CHAPTER THREE>

While I'm in this full disclosure mood, I have this disease or, at least, I've been told I have this disease. Shortly after Beth died and I took to drinking more than usual, Dr. Dan, my GP, who mostly tends to my Type-2 diabetes and vainly lectures me about smoking and drinking, sent me to a psychologist in nearby Peterborough. I went, largely because Dr. Dan said he was worried about me and that was kind of touching.

Shirley Playfair, my new psychologist, was a nice woman, of the sort that quietly gushes concern. She spoke in plurals—supports, strategies, behaviours—as she unleashed the catalogue of ills and challenges she thinks I may be facing. Childhood disintegrative disorder, schizoid personality disorder, attention-deficit hyperactivity disorder, obsessive compulsive disorder, semantic pragmatic disorder, multiple complex developmental disorder and nonverbal learning disorder, bi-polarity, autism, and manic depression. I looked them all up which made me manically depressed.

Eventually, we settled on low-grade Asperger's with a dash of OCD as the explanation for the unbalanced chemicals in my head and the often weird shit I sometimes do or think as a result.

She also declared that there's a particularly odd anomaly to my condition. Shirley has divined that, despite my rage and grief over Beth's dying, I actually have empathy for the human race and, sometimes, even for individual members of that species. I begged to differ, claiming that me figuring out the origins of person's particular brand of humanity is just an intellectual exercise to pass the time. To sum it up, go to Cohen's *Sisters of Mercy*: "Well, I've been where you're hanging; I think I can see how you're pinned."

"That's empathy!" she pounces.

Shirley also talked about cognitive therapy and drugs. As a chain-smoking, practicing diabetic, I've always been pretty stingy with my time and money. Besides, she couldn't give me drugs; a psychiatrist had to do that, which means I'd have to go see one and then I'd have to talk about myself all over again to another stranger before he or she could hook me up with the pharmaceuticals which I don't particularly like to do—either taking more prescription drugs than I already do for my diabetes or talking about myself—despite the fact that I'm writing this tale down and despite the fact that I don't particularly like run-on sentences either.

I had another solution. Call it alternative therapy. I joined a boxing club.

My interest in the pugilistic arts goes back more than forty years. Let's just say that when I was a teenager I had what they now call an anger management issue. Back then, they called it being a drunken asshole issue. And that led to a couple of assault charges, one for a beat-down at a party when I decided to take active exception to a guy hitting on my girlfriend at the time and once on a complete stranger standing beside me at urinals in a tavern washroom. This last event took place in the mid-70s when my long hair actually did piss some people off. Even though his rhetorical musing—that he was surprised I still peed standing up—struck me as pretty funny, my witty comeback—something along the lines of "Fuck off, red neck!" —led to an escalated confrontation where I popped him after he swung at me.

At any rate, that's all in the past, no sense crying over spilled milk, water under the bridge and so on. Particularly after I spent some thousands on lawyers to expunge—I love that word—my record with the US powers that be so that I could travel there and not be perceived as a threat to the Republic.

It also scared me enough to do something about it. Rather than go all Buddhist—the religion of self-involved Whatever-the-Fuck—I learned to fight. After hours and hours spent in sweaty gyms, punching bags and then humans, I got pretty good. Being a southpaw didn't hurt although getting hit did. I got good enough to claim that I was mediocre when I quit the "serious" fight game at age 19 with a 4 and 4 record and a nose that wasn't exactly between my eyes anymore.

Since I hung up the gloves, I hadn't hit anyone in anger.

But fifteen years ago, I started to want to hit people again.

So, rather than taking swings at guys talking on their cell phones in theatres or pummeling tailgaters, I decided—without much deliberation—to go someplace where hitting people was the whole point and so started boxing again, at whatever rank is below amateur. Another addition to my bag of habits, things I just do without question or analysis.

Given all my other habits—Hey! Smoking and drinking! I'm talking to you!—it's probably better than most of my rituals. It's kept me reasonably fit, reasonably quick and alert, and it keeps me close to one of the most brilliant philosophical, psychological, sociological, and anthropological observations ever made: "Everybody has a plan until they get punched in the mouth."

That gem from Iron Mike ranks right up there my other guiding principles from two of the 20th century's greatest thinkers: Popeye's declaration that "I yam what I yam," and Doris Day's broader ode to stoicism: "*Que sera, sera.*"

The day after I'd read the news about Alistair, coming home from the Angler Arms with Carl, I was surprised to see a car in my driveway. It was an unmarked police cruiser—that much was obvious from the shitty hubcaps.

Halley was sitting on my front porch.

"Drinking and driving again?" my daughter asked, as we piled out of the truck.

"Not me, kiddo! The Vibe-rator's right there. Go ahead, touch the hood. Cool as the proverbial cucumber. It was that big bastard, Carl. I tried to pull a citizen's arrest on him but he threatened to beat the chicken soup outta me. And he'd do it too, that big bastard."

"Why don't you just walk, dad?"

"We do!" I insisted. "Sometimes. Oddest thing though: eleven minutes there but seventeen coming back."

"More like eighteen," Carl piped up.

"Seventeen!"

Halley rolled her eyes at me, a practice she had perfected and I had richly earned many years ago. Carl slunk off to his boat—I won't say stealthily because that implies some grace and he was easily as shit-faced as I was.

Father and daughter watched his huge teetering frame trying to get his motor started.

Halley is 28; her name was my wife's choice in recognition of the comet's appearance around her birth. I do remember noting that Beth must've been glad that Kohoutek hadn't passed by that year because our kid would have been in for a real hard time at school.

Halley was the most organized child I'd ever met. And she wanted to be a cop all her life. I'm not going to spend any time analyzing why, beyond assuming that it would bring order to her life and answer her need for something like justice.

She's a smart kid—a whole lot smarter than her old man. And tough—a whole lot tougher than her old man. She has to be to have the father she has and to get along in her life as the youngest and femalest Detective Sergeant in the Toronto Police Service, where she's constantly surrounded by dirt bags, some of whom commit crimes.

I don't see her much. Actually, I don't see anybody much as what started out as a choice has now become a habit.

I assumed she had a "project" for me. From time to time, the police—sometimes Toronto, sometimes nearby Peterborough, sometimes the OPP provincial force—hire me to take a look at one of their cases. The people who pay me call it having another pair of eyes. The investigators I sometimes work alongside call it being interfered with by a fuckin' nutbar. The money's shit and there's nothing exactly glamorous about the work.

These occasional gigs pre-date Halley's involvement with law enforcement. Years ago, I had wandered into the Peterborough Police station with an armful of print-outs more or less proving that a "person of interest" in a timeshare Ponzi scheme—a guy whom they had recently released—ought to be re-examined. For no particular reason I could ever discern, I had spent something like three days tracking his various ownership and directorship positions in a very long chain of increasingly obscure and often just numbered shell companies. "104562960 Ontario corporation doing business as . . . " sort of tracking which laid out a trail of cheque-kiting among the guy, his lawyer and a cousin-by-marriage whereby they paid back rental income to investors on a small apartment complex in Puerto Morelos which they didn't own. That I discovered when the Mexican *Ministerio de Asuntos Exteriores* told me there was no registered *fideicomiso* for that property.

The cops and the crown attorney were grateful but, at the same time, obviously surprised and a little pitying that a rumpled stranger would devote all those hours for no apparent reason.

Nonetheless, word got out that there was this oddball who, through some combination of maniacal research abilities and an innate sense of why people do the things they do, might be able to help out. Not on really high profile cases—but stuff like unfrocking an Anglican minister who had plundered the church kitty to feed his gambling kitty or finding out that the head of a Rotary Club is the piece of scum that scum wipes off its feet owing to his predilection for kiddie porn and frequent "Christian" missions to Thailand.

I might not have much in the way of any discernible talent but, boy, can I find my way around Google or any other search engine. Ask the same question different ways and you get all sorts of different responses. Page after page of increasingly vague suggestions but, every once in a while, exactly the right answer.

What matters is the time and inclination to go through them all. I have that kind of time now. I've always had the inclination. You can go ask Alanis but it's very possibly ironic that this time and this inclination are the very things that were about to land me in an impending shit show.

So, sweetie, this is a swell surprise. What brings you out of the city?" I asked.

"Alistair MacNeil."

"Why are the police interested? The paper said natural causes."

"That's what we think too but, still, there are some odd things about this."

"Like?"

"Like I'd rather not say."

"Hey! You guys hire me sometimes; remember? So spill!"

"I can't. It's a little close, don't you think? I mean, you worked for him."

"Yup. Full-time more than seventeen years ago and on a short contract four years ago, your honour."

"What was he like?" she asked.

"What was he like seventeen years ago?"

"Don't you always say people don't change?"

"Objection, Your Honour! Blatant smart-assedness. Are you looking for an in-depth character study?"

"Something like that."

"OK. He was a dick."

"Do you think you might be able to expand on that a bit?"

"He . . . was . . . a . . . dick."

"Thanks, dad."

"Alright, alright! Actually, he was a pretty good guy. He just seemed like a dick sometimes because . . . because . . . he was a hard man. I never had a beef with him. Even when he fired me. Both times. He was tough but fair as hell. And he was good to your old man."

"Any enemies?"

"Are you kidding? Lots of money means lots of enemies."

"Anybody stand out?"

"Nope. A blur of pissed-off bankers and investors from time to time. Why are you asking?"

"Covering all the bases. That's all."

"You think someone whacked him, don't you?"

"Covering all the bases, I said."

"Give me something, goddamnit!"

"Fine. I will. They found him in his lakeside condo, collapsed on his treadmill. He'd been dead at least two days. Autopsy says he died of severe hypoglycemia."

"And that's odd how?"

"We don't know. That's why we're checking."

I wasn't particularly in the mood for solipsism but I was hungry.

"Stay for dinner?"

"What kind of Hamburger Helper are you having tonight?" she asked.

"That hurts, daughter. It's Sidekicks. And I'll have you know I'm whipping up their new Cheddar Chipotle. With cut-up hot dog wieners, may I add."

"Oh, dad."

"Oh, dad nuthin'! It's brand new, likely the product of years of research. And it's really quite good."

"I'll pass. I've got a long drive back. And these days it's a 24/7 rush hour on the 401."

"Sorry I couldn't help more."

We hugged and had that instant connection when we pulled away and our eyes met. I like to think that, mostly, she's forgiven me for being such a shitty father. I should ask but I don't.

After she left, I felt a little remorseful that I hadn't mentioned to her that Alistair had called me six weeks earlier. Out of the blue after four years of silence. It had been an odd conversation but they were always odd when he tried to be affable, almost like an alien pretending to act like a regular human. It was odder still because his voice just didn't have the crispness, the clipped tones I remembered so well.

Now, all evidence to the contrary, I think a lot—although to be accurate, my thinking just goes around in circles and occupies my time. Alistair was always thinking too, but in a straight line to how he could do what he wanted to do.

So our conversation immediately sounded as if he had timed it out beforehand. First, 2.5 minutes of personal chit-chat. How's the kid? What are you doing? And strangely enough, what about them Leafs? Strange because I knew he knew squat about hockey.

Then the wind-up and the pitch: "What would you say about coming to work for me again? I have this new venture."

"What new venture?" I asked.

"I can't tell you . . . yet."

Then another 2.5 minutes about how it would be completely illogical of me to turn it down. Great money, freedom to call the PR shots, hardly any travel.

I can't say I was tempted. Even a little bit. The prospect of having to cut my hair and clean up, show up when other people wanted me to in places I didn't want to be did not appeal to me. Dealing with reporters again wasn't on my bucket list either. And I knew he was bullshitting about travel. Everything he ever did involved traveling to other cities—we used to refer to them as going out on a raid. And all for a job doing something, I didn't know what?

"You fired me," I reminded him. "Twice."

"I did you a favour. Twice," he said, hinting at the huge severances he'd granted me.

Ah, the trump card. Everything was debits and credits with him and, somehow, everybody else was always on the red bracketed side of his ledger.

"Let me think about it," I said.

"I can give you the rest of the day. If you need it."

"In that case, the answer's: thanks but no thanks."

There was the slightest of pauses, not even long enough for me to guess the number of computations he was performing.

"Well, goodbye," he said.

Click.

What Halley had told me had only added to the puzzle. It made no sense that the normally fastidious billionaire had not known his blood sugar had dropped like a stone.

And how could the body of this fastidious and always plugged-in billionaire with a family not be discovered for two days?

Despite the fact that it's sort of a big deal to get me away from the lake, I decided it would be a swell idea to go to Alistair's funeral. Even though I was pretty sure it didn't much matter to him anymore, I felt it was something I should do. Pros and cons can fuck off after I've made my mind up. It's like going with your first hunch playing Trivial Pursuit. Don't question; just answer. The rationalization can always come afterwards. Or not.

Unlike a real grown-up, I usually get all freaked out in a city even though I was born, raised, and worked in one. The pace, the driving, the noise, the volume of people and cars, everything, the size of the goddamned buildings, even the width of the streets have always frazzled me beyond reason. Now add in my years of splendid isolation. Let's just say that by the time I got to the old Presbyterian Church just off St. Clair I was a mess.

The funeral was a small affair. Alistair was pretty famous but also pretty friendless. There seemed to be almost as many media as mourners in the half-empty church.

Sarah, Alistair's second wife, was there with two of their three kids. Both Alistair's grown-up daughters from his first marriage were there. Of course, Mike Coulson was there. We had joined Montrose together. At the time—that would be 1984—we were both young and keen. He had quickly become Alistair's right-hand financial guy because he was an accounting whiz who spoke Alistair's language. I was an alleged PR guru and I quickly became the court jester. My decade and a half with Alistair paled in comparison to Mike's thirty-plus years.

While not exactly the Glimmer Twins, we had been close until a thoroughly stupid little spat had morphed by mutual intransigence into an uncrossable abyss.

Scanning the crowd, I saw Donna D'Angelo, Alistair's long-time secretary, Peter Wachefsky, his long-time personal accountant and Jeff Sears who was Montrose's long-time president and corporate lawyer. The legal representation at the funeral was rounded out by Mary-Ellen Thompson who handled all the big contracts, licensing agreements, and intellectual property work for Alistair's technology companies, first as an employee and later as outhouse counsel.

Interesting, I thought, that Alistair had so many long-time camp followers. Particularly these days, as corporate loyalty has also apparently gone the way of rotary phones and getting hammered at lunch.

I was sort of surprised to see Alexandra Simpson there. She was a Boston-based technology analyst way back when I was gainfully employed and there were about twenty such self-identified analysts on the planet. Now everybody's a fucking technology analyst, getting richly rewarded for guessing about the next big thing. And usually guessing either wrong or obviously, may I add.

I think she tried to seduce me once in New York. I've always been a moron about things like that. At any rate, she and I would talk regularly. She would call me all the time, fishing for tidbits that would cause her to feel better about her recommendations.

Back then, just before our IPO, I had been deputized as the Investor Relations Manager, like I had a fucking clue about P/E ratios and convertible subordinated debentures. But, if you hum a few bars, I can usually pick it up. She had always recommended whatever stock Alistair had on the go. Alexandra was crazy in love with Alistair's brain. She had made millions for investors and she probably lost as much because her unwavering confidence in that brain made her publicly support his latest stock play long after its "best before" date.

She was already inside the church so we could only nod and smile at each other. From a distance, she looked great.

And I was really surprised to see Nigel Hayward was there, given that he and Alistair had been embroiled in a really ugly and public tiff a few years back.

Ah, *Doctor* Nigel Hayward. He'd say "doctor" as if it were in italics, lest any mere mortal hatch the notion that he or she was in any way a peer of his.

I met Nigel four years earlier during my last brief employment with Alistair, just before I got fired again. Nigel is one of those complete overachievers. Normally I can't stand these guys, largely because they're usually talking about what they had just overachieved at.

And, well, because I'm jealous.

This guy just did it all. He'd climb mountains, go rafting on the Orinoco, and win tango competitions, serial-date gorgeous women. He could even drink like a world champion. He had that ruddy Anglo-Saxon complexion, suave good looks, a booming voice, surprisingly good teeth given his UK birthplace and a sardonic sense of humour that almost made up for his arrogance.

Nigel was one of those Brits who, Graham Greene-like, would live anywhere but Britain. He had had a thrilling career all over the world as a vascular surgeon and was now applying his prodigious medical experience to developing devices that prevented or managed all bad things blood-related. After stints doing stents in South Africa, Hong Kong, London and the Cleveland and Mayo Clinics, he had settled on Toronto about five years ago for what I'm sure he believed would be a hugely lucrative deal with MacNeil.

Alistair had used Hayward as the centrepiece for much hoopla surrounding the re-launch of a medical devices company Alistair had acquired. The new and improved Bio-Watch Corp was to feature Nigel's remotely monitored doo-dads that could track everything from blood sugar levels to heart rates to, I suppose, fart intervals.

Alistair had brought me in on a fixed price contract to prepare all the road show materials and, generally, to find ways to talk up the company in advance of another share offering.

Towards the end of our brief association, ol' Nige decided he had added prose-writing expert to his book-length résumé. He had to point out that I couldn't be taken seriously as a writer because my post-graduate degree was from Queen's, not the University of Toronto. Coming from a "second-tier" school, I obviously needed his help. So he'd mark up my press releases after they went out (never before) to show me how "colonial" my writing style was. I, of course, couldn't let *that* slide—had to point out the perfectly acceptable "you say tomato, I say tomawto" options, and the fact that we were really writing to a US crowd and didn't he have anything more pressing to do than play after-the-fact editor. And I couldn't help but note that his doctorate was from Cambridge, the centuries-old also-ran to Oxford.

We got along just fine after that.

Hayward had been working on a radically-updated monitoring system that replaced the current generation which, when tied to manual pumps, told you to immediately adjust your insulin doses if your blood sugar levels were too high or low.

I didn't know all the details but I did know MacNeil. It had to be a back-ended deal where the real money would come only after the devices starting selling. That could be years away, and that's why you stayed.

Years earlier, this enticement tactic worked on me too. Montrose didn't have a pension plan—hardly anyone in high tech did back then. So Alistair promised me a huge cash bonus based on the share price if I stayed three more years. Of course, the market and our stock price cratered weeks before my three years were up. And of course, I got squat.

At any rate, Nigel held the patent personally before he came to Bio-Watch. He'd traded it to MacNeil because Alistair had the sole patent on the uninterruptible power source. And without a dependable power pack mounted inside a human torso, you really couldn't use the monitor effectively. In return, Hayward was to get a hefty percentage of the joint sales and MacNeil (and his estate, well, now Sarah, I thought) could charge whatever they wanted for the device/power source combo.

That's why Alistair bought Bio-Watch in the first place. According to Alistair, the techies who made up the company didn't truly understand the value of what they had invented.

They had come up with a lithium carbon fluoride battery that used a solid lithium thiophosphate electrolyte. So what's the big fucking deal about thiophosphate electrolytes, you reasonably ask? Well, I'll tell you. Cooperative interactions between the electrolyte and cathode are caused as the battery discharges, generating lithium fluoride salt which further catalyzes the electrochemical activity of the electrolyte relationship thus converting the electrolyte— conventionally an inactive component in capacity—into an active one.

That actually sounds like I might know what I'm talking about, doesn't it? Well, I don't. Thank Christ the engineers do, but despite their arrogant claim to omniscience, they're as dumb as day-old bunnies when it comes to answering the one question everybody else needs answered.

So?

So that's why I got paid.

So, their invention would, theoretically extend battery life by a factor of at least three and as much as five.

So?

So there's nothing on the market that has near that extended life.

So?

So imagine an implantable battery that'll last up to fifty years. For openers, imagine a pacemaker you don't have to dig out your chest every ten years. Or a permanently-working device to monitor everything going on in your body for as long as it was vertical and mobile.

Nigel believed strongly—and wrongly—that he was as smart as MacNeil. Actually, on some subjects, he probably *was* smarter—for instance, in his knowledge of 14th century Italian madrigals. But I didn't need to see the exact wording in their agreement to know that Nigel was in way over his head at deal-making. MacNeil would've kicked his ass till his nose bled.

The FDA and Health Canada hadn't approved human trials. Never mind Europe and the rest of the planet. Alistair's optimism was unflagging. In any interview or piece of commentary I arranged, he was sure the government nod would come "in a timely manner."

In a timely manner. That was one of his favourite bullshit PR phrases. Timely compared to what? The life of a fruit fly? The end of the universe?

Months turned to years; the stock dropped and there was a reverse one-for-five split.

With no discernible progress and working for salary alone, Nigel quit about two years ago and went to work for Concord Medical Systems, a smallish subsidiary of giant WesCor, which made similar such things. He apparently left behind his patent and a bunch of hard feelings because he sued, believing he had sold his cow for some magic beans. I had always reckoned that he was mostly enraged over Alistair's quote in the press release announcing Hayward's departure. "We wish him the best but understand his utility to the company was complete."

Nigel lost the pissing match and, surprise, surprise, Alistair won with his countersuit against him for non-performance.

That's why I was taken aback to see Nigel at the funeral. Unless he wanted to be sure that Alistair was, in fact, dead.

Steve Golding was there and I was instantly warmed. Steve was an "old style" reporter, one of the few I had completely gotten along with. Back then in the mid-80s, he was one of only a handful of media guys in the country who understood both business and technology, so he was treated with the kind of reverence and awe you'd be accorded in the Middle Ages if you were a successful alchemist.

He was big-league smart and a big-league journalist with a big-league drinking problem. Specifically, his problem was that his bosses at the *Globe and Mail* never liked his prodigious consumption. On the other hand, I did. And with my unquestioned expense account, we would, from time to time, spend hours drunkenly dissecting the markets and the next technology trend and the Leafs' chances that season.

Such beer-infused discussions did not lead to favourable treatment of Montrose by him in the *Globe*. But it did produce fairness, a tacit agreement that I would never jerk him around and he would never play gotcha journalism. The result: I was content with whatever "job" he did on us in the paper. "Neither hammer nor blow" was our motto.

Because I trusted Steve, I was able to convince Alistair to trust him too, with the result that he had tallied a lot more one-on-ones than his fellow reporters scored.

Career-wise, Steve's "Best Five" years were long past him, but he had them under his belt. About 100K a year back then when he was every PR slut's nightmare. Years ago, he told me that he wouldn't mind playing out the string. And, near as I could tell, that's exactly what he was doing. He had two decades in the Business sections of the big-league papers, passing through the *Globe,* the *National Post,* and the *Star.* Next stop, Triple A as a crime reporter for the *Toronto Sun.* I was betting he understood his downward trajectory but didn't give a shit. His "Best Five" would give him at least 50K-a-year pension—indexed for life—when he either packed it in or got whacked again.

He, like me, aimed low in life. And, it seemed, he, like me, hit the mark.

We kept in touch for some time after I exited Montrose, mainly by e-mail, but that faded away after I lit out for the territories.

I felt a little guilty treating the funeral as something of a reunion instead of a display of reverence for the dead guy I had known for so many years now laid out in the long box at the front of the church.

And I knew why I was acting that way. The last funeral I had attended was fifteen years ago. I couldn't stop staring at the coffin on that day.

<CHAPTER SEVEN>

The service was exceedingly long and sad. His family and a few friends all got up to speak and that's what made it sad. Everybody told anecdotes about Alistair, but these small stories did not amuse or get you choked up, although they plainly were intended to. And that was the sad part. No great insight, no touching humanity, no real laughs. I don't know to or for whom, but it was almost embarrassing.

I was sitting in the back and when a cousin of his started talking about summer jobs on the family farm, I slipped out for a cigarette. Steve Golding was already outside and smoking. Another thing we had in common.

"I'm pretty sure they barred the media from this event," I said, as we briefly embraced.

"I'm not working, just paying my respects. I liked the guy."

"Me too."

"Lunch?" he asked with his eyebrow arched in a Nicholson kinda way that always made me laugh.

"Well, why wouldn't we do that?" I said. "Let me talk to some people first, OK?"

The mourners filed out spreading around the hearse while the coffin was loaded.

Nigel Hayward came up to me, bestowed one of his hearty handshakes that threatened to turn into an arm wrestle. After we quickly established that we were respectively doing "good, good" and "fine, fine," I couldn't resist asking him what he was doing there.

"I was in Toronto on business. And, there are people I know here, old boy."

The "old boy" was said rather pointedly, I thought, as he studied my greying hair. Bastard still had his curly blondish hair even though he was exactly one year younger than me.

I hugged Sarah. It was awkward—as if it's possible to be graceful at a funeral. She was dry-eyed but shaking, as though she might collapse.

She was still pretty—tired-looking and thinner than I remembered—but still pretty. I always liked her. We used to go outside and smoke together during official functions, like annual meetings and such, and talk about stuff that had nothing to do with either technology or dollars.

By the hearse, I was quickly introduced to her two children with her, Lana and Laura, mid-teen girls who closely flanked her. The trio seemed to be propping each other up, like gladiola stalks in the wind. Jason, her third kid with Alistair, was the only one I actually knew and he was missing. Stupidly perhaps, I asked Sarah where he was.

"He has . . . challenges," she said. "Hey, are you staying in the city?"

"Don't think so."

"That's too bad. Dinner would be nice."

"Are you sure?" I asked, thinking she might have other things to do after her husband's funeral.

She smiled.

"I'm not going to sleep with you, if that's you mean," she whispered. "I just wouldn't mind an old face to talk to."

"Give me your number; I'll see what happens."

I was glad Mike came up to me afterwards with his hand extended, in a let-bygones-be-bygones kind of way.

After some trivial chit-chat, Mike leaned into me and whispered: "I need to talk to you."

"Sure, bud. Let's talk."

"Not here."

Well, that intrigued me. He gave me his address and directions and we set five o'clock as a time.

All us mourners milled around a bit exchanging handshakes, kissy-faces, and small talk. Nobody ever says anything smart or helpful or important at times like these, but it's connective. It was good to see Alexandra, albeit real briefly, and I had even exchanged pleasantries with Nigel Hayward.

Donna worked her way through the crowd picking out people to tell that some of us were invited to a sort of informal reception at sort of a nearby bar. I went because I had been part of Alistair's supporting cast of characters.

There were hugs and handshakes all 'round. These sorts of gatherings always fuck me up a bit as you engage in what's referred to in football as incidental contact. Irony #68: my chosen profession was *public* relations.

I don't think there are a lot of technology company reunions. And here we had one because, quite suddenly, here we all were, all linked again by the fact that we were related to a company and a CEO many years ago and, for many, still.

There's always something intrinsically warm and close about a high school reunion. Despite the weirdness of reconnection after twenty-five or thirty-five years, everything petty is forgiven or forgotten and everybody is wreathed in good will. Suddenly comrades after all those years for having survived the changes that everybody was going through at the same time, spending most days together in the same building. Except for the dead ones whom you find out about when their names come up.

Company get-togethers don't feel like that. The difference in tone is probably due to the fact that we didn't get paid to go to high school.

For a moment, however, there was a warmth but there wasn't a lot of grief, as there often isn't once the churchy stuff is over. More it was a sense of being lost. Everyone seemed a tad aimless now that the nominal patriarch had passed, the reason that everyone knew each other, and had a job, and it seemed that it would and should last a whole lot longer.

As it turned out, I was about the only one who had left the fold. Mike Coulson, I knew, was a lifer but there was Donna who, up until the moment of MacNeil's death, was his executive assistant. Foul-mouthed and ferociously protective of MacNeil and his frantic schedule, she was both unfailingly efficient and remarkably discrete. I knew a lot of stuff that went on behind the scenes but she knew *everything*.

Jeff Sears was there. He once was known as a big swinging dick. I don't know if he had one, but he sure was one. With an encyclopedic understanding of securities law on both sides of the border, broad knowledge on the day-to-day operations of Alistair's companies, and a horse-trader's shrewd sensibility, he was perfect as MacNeil's chief negotiator ironing out the many details to the labyrinthine financing deals that Alistair had sketched out on his mental napkin. As he did with everyone else, Jeff addressed me by my last name even though we worked together for about a decade. We'd brawl over wording in press releases but other than that, got along just fine.

Mary-Ellen Thompson was there. I had followed her career a bit. About ten years ago, she had left Montrose to hang out her shingle as a one-lawyer boutique firm specializing in technology patent law. A few years back, I saw that her boutique was on the verge of becoming a big box store when she announced the hiring of their 100th lawyer. Such was the booming business of protecting the stuff you had invented from people not smart enough to think of the stuff you had invented but keen to steal yours. Despite her ceaselessly pleasant demeanour, I knew she could grow a fin in a civil case and I always pitied the poor bastards facing off against her.

Peter Wachefsky was also in attendance. As Alistair's personal accountant, Wachefsky wasn't ever around the office that much. You'd see him mostly around tax time when you'd also hear him behind MacNeil's closed door, loudly arguing because he did everything loudly. After all these years, I bet his entire client list consisted of one name: Alistair MacNeil.

So there we were, standing around in a circle, everyone but me with an actual job, everyone but me in "business attire, and everyone but me holding a non-alcoholic beverage. I just couldn't resist filling a pause in the conversation with a badly-sung tune.

> One of these things is not like the others;
> one of these things just doesn't belong . . .

Everybody chuckled and some ice had been broken. Again, I was reminded that I really do enjoy getting a cheap laugh. If pressed to sum up my human relations in a single movie scene, I'd wanna say Costner in the bath with Susan Sarandon in *Bull Durham*. The truth, however, is closer to Belushi crushing that beer can on his forehead in *Animal House*.

Que sera, indeed.

I said my good-byes and agreed—because what else can you

say?—that, yes, we absolutely must stay in touch and went off to meet Steve.

Our late lunch was a crushing disappointment, mainly because I learned that Steve had stopped drinking years ago. I'll concede that a DUI and the near failure of his liver may have played some small part in his decision, but still.

So I drank beer and he drank tonic water and lime. For the scurvy, I assumed.

Other than our shared interest in absurdly inhaling noxious substances, Steve had undergone quite the transformation since our PR hand-to-hand combat days in the 80s. It wasn't just his newfound seat on the wagon. For one thing, he was in great shape, obviously having got that way through something known as exercise and healthy eating habits.

His response to me chiding him about hypocritically still smoking, however, made complete sense to me:

"Playin' for the tie, just playin' for the tie," he said.

Not too surprisingly, we talked a lot about Alistair.

"He was the end of an era. You know that?" Steve mused.

"He was, wasn't he? Old school kinda guy, principled, a true businessman."

"Not like all the young arrogant billionaire techno-pukes and their legion of wanna-bees intent on changing the world. Believe me; I had my fill of 'em; that's why I left the tech section."

"Plus, they fired your ass," I said, reminding him of his one drunken lunch too many that brought the publisher's wrath and instant unemployment down on him.

"After they fired yours," he said, pointing out my own shit-canning as one of the conditions set by an investor in Montrose.

"Touché, you little monster. The crime beat must be a whole lot easier. Bad guys, good guys, people with guns, what's not to like?"

"Actually, I'm working on a series you might appreciate."

"Try me."

"Technology and crime."

"Punks fucking around with other people's computers? Now *that's* exciting! What's next? A series on graffiti?"

"It's a whole lot more than that, you fucking moron."

I smiled at his use of this longstanding term of endearment.

"Hackers. Pretty sophisticated," he continued. "They're doing all sorts of advanced stuff. It started out that they broke into systems just to prove they could do it. Used to be a single guy in his mom's basement. But now they're getting a lot more organized. And a lot of them are idealistic too."

"Like we used to be?"

"When?"

"Good point."

Years ago, we had compared notes; it had been obvious to both of us that he and I had been born under a cynical moon.

Another beer came for me and Steve turned serious.

"Jake, have you ever thought about writing a book?"

"I did."

"Oh, that's right, your novel. I read it."

"Liar!"

"I did!" and he recited a few plot points which he couldn't have stolen from the back cover blurb.

"Well, congratulations for joining such a select group!"

"I liked it."

"Don't bullshit me."

"No, I did. Really."

I have a tough time with compliments—probably because they're so rare—so I brought the conversation back to the present.

"You mean do a book about the good old days?"

"Yeah . . . the good old days would be in there. We could write it together."

"Absolutely no one would read that," I said. "Not even me."

"But you know stuff."

"I'm old; I forgot it all. Why don't you write it? You know even more *stuff*. And you may be a little more clear-headed these days."

"A friend of mine once told me that absolutely no one would read that."

"Smart friend."

"No, I'm not kidding here; we should do something like that."

I have to admit, the idea appealed to me, more for the fact that we'd get to hang out and work together.

But of course, I was also skeptical.

"Why are you asking me? You don't need anybody to do this with."

Steve paused.

"You're a better writer than me."

That's the closest we got to maudlin and sentimental, so I nipped that in the bud.

"Suckhole."

We swapped "co-ordinates" as they say, along with a sort of hug. Back then, I always believed that we would have been even better friends if we didn't have to go at each other as PR Slut and Digging Reporter. It wasn't exactly Spy Vs Spy but close. And yet we were friends. More than any reason for the fact we gave as good as we got which made things fair, and things should be fair.

I like fair and I really liked the guy. Even sober. Not me. Him. I don't much care for myself when I'm sober.

Mike's house was in Rosedale which is not a chic, recently-gentrified neighbourhood in Toronto, just a stinking rich one. Always had been and always will be. No modernistic in-fills here. Just winding road after winding road of squatting mansions with stone turrets crawling with ancient ivy and set in meticulous lawns, all discretely hidden by stately elms. The barns here go for about two million and up.

I parked my silver Vibe beside his silver Z4 Roadster.

"Loyalty has its privileges," I remarked as I walked across the grand foyer's gleaming tile floor.

"Outside?" he said.

"Sure," I said, lighting a cigarette as I followed him through the gigantic French doors leading to the backyard. Wait, it wasn't a backyard; these were grounds.

Mike looked like I'd just waved a turd under his nose, the way he always did when anybody smoked around him. I knew he would because Mike was what's regarded as an early adopter. That's what had ended our friendship. When the city banned indoor smoking, he'd yelled at me through the stall door in the company washroom just as I was enjoying the nostalgic wave of sneaking a cigarette as if I were back in a high school can.

"They could fine us five thousand bucks, asshole!" he had shouted through the cubicle door.

"I'm good for it, OK? Now fuck off!" I had yelled back.

He tried to make up for or at least explain his anger by telling me his dad had died of lung cancer. I was still pissed off at his prissy outburst so I said that he was lucky his father hadn't died in a car accident because Toronto was a tough place to walk everywhere, what with him, on principle, being forced to give up his BMW and all.

That really did us in as friends, which—if you think about it—is a classic example of pettiness on both sides. Not long after that I got whacked by Alistair. Neither Mike nor I said good-bye and, before you knew it, almost two decades went by as decades tend to do. Which is why I was surprised to find myself sitting amid his manicured backyard.

We didn't spend much time catching up. I knew what he did because I can read and he likely couldn't give a sweet shit about what I did because he either didn't want to embarrass me for the way I was dressed or because finding out about how the last eighteen years had turned out for me made not a bit of difference to his life. I'm thinking the latter.

After he bought Bio-Watch five or six years ago, Alistair installed himself as Chairman and CEO, Mike as the COO, packed the Board with his hand-picked usual suspects, brought in Hayward, took them public, and—voila!—made a shitload. Mike had been in California during the short time I spent at the place four years ago on my consulting contract that ended prematurely after I got into a loud brawl with their young, inexperienced, and baselessly arrogant full-time PR slut.

"How's Robin?" I asked.

"I have no idea. We divorced three years ago."

"So this is just one-half what you used to have?" I asked, looking around. "Jesus!"

Mike smiled for the first time. "I always did what Dad asked. I knew it would be legal, I knew it would be creative and I knew it would make him and therefore me a lot of money."

We used to call Alistair "Dad" because, in many ways, he acted like a father to us, shepherding us into our corporate futures, grudgingly appreciative when we did good, stern with us when we fucked up—well, when I fucked up. If Mike did, I never heard about it.

Looking around at his place, Mike's career theory had proven to be wildly successful. It was like that alleged team building exercise. I don't know if they still use it. You fold your arms. Close your eyes and fall backwards and the guy behind you is supposed to catch you. Mike had been falling backwards for three decades and Alistair had always caught him. Me, for better or worse, I could never trust anybody like that.

I don't care what anybody claims: considering other people's expensive pretty stuff causes jealousy, and I was feeling a tad envious. I could always understand why Mike had outlasted me and everyone else. It was just a great distance from the time when we had christened ourselves Pip 1 and Pip 2 after Dickens' young character because we too were living on the fringes of the rich and famous.

Since then, he had moved inland and upmarket.

"I think somebody killed Dad," he simply stated, interrupting my contemplation of his stuff.

"I agree. Something's not right."

He didn't look all that surprised.

"Why do you say that?" he asked.

"Remember Halley?"

"Your daughter, Hailey?"

"Halley."

"What about her?"

"She's a cop now."

"So what do the police think?"

"She didn't say too much. I'm guessing they want to be sure that his death was accidental."

"Did she offer up any theories or anything?"

"No."

"Any idea what they're thinking?"

For some reason, this post-mortem chat was turning into something resembling a clumsy investigation. I can smell them a mile away. Reporters used to wander around a subject with me—especially after I had been out for lunch—before pouncing.

"Why are you so sure he was murdered, Mike?"

"Jake, you know him . . . *knew* him; he just wouldn't screw up or forget."

"Yeah, but what if he killed himself?"

Mike looked as though the very possibility was absurd.

"Absolutely, positively, not a chance," he declared.

I had to agree. Alistair never seemed all that happy but he never seemed all that sad either. I'd seen him personally lose 100 million on paper in the stock market in a week and I'd seen him make that much in a day. You couldn't tell the difference by looking at him. Steady as he goes. There might've been a raging firestorm of existential angst inside him, but I doubted it.

"And besides, he was on the verge of a huge deal with WesCor, through Concord Medical. *This* close," Mike said.

"C'mon, Mike, he was always *this* close to a big deal. And didn't WesCor tell him to fuck off a few years ago?"

"It's business, Jake. No one takes it personally; you never learned that. And anyway, Alistair was the one who told them to fuck off. But about year ago, they came sniffing around again and tried to buy a majority position in the company."

"Don't tell me: Alistair wouldn't sell."

Of course he wouldn't, I thought. He once told me the only corporate ownership positions that made sense to him were either 100 or 50.1%. Everything else was just fucking around.

"But they wouldn't go away," Mike continued. "They offered a ridiculously large amount of money. About the same time Ulti/ME showed up expressing their interest."

"Ulti/ME? The social media company? Why would they be nosing around?"

"Apparently, they're keen about branching out, getting more integrated, as they say."

"A good offer?"

"Decent, but nowhere near WesCor's."

Mike told me that, eventually, both companies 'fessed up that they thought Bio-Watch was years ahead of the competition with the combination of long-lasting power source and Hayward's advanced monitor.

Even I knew that kind of technological lead was important, especially now that the jump on the market was being measured in months, even weeks.

"And I bet Dad still wasn't interested in an auction, was he?" I asked.

"Nope. Instead, he came up with a complicated per transaction licensing agreement that could be worth hundreds of millions, probably billions and still let Alistair keep Bio-Watch. He offered the deal to both companies. They both passed. They both wanted to buy us outright."

"And Dad wouldn't do that."

"The way he saw it, he had all the cards. He knew our technology was a game-changer. He knew they both really wanted it, and he knew that they both had just about bottomless pockets. He told our shareholders that we could afford to wait them out."

"And could he?"

"In my view? No. The news of a possible sale barely moved our stock. It was being discounted as just some more of Dad's over-optimism."

"Where's Jeff Sears on this?"

"He ran what numbers he could get from WesCor. Thought they could do better than Ulti/ME who have zero track record in this kind of deal."

"Any idea if Sarah's on side?"

"I don't think so. She wanted the Ulti/ME deal right from the start. Not that that matters a whole lot. As usual, Alistair decided everything himself."

"And you?"

"I have to tell you, I'm getting tired of all this complicated per transaction stuff. Even before Alistair was . . . even before he died, I'd rather have gone with WesCor too. Nice and clean. And very, very profitable."

"So you're nowhere right now."

"Yes," Mike said, but something was not right in his tone, in the way his eyes had suddenly shifted away from me. And, for the first time, he was drumming his fingers on the glass patio table. Years ago, I had media-trained him and that was his "tell."

"Mike, you're leaving something out, buddy."

He seemed in some way relieved for getting called out for using the company line.

"Truth be told, Jake, I think he was starting to listen to me. Just recently, he'd been in contact with WesCor to revive talks. You do anything with this and I'll turn you in. I swear to God, I will," he quickly added.

"Understood. So it's a one-horse race now."

"I think so. Months ago, he had even sent WesCor a unit to play around with."

"That doesn't sound like him."

"I was against it, but he wanted to show them what it could do and was convinced that our patent lawyer was better than their patent lawyer. Besides, he got them to send the latest version of their monitor so we could see how it stacked up against ours."

Mike told me that Alistair was personally trying out WesCor's remote blood monitoring system for his advanced Type-2 diabetes. It had been touted as this giant leap in reliability and accuracy, a total redesign of their previous offerings. Alistair's verdict: it did some things better than Bio-Watch's, some things not so good. And for sure, its power source was lacking. It too didn't have all the approvals needed to sell it.

So Alistair had become a subject for what was, in effect, an experimental device.

"Why would he take that chance, be a guinea pig?" I asked.

"You remember. He *had* to be first."

Mike was right. If there was some advance that would take away the pain in the ass of sticking yourself with needles several times a day to test blood and then fuck around with those expensive test strips, he'd jump at it because he was impatient all the time for everything, an early adopter of all technology, even though he didn't understand any of it.

"Maybe the thing fucked up," I said.

"That's the point. We know—absolutely know—that it didn't."

"So the monitor was working. And suicide or accident is unlikely. That makes it curiouser and curiouser."

"Doesn't leave many options, does it?" Mike asked.

"You tell the cops what you think?"

"No. The stock price is already taking a pounding over his death. But murder? That'd kick the shit out of it and who does that serve?"

I fought the urge to point out that he was surely among the least "served" by such a speculation, owing to the millions in stock options he probably been granted.

"So why tell me?" I asked.

"I don't know . . . You had a relationship with him that nobody else had."

"I did?"

"Yeah, you did. To be frank—"

"And I'll be earnest—"

"—you never valued it. And that's a shame."

"It's only a shame if I think it's one. Appearances to the contrary, things turned out OK for me."

"But they could've been a lot better."

"Maybe. Maybe not. I don't know and, *for sure*, you don't know. Maybe everything does happen for a reason."

"Even if that reason is you're dumb and make bad decisions?"

"Technically, that's a reason," I pointed out.

"Anyway, when I saw you at the church, I guess I thought you should know."

"Mike, besides this possible WesCor deal, what else did Dad have on the go?"

"I can't tell you."

"Aw, for Christ's sake, Mike; he's dead!"

Mike lowered his voice as if someone could hear him two hundred feet away from the other side of his tall and thick hedges ringing the yard.

"He was going to buy the Leafs."

"Get the fuck outta town! You kiddin' me?"

"The deal with WesCor or even Ulti/ME would've paid for it. He was also looking at a pharma company."

"There's a combo. Watch the fucking Leafs long enough and you're going to need some drugs."

"He just figured that entertainment and pharmaceuticals were good things to invest in these days."

"And, of course, that's logical. Of course. Is the WesCor deal dead, as it were?"

"Maybe. It still makes sense, at least to me. We'll see."

"We'll see" is one of those statements that effectively end a conversation. We sort of looked around the yard for a bit. I was wondering which job Alistair had tapped me for—hockey or legal drugs. I assume Mike was busy imagining shipping containers full of cash.

"You going back to . . . to . . . ?" he finally asked.

"Mississauga Lake. Naw. Traffic's a bitch right now. I'll probably stay downtown."

"Let me know, if you hear anything, OK?"

"Sure."

I picked up my cigarette butts, stuffed them in my jacket pocket and left, but not before I loudly revved the Vibe a few times.

Christ, I really am a child.

<CHAPTER NINE>

Just about the last thing in the world I enjoy is being stuck in traffic. I could easily be the guy you read about crashing his SUV into a crowded shopping mall in a fit of road rage. It was 6 o'clock and the 401 eastbound would be stop and go—mostly stop—as the city disgorged its hundreds of thousands of worker bees.

So I went against the flow, drove downtown, and checked into the Royal York, that grand old lady, and the one hotel in Toronto where I knew the windows opened. I had spent a large part of my life hermetically sealed in hotel rooms and office buildings all over the continent and I just never liked it. Whenever things got intense at work—the near all-nighters we used to pull in the early years—I'd book into the Royal York rather than drive out to the 'burbs, because I knew a few hours later I'd have to be back at my desk.

I sat on the hotel's wide window sill, smoking and listening to the sirens and traffic. I was up high enough to see the Air Canada Centre, or whatever they changed its name to. The building and the hockey team playing inside it were worth well over a billion dollars. And the value of rabid fan allegiance for a team that hadn't had a sniff of the Cup in almost a half century? Priceless. Imagine your hand on that PR and marketing throttle.

My reverie which had turned into re-living my life-long fantasy of starting in goal was interrupted by the phone ringing. It was Sarah.

"How'd you find me?" I asked.

"I took a wild guess."

"Sure you did."

"Mike mentioned you might be staying in town."

"Mike?"

"He called me after you left. To see how things were. Anyway, I figured the Royal York. Have you eaten yet?"

"Nope."

"Barberians in an hour?"

"Are you sure?"

"Stop asking me that! Dinner or not?"

I smiled as I agreed. Barberian's was as old school as the Royal York. The near-extinct species of restaurant known as the steakhouse where the cuisine was about as nouvelle as buggy whips are to transportation.

I decided to walk. Yonge Street had retained its quality of a carnival midway or a zoo. A ribbon of artificial daylight under blinking signs. Throngs of people seeing and being seen. The hipsters and the homeless. Out-of-towners gawking.

Along the way, I made up my mind not to pass along Mike's murder theory to her. What possibly could be the point?

She was already at the restaurant. A little kissy-face, a little hug, and a little smile on my face when the tuxedo-ed waiter told me they had Molson Ex.

"How are you holding up, kid?" I asked.

"Pretty good. Not to be harsh but let's face it: it's not like he was around much. He never was a huge presence in our lives."

Whenever people start a sentence with "Not to be harsh," it's harsh.

We briefly studied the menu. I was in sticker shock at the prices. I looked around to see if they had a loans officer.

"I just want a little part of the cow, not the whole thing," I said.

"Don't worry, Jake; I got this."

I still ordered as cheap as I could. Sarah picked out the lobster thermidor with the nonchalance of someone who did not ever worry what the "Market Price" might be.

She leaned toward me. I did the same and my heavy linen napkin slid off my thigh onto the floor as it always does.

"The police talked to me," she said quietly. "I get the feeling they think someone may have killed him."

"Oh?" I said. "I'm sure they have to look at all the angles."

"Do you know that Alistair left me everything?"

"Well, you *are* his wife."

"Actually, I'm not. We've been separated for over a year. The divorce would have been final next month."

That kind of stopped me. Nobody had mentioned it, and yet there she was at the funeral, as if nothing had happened, other than her soon-to-be ex had died.

"I hadn't heard . . . but . . . well, he *was* crazy about you."

"At one time, probably. But it doesn't make sense now. The patents, the intellectual property too. Everything. And Jeff Sears told me it was a new will."

"Look, I knew him . . . sorta. He would've been fierce about taking care of the kids. Maybe he didn't trust anyone else but you to do that."

"But it means getting it all now instead of half in a few weeks. That makes me a suspect, right?"

"Only if it was murder."

"Well, for argument's sake, say it was."

"I don't have any inside knowledge but think about it: *of course* you're a suspect. Rich guy dies, they look at the wife. You still don't watch TV, do you?"

"Have the cops talked to you yet?"

"A bit. My daughter Halley's with Metro."

"I was wondering about that. A couple of months ago, I think I saw her name in the paper and Halley Lydon just isn't all that common. So . . . what did Halley think?"

"Not much. They're gathering info right now. Do you mind if I excuse myself. I need some fresh air," I said, tapping the pack of cigarettes in my shirt pocket.

"Mind if I join you?" she asked, getting up.

Sarah still smoked the way she used to, which is to say: not all. She didn't inhale but, geez, she was sexy with her long fingers and blood red nails wrapped gingerly, delicately around the white tube. I loved how she didn't even try to pretend she was inhaling, the way some dilettantes do.

Certainly, she was adding some by-gone class to Elm Street.

At least that's what I thought.

Apparently, us standing there having a butt didn't strike everyone as aesthetically pleasing because a largish woman in I'd say her late 30s, with about a six-year-old boy in tow, took it upon herself to cross the street and approach us to let us know what an unhealthy and disgusting habit it was—assuming obviously that she was bringing a valuable and astounding revelation to us.

I don't control myself well in these such situations.

"Look, lady," I said, "another unhealthy and disgusting habit is lecturing a complete stranger who may or may not be mentally stable about something that matters exactly fuck-all to you. But since we're in a sharing mood, doncha think you could stand to lose a few pounds? Much healthier for the ol' ticker, you know, if you back away from the fridge once in a while."

I mean *really*, I thought, as she stomped away dragging her kid.

"That was a bit harsh," Sarah said and smiled.

"I did her a favour. Whatever happened to leaving people the fuck alone? It's probably too late for her. She'll be on the ol' dinner party circuit telling everybody about the barbarian she met in front of Barberian's. But maybe the kid'll learn some sympathy, or at the very least, some restraint."

Dinner was arriving as we re-entered. Both of us were toying with food that cost more than a month's grocery bill for me.

"How are your kids doing?" I asked.

"OK, I guess. The girls are great. You know he could be a hard man, remote. He wasn't seeing them much after we split up."

"How's Jason?"

"Not too good, I understand; we don't talk a lot."

"How much?"

"Not at all for about six months. Except one call. A couple of weeks ago. He didn't sound very well."

"Some kind of trouble?"

"No. I don't think so. Just nervous."

Jason was five or six when I last saw him and, in the way we freeze people after years of separation, I thought the only challenge he had back then was being a spoiled brat under Sarah's dotage. Her kid and my kid were about the same age.

"I'm sure he's just got to work some shit out; he'll be fine," I said.

I mostly meant it. A lot of teenagers, me included, went through a big rebellious stage—as teenagers. These days, a combination of excessively smoking excessively powerful dope and financial excess had retarded (that's right, I said retarded) kids so that, near as I could tell, they hit their "up against the wall, motherfucker" stage some years later than we did. At about the age Jason was now, I reckoned.

"So what are you going to do with it all?" I asked, wanting to change the subject.

"For sure, I don't want to run the business," she answered. "After that, I really don't know. What do you think I should do?"

"Sell it all, move to the Dominican with me and finance the best beach bar in the Samana peninsula. C'mon, whaddya say?"

"It's a little more complicated than that."

"No it's not," I insisted. "I mean, summers are hot and then there's the odd hurricane, but other than that . . . "

I was only half-kidding with my suggestion and I think she was only half-serious in dismissing it; such was the flirty way we had, and apparently still had after these many, many years.

She drove me back to the hotel and we sat for bit in the No Stopping zone. We had this sweet little awkward moment that featured a peck on the cheek from her and my expressed hope that she take care.

I fell asleep thinking about Sarah's statement of innocence. It was odd. I hadn't really considered her guilty of anything, most likely because I—and just about every other guy—do not think pretty women can do bad things.

But I reminded myself that, even though she wasn't as beautiful as Faye Dunaway, Bonnie Parker was kinda cute.

Next morning, I was thrilled to be out of the city. I'm not picking on Toronto. My elation at leaving large collections of humanity applies to every city because they all give me the heebie-jeebies. Every city, that is, except San Francisco and New Orleans. Those places give me a hangover.

As I'm leaving the people coagulation, as the roads narrow and cars become fewer and more green appears, Jerry Jeff's line invariably comes to me: "If I could just get off this LA freeway without gettin' killed or caught."

In the two hours it took to drive from downtown Toronto back to the lake, I had time to think about a bunch of things, about the warmth or something like that of seeing people I hadn't seen for years. All brought about by a man who drew us all together and set in motion our dealings with him and with each other. A man who was now occupying an urn.

The prospect of writing together with Steve was, at once, appealing and repugnant. Appealing because it was a chance to be around a guy I always liked, yammering about a subject I was keen on, and it was repugnant because little Jakey just doesn't play well with others.

Alistair knew that. He was smart enough to foresee the HR disaster-in-the-making if he ever let me build a department. Well, actually, he also had proof. He gave me an assistant once, but that didn't work out.

After weeks of what I took to be harassment from her to provide a detailed written job description against which she would be measured in our semi-annual performance reviews that I knew I wouldn't do, I stopped long enough to explain to her I had formulated a full accounting of her duties.

"Karen. Here's your job. You do *everything* I don't want to, OK?

Here, let's put it another way: imagine it's February during the worst fucking winter anyone can remember. There's a computer show in San Francisco and one in Saskatchewan at the same time. Guess which one you're going to."

The flood of memories continued as I was sitting on the porch.

Take this: I didn't have diabetes when I worked for Alistair but I knew he did. Some years after I was diagnosed, I sent him an e-mail accusing him of giving it to me. He wrote back "*Ha!*" That was it.

For all the public presentations, editorial boards, annual meetings, investor chit-chats I'd seen him give in his rapid-fire, dazzlingly-delivered style, I was always struck most by the moments I saw him at rest. Donna the Gatekeeper would normally greenlight me into his office to discuss the latest PR disaster I had no doubt helped to create.

He'd be sitting in his huge but sparse office, staring out the window not daydreaming, not ever daydreaming, but imagining big things like how computers ought to make things better in certain jobs. Even though he had no technical background whatsoever, he had the habit of think-think-thinking about something and then picturing what it could look like. Way back in the mid-70s, he thought computers could make maps better. Not just drawing them but making them able to predict tree growth or future demographics by adding as much embedded detail as you could think of. Same thing for the office, any office. Take what we used to call dumb terminals, connect them, and make them smart.

Or he'd be thinking about ways to make money off his ideas or somebody else's. Complex deals all in his head. It struck me then and still strikes me that he never got enough credit for causing or helping things to happen the way they did.

Must've been the fault of that dissipated douchebag he had in charge of PR.

I called Steve to shoot the shit about our alleged book.

"Like we talked about, I think we should start with Alistair," I said, "And some of the other pioneers . . . "

"But it can't be just a history."

"Agreed. Technology is the one area where no one gives a shit about history."

"So we morph it into the next generation and then the next generation of high tech. Where it's going and how it's getting there. Wherever the fuck 'there' is."

"Anybody who claims to know where things are going with technology is full of crap," I said. "Think Apple now involved almost exclusively with making entertainment toys, think Amazon sending drones to deliver stuff or selling food and lawn furniture, for Christ sakes."

"OK, but I want to get to talking about what it all means. The result of all this shit that's being invented."

"What? Like fewer bank tellers?"

"Not exactly. Jobs being erased are the easy stuff. There aren't too many blacksmiths around anymore either; that always happens with new machines. It's a bitch for a while. Some people get nostalgic and then hardly anybody even remembers what it was like to have somebody wander out and pump your gas for you. That kinda technology was *meant* to get rid of jobs. I'm more interested in the unintended consequences."

"Like thalidomide?"

"Yes! These days, absolutely everything is brand new. And it's not backroom stuff. It involves everybody. But meanwhile, nobody really knows what the effects will be. What it's all doing to our brains, to how we deal with people, how we pass our time."

"Ya know, there just might be a tiny, miniscule, negligible shred of wee merit in the idea," I admitted.

"So, let's write a book, shall we?"

"How hard could it be?"

"And we don't actually have to see each other do we?"

"Not if I can help it."

"Perfect!"

Steve told me he had already started pulling some things together, had a bunch of notes, observations, background. He asked me to put lipstick on the pig by making sense of his collection and then producing a detailed outline for a publisher. Oh, and could I fill out some of the research.

"What the fuck are you going to do?" I asked him.

"Imagine the royalties."

"How about imagining a publisher?"

"Already done, friend-o. Small press in BC. They published my first book. I called them and they're pretty interested. They want to see what I—we—have."

"What's the advance?"

"My Christ, you're out of touch. There's no advance."

I knew from my own book that there wasn't going to be any advance.

"So, are you going to do anything?" I asked.

"Look, I have an actual job. Just play around with it, will ya?"

Out of guilt, I thought I'd better first catch up on the book that I didn't even know he had written. I found it on the web, and popped for the 7-dollar download. I made a note to myself to give him a hard time for calling himself "J. Stephen Golding."

Tradeoffs was another post-mortem on the financial flame-out from the late aughts. It was pretty good, actually, not because it was a screed about why the bankers should be jailed—which, of course they should—but because it tied in technology as the great enabler of all the madness that nearly fucked everything up and could very easily do it again. Program trading down to the nanosecond that caused instant euphoria or panic. Bundled-up assets electronically whizzing around the world, being picked up by Icelandic fishermen-cum-bankers or Europeans who used to think anything American must be worth a shit-ton.

Steve must have been attacked by a wild pack of adverbs, adjectives, and commas when he was young. It was all noun-verb-noun which, in my never humble view, made for a tough slog over 80,000 or so words.

I checked my e-mail and found a string of notes from Steve, all with giant attachments representing his research. I dove in. His stuff was fascinating. And it was bound to be controversial. At the very least, highly argumentative.

His basic theory—not completely unheard of—held that technology was doing a whole lot more than just making it easier for us to bank, travel, shop, and watch videos of baby Pandas and crazed Russian drivers. It was transforming the way we dealt with each other and it was actually re-wiring our brains to create a planet of, in effect, ADHD sufferers. He had the links and the articles from neuroscientists and the psychology studies arguing that we were all developing the attention spans of hyper-nervous hummingbirds.

Like I said, none of it was really all that revolutionary and normally this "sky is falling" kind of bullshit bores me stupid, but what I found interesting were nuggets suggesting the side effects from this great steaming pile of technology. One, the exponential explosion in pharmaceutical sales to help keep us focused amid the constant barrage of images. Or the skyrocketing sales of other drugs that calm us down after reading all the alarmist crap hurtling at us. It wasn't just the stress from big stuff like reading/seeing/hearing about gun violence or natural disasters or the new robber barons and the useless governments letting them do the robbing that was killing us. It was everything. The litany of news items that in one day, an average day, documents things like an anti-religion blogger hacked to death in Bangladesh, an earthquake in Chile and a mass shooting in rural Missouri. All stuff you wouldn't even hear about 100 years ago, now just an incessant and instant stream of tragedy and viciousness.

Secondly, this reliance on technology and just reading reading/seeing/hearing about things instead of actually doing things was leading to the creation of a class unable to care for itself at the basic human level if the shit ever hit the fan, at the exact time when it was more likely than ever that the shit *would* hit the fan, what with the prospect of global warming, water shortages, crashed power grids, super-viruses, never mind the political upheavals or the chance of Menudo getting back together.

This prospect of doomsday, I mentally added, had to be abetted by the Born Agains who, if serious—and I always saw them as deadly serious as cancer—had to be positively giddy about not being left behind real soon.

Broadcast that often enough and it also begets the nutjob survivalists and conspiracy theorists who now learn everything they think they know from the Internet which has proved to them that 9/11 was an inside job, our weather was being manipulated by NOAA, and Ringo Starr was Yasser Arafat's body double. While some of these people are now living off the grid in cabins in Wyoming smug in their preparation for apocalypse right the fuck now, there are lots of middle-class families living down the block that were gleefully and matter-of-factly spending every waking moment and dollar on getting themselves and their family ready for *Mad Max* every day.

At the other end, the new mega rich seemed equally convinced that the end was nigh. Their response: git while the gittin's good. And then build high-walled oases to protect the oodles you had just gotten from the packs of disenfranchised marauders that were sure to be dropping by any day now.

He tied all these doomsday scenarios into a package that essentially concluded there was one common element: greed. Prattle on all you want about the psychology or the sociology and or any other fuckin' ology, it's really all about the cashology. Technology races, legal drug wars, gun sales, environment raping, banking bonanzas, and bent brains were being fueled by the insatiable lust of shareholders for quarter after quarter profits. While it was tempting to write off Steve's conclusions as the rant of a Commie bastard, it was equally tempting to see that he was right. Money was the insane incentive that was driving us, lemming-like, towards self-destruction.s

I actually had some historical framework for this view. Attributed to King Philip of Spain in the mid-1500s was this killer one-liner that still held up, that would *always* hold up.

"Everything is about one thing: money and more money," ol' Phil was supposed to have said.

So if End Times weren't just around the corner, at the very least, it was going to be a pretty fucked up way to live for a lot of people.

This could be good.

I told him so in an e-mail.

"Dude," I wrote. *"Got the title: "How technology is ruining me and you . . . and the universe." Catchy, huh?*

"No, no," he wrote back. *"That can be the subtitle. Every book has a subtitle now that follows the main grabber and pretty well reveals what the book's about. There's one every week. Just watch late night TV. So keep working on it. I'm not a headline writer."*

I did think for a bit and, as usual, fell in love with my first hunch. I called Steve.

"E-pocalypse Now!"

"Better . . . much better."

"This shit just comes to me! Now, can I have the rest of the day off?"

"Jake, are you going to be serious about this?"

"Hell, yeah. You?"

"All in."

We decided that this thing couldn't all be yelling from a soap-box with a sprinkling of some short anecdotes. We had to take what we thought we knew and spin it outwards. Do solid research, prove the title.

"Where do we start?" Steve asked.

"How about with what we sorta know? Maybe use WesCor and Ulti/ME as a starting point. Who's going to win?"

"Who cares?"

"You, sir, are the fucking moron," I said. "That's *all* a lot of people care about. They want to see a game with everyone belonging to teams. Winners and losers. And with our whole industrial base shifting, we need to pick 'em."

"And ultimately, it's about who you trust. An old style company like WesCor that makes stuff?"

"Which breaks."

"And needs to get fixed by the people who made it. Or a next-wave company like Ulti/ME which doesn't make anything but which has millions of subscribers, all afraid they're gonna lose out if they don't sign up. So they join and turn over a big bunch of their lives to what? A website they think they can trust?"

"I couldn't trust anyone like that," I said.

"Not even me?"

"Alright, alright, I trust you."

"Jake, do you think maybe we're a little too cynical about all this tech stuff?"

"What do you mean?"

"Well, we probably get along because we're both curmudgeonly old farts."

"Like those two old guys in the balcony on the Muppets."

"Yes! But we just can't kick the shit out of everything."

"We don't have to," I said. "We can write chapters on all the good stuff."

"Like all of medicine," he suggested.

"Like *most* of medicine. I think we have the boner challenge whipped and we could probably stop investigating restless leg syndrome."

"OK, what about all of science?"

"Whoa, again! Like *most* of science. Having a research *team* spend months or years proving that dogs can recognize if their owners are pissed off or happy seems to me exactly like having an English major spend a year of his life dissecting the stage directions of *Troilus and Cressida*."

"And then you have those huge R&D departments of the largest companies investing shitloads into making what amounts to new toys. How many different kinds of headphones do kids need to listen to their shitty music?"

"For the rest of my life I will remember one of the greatest comments ever on this fascination with electronic toys."

"Hit me."

"*3rd Rock from the Sun*," I recalled. "The episode where the alien family discovers both credit cards and big home entertainment systems. They spend tens of thousands on the full monty—speakers, amps, giant screen—back when all this shit was really, really expensive. They're sitting their awestruck, completely gobsmacked, commenting wondrously on the colour, the clarity, the sound. And then Tommy says: "Guys, guys. It's *Leprechaun 2*!""

"So yeah, we can do something on how diversion isn't diversion anymore; it's preoccupation. Not with the content, but the delivery system. Watching *Lawrence of Arabia* on a phone?"

"You can't possibly get absorbed by the film; you just pick up bits while you're doing something else."

"Same as scrolling through a 5,000-word article on Mid-east interventionism."

"Just taking away a few more bits."

"And when you talk about it, it's just those bits."

"Plus, what can you possibly say in 280 characters?"

"Exactly. Just yell!"

"There's a chapter for the book: The Death of Nuance."

"So compare and contrast with what WesCor does. It makes stuff that actually does stuff."

"God, I love it when you talk technical."

The next morning, I was still cranked as I sat on the deck, drinking coffee and thinking.

When I get to thinking about something, I wind up looking into it. True fact: I once spent an entire day in our Washington office going through months of the branch's phone records trying to find a suspected leak to a New York short-sell analyst who had the uncanny knack of kicking the crap out of our stock a few days before we deserved to get the crap kicked out of it. P.S. I found the employee. I mean, the ex-employee.

Thanks to the Interwebs, my odd kind of diligence has moved onto a whole new plane. A half a lifetime ago, I could spend all day in a library, rummaging through those file cards packed into little wooden drawers, digging through stacks, and making librarians crazy with obscure requests.

As a result of my library-dwelling and a life-long fascination with trivia, I know lots of things, arcane facts mostly. But other than gardening and a bit of carpentry (adhering to my infallible motto: measure once; cut twice) I don't really know anything of any value. And even my trivia mastery is pointless now that it takes a nanosecond to find out who engineered the early Doors albums (Bruce Botnick, to save you a few keystrokes. You're welcome).

I always start my research by cutting and pasting bits of articles or whole documents but that usually results in pages after pages of word docs to comb through later to re-sort again. As I get more immersed, I switch to those yellow legal pads and my barely legible handwriting. And then come the largest Post-it notes whereon I jot down fragments and date them—or in this case—timestamp them so I can revisit them chronologically.

It all may sound organized but it's not. Soon there are Post-it notes everywhere—walls, lampshades, the edges of the coffee table. The whole place looks like it's been buried in giant yellow confetti.

By the end of the first day, I could see a pattern emerging, was convinced that contrasting WesCor and Ulti/ME would serve as a sturdy metaphor.

Despite all the advanced technology they developed, WesCor was as old school as a business can get. Closed loop, as they say. Through their subsidiaries, they designed, built, sold, and maintained a huge range of machines and devices. They just wanted to make actual things. And they did so for just about every industry—military contracting, energy, aerospace, manufacturing, transportation, and health care.

The sheer volume was huge, the business model simple. We make 'em for x. We sell 'em for x + y and we keep the y. How much was the y? None of your goddamned business because all these companies had another thing in common: they were all privately owned by WesCor's founders, Wesley and Cortland Reed.

They didn't have to tell anybody anything. And they didn't want to be owned by anybody. You only ever heard about what they did in the form of rumour and gossip columns in the business press. Or if they acquired somebody who was publicly-traded and, therefore, had to disclose that their asses had just been bought and privatized.

Concord Medical Systems, the medical devices company that Alistair had been dealing with, was the anomaly. A relatively small part of the WesCor empire, it was their only public company. The Reeds owned about 32% through WesCor. The rest was allegedly public but not really. The shares were very thinly held by a few institutions that, coincidence among coincidences, were also the firms that shared the underwriting of their IPO.

From my short stint with them, confirmed a few days ago by Mike, I knew that MacNeil and Bio-Watch had the critical piece, the power system. If Mike were to be believed, it worked better than anybody's, had been humming along on a lab bench for years. Alarms were perfect, mechano worked, and it was easily controlled and re-charged, with at least five times the longevity of any other battery. But, Mike said, Alistair wouldn't sell. Yet.

On the other hand, Ulti/ME was the way new technology was going. Mostly because Little Jakey doesn't like sharing, I am repulsed by the new wisdom that says we have to tell everybody everything that's going on with us. Share everything all the time and just wonderful stuff would happen. They'd point to things like the Arab spring. Gosh, that worked out well, didn't it? And even if it had, those kinds of things are pitifully few compared to the blizzard of insignificance and self-indulgence we trudge through on the web. Even if you were the very best friend I had on the planet, I still wouldn't give a shit what you had for dinner last night.

In capitalizing on this wave, Ulti/ME was that swinging-for-the-fences, one-in-a-million start-up that pans out—a serendipitous combination of a strong idea, determination, and hitting the sweet spot of timing. All being orchestrated by Josh Steinman, their enigmatic boy wonder founder.

Digging around a bit in their history, I had to smile as I re-read the report Alexandra Simpson wrote six years ago when they were just starting up. She had tapped them as the next big thing.

It struck her—and me—that Ulti/ME was smarter than the rest even if it didn't take a genius to figure out where it was all going. After people got through trying to buy things cheaply with instant coupons, liking or unliking people and things they really couldn't care less about one way or the other, posting endless vacation photos, and tweeting inane inspirational statements, they were going to focus on their Number One concern: themselves. And that meant they were going to become even more obsessed with their health.

Oh, goody.

This being the age of impatience, it was obvious that people weren't going to wait for poor and hopelessly stalemated governments to actually do something about it. Why not turn to the sort of folks who changed the way you listen to music, watch movies, deal with people? Just pay a fee, file your medical records with them, get advice, and build so-called communities of interest where *moi* was the only interest.

Given Ulti/ME's designs on Alistair's Bio-Watch, and, presumably with other similar companies, Ulti/ME was about to take the next step. Why not have your blood sugar or heartbeat monitored by a big pro outfit that could hook you up to alarms to keep you right?

And what an upside. Why not go on to write prescriptions for the whole class of drugs that millions needed but which weren't either glamorous or dangerous—like statins and metformin? Then, why not fill those prescriptions yourself? Free shipping thrown in. While you're at it, why not file all the paperwork with the government or the HMO? You actually didn't need doctors; you needed doctor-approved algorithms, to stay within the range that's been pre-set for you. Theoretically, you needed one doctor in every province and state with his or her name e-signed.

All wired in. Encrypted. E-nudging you to take your meds, book an eye exam, do something about the pounds you were packing on. Just like the ceaseless robocalls you get from your dealership telling you need your motor oil changed even though you've owned cars for forty fucking years. Go another step and why not perform almost all diagnoses by HD camera 24/7, in the comfort of your own home, whenever you want to?

One obvious next step—and the subject of much speculation—was the imbedding of devices that actually administered all the drugs you needed—or had been convinced you needed.

A happy by-product of all this self-diagnosis and self-medicating? It would take all the heat off the medical system. ER visits would have to plummet because the information you could get on-line about your malady would easily be as good as what the beleaguered interns will tell you at 3 AM in the crowded Emerge, as they deal with gunshot or stab wounds or traffic injuries, or all the other damaging things that can happen when humans come into physical contact with each other.

It all hung on a concept whose very mention causes a gag reflex in me: empowerment. Taking control of your health, it was called. People would line up to spill their guts about what was going on with those very same guts. They could and were updating their files electronically. Why not be able to request and be billed for a doctor to review?

It struck me as brighter than hell, much the same way they got people to pay for and then bag their own groceries without the intervention of store employees, except the ones who had to help useless tits such as myself.

You'd think people would care about this automation. Maybe the older farts like me prefer pointlessly sitting around in waiting rooms thumbing through old *National Geographics*, but, once again literally, we're dying off.

All of us old folks are being replaced by people with absolutely no shame and no interest in privacy.

I can't prove it (well, I suppose I could), but people now trust companies more than they trust governments. Orwell was waaaay wrong. It's not governments ruthlessly seizing power through technology to create a few superpowers. It's companies ruthlessly seizing power through technology to create a few superpowers.

No, that's not right. They aren't seizing anything. They're being *offered* the power. Just sign the waiver. You know, the one on the website marked Accept/Don't Accept the electronic reams of small print contract terms you never read but come into force when you make that one keystroke.

All that seemed to matter these days was if people liked your company. If your "brand" gave them warm and fuzzy feelings you were in like flint.

Ultimately, Ulti/ME was logical extension of this self-absorption, this self-interest.

Big Pharma companies had to love it. Even though it would likely drive prices down somewhat to keep everybody competitive, they'd get to talk directly to people who have a stake in talking back because they have the condition you claim to fix. And make sure they receive a tailored news stream of articles telling them they better do something about it right the fuck now. Here's your choice, here's the side effects, here are the studies we'll let you see, here's the cost, and did we mention free shipping.

Ulti/ME had to really love it. Now fight, ya bastards, for advertising space.

And to make this unholy marriage between Big Tech, Big Pharma and Big Insurance more friendly, give it the patina of societal concern. Want to make a donation to a medical cause? There's another app for that.

I was jacked and it felt great.

I have this ritual—big surprise huh?—have had it for decades when I'm pumped about a project. It could be an addition to the deck, could be a big writing gig. It's the moment when I know, absolutely *know* how a thing will look or sound. How the start, middle, and end will fit and turn out before I even begin.

I always put on the Stones' *Time Waits for No One*, crank it up, and play air guitar under whatever stars happen to be above me at the time. Six and half minutes of jazzy groove and Mick Taylor's guitar magic.

Before I turned in that night, I grabbed another beer and my trusty yellow legal pad, and starting writing questions down for my next day's self-assignment. Questions about what Steve had dug up, questions about what I knew or thought I knew or needed to know.

The questions started piling up, filling one page and then another and then another. The beer empties piled up too, to the point that, when I finally went to bed, I had a pretty good hum going. I fell asleep and/ or passed out with a smile on my face because I was sure we were onto something. We just needed more answers.

"The dreams of the night time will have vanished by dawn," sings Sir Mick.

Well, let's see about that, shall we?

The knock that woke me up sounded angry and made me likewise. Pissed off, I stumbled to the door and whipped it open.

"Carl, what the fuck—"

It was Halley and she looked a whole lot more pissed off than I was. She swept into the place and was about to start speaking when I shushed her.

"Coffee," I croaked. "Must . . . have . . . coffee."

She swept out of the place and onto the back deck while I shakily went about preparing my caffeine fix. I debated dispensing with the water; I mean, why cut it?

As I knew she would, Halley started in on me the second I closed the patio door.

"What did you and MacNeil talk about, on the . . . " she said as she flipped open her notepad, " . . . on May 13th . . . 5 weeks before he died."

"You knew he called me?"

"C'mon, dad! You watch cop shows. Phone records are pretty easy to get."

"Mine or his?"

"His. We're not checking up on you. Yet."

"And you didn't tell me?"

"Dad, how about you don't start with that mock indignation? Why didn't *you* tell *me?*"

"It was nothing. Not worth mentioning. Maybe three minutes of bullshit."

"Four minutes and 28 seconds," she said, referring again to her notepad.

"Alright. Four minutes and 28 seconds of bullshit."

"Odd bit of coincidence, don't you think?"

"Random nature of the universe. A tear in the fabric of time. That sort of thing."

"Dad, fuck off, will you? What did you talk about?"

"Nothing!" I repeated.

I knew I was sounding like a teenager with the multi-purpose answer that hadn't, as near as I could tell, changed since the non-communicative 1960s.

What'd you learn in school today?

Nothing.

What'd you do last night?

Nothing.

And so on.

"Don't bullshit me, old man."

"Really sweetie, it was a nothing call. He wanted to see how I was. You know, catching up. He hinted about me coming back to work for him but I blew him off."

"Work doing what?"

"He didn't say. But he did sound a little funny."

"Funny how?"

"Kinda boozy. Trust me; I know that sound. But he didn't drink much, at least not back then."

She wrote something in her notebook, and then stared out at the lake.

"What do the rest of the cops say about his call to me?" I asked.

"They don't know yet. I recognized your number. They're working their way backwards through his records, probably running it down as we speak."

"Why didn't you say anything to them?"

She hesitated.

"I wanted to be sure you were OK," she said, "That you weren't . . . you know . . . involved."

"I'm fine and I'm as uninvolved as ever. Now, you go back right now and tell them about the call. Tell them you investigated me, tore my life wide open and your old man's as clean as a whistle."

"Whistle's are never clean," she said, staring at me a bit too pointedly for my liking.

That amped the old man up.

"Thanks a heap for moving me from dad to perp! Ya got me. I confess! I became so pissed off at him for firing me eighteen *years* ago and then having the nerve, the fucking gall, to offer me a new job that I drove to Toronto, found him—although I didn't have a clue where he lived—and murdered him in a way that the smartest cops in the biggest city in the country can't figure out. Christ, you're quite the sleuth!"

We sipped our coffee in silence, perfectly matched as our angry indignation subsided.

"Why do you think he wanted you to come back?" she finally asked.

"I'm absolutely outstanding in my profession? No, wait; that can't be it. Maybe he was just nostalgic? Naw, that's not it either. He was never a rear-view mirror kinda guy."

"Did you know," she said, "that Alistair was hooked up to an experimental device, something that not only told him what his glucose levels were, but that automatically injected him with the right amount of insulin to keep his blood sugar normal?"

"I did not."

Which was true. Mike said it was a just a different monitoring thingy, not that it actually administered the drugs on its own.

"Who made it?"

"Concord Medical."

"Find Nigel Hayward. He's at Concord. He'll know what happened."

"Old info, dad. He left six months ago."

"I saw him at the funeral."

"Really?"

She wrote in her pad again.

"At first," she said, "Concord claimed they didn't know how Alistair got his hands on one, let alone hooked himself up."

"That's gotta be horseshit."

"Turns out it was. The first guy we talked to was pretty low-level. Then, let's see, a Robert Howe, the chief engineer at Concord, called back all apologetic, said it was a hush-hush business deal. He should know."

"So the pump screwed up?

"That's what we thought. That it had to be a malfunction that gave him a huge dose. Autopsy said his blood sugar was below 2. It would've been even lower than that when he went comatose."

"Maybe it was hacked?"

"Considered that too. But we checked the logs that Concord sent—pages of print-outs going back three months. The sensors were operating exactly as they were supposed to, adjusting his blood sugar levels; the pump was working exactly as it was supposed to. And, the reservoir wasn't even empty. The dose that killed him would have had to have been at least the whole reservoir, probably a lot more."

"So, worst case, he'd get woozy, sweat like hell. All he would've had to do was have a glass of orange juice, lie down and he'd be fine."

I've had a few of those episodes myself; I know exactly what they feel like.

"What about the battery?" I asked.

"Nope. If it was run down—which it wasn't—"

"—he wouldn't be getting the insulin so his sugar would have been high, not low," I said finishing her sentence. "Did you find out who actually hooked Alistair up?"

"Eventually. It was one of his techies from Montrose. He had some kind of confidential private gig on the side as MacNeil's computer valet. We talked to him; he damn near broke down in tears as I was introducing myself. Through the blubbering, we found out that a) it's a pretty simple procedure as long as you had a halfway competent doctor—which Alistair did— and b) this techie wouldn't hurt anybody."

"OK, another possibility: It wasn't a secret that Alistair had severe Type-2. What if a bad guy got into his place and injected him manually with a bunch of insulin? You know, pulled a Von Bulow."

"We checked. No forced entry. No extra needle marks showed up at the autopsy."

"Maybe you weren't really looking? I mean, why would you? It seemed like a natural death."

"Trust me, we looked. The pathologist was 99% sure there was no external shot. There's a bit of doubt because of the implant site."

"So, in other words, daughter dear, you still got nuthin'?"

"Except the fact that the last dosage likely wouldn't have been fatal.

But somehow, it likely was."

"Likely" often has nothing to do with it. You can trot out the statistical probability proving that something likely will or won't happen. A kid growing up in the inner city is likely to have a crapfest of a life but not 100% of them do. Abused kids grow up to be abusers. But not all of them. And sometimes the overwhelming underdog wins the Super Bowl. Think about it the other way 'round: it's shitty odds but not even close to lottery-ticket shitty. That's where I like living. In that small area where something that was supposed to happen, didn't. I don't much care that 9 out 10 dentists recommend something. I am, however, intrigued why that one dissenter didn't.

I have no idea why this is so. And I'm way past caring.

"Why do you think he had such a huge Swiss bank account?" Halley asked, apropos of nothing.

"He did?" I smiled, remembering at least two trips to Geneva although we had no clients there. "Maybe he didn't have a choice, honey. I tried this experiment once. Every day, for about a week, I left big piles of peanuts out on the deck, handfuls and handfuls. Every day the squirrels and chipmunks would mob the place, cart them all away, and hide them for the winter. Next day, I'd replace the pile, and the next, until there must have been 20 or 30 pounds stashed around the place. Enough for the next ten winters. Turns out, they don't seem to remember where they hid them."

"So?"

"So they just can't resist a pile of peanuts."

Halley shook her head and rolled her eyes.

"Well, we don't think that's the reason."

"Alrighty then, even though I'm no financial genius, try this for a wild theory: I bet he saved the cash so he could spend it later."

"Then why is it all gone?"

"I didn't know that either. How much are we talking about here?"

"Near as we can tell, 122 million."

Even though I've never learned to do it well, I whistled.

"That's a lot of peanuts," I said. "Did you ask Peter Wachefsky, his accountant?"

"He seemed as surprised as you."

"What about Sarah MacNeil? She have anything to say?"

"Same level of surprise."

"Say, sweetie. Was your name in the newspaper a little while ago?"

"Don't think so. Chief hates to see an individual cop's name in print. Unless it's a . . . "

"PR slut?"

"Exactly. And I wish you'd stop using that word."

"I had that expression years before it became uncool, works for all genders."

"Why'd you ask about a newspaper quote?"

"Sarah thought she had seen it."

"What's your deal with her, if you don't mind me asking?"

"I don't, and there isn't any 'deal', as you put it. You prying as a concerned daughter or a nosy cop?"

Halley didn't answer.

Again, she passed on the opportunity to partake of my culinary expertise but mercifully Carl came by and we drove to the Angler Arms and got semi-loaded, arguing about the how the NFL draft turned out compared with all the punditry leading up to it. As usual, I thought some third and fourth-rounders were the best prospects and, as usual, Carl thought I was full of shit.

I spent some time debating with myself over how much to tell Steve about what Halley had revealed concerning Alistair's death. Even though I did trust him and it sure was tempting, it was also something that Halley probably shouldn't have let slip. I decided to hang on to that gem until it eventually came out, as I figured it would. Tell more than one person anything and it won't ever stay a secret.

The irony of Alistair's death maybe having been caused by a malfunctioning piece of technology when he had made his fortune from technology was macabre perhaps but no less true. How's that for an unintended consequence?

Normally, I love irony. Except when I practice it on myself and get caught. Like, for example, my obsession with gardening. Years ago, when I took it up, just after Alistair fired me the first time, I had lots of time and lots of severance money and it was spring. Beth smiled and shook her head and indulged me as I began transforming the little lot surrounding our bungalow in Don Mills into a botanical wonderland.

That was the plan, anyway. Truth be told, it was a crazy quilt of sun-loving plants which I expected to live in the shade and vice versa. But I got better as everyone—except the fucking Leafs—gets better at anything they do over and over again for years.

Some people, early on myself included, refer to gardening as a passion. That's bullshit. Addiction is closer to the truth. I know the difference. The local nursery owner—who I bet owns a condo in Barbados thanks to me—will sometimes slip me a few bulbs of a new lily variety that's allegedly resistant to those fucking red beetles that can strip a stalk in an afternoon. He smiles and waves away payment. Goddamn the pusher man.

My lawns down to the lake are stunning. After twenty years of blood, sweat and beers, they fucking well better be.

The irony of course is that no one except Carl regularly visits and Carl couldn't care less about the *psychocarpus opulifolius* I brought back to life or the new stone wall I built. He just shakes his head.

I tell him that it'll help resale, but even he knows I'm coming out of this place on a plank.

<CHAPTER FOURTEEN>

I got deeper and deeper into the research. For that day and the next and the next, until I had eyestrain, back spasms and my keyboard was lightly dusted with cigarette ash, I worked Google like a madman. So much so that I had forgotten about earning a sort of living.

I was going to pass on the six or seven hundred bucks I could've made that day. From time to time, I get hired to write complicated scenarios for crisis communications training at a big PR firm which has built quite the reputation for schooling companies on what to do and say when the shit hits the fan.

I had earned the nickname "The Master of Disaster" at the agency which, while not necessarily a comment on my family affairs, described the entire scope of my business—such as it is.

It takes a long time for me to write things for a client. I'll stare out at the lake or the ocean for hours sometimes, building a movie shot-by-shot about whatever disaster I had been asked to simulate. Imagining the wreckage/carnage/financial ruin/injuries/oil spill/stock swindle/hotel fire/murder on campus was now my stock and trade.

I always love it when a client says: "That couldn't happen." There's only one reply: "In your entire life, have you ever heard of . . . ?" then mention a famous calamity.

They have to nod their heads because it's not like I use alien invaders in my scenarios.

"So," I continue, "we've just established that it *could* happen. Now, all you can say is: it just hasn't happened to me . . . *yet*."

That was the key. It all had to make sense. No matter how outlandish, every piece of the scenario, every action and reaction, had to have its own internal logic. And not just the original problem, because the tragedy had to escalate, as these things *always* do.

Jenna Milne conducts these sessions in person at the client's site, wherever that happens to be. Calgary, Los Angeles, Dubai. She hands out the first part of the scenario to her corporate pupils and gives them twenty minutes to think up the company's public response to the horror story that just happened to them. Then I pretend to be a snotty reporter phoning in to demand answers. After that round of questioning, the crisis gets stepped up with the second part of the scenario and again I call, being even snottier.

Now, I have never been a snotty reporter but I've met my fair share so I know how they work. Plus, in my spare time, I'm generally pretty snotty myself.

I never actually go to these places where the sessions are held. I truly do hate traveling unless Mexico or the DR is the destination, which works out well because years ago Jenna came to realize that I ought not to be presented to clients. "No good can ever come of it," she said once. I had to agree.

In the course of my snotty interviewing, I've been cursed at, had the phone slammed down on me by Senior Vice-Presidents, and made newly-minted managers cry. All during a pretend exercise.

It's not ever the first question that gets them. Almost everybody's smart enough to get past the first question.

Before every session, Jenna and I agree to a code phrase she'll use when she wants me to be particularly hard on a trainee. We do a recap afterwards where I find out why she targeted someone for nastier treatment. Invariably, it's because the guy fancied himself an expert with the media. Just as invariably, he isn't.

This particular assignment was relatively simple: peaceful environmental protesters at an oil refinery. Now what if they were mostly Aboriginals? What if they had got their hands on an internal company report talking about how much damage the tailings ponds were doing to the nearby river, their main water source? What if one of the protesters got badly hurt climbing the stack? What if the plant manager told his employees not to help him? What if one of the protesters was a police informant?

But this possible book with Steve now had me on a single track and

I wouldn't—or couldn't—switch back to my paying gig. There were a couple of harrying e-mails from Jenna, whom I hate to piss off, so I played the under-the-weather card and bought myself a reprieve.

I headed back down the Internet rabbit hole. When I'm on a research jag, I become obsessed. Nothing else matters except smoking and coffee, then smoking and beer. Not time, not nutrition, not hygiene, not taking my meds. At points, it gets pretty frenetic as I try to separate the germane from the trivial, heading up e-tributaries, following Wikipedia footnotes, combing through the archives of obscure journals, finding industry bloggers then rifling through past articles and then the links embedded in them.

Biographical sketches and texts of speeches made by the main players fascinate me. I also listen to podcasts and recorded analysts' teleconferences because you can see the flesh involved, hear the cadence and inflections in their voices, the way their eyes moved, what they thought was funny. You could approach some kind of clarity if you could get past the PR lipstick being smeared on the pigs, the dumbing down in the general press, the lameness of the pronouncements after the lawyers and bean counters got through neutering them.

Talk all you want about events and trends and movements, these are not impersonal things; they are the result of a relatively small number of real, live, breathing humans driving them, reacting to them.

Because I used to write them, I also had a fairly good knowledge of the weasel words in press releases, where the truth lay, what the inference was of the quotes, the importance of the dates, before you slide down to the standard legal caveat about forward-looking statements when everything was a fucking forward-looking statement. That's after all why you issued the release in the first place: you were looking forward to your stock going up.

The real trove, if you had the time and interest, lies in sifting through the 10-Ks that public companies have to file annually with the Securities and Exchange Commission. They always give a drier but more accurate picture of what was actually going on with public companies and what their managements were planning.

The next morning, early as is my wont, I started back on the research. I tried to focus on the legal aspect.

The pace of change required another explosion, this one in the legal profession as tech companies sued each other ceaselessly over real or perceived patent infringements surrounding the tiniest little technical advance over a competitor's doo-hickey. This wasn't millions at stake; it was billions.

Some companies that used to actually make or do stuff had stopped making or doing stuff and had become patent licensing outfits that spent their time scouring the technology landscape and buying up patents filed by small companies who couldn't get their latest and greatest gizmo launched. They then turned around and charged the big boys great gobs of money for the right to revive the abandoned dream. That was a business? That was like a vulture selling rotting carrion to hungrier vultures.

And then there were the myriad, nay, the plethora of lawsuits between and among the big players. Paper wars on an international scale, hordes of litigant and defendant lawyers waging bloody duels, hop-scotching around the world like Risk armies, trying the same cases in different jurisdictions, winning in San Jose, losing in Seoul.

And this didn't include the thousands of wrongful dismissal suits, the I-didn't-get-the-respect-and/or- share-options-I-deserved suits versus the you-were-so-useless-we-had-to-fire-your-ass countersuits.

It all reminded me of watching squirrels brawl, something I've spent an inordinate of time doing at the lake. Without knowing the motive for their dispute, it's entertaining as hell trying to follow their frantic chases. Tree to tree, they zip up and down the branches, frequently changing roles. On a dime, the pursuer becomes the pursued and off they go again at top speed, shaking the branches, never falling, and hell bent on capture.

There really isn't much of an on-line depository for legal stuff in Canada; the US is a lot more open about their court proceedings. Want to know who's zooming who? Criminal or civil? You can find it all for a price on pacer.gov in America.

That's when it got interesting. At least to me, anyway. Concord's last 10K had specifically referenced a lawsuit against its parent company. No detail, other than the suit was, in the opinion of management, "vexatious", likely to be unsuccessful, and would be "vigorously defended" (as opposed to, what, "lackadaisically defended"?).

I dug up a civil proceeding originally filed six months ago in Massachusetts and still winding its way through the judicial system. Owned by a former Concord employee, a company called East Anglia Holdings was suing WesCor and the Reed brothers personally for patent infringement and for wrongful dismissal. There was a countersuit from the Reeds against East Anglia, claiming that it had violated confidentiality agreements and non-compete clauses.

East Anglia's owner/employee wasn't named but I could guess.

For reasons known only to neuroscientists, I remembered that Cambridge University was in East Anglia and, further, I knew just one graduate of Cambridge University involved in the medical devices industry.

A little more digging in corporate records yielded the name of the president, director, and sole proprietor of East Anglia Holdings.

The plaintiff in the first case and defendant in the second was Doctor Nigel Hayward.

Sonofabitch! He was doing it again. He had lost his lawsuit against Alistair, and now he was going after the Reed brothers who were also retaliating.

What struck me as odd was that Hayward seemed to suing for the same thing.

To confirm that, I spent the better part of the day toggling back and forth between Ol' Nige's case in Canada and his lawsuit in the US. Sifting through hundreds of pages of pre-trial hearings and discoveries is exactly nobody's idea of fun. An hour into it and I was convinced that I'd soon regret pissing away this much time on what, in the grand scheme of things, looked like a minor spat. But, like just about everything else I say or do, I couldn't help myself. I had to see it through, get to the nub of the thing.

As near as I could tell, the nub was this: Nigel had sued Alistair. Lost. And in the bargain, the Canadian court upheld the agreement he originally signed giving up world-wide rights to his patent for his advanced monitor.

Now here he was, suing the Reeds even though, by court order, he didn't own the patent anymore.

It got weirder.

Switching back and forth, it was clear that Nigel had cut and pasted pages and pages of his Canadian motions and filings into his US case. Word for word, with identical engineering drawings; he hadn't even bothered to switch to American spellings.

And then weirder still.

In Canada, every time Nigel made any legal move, filed any amendment to the suit, Alistair would play whack-a-mole and issue nasty, detailed responses. In the US, the Reeds seemed as though they were barely acknowledging the suit.

I wanted to confirm with Mary-Ellen Thompson that if Doc Hayward lost in Canada, he couldn't try it again in the US. After all, she would've helped win the Canadian case.

I reached her just after five. We shot the shit for a while. Mary-Ellen was always nice enough to talk baby talk to me in explaining the various ins and outs of patent law and civil proceedings.

She told me that Hayward could sue for essentially the same thing in a different jurisdiction—Apple and Samsung had been foitin' 'round the world over similar matters for years. However, it was exceedingly rare in Canada/US situations.

"In other words, Hayward knew he was likely to lose?" I offered.

"He had to. He didn't have the patent."

"And the cost?"

"It's a lot more complicated now. It can take years and cost millions."

"And he'd know that too?"

"I can't see how he couldn't."

"Any idea why the Reeds couldn't see what was going on? I mean, this amounts to selling the Brooklyn Bridge over and over again, doesn't it?"

"No clue. Hubris, maybe. From what I understand, they aren't used to losing."

"And Hayward. What the hell was he thinking?"

"No idea. Rumour has it, he's gone over to Ulti/ME, so maybe he just screwing around the Reeds as a favour to his new boss."

"I did not know that."

"I don't either, for a fact. But maybe he's dead serious with the lawsuit. He's taking a huge chance, but he could be betting a US judge would side with the little guy no matter what had gone on up here. And, frankly, he might be right."

I too had been right. I had pissed away an entire day trying to understand this case. The only tangible result was my grudging admiration for Hayward and the balls it took to attempt this legal caper. But it fit. The guy was something of a gambler and an adrenalin junkie.

And it did get me thinking about another unintended consequence of the technology arms races: legal manoeuvring. Lawyers were flocking to patent law with the same kind of greedy glee with which gold prospectors descended on Sutter's Mill. Not exactly exciting stuff to watch, but this was, after all, big business, with huge implications for the winners and losers.

While Concord only talked about that one law suit in their 10-K, I decided that Ulti/ME's legal situation also bore investigation. So I went at their SEC filings the next day.

Whoa! They must have had hundreds of lawyers on staff. And at least a mid-sized San Francisco law firm on retainer. Scores of lawsuits, some petty, some significant, were on their books.

Some of the cases were pretty famous. Like Steinman being sued by three college buddies claiming they had come up with the idea for the whole shebang and were therefore entitled to several billion dollars for what I imagined could very well have been was a few minutes of drunken frat house chatter.

And then there was a major data breach at Ulti/ME a couple of years ago, resulting in a class-action suit brought by hundreds of people who believed either that every friggin' right they had under the Constitution and its Amendments had been violated or that here was a solid chance for some quick cash spurred on by lawyers on late night TV advertising as loudly as they could and with the same vigour they recruited mesothelioma victims. "1 800 ULTIBAD. Call now. Our operators are standing by. That's 1 800 ULTIBAD."

A case caught my eye, only because I had just heard one defendant's name from Halley.

Ulti/ME v. Robert Howe, Cortland Reed and Wesley Reed.

For several years, Howe had worked for Ulti/ME who was now going after him for corporate espionage, alleging that he'd walked out the door with reams of proprietary plans for Ulti/ME's health care division before taking up his current position as Head of Engineering for Concord Medical Systems. Further, they claimed that Howe had planned his theft and that it had been directed personally by the Reeds.

Early on in the paperwork, the suit referred to a criminal investigation by Santa Clara County and the California DOJ.

I switched over to a few news gathering sites.

Initially, with its explosive accusation, the story had been business section banner headline stuff for the San Jose *Mercury News* and more than a few tech media sites. Howe's alleged theft involved hundreds of documents and high level e-mails in which were laid out Ulti/ME founder Josh Steinman's long-term vision for his company.

Alistair's take on revealing business plans to competitors had been refreshing. He'd give his senior executives heart palpitations by openly discussing his plans with the media and analysts. In bullet points, he once laid out to me why he wasn't concerned at all with what one of our vice presidents had likened to the Allies telling the Germans about Normandy, complete with code names for the five beachheads.

"In the first place," Alistair said, "you have to assume that our competitors are able to understand *exactly* what we want to do. Secondly, they'd have to duplicate it *exactly*. Thirdly, why should we ever be afraid of any company who would throw away everything they were doing just to copy us? And lastly, what if I change my mind or was just bullshitting?"

The duel between Josh Steinman and the Reed brothers soon descended into a "no, I didn't/yes, you did" wrangle that petered away when no charges were laid.

Likewise, the civil case, which sought a billion dollars in damages, ended quietly with a sealed settlement.

How do companies stay in business with all these legal daggers hanging over them, I wondered. Wonder no more, Jake. Talk to a business and legal guy.

I was a little surprised that Jeff Sears took my call. He had to be a busy lad, keeping tabs on all Alistair's subsidiaries, supplying the operational info, as well as taking care of the financial reporting, all the while dealing with Alistair's death.

"Lydon! Whaddya know?" he said, the way he always did when greeting me.

"Everything and nothing," I answered, the way I always did.

I told him I was writing a freelanced piece about how the legal side was affecting commerce. As I suspected, the potential smack on the bottom line was built into the top line. Jeff confirmed that companies had to spend a whole lot more energy on forecasting what their legal expenses *might* be—lawyers, possible settlements, likely wins and losses—and tacking those expenses onto whatever they sold.

"Cost of doing business these days," Jeff said. "Like rent or watering the plants."

"Like the way banks are paying multi-billion dollar fines without a hiccup, just by passing it all on to their customers?"

"Yup."

"Can I quote you?"

"No, you cannot . . . You're not writing about Montrose, are you?"

"A bit. Only to prove how much things have changed since then."

"Be careful, Lydon."

"Of what?"

"You signed a confidentiality agreement. They don't go out of date."

"Actually, I didn't. I never had a contract."

There was a brief silence.

"You didn't?" he asked.

"Nope. I think I was Alistair's little side project."

"Well, it's certainly implied that you have to keep quiet."

"It was almost twenty years ago, Jeff, and you know how much I liked Alistair. I wouldn't do anything to piss on all he did."

"Just be careful," he said.

I couldn't decide if Jeff's warning was friendly or ominous or both. I took it as a sign of our litigious times.

CHAPTER SIXTEEN

Pretty excited with my progress, I called Steve.

"C'mon up to the lake, I'll lay it out for you," I said.

"No. You come down to my lake."

"Fuck that. I'm not going to Toronto twice in a month."

"Meet me half way then."

He picked the day and time and I chose the Denny's off the 401 near Oshawa.

I collected all the Post-it notes I thought mattered, stuck them like roofing shingles to a clipboard and I grabbed one legal pad full of hand-scrawled, potentially relevant stuff. I decided against taking my laptop because that just gets distracting and I wasn't going to be writing really, more organizing. Plus, I know exactly what happens to a keyboard when I spill beer or coffee on it.

I arrived at the Denny's just off the 401 at mid-morning. Steve was already there, sitting in a big booth, with papers spread out around him. It was good to see him.

"Shut up until I get a coffee, can ya?" I warned him.

"Rough night?"

"Rough life."

"You're breaking my heart."

Hours went by and our working breakfast turned into a working lunch. As I expected, things got heated a couple of times, the volume rising to the point where our waitress had to intervene to remind us it was a family restaurant. We're both pretty stubborn and we were both pretty charged up. A lot of people don't, but I always take this sort of friction as a positive sign.

Our louder disagreements were over the basic theme for the book.

Steve's original premise—technology's re-wiring of our brains—and how that would play out—won the day. Eventually—and not easily—my focus on changing business models and legal stuff was defeated by his intricate and well-reasoned argument that my suggestion was "boring as piss on a plate." The WesCor-Ulti/ME struggle still worked as a starting point but after that, it was the effect of tech on the individual—rather than corporations and government—that was going to be the heart of the thing.

I was a little pissed that my days of research and reams of Post-it notes would be reduced to a couple of anecdotes. However, the health aspect—how everyone was becoming even more obsessed with themselves—survived, as did the overwhelming profit motive that was driving the bus.

We divvied up the tasks ahead of us. Steve was going to work the phones, interviewing people who might have something to contribute. That was fine with me because it was a job I wouldn't do. Never mind the legwork of tracking these sources down; the prospect of talking to humans—lots of them—didn't intrigue me at all anymore. I used to do that for a living but, as soon as I didn't have to have a beige piece of plastic growing out of my ear, I quit. It was sorta like how, after years of using a chainsaw, I just stopped. Odds can only be pushed so far. I don't hitchhike anymore either.

Plus, Steve had a decent contact list and the magic passport of being able to identify himself as a reporter. Forget about those news clips of a media target brushing past reporters or taking a swing at a photographer. The fact is, most people love the chance to talk if they think it'll wind up in print or on camera.

In return for Steve's hunting and gathering, I was going to handle the bulk of the early writing because, he contended that, as a writer of shorter news items, he was pretty well shit after a thousand words. I also volunteered to continue with my research, particularly on the health angle.

Around 4 o'clock, we emerged from the restaurant brimming with coffee and optimism.

I came home and walked around back to the deck and, more specifically, to the fridge I have under a little lean-to that keeps the rain off.

Even though my regular fridge inside is pretty much empty all the time, this back-up is a summer luxury I can afford. I reasoned that it saves me close to sixteen steps and the wear and tear on the screen door plus the aggravation factor of blood-thirsty mosquitoes getting inside to deliberately torment me while I slept.

I sat on my porch and stared at the lake, feeling pretty good about where we were with the book. At this stage, it was more conjecture than anything, but the skeleton of it was now growing some muscle, some nerves.

I thought of all the new questions that needed answers. I mentally started to categorize the likely answerers of those questions. Industry analysts, medical ethicists, academics, government policy wonks, social activists, union leaders. And so on.

I knew I had to write it down before I forgot it all, which seemed to be happening a lot more frequently these days. I finished my beer and went inside, looking for one of the yellow legal pads.

That's when I found the dead guy in my living room.

CHAPTER SEVENTEEN

The dead guy looked like he might have been sleeping off a bender. Except for the large pool of blood by the ragged and bloody perforation in his skull, and a couple of flies buzzing around that weren't ever going to wake him up. Stuck to the stained carpet was a bunch of small white feathers.

After the initial jolt of my discovery, I walked around the corpse, knew I didn't know him. Knew I had to do something. But as I picked up the phone, I heard sirens. At my front window, I watched as three police cruisers screamed up to the house and braked amid a shower of stones and dust.

Why do they do that anyway? To heighten the drama, I suppose.

At any rate, a bunch of black-vested cops poured out of the cruisers with their guns at the ready. Jack Snap, I was outside with my hands over my head. I might as well have been aiming an assault rifle at them instead because, even though I was trying awfully hard to surrender, they were on me, yelling for me to get down, shut the fuck up, roll over, beg, and a bunch of other commands I didn't understand because they were all shouting different things at the same time. It hurt like hell as they pulled my limbs this way and that. With a knee in my back, I went limp and let them do what they'd been taught to do.

Hand-cuffed and lying on the grass, I was staring out at the lake and Carl's island where an OPP patrol boat, the kind that wanders the lake looking to fine lads for drinking or illegally fishing, (please, they're *always* lads), was parked at Carl's dock. I could see them hustling Carl on board for the short run to the mainland. I could also see that Carl was the opposite of me, completely tensed. And when Carl, the big bastard, tenses, it's a trick to get him to loosen up.

I was being hauled to my feet just as they were wrestling Carl to the ground. The cops looked like they were trying to take down an oak. All but one of my guardians went to help.

Even though I was as passive as an etherized bunny, the cop who stayed behind was clearly pissed to be missing out on the action so he yanked me around a bit.

I looked at his nameplate.

"Dysart? Any chance you're related to Richard Dysart?" I asked.

"What the fuck are you talking about?"

"You know, he played Leland Mackenzie on *LA Law*. Dysart's not a very common name."

I'm pretty sure that got me the bump on the head as he pushed me into the cruiser. I'm also sure their display of firepower and sounds and lights wasn't going to help my standing with the cottage owners' association as the cruisers screamed back up the narrow lane and onto the main road heading to Peterborough.

Carl and I were in the same cruiser. Evidently, the cars ahead and behind us were just for show, sort of a miscreant's cavalcade.

I looked at Carl.

"Bud, did you—?"

"—Shut the fuck up!" cautioned my old pal, Constable Dysart, from the front seat.

Carl didn't say anything, just shook his head "no" which was good enough for me.

"Where are you tak—"

"—I said shut the fuck up!"

That kind of direction always works well with me.

"Can we have the radio on?" I asked pleasantly. "Not the cop radio. The *radio* radio. Doesn't matter what station. Except country. I fuckin' hate new country music."

"Last warning, asshole: shut the fuck up!"

Dysart was spitting now but, despite his assertion, I was pretty sure he had at least one more warning in him. And, no matter how badly the cops may have wanted to, I just couldn't see them stopping to pound the piss out of me or execute me by the side of the road. We were expected.

"You know," I mused out loud, "a Tim's would be great right about now. Regular coffee. No sugar, lots of cream. Not that weakass skim milk."

Not altogether surprisingly, there was a mob of reporters at the police station to witness my perp walk from the cruiser to the jail. Well, not exactly a mob, more like four or five reporters, two with cameras. A lot of the print reporters are now called video journalists because they have to lug a camera along with their pen and pad. After all, no one can wait until the next day for the story. I know I can't.

I was, however, surprised to see that Steve was part of the media mob.

As I was being frog-marched past him, Steve had an odd look on his face, like what the fuck?

I couldn't help myself. I smiled and nodded at him and, of course, that's the picture that showed up next day in the papers and online—making me look like one of those psycho killers who are amused and pleased by the notoriety they'd gained—the notoriety they sought that was often the point of their madness to begin with.

I was in more of a daze than usual throughout the booking and fingerprinting. They kept Carl away from me, but I presume he was a tad more resistant.

The only other time I'd been in a jail cell was an overnighter in Niagara Falls for underage drinking almost forty-five years earlier. Apparently, in the intervening four and half decades, there hadn't been a renaissance in jail cell-decor philosophy. The same iron cot suspended from the wall, the same scratchy blanket and smelly toilet, the same sort of light green caterpillar's guts paint colour on the cinderblock walls and not much else.

What had changed was my level of preoccupation. I was so fucking bored. No one to talk to, nothing to do, and no computer. Back in my drunken teenage years, I at least filled the hours of my unfortunate incarceration by imagining a movie starring me as I got used to a life in the big house. Here, I didn't have a harmonica or even a tin cup to run across the bars.

Or a smoke.

How is it that, in one moment, everyone nods their heads and agrees that nicotine is harder to kick than heroin but, the next moment, are fine with the idea of putting criminals together and forcing them to go cold turkey and, in the moment after that, wondering why things seem to be a little edgy around the old cell block. And second-hand smoke? Puh-leese. That's way down the list of health worries in a jail filled with pissed-off bad guys.

One of my few talents—bordering on a superpower—is my ability to fall asleep just about anywhere. Even though the thin blanket made for a shitty mattress, it took me about two minutes to go under.

I was awakened the next morning by the angry sound of iron doors clanging open. And there was Halley.

Although it doesn't happen often, I was embarrassed.

"Oh, dad."

"Oh, dad, what?"

"How are you doing?"

Her concern was evident and it was touching.

"I'm fine. Besides me and Carl, I think the only other guy in here right now is an old drunk. Don't worry, hon; I won't let him make me his bitch."

I have this habit of making light of things. The nastier the situation, the more extreme the jokes. I don't know why. It's as if I want to reduce the seriousness of the mood. Smooth over all the bad things going on. Everything's going to be fine, just fine. Even if they weren't.

Halley seemed speechless.

"Any idea how this happened?" I asked.

"They got a 9-1-1 tip about some guy in a Hawaiian shirt waving a gun around."

"Who called?"

"They don't know. Cell phone for sure. They're working on it."

"I wasn't even at the place for most of the day."

I described my hours with Steve at the Oshawa Denny's, coming home in the late afternoon, sitting on the deck until early evening.

"So, anybody other than Steve know when you left?"

"The waitress, I guess. Wait! Not Steve. Not a chance!"

The prospect of Steve setting me up was too absurd to consider. And yet. And yet that's exactly what I found myself doing. The numbers didn't add up. I had been cop-invaded around seven o'clock. Steve's drive west from Oshawa to Toronto then back north-east to Peterborough to be among my jailhouse reception line would've taken longer than the three hours since we left the restaurant. And that meant he would've had to have been driving to the jail *before* I even found the dead guy.

"I just can't see it, Hal," I said, trying to convince myself as much as her. "What about the shot? Anybody hear it?"

"Not that we've found, which is strange because you do have neighbours."

"Carl's closest to me. He sure as hell didn't call the cops, but he would've been over in a flash if he heard anything."

"We talked to him. He says he was at his woodlot most of the day."

"Well . . . well . . . do your thing. You know. GSR test, angle of the bullet, time of death. All that."

"We will, dad."

"This just stinks, Hal. You know it does."

"Yeah, I do."

I was grateful that, whatever my failings as a dad or as a human, she didn't think I was capable of murder.

<CHAPTER EIGHTEEN>

After Halley left, they took me to a sparse interrogation room. Staring at the drab walls, I was disappointed there was no big one-way mirror. Two detectives came in and politely introduced themselves.

They stumbled around with pleasantries for a bit, the way some reporters used to do with me. These cops had all the time in the world for this cat and mouse thing. And come to think of it: so did I. That's why I played along, stalling my demand for a lawyer.

There was a sharp knock at the door; I was hoping it might be Steve, the crusading journalist who nobody dared fuck with. Instead a short and sort of round guy in an expensive suit brusquely entered.

"That's all for now, gentlemen," he said to the cops.

"Who the hell are you?" asked one of the cops, pretty upset that his afternoon of interrogatin' was apparently being cut short.

"Yeah. Who the hell are you?" I echoed.

"I'm Mr. Lydon's attorney. Martin David."

He took a business card out of a slender silver case and crisply presented it.

"Camera off," Martin David instructed.

"Legal aid must be paying a whole lot better these days," I said, admiring his suit.

"Not legal aid. Courtesy of a friend."

"I don't have enough friends for a game of checkers. Who was it?"

"I'd rather not say."

Well then, I'd rather you fucked off right now. I can handle this."

"Very well. I'm here courtesy of Sarah MacNeil and, no, you *can't* handle this."

I had to smile. This 500 dollar-an-hour gift from Sarah was a little rich.

"Some privacy, please," my new lawyer said and the cops filed out.

"She could've saved her money, you know," I said to him as soon as we were alone. "I was just going to tell them exactly what happened."

"No you won't."

"Why not? Truth will set you free and all that."

"In the legal profession, we have another saying: shut the fuck up."

"Funny. We have the same one in PR," I mused.

"We need to see what they have," he said, ignoring me. "I'm betting it's not much. Arraignment's Monday morning. You'll be out by noon."

"On a murder charge?"

"No chance of that coming. From what I understand, the charge will be manslaughter. Self-defence. A home is a man's castle etcetera, etcetera."

"But that's not what happened!"

"You mean you really did murder the guy? No, wait! Don't tell me."

"I didn't murder anybody! I found him! And what about Carl? He didn't do anything either."

"They'll probably let him go. For some reason, they seem sure it was you and there's no way they can suggest that you both held the gun at the same time."

"We are pretty close."

"And no talking to the media."

"Wouldn't think of it."

I was settling back into my cell when the guard told me I had yet another visitor. So much for solitary confinement; they needed to form a goddamned receiving line for me. They hustled me out of my cell again and took me back to the interview room.

This time, it was Steve. Even though I was sure that he could still be a prick when he wanted to, I was equally sure that he got along with cops to have held his crime beat for so long.

"Is this business or pleasure?" I asked.

"Business," he said quietly as he pulled his wire-bound notepad from his jacket. "I have to do this, Jake. You know the drill."

"No. No, Steve, I most surely do *not* know the drill!"

"Awww, c'mon. I gotta ask."

"Looking for a jailhouse confession are you? Ask away."

I told him everything I knew. There wasn't much to tell. Coming home from our meeting, having a beer or two outside then finding the guy. The cops just showing up.

Let Martin David earn his retainer, I thought. I was pretty sure I had nothing to lose by telling the truth.

"My turn," I said. "What are the police saying?"

"Not much."

"That's it? Not much?"

"They're not in a giving mood."

"OK. Then answer me this: how did you know I'd been arrested?"

"My police scanner. Mississauga Lake. Hawaiian shirt. You know, two plus two."

"What time?"

"I don't know. Around six, I guess."

"Did you know I hadn't even found the dead guy by then? Did you know the cops came because of a fake 9-1-1?"

"What!? No! What the fuck are you talking about?"

"Steve, how could you possibly make it to Peterborough that fast?"

"I never went back to Toronto. I was in Oshawa. At the mall."

"Steve, did you make that 9-1-1 call?" I had to ask.

"NO! Christ, no!"

There was anger and hurt in his eyes.

He hadn't looked away the entire time I was asking questions. He didn't hesitate. He didn't fidget or exhibit any of the classic tells.

I believed him.

"Well, somebody did," I said.

"It wasn't me."

"I know, I know. But this whole thing is getting more fucked up by the minute."

"I'll see what I can find out."

The night was not pleasant. Never mind the setting, the circumstances which had taken me there overwhelmed me as I was trying to sleep on the iron shelf they called a bed.

Maybe it happens to a lot of people, but it sure hadn't happened very often to me that I'd found myself in situations where I didn't have a fucking clue as to how I'd got there. Beth dying, that was the main one. And a few alcohol-fueled evenings, but that's it. In my shitty cell for the second night, any attempt I made at backtracking, re-tracing my steps did not contribute a thing towards explaining why I was in this shitty cell.

And then there was the issue of who to trust. More than anything, that bothered me. Maybe Steve had lied about being in Oshawa when I was being busted and was a better actor than I thought. Maybe he *had* called 9-1-1? If so, why? How, and for that matter, why had Sarah acted so quickly and so generously? And where was Carl during all this?

At the best of times, I don't have faith in much, but foundations were being shaken.

Other than listening to Martin David bitch about Peterborough's lack of fine dining, my arraignment the next morning was uneventful. Hours spent sitting around before I got to stand up and proclaim my innocence. It was a whole lot less dramatic than, say, pre-guillotine

Sydney Carton in *A Tale of Two Cities*. Martin David could sense I was about to launch into my version of "It is a far, far better thing that I do, than I have ever done." He forced me to my seat, rather roughly, may I add.

Bail was set at 50 grand, the gavel came down and I was shuffled off to my cell, pissed off that I now had to mortgage my free-and-clear house.

Martin David said he'd handle it all.

"Then that's that?" I said.

"No, Mr. Lydon, that is decidedly not that. There's still going to be a trial and if you're convicted, it's a *minimum* four-year sentence."

"What!?"

"Manslaughter with a firearm."

Suddenly, there wasn't so much to joke about.

When they let me out the next morning, I was surprised to see that Steve wasn't there, but happy and surprised again to see that Halley was.

"Thanks for posting bail, sweetie. I'm pretty sure that's every dad's dream."

"But I didn't."

"Then who? Sar . . . "

"The clerk told me it was a Michael . . . Coulson."

"Mike?"

"You know him?"

"Yeah. So do you, actually. I worked with him years ago at Montrose. He used to come to the house sometimes when you were a kid."

"Must've read the article in the *Sun*."

"They spell my name right? I'll fucking sue if they didn't spell my name right."

"Shut up, dad. Let's go home."

"Just a minute," I said, as I was swooning over the nicotine rush of a cigarette.

Carl strolled out of the building and joined us by the car.

"You OK, bud?" I asked.

"Helluva way to spend a weekend," he said. "Thank you for that."

"Jesus, buddy, I'm sorry. But at least you're in the clear."

"Nope. They piled me with a bunch improper storage of firearms charges or some such horseshit. Could be five grand in fines. They wanted to nail me for resisting arrest, but your lawyer killed that. So, thanks again, I guess."

Carl didn't look all that grateful and I didn't blame him. We drove back to the lake in silence.

At the end of my laneway, I became intent on the damage. Even though I'm pretty much a slob, I prefer to be the one slobbing the place up and I have a pretty specific order to my strewing hither and yon. I certainly didn't like the police tape lying all over the place as though a giant but really skinny yellow snake had shed its skin.

The damage that the police and reporters had done to my gardens during their hunting and gathering of evidence after my arrest was actually pretty minimal—a couple of hours' work maybe—but it pissed me off mightily.

"Son, mind runnin' me back to my place?" Carl asked. "Don't feel up to the swim."

Normally, I'd tell Carl to go fuck himself, but nothing felt very normal.

"Dad, I need to speak with you. I'll wait," Halley said.

Carl and I didn't say anything as we went through the ritual of me trying to start my little 5hp motor, him taking over and getting it going with one powerful yank, then me almost piling into his dock.

In the normal course of events, we don't talk all that much but this time our silence was different. A brief glimpse into each other's eyes and we knew things had changed between us. Suspicion of the other, anger at being drawn into something beyond our pleasant routine, our pleasant lives. All unspoken but as solid as the lake ice in winter.

All I could think of to say was that I'd pay the fines, whatever they were. Carl didn't say a word.

I was in an extremely foul mood upon my return, made fouler as I studied the rust blood stain on my carpet, the carpet with a square cut out and a few feathers the cops hadn't collected lying around. Overall, the heightened sense of disruption and mess around my small cottage was depressing as hell.

Halley was trying to straighten things up which upset me more; I told her stop.

I surveyed my living room again. The anchors of my life—my shitty computer and my ridiculously large TV—were where they were supposed to be. But something wasn't right.

Then it struck me. All my precious Post-it notes that I had left festooning the furniture and walls were gone. So too was my stack of writing pads.

"Fuckers took all my research!"

"What?"

"Notes, papers, the cops took it all."

"Are you sure?" Halley asked.

"Well, they're not here."

"Were they there when you found the vic?"

"I don't remember. Maybe not. Now why the Christ would—"

"—just a second," Halley said, holding up a finger to silence me.

Halley brought out her phone and went to the deck where the reception is better. The screen door off the kitchen loudly whapped shut behind her, even though I must have told that girl a million times to close it gently.

After a few minutes, she came in all excited, looking the way she used to as a little girl holding a particularly large toad or a jar of fireflies.

"Now, dad, are you absolutely positively sure those things are missing?"

"I'm sure I'm sure. I swear on a stack of Stones records."

She smiled for what seemed like the first time in a long time.

"Peterborough police say they don't have any of your papers logged in as evidence," she announced as though confirming winning lottery numbers.

"So you caught them lying, so what?"

"No, dad; they're not lying. It's a whole lot better than that. Unless the guy had time to call a courier to pick that stuff up before he got shot . . . "

" . . . he definitely had someone with him!"

"We thought there could've been another guy but didn't have proof. No extra prints. The neighbours we canvassed hadn't seen anything. No conclusive tire tracks in your laneway. We didn't find a car or boat unaccounted for in the neighbourhood to explain how the dead guy got to your place alone but maybe that meant it was too well-hidden."

"So that's good news, right?" I said.

"The best you've had so far."

"Beer?" I asked, because it sounded like something we should celebrate.

"Better not."

"On duty, right?"

"No, dad. It's 10 AM."

We stared out at the lake and I drank my beer, just as I had been doing two and a half days earlier while a stranger was being dead in my living room. The memory bothered me. He may have been beyond caring, but I wasn't.

"What are working on?" Halley asked.

"A book about why technology sucks. Harmless stuff."

"Think, dad. They had to believe you had something worth stealing."

"Trust me; I've been wracking my wee brain."

"Do you have any idea who would do this?"

"There are a couple of old dolls around the lake who, apparently, aren't Stones fans, but I can't see them taking out a contract on me."

"Anybody else?"

"Oh, and the Volvo-driving guy next door who singled me out for my shoddy recycling practices. You might check him out. But other than that . . . Now what did you want to talk to me about?"

"There are some things you should know, dad."

"Like what? You got the guy who did this?"

"No. But they found a gun."

"And?"

"And they found it stuffed under your mattress. A .25 calibre."

"Well, someone must've planted it."

"It's registered to Carl."

"Well, now you *know* Carl didn't do it," I said, remembering.

"Why?"

"He never used that gun, for anything. Said it was a pain in the ass to clean, couldn't hit anything with it so he gave it to me. I don't know why. I couldn't really refuse a gift, could I? That was years ago. Ten, at least. I don't even remember where I'd put it."

"Dad, it had been fired."

"What? Not a chance! I've never shot that gun! I didn't keep it under the mattress and I sure the fuck didn't kill that guy! I'm being set up! And . . . and . . . if I *had* shot the guy, all I had to do was toss the gun into the lake."

She patted my arm trying to slow down my blurted defence.

"Dad, dad . . . I know. The head shot was a much bigger calibre. They're not gonna argue you shot him once with the .25 and then switched guns. And they're not going to argue that you and Carl gunned him down together."

"And besides," I added, "if Carl said he was at his woodlot most of the day cutting firewood, then that's what he was doing."

We sat in silence for a bit.

"Peterborough cops turned all the lab stuff over to us; we'll figure it out, dad."

"Right now, all I care about is you figuring out it wasn't me. Because it wasn't."

"We should have something by end of day tomorrow. I'll call."

In all the hub-bub, a thought came to me.

"What about some of that good ol' police protection? After all, there *is* another guy out there."

"Not possible. You're the accused, remember? If it helps, I don't think he's coming back. Let's bet he either found what he was looking for or it wasn't here."

I locked the doors after she left and that pissed me off.

I never lock the place when I'm here, just like I never lock the Vibe. Why sacrifice a door or a window? If someone wants in, they'll get in. From the road or the lake, they'd be unobserved for hours, unless Carl was out and about. They could take leisurely hours to break in. Forget smashing a window; they could use a dull Swiss Army knife to whittle their way through the logs. They could gouge away, go home, and come back the next day. And then do what? There was nothing to take, other than my elderly and ridiculously large television and a shitty antiquated laptop that the discerning young lads (please, they're *always* young lads) wouldn't bother to steal for fear of getting laughed out of their little techno-theft ring. Maybe a tequila bottle or two, a half carton of smokes.

That's it.

And my car? Who the hell steals a thirteen-year-old Pontiac Vibe? And, if someone did, it means they needed it a whole lot more than me.

Fact was: I was pretty rattled about the whole thing. I had been involuntarily submerged in an unreal, surreal, disreal situation and then I was supposed to snap back to "normal" as if nothing had happened? All the while facing the prospect of four years in the big house?

Turns out, I couldn't do it.

I lay awake in the dark listening to the many sounds any old cottage makes, sounds you used to ignore that now seemed to announce an army of clumsy ninjas creeping the joint. Rather than get up and investigate every creak and snap, I did the only logical thing: I pulled the sheet over my head. That worked for a few seconds, until I sat up and spoke out loud.

"Stop being such a fucking drama queen!"

I got up, checked the locks, and went to the kitchen. My hand was shaking as I poured a generous, oh, let's call it a philanthropic shot of my infallible 100% blue agave Cazadores Reposada sleep aid.

The next morning, having not been murdered in my sleep, I was back at the keyboard, not for the book but for finding out about me. I got to watch me on the web. I looked dishevelled (as if I've ever been shevelled), almost Nick Nolte-like as I was being frog-marched into jail. I chided myself for the rookie mistake of not covering my face as the cameras rolled.

I also got to see all the cops climbing under the police tape and trampling all over my gardens as they took footage of the crime scene.

And of course, there was the obligatory neighbour, sadly noting that this sort of thing never happened in his 'hood.

Then I read Steve's story. As I had expected, it was all pumped up as a cell block exclusive. Of the "he said/she said" variety that lets the media keep the story going. Assertion/denial/stay tuned. He got down the facts I'd given him but I didn't care much for the headline—which I knew he hadn't written. Over my mug shot was the banner: "Murder or Standing His Ground?" What the fuck did I expect in an age where the mildest public disagreement is reported as "Lashing Out" or "Hitting Back" or "Slamming" or "Eviscerating" or "Blasting"?

The "Comments" trail after the article was the usual misinformed bullshit as the conversation we're all supposed to join devolved into the same old tiresome hobbyhorse jousting over everything from gun control to cuts in police budgets to mental health spending to the obvious fact that I was a "d*bag."

Two other accounts, one from the *Peterborough Examiner*, the other the *Toronto Star*, were a lot more sketchy but no less dramatic. Small consolation: I knew that, as I was reading them, editors of both those papers, as well as the news directors at the local TV and radio stations, would be lashing out, hitting back, slamming, eviscerating, and blasting their news departments for being scooped by Steve.

I wrote to Jenna at the agency, saying that "owing to circumstances beyond my control" my assignment was going to be a little late.

She wrote back, telling me that my services were no longer required. Fuck!

But, really, what did I expect? I would assume that employing an accused murderer—OK, manslaughtererer—didn't add a lot of cachet to the agency's reputation.

I spent the rest of the day outside, trying to distract myself by being a yard ape. Usually getting myself dirty, turning my fingernails black with earth, transports me, calms me the fuck down. Not today. I was repairing stuff that I hadn't broken or neglected and I loathe cleaning up other people's messes.

Most times, if I think-think-think about some problem, an acceptable answer or, at least, some clear options come to mind. Not today.

The phone rang and I raced to the house, Pavlov's paunchy greyhound.

It was Halley and she was all business.

"We haven't identified the John Doe yet. No ID, no prints in any database. But here's what we do know, dad. Like I told you, he had been shot twice. Autopsy puts the time of death at least two hours before you got home."

"So you're starting to believe the old man?"

"Well, not exactly. We checked with the waitress in Oshawa and the time stamp on your Visa."

"Thanks."

"The bullet to the head that killed him was from a .38," she continued. "The second shot, your .25, to the chest had been fired post mortem by quite a bit. Hardly any blood so it came at least an hour after."

"You can figure that out?"

"Imagine. Anyway, looks like someone—the killer or the victim—found the .25 earlier and then the shooter had the thought and the time to use it. He picked up a cushion and put a round into the corpse."

Halley's voice trailed, almost distractedly. It was the same sound she'd make when she was trying to evade my questioning about a homework assignment or what she had done on a date.

"Annnnnd . . . ?" I prodded.

"And from the marks on the slug, the .38 was fired through a silencer."

"Which means . . . ?"

She hesitated.

"Dad, pros use silencers."

I let that sink in.

"Hit men on Mississauga Lake?" I asked.

"We don't think so. Contractors wouldn't have screwed up this bad. Sorry, but if they wanted you dead, you'd be dead. More likely, armed plumbers who had a specific job. Like stealing your papers."

"Isn't that just wonderful news? Anything else?"

"The John Doe had a gun too, still in its holster."

"So there! That's the end of it."

"No, dad. That's the start of it."

Of course it was just the start. Two unidentified guys crawling around my shitty cottage, both with guns, at least one with a silencer, for Christ's sakes. Not exactly your typical home invaders. And what if I had been there—as I usually am?

And then there's the identity of the bastard who called the cops.

"What happens next?" I asked.

"First off, the Crown will drop the charges; they know they don't have a case. Any time now; they'll come by with an official notice."

"Do me a favour? Could you ask around, make sure that Constable Dysart delivers it?"

"Why him?"

"We seemed to really hit it off in the squad car. I know he'll be pleased."

"Listen, dad. If you hear or remember anything, you'd better tell the police. OK?"

"Sure, hon."

"And, dad, they pulled me off the case. Our family connection isn't helping either of us."

"I'm sorry, Halley. I really am."

And I was. She was smart, hard-working, and keen. Shit like this follows you around.

<CHAPTER TWENTY-ONE>

I blog. There. I said it. I blog. Said it again.

Some people call me a cranky old man, but most don't know that I was a cranky young man. I just grew into it. So late at night, usually with a head full of Cazadores, I'll bash away. Three hundred and sixty-eight people in the world "like" me. Maybe there's more, but they just don't want to publicly commit, or maybe there's a lot less. Three hundred and sixty-eight people liked me a year ago but perhaps they don't anymore or they died or they went off the grid or realized they had made a huge mistake. Who goes back into something and "unlikes" it? I also have a traffic counter. That won't tell me if it's one strange little person returning over and over again, but it will tell me how many are knocking on my cyber door. Three hundred and sixty-eight. A few less than bought my novel.

Little Blog Cabin is the name for my on-line rantings. I don't know what the fuck I was thinking when I came up with that cutesy title.

I e-yell about "Big" things. Big Pharma, Big Oil, Big Government, Big Insurance, Big Banks, Big Religion. I leave out Big Tobacco, mostly because I smoke, and, for at least the last thirty years or so, there can't be a less deceptive industry in the world. Buy our stuff and you'll probably die much sooner than you'd planned. A short, direct, and utterly honest value proposition.

I won't claim anything startlingly or even marginally original in anything I write. I intersperse the rants with mostly small stuff. Calculating that because there's about 130,000 self-help books listed on Amazon, if each sold just 262 copies (261.53846, actually) to a different person then every man woman and child in Canada would be self-helped and with that kind of moral, psychological, intellectual, and spiritual strength,

Canada would be back to punching above its weight in the global ring.

Or I wonder why faith-healing televangelists don't just camp out at ERs and cancer wards where they could pick up a ton of converts, make lots of families very happy, and save the national medical system, all at the same time.

On this day, I was going to write about my unfortunate incarceration and all the thoughts I had about the judicial system and law enforcement and the bilious paint colours they use in our jails.

But each time I'd start, I'd highlight/delete, highlight/delete. I was embarrassed and angry and confused and I just wanted for it to all go away.

I called Mike at Bio-Watch to thank him for the bail bond, didn't reach him as people rarely get their phone target on the first try, so I left a message. Then I called Sarah to thank her. Ditto with the message, then I sat on the deck, staring at the slight, gun-metal grey ripples on the lake and wondering how and when—and even if—everything might return to the innocuous pattern that was my life.

I decided I needed an action plan.

Clearly, there was only one thing to do: drink. Which I promptly did. I walked down the dirt road and sat by myself on the patio of the Angler Arms staring out at their slight, gun-metal grey ripples on the lake which were an awfully lot like the slight, gun-metal grey ripples I had been viewing from my deck a little ways down the shore.

As usual, the service at the Arms was prompt, but not as usual, there was no cheerfulness from Carla as she served me. I didn't blame her for treating me more like a leper than a customer. I really didn't. On the upside, a couple of regulars who also lived around the lake came up and congratulated me for defending the sanctity of property and, sure as shit, no one was going to pull a B & E around here for a while.

I reckon I was moments away from viewing the lake at a 90-degree angle, my cheek comfortably resting on the tabletop, when I felt powerful hands upon me.

"C'mon, son," Carl said as he effortlessly hauled me to my feet and steered me to his truck.

I view my mini-benders as the same kind of tactic as sleeping your way through colds or the flu. Sink into oblivion for a while until you disgust yourself with your inertia and your shameless expense of time and spirit and then snap the fuck out of it.

The next morning, the jangling phone woke me up. Although it killed all those movie scenes where the cops feverishly try to run a trace, call display is one of the best inventions of our time. Right up there with cablevision and non-stick cooking spray, it truly separates us from the great apes.

Most times, I can see who I'm ignoring. This call I was going to take.

Uncharacteristically, Halley didn't offer up so much as a "Hi, how are ya?"

"Dad, why did you have to write that?" she demanded.

"Write what?"

"Your blog about MacNeil's death, that's what."

"I didn't write anything! I swear! Gimme a minute to find it."

I went on-line to see what I had supposedly written, recognizing the distinct possibility that my cunning password—1-2-3-4—might have been cracked.

Not bad, I thought, as I read about "my" theory on how Alistair MacNeil had finally had enough and logged himself off for good. His fortunes made and lost were described in some detail followed by the insinuations that both his marriages had been disasters and that he had crappy kids, and so on. There was some inside skinny but there were also major errors in basic facts that no one who knew him well, particularly in the early years, would get wrong.

The smart-ass tone was surely mine but the style wasn't. The article was mostly subject-verb-object sentences which I don't do very much. I used to argue with Steve about this writing style because reporters use it all the time. That's why they all loved Hemingway. And why I didn't. I like to mix things up a bit, Bend the rules. Decorate the final product. Just the facts, ma'am, is, to me, boring as shit.

"I did not write this, Halley. Get one of your analyst geeks to go over the millions of words I've puked out for clients."

"Truthfully, that was my first hunch, dad. I know you don't write anything that looks like a normal sentence."

So there it was. Less than a day after I had been on my blog site, someone somewhere had planted a story on it.

That's scary fast.

The speed of everything these days (except old people driving white Buicks) really floors me. But the speed with which I had been set up—again—was frightening.

I was at loose ends in the immediate aftermath of my unfortunate incarceration. Other than rescuing me from public unconsciousness, Carl was keeping his distance. Neighbours on the road either stared icily at me or looked away—although that didn't bother me much as I never talked to them anyway. My crisis scenario work was in crisis.

Normally, time is real elastic for someone without a steady job or a steady family. I freely acknowledge that I'm bone lazy, but things were off-kilter enough that it was no longer a desire to work on the book but a necessity, if for no other reason than to evade the clown show I had found myself in.

I needed to be absorbed and not just diverted. Before this, I was being diverted to death by exploring my subject de jour: watching web videos of squirrels water skiing. By the by, I don't see what the big deal is; they're not very good. I haven't yet seen one jump a sizeable wake.

Please, I prayed, somebody or something interest and amaze me. I like being amazed at stuff. Even beyond how they get the caramilk in there. For example, I'm still awe-struck I can make it to Las Terrenas in four and half hours, which can be the duration of a pretty good winter traffic jam on the Don Valley.

And I, literally, can spend years at something that interests me. Until it doesn't. I'm also cursed with enough self-knowledge to know that what usually keeps me interested in something is the opportunity it presents to get into a fight with conventional wisdom.

Take the fact that I've been brawling with the Canada Revenue Agency for over four years—not counting my time in the Dominican during which I send the odd snot-o-gram just to keep the pot stirring—when the obvious course of action is to pay up and shut up. It took three years to end my dispute with the Ministry of Environment over the placement of the dock I barely use because their rules just seemed out-and-out dumb.

It took me five years to write my goddamned novel suggesting that the Great Depression was actually an exciting time for lots of young people who were forced into adventures.

In grade five, my classroom teacher wrote the following under my photo in the yearbook:

"For e'en though vanquished, he could argue still."

Fucking Oliver Goldsmith.

But I couldn't argue with that one.

The book was the only thing I had on the go. In a rare display of self-discipline, I managed to set aside all the big and little shit going on in my life and concentrate on making the thing I wanted to make.

A week went by and I was back on a writing jag. I have pretty good recall, so recreating the stuff I had derived from Steve's research wasn't all that hard. It took a bunch of time but time I had in spades.

About the only person I spoke to in-person during that week was Constable Dysart, who did indeed come by with formal notice dropping all charges against me. I'm sure he wanted to just tie the paperwork around a good-sized rock and heave it through a window but, to his credit, he did present it to me face-to-face.

I invited him in to watch a re-run or two of *LA Law* but he declined.

Other than that, I was on my own for a blissful week, free from all the entanglements, expectation, and disappointment of human contact, rolling around in the research and mulling over any number of themes I could make fit to the facts and opinions I was gathering.

The possible Ulti/ME-led health care revolution could be the subject for a whole other book. The legal aspects had to be covered but only as tactics for the real point of commerce, e- or otherwise: creating piles and piles of money.

The flow of big money being generated by technology both intrigued and angered me. When did billions become the new millions? And all this money meant that there was now way too much of everything. From yachts longer than a football field to maybe thousands of different kinds of pet food to advancing razor R&D. I'm sure someone somewhere is on the verge of breaking the 10-blade barrier.

I don't subscribe to the argument that all this consumption means that dollars are circulating. Yes, people now have jobs covering foyer walls with manta ray skin and gilding bathtub taps. So, admittedly, that makes it better than Ritchie Rich or Scrooge McDuck just wallowing around naked in vaults filled with dollar bills.

But not by very much.

Sour grapes? Fuckin' right it is. Sour at the scale of everything now. This isn't creeping inflation; it's orders of magnitude. $25 million apartments? $38 million cars? $22 million for a diamond not called Hope? Three million bucks for a comic book?

I can hope all I want that the sellers of all this financial overkill took their winnings and put them into drilling water wells in Africa, but I somehow doubt it.

What was clear to me was the fact that the hi-tech stars appeared to be the least garish of the rich bunch. Unlike Russian oligarchs or oil princes or New York hedge fund managers, people like Gates, Jobs, Ellison, Steinman, the Reeds at WesCor, and even some of the startlingly rich guys from Amazon, Google, and Facebook weren't as ostentatious as I first thought.

They all lived really well; I know because I e-staked out their homes on Google Earth. But they seemed more intent on spending the money which their companies had generated for them—through ridiculously high valuations—on legacy/vanity projects that either might eventually actually matter to the world or just wind up being big circle jerks.

The one guy who truly stood out—who could accurately be called frugal—was Josh Steinman. Not Warren Buffett frugal, but there was just no evidence of what he did with a fortune estimated by *Forbes* to be worth somewhere north of twenty-five billion dollars.

At the end of the week, I knew there was at least a chapter on where the money went and what it bought. I titled it with a quote attributed to David Lee Roth. "I know money can't buy me happiness. But I can sail my yacht right up beside it."

One evening, Sarah called to say "you're welcome" for supplying the services of Martin David, the legal clotheshorse who had sprung me.

When I spend days in monkish silence, it usually takes me a while to converse coherently, but the timing was perfect. It was a warm clear night, it had been a good day's work, and I was drinking beer on the deck.

We chatted amiably for quite some time. I asked her if she had finally made up her mind to get into the Dominican bar business with me. She got all serious.

"Jake, I think the girls and I are moving."

"Where to?"

"California."

"Why the hell would you go there?"

"There's really not much here for us anymore. Time for a change of scenery. The estate's close to being settled so obviously money's not a problem. Good weather, good schools. Exciting place to be. Lana and Laura are very keen. So really, why not?"

"What about Jason?"

"Jason detached himself some years ago. He's a man now. He likes being on his own and he's doing fine. I can mother him through e-mail. Or Skype my lectures. And he can travel to me."

"So you've talked to him."

"No. But I know him. I *am* his mother."

I wished her good luck and we offered up that "let's stay in touch" pledge.

My conversation with Sarah, the warmth of the night, and the coldth of the beer had me in a Chatty Cathy kinda mood so I called Mike. And got him at home.

Big mistake.

After I thanked him for springing me, there really wasn't much to yak about beyond the situation with people we knew.

Right away, Mike wanted to know if I had heard about further police doings or anything else surrounding Alistair's death. And that made me want to ask why.

"It matters to Bio-Watch . . . and to me," he answered.

"OK, my turn. Did you know that Nigel's with Ulti/ME?"

"Yes."

"Just before Dad died, did he have any meetings scheduled with him?" I asked. "He was in Toronto for the funeral."

"Not a chance. He was shrouded."

That made sense. Typically, when Alistair wrote you off, you were gone. And you stayed gone. Except for his love of country music, the only other irrational thing Alistair ever did was stick to his iron-clad rule that dictated once he had cast you out into the desert, you had better get used to eating sand because he wasn't ever going to change his mind about you or admit that he'd made a mistake.

"Do you mind me asking if *you* had set up a meeting with Nigel behind Dad's back?"

"Christ, no! Dad would've fired me on the spot. You know how he was."

"Then how'd he make the back-up deal with Ulti/ME?"

"Directly with Steinman. He would only talk to Alistair and Alistair would only talk to him."

Josh Steinman was the enigmatic founder of Ulti/ME, a boy genius who had come up with the concept when he was in school, built the first site, and never looked back.

"In fact, one of the conditions of the deal was to fire Hayward," Mike continued.

My brief chat with Mike had turned my mood, reminded me of my tiny universe whose sun had recently imploded into a black hole, reminded me that there were some unexplained mysteries in that universe.

And that just pissed me off. The attempt to frame either me or Carl or both for a murder pissed me off, the hacking of my blog pissed me off. And the fact that everybody seemed to want something from me or know something or think that I knew something. That *really* pissed me off.

Some people might label these nefarious doings as pretty interesting. I did not. Nor did I think that they were in any way amazing, because, sadly—or perhaps not—I'm not amazed by people. Once you know the back story, it's usually not too tough to figure out what they want and what they may be willing to do to get it.

Maybe it's experience or maybe it's too many *Law & Order* re-runs, but it all goes to motive, Your Honour.

And right now, for the life of me, I couldn't figure out anyone's motive.

And that, as I may have mentioned, pissed me off.

<CHAPTER TWENTY-THREE>

We gots us an interview with the Reed brothers!"

Steve was more cheery and excited than anybody should ever be on the phone.

"Well done, dude."

"It was one of those long-shot things; I didn't really expect them to say yes."

"Conference call?"

"No. In person. That's the only way they'll do it."

"When do you leave?"

"Not me. You."

"You're the goddamned reporter. Why don't you go?"

There was a pause.

"I don't fly," he said quietly. "Haven't for years."

"What?"

"Y2K."

"Are you fucking kidding me?"

"I know, I know. It all turned out to be bullshit. But I just can't get rid of the picture of planes falling out of the sky like lawn darts."

"Thanks a pile for that image. And for reminding me about lawn darts and the genius who thought that throwing heavy, steel-tipped darts into the air around groups of children was a terrific idea."

"Plus, I looked into it. The air traffic control systems down there are crap. Old crap."

"So drive."

"One—Homeland security hasn't forgiven my DUI yet. Two—I can't get the time off and Three—the interview's the day after tomorrow. So you get the ball on this one. Start packing, sunshine."

Me packing for a business trip?

As I stuffed clothes and meds into my trusty bowling bag-type carry-on—the only luggage I ever travel with—I shuddered.

No, I winced.

It was weird to find myself in Logan Airport for the first time in over eighteen years. Of course, it didn't look anything like I remembered, just as nothing from almost two decades earlier ever looks exactly like you remember it.

Visuals aside, I felt like—and actually was—a total moron as I rented a car, something I hadn't done in twenty years. I was fucking Starman, an alien trying to figure out all the now-automatic functions that everybody—except me—knows about. The car itself—a Ford Focus, for Christ's sake—had a lot more buttons than, I was sure, most passenger jet liners. I had no intention of using them anyway. Automatic parallel parking? I prefer to do a shitty job of backing up on my own. Bluetooth? I didn't need to be connected to anything. Even if I had a cell phone, I just can't imagine wanting to talk to anyone when I'm driving (now against the law in lots of places, as it fucking well should be). And docking my "personal device" wasn't high on my list of things to do.

Why put all this shit in new cars that doesn't have anything to do with driving and then bitch because people get distracted? The answer, it turns out, is to put even more shit in cars to help you do basic stuff like stay in your own goddamned lane.

And, I was informed, they'd bill my credit card a hundred and fifty bucks if their forensic maintenance guys found a trace of cigarette smoke in the car, which meant I was going to have to drive with my head hanging out the window like a panting Irish setter.

Getting into and out of Boston wasn't the same either. It's amazing what 20 billion or so will buy in the way of highway construction.

I was a little wistful as I drove past downtown Boston, past the newish TD Garden, on the freeway. Back in the good old days when I'd be there on business, with the right bit of planning a lunch in Quincy

Market could consume an entire afternoon. Instead, here I was being all purposeful on Hwy 93 snaking north and then west for a bit on the 95/128 that I swear used to just be called Route 128.

It was also very strange to find myself on that road again, Two decades earlier I was here once a month. All our tech partners were around there. Wang, DEC, Data General—the so-called iron makers. Now, all on the scrap metal heap, unlamented and gone.

They have all sorts of historical markers and tourist attractions commemorating the cotton and clothing industries which once thrived here in Dickensian workhouse splendour a hundred and fifty years ago, but, I'm betting, there will be no such memorials to the tech companies that at one time employed hundreds of thousands. They're all just gone now. Except for WesCor and a handful of niche players, manufacturing is pretty much all off-shore and even then, it's all disposable as all technology has become disposable, because something new is coming in three months so line up, ya bastards, like you once did for Cabbage Patch dolls.

Now, the whole region was re-inventing itself again with software and communications companies in a bid to compete again with Silicon Valley around San Jose. Oh, and "solutions" companies. Lots and lots of solutions companies. I wouldn't be surprised to see that McDonald's around here had positioned itself as a "hunger solutions" company.

I hadn't come across very many English majors in the tech world, and could not imagine that their literate numbers had swelled in the intervening years, so the grandest irony of all, the location of Walden Pond in the midst of all this complex technology, was likely still lost on most.

WesCor and its Concord subsidiary had taken over progressively larger quarters in an old textile mill on the banks of, surprise, surprise, the Concord River. They then had tacked on modern windowless office blocks, all of it pretty much hidden from the road by sweeping, pagoda-type evergreens.

The security procedures at the old mill were pretty rigorous, from the gated and guarded entrance to the metal-detecting and ID-badging. I was even offered my choice of a pat-down or x-ray. Want fries with that groping?

A sour-looking PR assistant named Gillian retrieved me from the waiting room.

Now maybe ol' Gillian was having a one-of-a-kind horrendous day. Bank foreclosed, cat died, husband served divorce papers—that kind of day. If so—and I doubted it—she had failed to learn the basic personal conduct rule for all public relaters: Suck it up, buttercup. Be human on your own time.

More likely, she was a naturally crisp, cool, humourless, and efficient PR slut. I had been one and I've dealt with many more. But like a bunch of other stuff, the trade was changing for the worse. There was nary a pretense of affability as we walked and she talked about all the rules for my upcoming interview. I was given a list of subjects not to be brought up—personal wealth, political affiliations, family stuff—and I was told several times how lucky I was to have been granted an audience.

Me asking: "Is there a ring I'm supposed to kiss?" didn't warm things up between us.

She stood before a large wooden door and did some retina scan thing that I found nifty in a James Bondian kinda way. As we walked through the minion compound, I couldn't see any skateboarders there, no pets, no basketball hoops, no sign of a day care centre, no baristas doodling on the latte, and no evidence of video gaming or anything else of what I'd been led to believe was the new way of working. Instead, there were giant monitors with engineering drawings and hushed conversations between well-dressed employees.

As we walked, I reviewed what I knew about my subjects. The Reed brothers weren't anything like the prototypical tech whiz kids these days, the ones who toss around billions to get people social and who ooze a tiring evangelical zeal. For one thing, they were about my age which made them complete dinosaurs in a time when you were considered a grizzled vet at thirty and over the hill at forty. They were also wicked smat, as they say in Boston. They were both engineers—one from MIT, one from Harvard—but they weren't anything like the proverbial peas in a pod.

Cortland Reed was the dumpy, rumpled, and reclusive genius of the pair. You rarely ever read or heard anything about him except in tech magazines extolling the elegant intricacies of the latest thinga-ma-bobby's design. Wesley was the tall, patrician, and photogenic public face of the empire, giving speeches, attending conferences, and generally being the bon vivant around town, at art gallery openings, charity galas, at Bruins, Red Sox, and Patriot games. He'd even been invited to the White House.

I was ushered into an executive meeting room—all sorta retro 90s-looking—with its beige brick and black-edged, floor-to-ceiling windows overlooking the river. Greening up the joint were ferns—tons of what else?—Boston ferns.

"Nice plant choice," I said as I shook Wesley's hand. He smiled at my leafy observation. Out of the corner of my eye, I saw Gillian start at me for going off-script.

"Horticulture jokes weren't on the list," I said to her.

She quietly took a seat and immediately began playing with her smart phone, the way I see teenagers do at the mall . . . well, everywhere.

Along one wall were expensively-framed player jerseys. Larry Bird, Yastrzemski, Steve Grogan, and Bruin immortal Bobby Orr. I was compelled to stare at them because I've always been a sucker for this kind of memorabilia.

"We can give you an hour," Cortland said as he glanced at his watch. I couldn't help but notice it was a cheap one, maybe twenty bucks.

"Those are all game-worn, aren't they? I asked, indicating the jerseys.

"Yes, of course," said Wesley, beaming. "Feel free to take a closer look."

I walked along the all-star row, stopping at the #4 hockey sweater of Bobby Orr, the pride of Parry Sound, Ontario.

"When I was in the newspaper delivery business as a kid," I said, "I won tickets to see the Bruins and the Leafs. Even up in the nose-bleeds, you could see Orr control the whole goddamn game."

"I know what you mean. But at ice-level, he was even more impressive," said Wesley.

"You saw him?"

"Many times at the Garden. And last summer, we had him on our boat. Tremendous gentleman. And the finest pure athlete to ever wear a Boston uniform."

"Fifty-seven minutes," Cortland announced, bringing us back to the business at hand.

"I have a tape recorder. Do you mind?" I asked as I sat down.

"Not at all."

"Just a minute," Gillian piped up.

She produced her own tape recorder.

"Duelling tapes of the same conversation?" I said.

"Tapes can be altered," Gillian said.

I was about to mention that her precious tape could just as easily be doctored, but Cortland cut in.

"This is on spec?" he asked.

"Not exactly," I said. "We've got a publisher lined up."

"Fire away."

"Ok . . . first question: why are you talking to an old guy from Canada for a book that won't be out for months?"

They seemed taken aback—which I always like.

"We're talking to many people and it's only an hour," Wesley said. "Of course, we looked into you. You and your writing partner know the ropes. You can provide some perspective on our situation. A little outdated now, but I quite liked some of your columns for *Tech View*."

"What else did you learn about me and my partner?" I asked.

"Well, you had a recent . . . situation with the law," Wesley said.

"You were in jail for killing someone," Cortland said, cutting to the chase.

"Longer stretch than Johnny Cash, shorter than Martha Stewart. And yet you're still talking to me."

"You were exonerated, weren't you?"

"Clean as a whistle."

"Fifty-four minutes . . . ," Cortland, our official timekeeper, chimed in.

"Alrighty then . . . why do you think your technology business model isn't doomed because you stick almost purely to manufacturing?" I asked.

"Manufacturing of highly advanced technology," Wesley said.

"Sitting or standing or walking around while you endlessly click through websites isn't an economy; it's a diversion," Cortland added.

I was warming up to ol' Cortland. Everybody, it seemed, was scrolling through the park, the only variance was if you were sliding screens up and down or across. And what do you do with all the vacuous content you're discovering? Why, post, re-post, re-post, and, oh hell, re-post again. The opinions people seemed to have were either so malformed or so unconfident or maybe everyone's getting lazier and lazier that they can't be bothered to work out a thought. It's just so much easier to re-post, re-post, re-post articles, essays, inspirational placards, as if we're all searching for more eloquent ventriloquists to transmit their views through our wooden heads.

"We live in a physical world. You have to make physical things," Cortland added.

"And you make those things in the US?" I asked.

"You're damn right we do," said Cortland.

"Patriotism?"

"Partly. Call it enlightened self-interest. We have plants all over the country," Wesley said.

"Mostly south of the Mason-Dixon," I noted.

"In our view, the right to work is infinitely more preferable than the right not to work," Cortland said.

"As I was saying," Wesley continued, "these plants employ a lot of people, pay a lot of taxes, and have rescued a lot of towns, so we're not going to apologize for that."

"And yet I walked through Concord Medical on my way to this office."

"We had the space; we had the Yankee know-how right here."

"The point is: we have complete control of the process," Wesley said. "No chance of interference by a foreign government or anyone else."

"That's right," Cortland said. "As you know, security will always be an issue with computer infrastructure. The more you make new things, the more ways in there are for the bad guys. Soon, you're spending most of your time trying to plug the holes."

I thought I saw a warning glance from Wesley to his plain-speaking and now more garrulous bro.

"Sort of like the little Dutch boy at the e-dyke?" I prodded.

Wesley chuckled.

"Something like that."

"So tell me this: why wouldn't MacNeil sell to you?"

That caused another hesitation.

"He's an astute businessman. He wants . . . wanted . . . to drive the price up."

"But, the fact is, we were offering him far more than *anybody* would or will," Cortland said.

"He was gambling that we couldn't build a good power source

ourselves or find another company who could," Wesley added.

"Was he right?"

"Time will tell."

"What Cortland means is that we have options."

"Like?"

"Like I can't say."

"Like possibly Bio-watch is more likely to sell to you now with MacNeil out of the way?" I suggested.

I didn't exactly mean to imply that they stood to gain from Alistair's death but, well, the fact is, they did.

The hitherto invisible PR assistant pocketed her phone and rose and whispered something to Cortland who, in turn, bent Wesley's ear.

"I'm afraid, Mr Lydon, we're going to have to cut this short," Cortland said.

"But you said I'd have an hour."

"Something's come up."

"I can wait around."

"No. This will take some time."

"Well then, we can pick this up again."

"To be honest, I doubt it," Cortland said.

"Any further questions, you can submit to Gillian here. She'll respond in a timely fashion," Wesley said.

"But . . . "

"We enjoyed meeting you, Mr. Lydon."

All I could think to say was: "The Leafs are going to kick Bruin ass this season."

"I doubt that very much too," Cortland said.

"Good-bye, Mr. Lydon."

I'd been tossed out of enough bars to know the feeling of a bum's rush. Gillian smoothly guided me back out the way we came, until I was standing in the lobby, forking over my security badge in return for her business card.

"So what's going on?" I asked.

"Nothing substantive."

"What's that you say, Lassie? There's trouble at the old mill?"

She looked at me blankly.

I was in yet another bad mood as I headed back to Boston. All that time—and money—just to get about twenty minutes of PR blah-blah horseshit.

Fuck it, I thought. There must be something else I could do while I was down here.

Alexandra. She used to work in Boston. Maybe, just maybe, she was still here.

I pulled to the paved shoulder near a "No Travelling in Breakdown Lane" sign. Even that had changed. It had replaced the more ironically contradictory "No Stopping in Breakdown Lane" that I had remembered. Like a monkey at a keyboard, I fucked around with various cockpit buttons trying to find her. Just before I snapped the steering wheel in half, I had an idea. I drove around Waltham until I found the public library.

After that, Alexandra was easy to find and, yes, she was still in the neighbourhood. Sort of. She was in Framingham, about half an hour to the south-west. She was listed as the founder and the tech analyst for an ethical investment firm called—rather cutely, I thought—the Fair Trading Group. That was an intriguing change from her superstar days working for the big houses.

There was some evident fluster when she came out to the tasteful lobby to retrieve me. I wrote it off to the way there always is fluster when people just show up unannounced, blowing holes in the tightly-orchestrated calendars everybody, except apparently me, kept these days.

As she swept towards me, I was quite stricken. The years had been kind, even overly generous to her. Tall, slender, unadorned, she was impressive as hell in a sort of Katherine Hepburn way. She had spent almost her entire adult life being feared and respected and catered to by thirty years' worth of tech giants. But she had likely been treated the same way on the playing fields and in the seminar rooms at Vassar or Bryn Mawr or whatever leafy campus she had attended. Thoroughly confident, self-possessed, and graceful, she'd be a natural force to be reckoned with, on a field hockey pitch or in a boardroom.

For both of us, it seemed, there was the issue of greeting etiquette. A handshake? That didn't seem right. We settled on a slight hug, a bit of cheek-to-cheeking. No more than a microsecond, but enough time for me to smell her light perfume, feel the leanness of her back.

"What the hell are you doing here?" she asked.

"I was in the neighbourhood so I thought I'd drop by."

"Sure you were."

"Sorry we didn't get to chat in Toronto."

"You seemed busy. What brings you to Boston?"

"Just had a useless chat with the Reed brothers."

"You did? You bastard! They won't even speak to me! I get Gillian."

"Well, I do too now."

"How long it'd take you to piss them off?"

"I must be getting mellow. Fifteen minutes or so."

She smiled.

"So what'd they say?" she asked.

"Just like the good old days, eh? Always fishing."

She smiled again. Did I mention she had a great smile?

"What'd they say?" she asked again.

"Not a lot. Why do you even care if you get to talk to that evil global megacorp?" I asked looking around at her modest office

"I hold my nose because they and companies like them are the ones pouring billions into R&D. You improve the health in developing countries and they develop a whole lot faster. If Concord were to succeed. Or Ulti/ME. Or anybody else, they might, with a little persuasion, have the sense to make available their devices at a decent price. Same with Big Pharma and cheaper drugs."

"You want to tell me all about it over dinner?" I more or less blurted out.

She paused.

"That was smooth," she said. "Where?"

"Your home field, your choice. As long as it's cheap and tacky."

"There's a place near here. I've got to finish up, but come get me at six."

"I most surely will."

I always like it when I've got a couple of hours to kill in a foreign place. A chance to explore, prowl shops, check out architecture. Invariably, these fact-finding missions conclude with a free real estate magazine and a bar. And all the better if, within that bar, there's a wise-ass bartender with whom to banter. The Colonial Tavern and Kirk, its youthful barkeep, fit the bill nicely.

An hour and two real pints, and a good-natured argument over Canadian vs. American beer later, I was back at Alexandra's office. She was waiting for me in the lobby.

"I thought I'd scared you off," she said.

"Not a chance . . . cuz I figure you're paying," I said, trying like hell to tamp down my eagerness.

A couple of minutes' walk took us to not exactly a dive but a place that had recently been done up to look like a dive. Real dives don't charge 23 bucks for a goddamned club sandwich.

The night was warm but cloudy. We sat outside and had the patio to ourselves.

I had a Philly cheese steak and she had a veggie burger and we traded carnivore and vegetarian insults. If this were public school, we would've been pushing each other into lockers.

It was a relief not to be on my guard any more, the way I always had to be cautious as a PR slut. Plus, if I remembered correctly, having dinner with a beautiful, smart, funny and tough woman is almost always pleasant. The goddamned twinkly lights strung on the trees around us didn't hurt the mood either.

We swapped a few anecdotes about Alistair, most to do with his utterly direct and often counter-intuitive statements about, well, everything. For both of us, these little stories were wreathed in some kind of wistfulness for his basic decency and as markers for the out-sized and lasting impression he'd obviously made on the two of us.

I told her about the limited edition booklet I had done up for the

20th anniversary of Montrose — "The Wit and Wisdom of Chairman Al", containing his alleged sayings, some real and some made-up.

"Given enough time," I quoted, "I can prove to you that Rhode Island is—"

"—bigger than Texas," she ended. "He sent me a copy; he really liked it."

"Funny, he never said a word to me."

"Just like my father would have done."

"And my real old man, too," I said. "A report card with mostly A's got me a "What the fuck's this B+?""

We figured out that we'd known each other for almost thirty years. Rather than despairing over the shocking passage of time, we skipped lightly along those years, filling in the milestones for both our career and personal history arcs. They were almost identical.

She too had a post-grad English degree (but in fucking Victorian lit). Then she sort of fell into hi-tech, as I had. So, at about the same time, we were learning the ropes when there wasn't much string.

"Alex, didja ever just close the office door, look at your pay cheque, and chuckle?"

"Yup. At the start. I was sure I'd get found out."

Eight years ago her marriage had dissolved but for less dramatic reasons than mine had.

"Turns out, he was an asshole."

Our histories diverged about five years ago. About the time I had perfected my isolationist doctrine, she had decided that she should actually make a constructive contribution to the world, experimenting with the wild notion that you could have a conscience *and* make money at the same time.

"You miss the bigs?" I asked.

"Not for a second. It's a good feeling when I can help raise money for, say, a coffee concern in South America or a wind farm in the Algarve. Better than just making rich pricks richer."

"In this day and age, that line pretty much identifies you as a goddamned pink commie bastard."

As we were leaving the restaurant, the black clouds opened up a bit and gave us a sort of drizzly night, the kind of night that coats cars and sidewalks with a soft sheen under the streetlights. Walking back to our cars, Alexandra slipped her arm into mine.

"Just like old times," I said, recalling a night on a Manhattan street decades ago when she had done the same thing walking back to my hotel and I'd left her standing kind of stupefied at the elevator. I had ridden up to my room alone, partly proud of myself for my moral rectitude and partly hopeful that she didn't hear the sound of me repeatedly bashing my head against the elevator door.

"You've got quite the memory," she said, as our eyes met then flitted away.

So here we were, two sixty-somethings standing by our cars in the soft rain, dancing around in the dark, and clueless about what was to happen next.

"Going home?" she asked.

"I dunno. Am I?"

"Follow me."

No FBI agent ever tailed a suspect with as much focus and deliberation as I applied to keeping up with Alexandra's Prius as it zipped through traffic to an old and heavily-treed residential neighbourhood.

You learn—or at least you think you learn—a lot about people by where and how they live. Alexandra's home was a small and completely renovated clapboard century home, all neat and extremely well-gardened. Inside, I was happy to see no trace of that modern minimalist shit with all the cold tile and stainless steel and white that transforms homes into sterile operating rooms for precious, self-identified idiot savants who claim they don't want their little brains to be sensorily-overloaded in their own goddamned house.

Here were wide honey-coloured pine plank floors, classic Shaker furniture, overstuffed chairs and sofas, and authentic-looking early Americana art and antique gee-gaws that you'd never call gee-gaws. All warm, comfortable, and Yankee as a hell.

You can also learn a lot by how people stock their libraries, assuming they even have libraries. So what really intrigued me were Alexandra's floor to ceiling bookcases and their contents. I couldn't see anything to do with technology and skipped over the mannered and boring-as-shit tomes by Austen, Eliot, Thackeray, and those dreadful Brontes. But, to my delight, she also had just about everything Marquez, Steinbeck, and Vonnegut ever wrote.

"Poo-tee-tweet?" I said.

Turned out that was a sort of secret password that got things moving as we were standing side-by-side, admiring the library.

Thanks, Kurt; I really mean that.

Except for pecks on the cheek with Halley, oh, and that smooch I gave Carl when the Steelers won the Super Bowl, I hadn't kissed a human since Beth. Getting face-to-face with Alex was simply wonderful as the pace picked up and we grappled our way up the narrow staircase to her giant four-poster bed.

It really was like bicycle riding after years away from it. Only a lot more fun. A little wobbly at first, but it all came back to me. And, near as I could tell, there was some Canadian-American reciprocity going on. All in all, just a truly swell time.

I got up.

"Are you leaving?" she asked, a cross between "how fucking rude" and "I'd rather you didn't."

"Victory cigarette," I said and I hummed part of the Rocky theme song which got a chuckle.

She joined me on the covered back porch. She was wearing a Patriots jersey and was sexy as all get out as she drew her endless legs up underneath it.

We sat in silence for a while, listening to rain drops as they gathered and plopped off the huge hosta leaves gleaming under the porch light.

"Wanna . . . I don't know . . . hang out tomorrow?" I suavely asked.

"Sorry, I can't. Got a flight to Dallas first thing."

"I suppose I ought to head back to Toronto."

"Let's go back to bed."

It was a comfort and a delight to sleep all wrapped up with her—warm, safe, and . . . alive.

The morning was sunny as we clattered around her kitchen, she making coffee and me pretending to help. There wasn't the slightest bit of awkwardness.

We settled down in the back porch.

"Funny, you being here," she said. "I've got a big report on Concord,

WesCor's med company, coming out next week."

"Can I get a preview?"

"Oh, I see what's happening . . . Thought you'd sleep your way to some inside info?"

"And did I . . . ?"

"You weren't that good," she joked—at least I hoped she was joking. "Sorry, Jake. You know the drill. Market sensitivity and all that."

"How about right after you publish?"

"Sorry, again. It wouldn't be . . . "

"Ethical?"

"I was going to say: it wouldn't be profitable. You aren't a client."

That smarted. She sensed it too for there was a pause that may have meant she felt badly over not sharing info, given the sharing we did the night before.

"If I were you," she finally offered, "and held Concord shares, I'd be selling about now."

"Why?"

"The Reed brothers are in big trouble on this one."

"Why?"

"It's in the report."

"Awww."

"OK, OK, their latest device failed."

"So a monitor failed," I said, playing along with the gag Halley had let me in on, that Concord was working on something a whole lot more complex. "That can't be such a big deal."

"You don't understand. It wasn't a monitor that failed; it's a remotely-controlled pump that was supposed to automatically inject insulin after a command centre here in Boston determined the patient needed a hit. WesCor's been working on it for years. The FDA let 100 late-stage diabetes patients from all over the country into a field trial after they signed the waiver."

"And . . . ?"

"It would appear that the machine killed some of them."

"Holy shit."

"There's more. It's not in the report, but I'm pretty sure one of them was Alistair."

"What!?"

"It looks like Alistair was test subject 101."

"How do you know?"

"I've got a source."

"You have to tell someone!"

"I'm telling you."

"That's not really someone."

"Look, the FDA sees this stuff all the time. They'll handle it."

"Sure they will."

She looked at the antique wall clock.

"Geez, I have to get going."

"I'll take off now . . . Alex, here's the part where I ask if last night was a one-off or not."

She smiled that great smile of hers.

"Let's see, shall we? Stay in touch."

So it goes.

‹CHAPTER TWENTY-SIX›

On the cramped commuter flight back to Toronto—after biting my tongue during the pointless post-9/11 security procedures—I tried to sort through both my unsatisfactory business stint in the US and my more than satisfactory interlude with Alex. Setting aside that pleasantness, I focused on Alexandra's reiteration of what Halley had told me. Two unconnected sources had confirmed it; Christ, I felt like a reporter with ethics and discipline and everything. It seemed pretty clear that Alistair's guinea pig adventure had ended badly.

Upon landing, I was pulled out of the normally perfunctory Canadian customs line and searched.

They didn't even bother to ask me if I had anything to declare. As often is the case, "What the fuck?" was the only thing I could think to say, as I watched the officious inspector tear apart my trusty bowling bag.

"There is no need for that kind of language, sir," I was sternly reminded.

I have never figured out why this now garden-variety obscenity seemed to particularly offend people in uniforms, well, anybody really. Have a politician say it and let the nationwide shock and howling outrage begin. Suddenly, it's the "F-bomb" or a "profanity-laced tirade." Doesn't anyone fucking watch cable TV?

"Alright, what the fff . . . firetruck? I didn't do nuthin', copper."

"Then what's this?" she asked holding up the carton of Marlboro Lights. "How long have you been away from Canada?"

"24 hours."

"According to your passport, it's been 22 hours."

I swore I thought Boston was in a different time zone, apologized for not being able to tell time, thanked them for their vigilance, and paid the duty.

In the terminal, after I was finally able to locate a payphone, I called Steve at the *Sun*.

"Sir, Minion Number 1 reporting in, sir!" I announced.

"Where are you?" he asked.

"Toronto Island."

"Well, happy to hear you're still at large. Why don't you c'mon over to my place?"

He gave me his home address at Queen's Quay Terminal and said he'd meet me there.

This country mouse was mightily impressed as I approached Steve's condo building perched and glittering on the lip of Lake Ontario.

While waiting for Steve, I shot the shit with the security guard. He was an older guy who looked efficient as hell as a presence but who confessed to being somewhat useless in the case of an incident. Night after night for seven years, he had manned his station. Over that time, he told me, there had been two, maybe three drunks, who needed tossing.

"It's quiet. Just the way I like it," he said, surveying the empty lobby.

This is the kind of guy I sometimes envy. He didn't ever lay awake at night, his head full of bees, worrying about the intricacies of his job on the following day.

We also talked a bit about the Leafs. Sorry, the fuckin' Leafs. I know, I know, they're getting better of late but it's hard to let go of decades-long pessimism.

Steve came through the front doors, almost marching across the marble-tiled lobby. Watching him in full stride, it occurred to me that, although he was my age, he moved and looked perhaps ten years younger than I did.

"I bet units here gotta be a mill," I said, as we ascended in the mirrored elevator.

"More."

"Some ink-stained wretch you turned out to be."

"Jesus, if you can't make money as a business reporter you gotta be pretty dumb."

"Or ethical."

An absolutely beautiful woman opened the door as Steve was trying to unlock it. He made with the introductions, labelling me his old, old, old, *old* friend.

"Kendra, this is Jake. Jake, Kendra."

I was tongue-tied, as I always am around gorgeous women. Tall, dark-haired, and I'd say at least twenty years younger than Steve. At least.

"Great condo," I said, surveying the sleek decorating with, thank Christ, a few splotches of colour.

Steve led me to his office which I imagined was a replica of the ones he would've kept at his various newsroom jobs. Stacks of papers, file folders, and books teetered on every available horizontal surface. Various framed awards, including not one, but three National Newspaper nods, a blow-up of a photo of him with Joe Strummer, as well as Karsh's famous black and white portrait of a sturdy and sober-looking Hemingway adorned the walls.

"Quite the shrine to self you got goin' on here," I said.

"It's actually hard to get things done while I contemplate The Glory That Is Me."

We were just settling down when Kendra appeared at the doorway.

"I think you boys will be more comfortable on the balcony," she said.

She slid open a glass door and we sat at a tasteful bistro table and chairs. A large glass ashtray was dead centre on the table.

On the balcony with the sun was setting behind our building, we smoked and watched as the sky in front of us darkened quickest where it met the lake horizon beyond the Toronto Islands.

Kendra came out with a cold, sweaty beer for me, soda water for Steve.

"She's beautiful," I said after she had retreated inside.

"She is, isn't she?"

"I didn't even know you had a daughter."

"Fuck off, jealous one."

I related in greater detail my experience in Boston, leaving out the delightful sleepover at Alexandra's. As I thought, Steve had that look of "I should've been there because I would have done it better" as he considered my failure as a reporter that had resulted in my relegation to WesCor's PR department.

"I've got a tape; you can listen to it," I told him. "Then you tell me what you would've asked differently."

"Well, it's done. Any chance you can get anything out of Gillian?"

"Doubt it. You can feed me some questions, Woodward, but I think there's a great, nasty stone wall looming."

"Well, at least you can fill in some local colour. We can tart up some conversation beyond what you got on tape, get the setting right."

I wanted Steve to know that my New England sortie had actually been quite valuable.

"But I did find out more while I was down there," I said. "Lots more. Do you know Alexandra Simpson?"

"Sure. From years ago. Heavy-duty analyst. I used to get quotes from her all the time. She was at the funeral, wasn't she?"

"The very same."

"And?"

What the hell, I thought.

"She told me that Concord killed Alistair."

"Really?!"

I explained that—according to Alexandra's report—MacNeil had conned them into letting him be part of these hush-hush field trials of a remote-controlled pump. And that it looked like the device had screwed up and killed him. And further, maybe its malfunctioning had killed a bunch of other people.

"How would she know?"

"A source. Wouldn't say who."

"Is this solid?"

"Think it is," I said, knowing that it was also based on what Halley had told me.

"*That*, my friend, is a big news story. I gotta write this for the paper."

"You don't *gotta* do anything. Don't fuck this up, Steve."

He knew and I knew he was right; it was big news. But he knew and I knew that it would pretty well mess up the book as we had it. What he didn't know is that any shot I might have with Alexandra would also vaporize.

"Look, Steve, nobody'll talk to us if you blow this up and get all speculative. You really have shit to work with. An unnamed source told somebody something. There's no way you can corroborate this. Alex won't talk."

"So it's Alex now?" he asked, with something resembling bemused curiosity.

"I've always called her Alex. Like . . . like I call you Steve, not J. Stephen," I said, trying to skip over his question. "Look. Reporters kill stories all the time. Editors kill stories. Goddamned publishers kill stories. Let's keep it for the book. Ya know, the big reveal."

"We should tell someone."

"The FDA knows. It'll get handled."

"Lemme think about it."

"Besides, you have no facts. And you'll get me in shit with Alex . . . andra."

"So?"

"So . . . we'll need her for the book. She's seen it all."

"She's not exactly a heavyweight anymore. Think anybody'll even notice her report?"

"She's the vet of the bunch; they'll notice alright. Any chance you can get a copy? You must have some bridges to your tech reporting days that you haven't torched."

"I don't think so, but I'll ask around."

We sat in silence. Steve obviously trying to curb his reporter's instincts for a story nobody else had.

"Want some good news?" he asked.

"What?"

"You're back up at the plate. You're going to San Francisco."

"Yay for me! What for?"

"I got us an interview with Cooper Stanley, the Exec VP for Strategy at Ulti/ME!"

"Actually, that *is* good news."

"Plus, there are some tech writers and a prof from the Stanford neuroscience department you can talk to. I'll send you the schedule I worked up."

"We can't do all this over the phone or by e-mail?"

"Some will and some won't. Stanley won't. So I figured you should go down there, soak up the local scene, you know, do the complete circuit."

"Do I get one of them silk tour jackets?"

"Asshole over America?"

"I want to talk to Nigel Hayward too. He worked for Alistair *and* for Concord. He's at Ulti/ME now."

"Perfect. You make that contact."

I didn't balk too hard at the prospect of visiting my favourite city in the world. I made a note to find out who had agreed to long-distance interviews so I could blow them off in person, in order to spend more time sittin' on the dock of the bay . . . with an Anchor Steam Ale in my hand.

"You're going to be a busy little Canadian beaver next week," Steve said.

"Next week?"

"Yup. It's all booked. Three days, two nights starting Tuesday."

"You could've checked with me first."

"Gee, I'm sorry. I know I should've, what with your frantic, break-neck schedule and all."

"Fuck you. Where am I staying?"

"Quality Inn in Sunnyvale. Belly of the beast. Free HBO and continental breakfast, may I add."

"I was hoping for the Mark Hopkins," I said, thinking back to my decadent corporate days.

"Dream on, champagne boy. It's beer budget time."

"While we're on the subject, any chance I can get some coin for the Boston expenses? That's about a thousand bucks for the flight, car rental and so on."

"Check your e-mail. Already done, my little jet-setter."

"The publisher won't cough up an advance but he will front the expenses?"

"I'm paying the freight. Call it a down payment; it'll come out of your share."

"We're actually doing this, aren't we? We're going to get a real live book outta this."

"We sure are, little buddy."

He put me up for the night.

Next morning, on a hunch, I strolled up to Adelaide Street to Bio-Watch's offices, amid the congested, honking, stinking, big, grim mess of morning rush hour. Christ, what a swell way to start your day!

Mike saw me right away. His white shirt was blindingly crisp. Everybody'd gone back to white shirts after a brief fling with coloured ones which, in retrospect, were a pretty pathetic stab at individualism.

I thanked him again for coming up with my get-out-of-jail card and made sure he had gotten his bond back. Then I asked him if he'd seen Alexandra's report because I knew interested parties usually got an advance peek if they knew someone who knew someone.

He hesitated.

"C'mon, Mike. This is important."

He brought out a rather hefty document, maybe a hundred pages, stapled together and stamped "Draft Confidential!" in red on every page.

"Alex sent it a couple of days ago," he said. "This has to stay right here."

The report looked like all other draft analyst reports I'd read over the years when it was my job to read them. I couldn't tell you, page by page, precisely what they meant. Then and now, all that seemed to matter to anyone was the last page wherein investors were advised to Buy, Sell, or Hold.

"Concord Medical Systems a Sell" was the subhead near the end. I backed up, read the section entitled: "Serious concerns over safety of RDC systems"

Here's the exact passage: "Serious safety concerns exist over the reliability of Concord's Remote Digital Control (RDC) software. In the field of medical devices, they can't afford to be right *most* of the time. People will live or they will die. We understand—but emphasize we cannot state definitively—that the FDA is currently investigating deaths in central Florida, Arizona, Oregon, and New Hampshire and that these deaths may be of field trial subjects with Concord's implantable devices. We also understand there may be more fatalities.

We believe the company's future is almost exclusively tied to the success of these remote digitally-controlled devices. Even though the eventual market will be worth billions, likely tens of billions, we do not think with these early results that Concord Medical Systems is a prudent or even speculative buy. Uncharacteristically, the Reed brothers seem to be in big trouble on this venture."

I looked up.

"You concerned by all this?" I asked.

"Not really," Mike said. "Desperate companies will usually pay desperate dollars."

"Did you read this? The section about the fatalities?"

"Yeah, it was a field trial . . . and?"

"Mike, did you know Dad was hooked to one of these actual pumps, not just a new fangled monitor?"

He looked genuinely shocked.

"No! I swear, I didn't."

"Apparently he had tagged onto that field trial disaster Alexandra talks about."

"I don't believe it. Are you sure?"

"Pretty sure."

Mike pondered for a bit.

"This'll probably screw any plans Alistair had with WesCor," he said.

"That would seem so. Your Board's going to find it hard to deal with the company that killed your Chairman. So now what?"

Mike thought for a bit.

"Not sure. Maybe Alexandra's source is wrong; maybe she's in bed with Steinman."

He really could've picked a better description of her relationship with Ulti/ME, couldn't he?

"Say she's not," I said. "On to Ulti/ME?"

"Maybe. But with WesCor out of the picture, the price just went way down. Looks like we head back to the drawing board."

Mike asked me if I had gone to any of my friends in the media. I lied and told him "no."

I took the Royal York shuttle to the parking lot where the Vibe squatted there, unmolested as usual. Except for the occasional "Wash me" finger-scrawled on her grime, nobody has ever messed with her. I paid the piratical parking fee—more than a month's rent for my first apartment (and that had a bathroom!)—and gladly headed towards the 401 and home.

I get as smug as a Prius owner or a former smoker when I'm leaving a city just as everybody's heading in.

There is this giant relief I always feel when I drive down my laneway. Olly-olly, oxen free. As if any kid says that today. Or even plays Hide n' Seek in the real world.

True to his word, Steve had sent me my itinerary, the Delta e-tickets together with electronic wads of cash and info about whom I'd be talking to and when.

"*Be sure to wear some flowers in your hair,*" he wrote.

I dug around Ulti/ME's website, found Nigel Hayward's address and sent him a note saying I'd be in the 'hood in a few days and could I drop by.

He wrote back in minutes. "*Brilliant! Just pop 'round. See you then!*"

Why is everything "brilliant" to a Brit? Probably the same reason everything was becoming "awesome" or "epic" over here when, in fact, not that much is awesome or epic or even brilliant anymore.

A little later, I sent Steve a note with my best guess as to how the coming WestCor shitstorm might affect the book. Essentially, I suggested that the likely Concord implosion was just one more bit of proof that—sadly perhaps—Ulti/ME or the next Ulti/ME was going to win over old school companies like WesCor.

There was zero surprise, a few days later, when Concord's stock tanked the morning after Alexandra's report came out. Cable snapped and the whizzing elevator hurtled towards the basement floor. It opened at $46, closed when the SEC suspended trading at 22.50, despite the denials, probably written by Gillian, that "the device is not even mostly our future . . . No clear evidence of failures . . . Simple rumor and speculation, etc. etc."

The stock re-opened the next morning when it continued its deadfall, dropping to 9 on huge volume. I bought in at 10.25. And I wasn't alone. The elevator hadn't splattered on the basement floor. Enough people bought back in to freeze it inches from concrete oblivion. The stock bounced around in the single digits for a while before it ticked up to the upper-teens the next day when I sold.

Whatever happened to reading balance sheets? Even my rudimentary math told me its hard assets and cash justified at least twenty bucks a share, never mind the patents. Don't hand me that bullshit about market logic. Near as I could tell, either panic or euphoria rules the market, with long intervals of just fucking around in between.

But, the fact was, on paper, somebody somewhere had lost north of a billion dollars.

In real life, I'd cleared just over 5K or about 150 cases of beer which really is the only worthwhile currency in my books. I even had a Dominican foreign exchange account—closer to 200 cases of Presidente.

Deciding I'd put in a good day's work, I wanted to celebrate. I figured that enough time had elapsed since our stint as guests of the Crown, that it was time to make up with Carl. I putt-putted over to his island. We never actually apologize to each other for anything; we just wait long enough so that whatever petty resentment or irritation we might have had dissipates.

"Thirsty?" I ask.

"Turns out I am."

So we motored down the shoreline to the Angler Arms where we spent an absolutely splendid afternoon—and evening—on the western-facing deck getting convivial as hell.

Just for shits and giggles and old time's sake, we decided it would be a helluva of a good idea to leave the boat docked at the bar and do our wandering-around-drunk-in-the-woods-at-night routine.

Although it was somewhat sobering—particularly because the big bastard hadn't brought any insect repellant and the mosquitoes were ravening—the experience was enjoyable. And I made it home before Carl did. He, of course, one-upped me by swimming back to his place, the water glittering under a full moon as he cut through the slight waves.

The next morning was depressive. A storm front had moved in overnight. Grey and rainy, too wet for any yard aping. That left research and writing.

The problem is, the older I get the more dedicated to procrastination I become, which of course is counter-intuitive. You'd think I'd be all keen to get as much done as I could within my tobacco-limited time remaining on the planet. But no. Especially not when I already know the outcome of things, as I thought I did with this book.

Fuck it. I decided instead to beat on a speed bag for a while. I drove to the gym in Peterborough. As with just about everything in my life, the gym is a throwback—perhaps to the 1890s. It's mostly populated by lacrosse players and junior or beer league hockey players who believe that boxing smarts might be handy in their sports but who can't afford or refuse to pay membership fees to an international chain of sleek "health and wellness" clubs. The gym also hosts a smattering of old tomato cans such as myself.

We all work our way through groupings of various bags and worn equipment that are scattered around the reason we're all here: the battered old ring squatting in the middle of the cavernous room. Before we step onto that canvas, we perform the Stations of the Right Cross, as it were. Here, there are few sounds beyond the "thwap, thwap" of boxing gloves on bags and the squeak and shriek of running shoes on the worn hardwood floors. Nobody says stupid shit like "namaste" in this dive or walks around with rolled-up yoga mats as though they were readying for a blissful Buddhist bivouac. Nary a $300, colour co-ordinated Lycra outfit to be found.

There's nothing like the stale, pervasive, almost nauseating smell of physical exertion to wake you up. It didn't take long until I was on the verge of puking up bits of lung and god knows what else. But it felt good, especially the speed bag where rapid-fire pummeling of something, anything, was exactly what I felt like doing.

A younger guy—well, they're all younger than me there, except the Burgess Meredith-type who empties the spit buckets and collects towels—asked me if I wanted to spar. I didn't recognize him, was pretty sure he wasn't a regular. A little shorter and lighter than me, I figured I could do alright in the ring with him.

I, of course, figured wrong. You might be surprised what little those puffy boxing helmets actually do to prevent ringing ears when you take a bunch of jabs to the head as I did in our one round of flailing away. I tried to plod into him, largely because plodding is my forte now that age has strengthened the hold gravity has on me. I managed to get in a few solid body shots, but mostly, he floated like a butterfly and stung at will like a hive-full of bees. I called it quits after he landed a stiff right on the ol' shnoz, that had me sitting splay-legged on the canvas, listening to the Notre Dame cathedral bells and watching more stars than turn up for the People's Choice Awards.

That kind of licking did not have me ticking but, I reasoned, every once in a while, I needed a lesson in humility—not that I ever actually go looking for lessons. Even though the gym facilities were, I bet, a little more squalid than most Mexican jails, showering off did feel good if for no other reason than it cooled the aches.

Dressed and on the way out, I passed the younger guy who'd just pounded the piss out of me. He was on the jump rope, hands crossing over, going faster and faster until the rope turned invisible, shit I couldn't even have done when I was his age. He stopped as I passed.

"We should do that again some time," he said, with what looked like a sort of cold smirk.

"No. No, we definitely should not."

I wasn't doing a lot of shoulder checks on the drive back home, such was the stiffness in my neck, well, all over really.

Pulling into my laneway I came upon one of those fluorescent lime-painted crotch-rocket motorcycles parked by the house which I found odd.

Odder still was the sight of Carl sitting at my picnic table, facing the lake. He never showed up just to sit there.

Oddest was the fact that he had someone in a headlock.

What the fuck?" I said.

"Easy there," Carl advised the kid, slowly loosening his grip as if calming a fawn he had captured.

This young deer was a skinny guy, dressed in black T-shirt, black jeans, and really nifty white and black sneakers. He had spiked dark hair and mournful-looking brown eyes. As he straightened himself up, I realized he looked vaguely familiar.

"Caught him nosing around the place," Carl said.

"Who are you and what are you doing here?" I demanded.

"I'm Jason MacNeil."

That stopped me. But I saw something in his eyes that reminded me of Sarah.

"Your mom's worried about you, you know," I said.

"*I'm* worried about *her*."

"Then you should call her."

"It's better if I don't talk to her right now."

"I'm sorry about your dad; he was a good guy."

"Not to be harsh; he wasn't really. But thanks."

Jason was pretty antsy, rubbing his palms on his thighs. You could see it was a habit of his because the black denim across the front of his legs was worn. At first, I thought he might've been high; I'd seen that sort of frantic nervousness when cocaine was the drug of corporate choice in the heady 1980s. He kept darting glances at Carl as though he was afraid my large, cantankerous neighbour would wrassle him again, which was entirely possible.

"Carl, it's OK." I said. "I'm OK here, right, Jason?"

"Yes."

Carl rose slowly.

"If you need me, just yell," he said.

Jason still had that chipmunk jumpiness in his eyes as he watched Carl leave.

"What's going on, son?" I asked.

"I can't tell you everything. But you have to stop digging into all that tech with Ulti/ME and WesCor."

That pretty well floored me.

"How the hell do you know about my digging?"

"I just know, OK?"

"No, it's not OK at all! How do you know?"

"My friends and I . . . we have a sort of club . . . we play around with technology."

"What friends?"

"The none-of-your-business kind."

"Anonymous?" I guessed, exhausting my knowledge of the hacker world.

"*Like* Anonymous. Look, the point is someone's fucking with you."

"Who?"

"I'm not exactly sure. It's not the government. We know that. But there are some systems even we can't get into."

"How did *you* get on to me?"

"Accidentally. I'm—I *was*—paying attention to some of the things my father was into. His phone call to you was strange in that you hadn't shown up for years. So I got looking into you."

I suddenly imagined how a bug under a microscope might feel, if bugs under microscopes had feelings. You spend your life in relative anonymity thinking that you're getting further and further off the grid, not in a batshit crazy survivalist way, but just in a place where you didn't matter and only a few people mattered all that much to you, and then, bang! You're in full Kafka mode.

"And what did you find, pray tell?" I asked.

"You've got some interesting search patterns. There's a logic to them but not a normal one."

"Thanks . . . I guess."

"More important, we could tell that someone was following you, going to the same places you went to, like a nanosecond after. It just couldn't be a coincidence, the odds are completely astronomical."

"But possible?" I asked, hoping he was wrong.

"Do you mean possible like the Raiders—that's your team, isn't it?—winning the Super Bowl this year."

Ouchie.

"Why are you even bothering telling me these things? I asked. "I'm a guy you don't even know."

He paused and stared out at the lake.

"When my father hired you a few years ago, I overheard him telling my mom that he'd brought you back. She was happy; said you were a good person. Then she told me that you had given me something when I was a kid."

"That stuffed rabbit?"

"Yes! That rabbit. I had Baba for years . . . So . . . I don't know . . . it seemed like it was something I should do. Warn you."

"Why didn't you just call? Or send an e-mail?"

"I couldn't, OK? You have to trust me . . . even though you don't know me."

The kid was right; I didn't know him at all. But here were a couple of simple facts: he knew what I had been researching and he made the effort to drive out here and give me a heads up about someone e-tailing me. And for no other reason than I had given him a stuffed bunny over twenty years ago. I didn't have the heart now, just like I didn't when he was a toddler, to tell him that the only reason he got the toy was that Halley hadn't liked the thing at all.

"If you knew they were following me, they must know you were too, no?" I said.

"Maybe. We're pretty good at covering our tracks."

"So what now?"

"I'm not sure."

"Well, I'm going to San Francisco."

"We know."

"Who's 'we' again?"

"It doesn't matter. What matters is we know. And if we know, they know. Any chance you could cancel and just lay low for a while?"

I thought about it. On one hand, I'm an abject coward. A running joke between Beth and I had been my general lack of bravery or any action or appearance approaching suave (pronounced swaw-vee). She contended, likely accurately, that if the two of us were ever captured by bad guys while we were trying to stop those bad guys, the first words out of my mouth would be: "Do anything you want to the girl, but, for Christ's sakes, leave me alone!"

However, on the other hand, I fucking hate being told what I can or can't do.

"No." I finally answered. "Things to do, places to go, people to meet."

"Then you have to take some precautions."

"Like what?"

"Like this," he said, fishing a cell phone out of his pocket.

I'm sure I shrunk back as if he were handing me a pissed-off scorpion.

"No way!"

"You need to get over yourself. You *have* to have this. It's the only safe way to communicate."

"With who? I won't have to talk to anyone."

"You might need to talk to me. Just in case."

"I already have a cell phone." I lied.

"No you don't."

Defeated, I took the thing from him, palmed it as if I were fondling raw liver.

"You call me on this number," he said, handing me a slip of paper. "Memorize it. And you *only* use that phone. It's a pre-paid cell. It's called a burner."

"I know what it's called. I watch TV."

"It's July 5th today," he continued. "This number's good until August 5. Then I'll get you another and another," (all of which I found off-putting, me who has had the same phone number for twenty-five years).

"Do you understand?" he asked.

"I understand that I just joined a group that includes drug dealers and terrorists."

"And people who don't need to be found."

Jason declined a dinner offer. The screaming whine of his crotch-rocket bike finally subsided. For someone keeping a low profile, he sure announced his arrivals and departures.

I considered another piece of irony. I was obviously being moved around like a dumb-ass marionette when I used to be pretty good at pulling the strings myself. With reporters, with investment analysts, even with fellow workers, devious little prick that I can be, I somehow had the knack of knowing what they wanted and what they likely were willing to do next to get it.

I hate being played. I don't mind playing, but I fuckin' hate being played. It's insulting. Steve, maybe Mike and/or Sarah, some unknown e-stalker, armed thugs, even my own daughter, all wanted something from me or for me to do something. My advice to all of them can't be better put than what Sean Connery's shaky character in *The Russia House* says as he questions the wisdom of his handlers:

"You're a fool to use me. I let people down."

From the air, the San Francisco Bay area dazzled me, as it always had. The huge, free-form multi-coloured salt ponds butting up against symmetric development, the needle-nosed Transamerica Building and other high rises bristling on the hills. Golden Gate hemming in Alcatraz, and Angel and Treasure Islands in the bay.

Owing to my newfound ability to actually rent a car, I sailed through Alamo, cutting the guy off as he tried to explain the technology in my Mazda.

As with Boston, the area on the east side of the San Francisco Peninsula was not the same as anything is not the same after twenty years, except maybe George Thorogood's music. It sprawled, one city spilling over into the next. Burlingame, San Mateo, Belmont, Redwood, Menlo Park, Paolo Alto, Cupertino, Mountain View, Sunnyvale all ran together along the west side of San Francisco Bay, draining south into a bigger pool of sleek anonymous called San Jose, each distinguishable only by the signs that you were entering or leaving one of them and their slightly different cop cars. A blur of buildings, business parks, six-lane boulevards, nifty cars, and overpriced real estate were the obvious amenities of this homogeneous, manicured hell.

And inside every one of those low rises were thousands of computer engineers and scientists and psychologists and programmers, each one of whom working for a company which just happened to be right on the verge, oh hell, were ideally-positioned to make a shitload off their latest idea of how we should, how we can, how we *must* change our lives.

All thanks to the Internet, which in my books is degenerating at an alarming rate.

When did the web turn so bossy?

29 Places you MUST see before you die.
40 things you've been doing wrong all your life
17 Next-Level Peanut Butter Desserts You Have to Try ASAP
Making ice cubes. You're doing it wrong
OK, maybe I made up the last one. Maybe.

And if article after article isn't involved with making you feel like an incompetent moron whose life has been an unending tribute to ineptitude, the web can turn all needy.

Jake, did you forget something?

No. No, I didn't forget anything. Why did you ask me in that unsolicited e-mail I just openeds?

This Mother's Day, Jake, you should give her that special gift.

My mom's dead . . . but thanks for reminding me.

Thank Christ the Internet compensates for its pushiness by offering me daily experiences designed to enervate and enlighten me, shaking me to my very soul.

According to, it seems, just about every site these days, I have only to read a story or click through a photo gallery and my jaw will drop, my gob will be smacked, my breath will be taken away, not to mention my speech. I will most likely cry and there's even the possibility my heart will break or even stop. Fuck, I must be getting jaded or maybe I'm just not human because none of those things have happened to me. Yet. I remain hopeful, as I idly click through the promises of the on-line carnival barkers.

I was depressing the hell out of me as I drove with the maddening stop and start waves of traffic. This place and a handful of others were responsible for spewing invention after invention into the marketplace to be endlessly analyzed, debated, and bought.

I can't tell you how glad I am to be getting old right now. Near as I can reckon, everybody's turning in on themselves, the way elderly people—like my mother—did leading up to their deaths. For old folks, what they ate, how their health was, what meds they were on, and, oh, look at the picture of their cute grandkid was pretty much the scope of their interests. Nothing outside their immediate experience. And that almost makes sense as they are about shuffle off their mortal coils. Because, at that point, who gives a shit about a heat wave in Europe or the latest Oscar snub?

But now, this insularity, this focus on self, is becoming every-body's normal. Most depressing fact: everybody seems to want it that way. Noise-cancelling headphones, tailored news streams, pre-selected music, wrist watches that monitor your bodily functions, and a device to endlessly scan while you're walking, sitting, standing does not, in any way, constitute living in the real world. And yet, that seems to be the goal. A life-long cocoon.

I'm full of shit; I know that. For one thing, I don't exist much outside my own head either. And secondly, I am usually impressed as hell by the very fact of human invention. I remember the awe with which I watched the first fax coming off on that waxy paper roll, the first PC, the ability to send messages instantly, the ability to book, print and pay for an airline ticket. OK, dog food over the Internet—that never really took off. Not yet anyway.

My first stop was Stanford and Professor R. David Bailey, he of several books on the subject on how technology was re-wiring our brains.

I drove around the huge campus for a while, an odd mixture of low, red-tiled Spanish-looking buildings and glass and steel abominations. I wasn't really absorbing the views of this legendary institution. I was just lost. I finally stopped to ask for directions and was rewarded with a smirk and a gesture from an undergrad pointing at the building I was parked in front of.

Professor Bailey was waiting—and none too patiently it would seem—because he was compelled to point out I was four minutes late.

He was a commanding presence, fortyish, trim, tanned and immac-ulately dressed in a tailored grey suit with a lavender tie and pocket poof. No rumpled corduroy and wild, frizzy hair here.

"Now, what can you ask me that wasn't in the books?" he began. "I assume you've read my books."

"Just the last one," I lied.

He recapped the book's main thesis that, deliberately or not, the brain changes with different kinds of activities. The more time spent on a particular neuron path eventually turns it into a paved highway. At the same time, roads fall into disrepair if they're neglected.

The problem is the destination of all the information we now have.

If you're doing one thing only—say studying—all the info goes into the hippocampus that's designed to store and retrieve it. But if you're studying *and* watching TV *and* checking your phone, all the info gets re-routed to the striatum that is downright shitty at storing facts and ideas.

But it gets worse, he explained. When you're focused on one thing, staying on task is controlled by the anterior cingulate and the striatum which actually reduce the brain's need for oxygenated glucose—the fuel that runs the grey matter. But going back and forth all the time makes the pre-frontal cortex and the striatum work together burning through glucose like a house on fire. In no time, you feel tired and confused because you've literally depleted the nutrients in your brain. This leads to fucking up your thinking and even your movements. Then what happens is the stress hormone cortisol comes flooding in and you start making knee-jerk and usually bad decisions.

"My students will actually brag about all the things they claim they can do simultaneously," he said. "They're kidding themselves, because they aren't doing any one thing particularly well."

"But isn't it true, Professor, that if you stop multi-tasking, the brain goes right back to the way it was?" I said, trying to impress him with the depth of my research and the intellectual exchange of different neuroscientific theories. Actually, I had read an extended headline somewhere—I don't remember where.

"That's that MIT asshole Donaldson!" Bailey spat. "He doesn't have a clue about reality. First, all this continuous multi-tasking is less than 20-years-old so we don't have any idea if generational repetition will lead to permanent re-wiring and, secondly, do you think there's any chance of stopping a kid from looking at the phone? Any chance at all?"

"But there's something missing," I said. "You don't really look at what this re-wiring will actually mean. What the world looks like. How people will spend their days."

"I'm not an anthropologist or a sociologist."

"But you must have an idea, a picture of how a day unfolds."

"What do you mean?"

"I mean . . . was Huxley right?"

"Who?"

"Aldous Huxley. Wrote *Brave New World* in the 1930s."

"Fiction?"

"Yes."

"I don't read fiction. Never have. It has nothing to do with life."

I couldn't see the point of discussing the lunacy of a learned man philosophically avoiding works of imagination, creativity and wonder but did my "elevator pitch" for ol' Aldous.

"He predicted that most of society would be peaceful and anesthetized, diverted by pleasure, consumerism, and a drug called Soma. All in all, completely ego-centric and passive. Meanwhile, a genetically-engineered underclass would do all the heavy lifting and the shitty jobs. Sound familiar?"

"I'll have to look that up. Spelling?"

"H-U-X-L-E-Y."

He immediately started tapping on his tablet.

"You know, I don't even have a cell phone," I mused aloud.

"Interesting. Why not?"

Apparently my explanation was in some combination too lengthy and too uninteresting, because Bailey went back to sliding through his tablet, not even looking up while he uttered sounds meant to signify he was listening.

"I find mental telepathy more effective," I suggested.

"Uh-huh."

"I used it a lot when I was running guns in Nicaragua . . . "

"Hmmm."

I'll easily admit that I'm not the most interesting or engaging person on the planet but, for Christ's sake, can you possibly find a more obvious irony?

"Thank you for your time, Professor," I said and saw myself out.

I then connected with Janet Hawkins, a blogger/journalist of some repute, known mostly for her close monitoring of Ulti/ME. Although I dutifully took notes, she really didn't tell me much I already didn't know. That wasn't her fault but nor was it mine. And she got a bit chippy when I didn't sound all that keen about Steinman's company's intention of ruling the planet. I can understand local boosterism when it comes to sports teams but it's just a fact that every company in your hometown isn't perfect.

That was it for me. Time to call it a day. With a bad case of road ass, I finally found the Quality Inn on El Camino Real. Nothing too monarchial about the place but I was tired. Not so tired that I couldn't find a liquor store for a six-pack of Yuengling rather than face the usurious mini-bar. I collapsed on the bed with some truly shitty pizza I had ordered in, as opposed to the frozen cardboard I always burn at home. In other words, it was a close approximation of a standard evening for me.

I wear out TV remotes at an alarming rate as I flick from channel to channel, usually the history or nature stations. For some reason, I still enjoy arcane facts. That night, I found out that regiments from the same state, Maryland, had fought each other at Gettysburg and that female Patagonian penguins will spend six months of the year swimming from southern Argentina to Brazil and back again.

Poor goddamned day if you don't learn something, as my father would say.

<CHAPTER TWENTY-NINE>

I was supposed to start my morning at DigIT, a data mining company getting a lot of press lately for having refined the way personal info can be extracted by zip or postal codes right down to a specific house. I decided I just couldn't do it.

Maybe I was in a bad mood because of the quality of my "continental" breakfast that, owing to the staleness of the croissants, made me believe the continent they were referencing was Gondwanaland. More likely, I realized I could never talk to a company like DigIT without getting into a brawl.

It didn't mean I was right or being reasonable—as usual, I was neither—just that I cannot think of any company using personal info like that as anything but e-stalkers trying to trick people into buying something using inside knowledge.

I e-mailed them my apologies and made a note to self to hand over interview chores to Steve.

After a couple of hours catching up with the TV version of all the trouble in the world, I checked out. With San Francisco less than an hour away, my last night in California before my flight back, was not going to be spent down here in motel hell after my interviews.

But first, Ulti/ME. To get to Los Gatos and their intergalactic headquarters at the base of the hills separating all of Silicon Valley from the Pacific Ocean, you had to drive through another conglomeration of connivers and prophets living amid more prosperous sprawl.

Ulti/ME headquarters were on what's called a campus. Low rises, beautifully landscaped, fake ponds with fountains and that self-consciousness that comes from determining they are going to look hip (if, indeed, anyone even says "hip" anymore) while they try to control the insane growth they wished for in the first place. Growth requiring many more accountants, and especially, many more lawyers, as you attacked competitors you think stole your idea, letting the courts decide if they actually had, while pulverizing them any way possible.

My self-righteous and dinosaurian bile had subsided in the waiting room where I sat for some forty-five minutes. Plus, I had time to fuck around with the receptionist. For whatever analysis-defying reason, I always mess around with the tangential people in my life. Restaurant servers, parking lot attendants, pay roll clerks, cablevision call centre techs, grocery store cashiers. And receptionists. All of them contribute to moving you through life. And all of them—well, most of them—like smiling. What's it cost? A few cheap jokes, a little bit of pleasantry?

I expected a PR slut would come to get me and take me to Cooper Stanley. I know I was visibly surprised when Josh Steinman himself sauntered into the antechamber. And with no handlers in sight.

"Jake? I am Josh," he said, awkwardly extending his hand. "Nice to meet you."

He looked like it wasn't at all nice to meet me. He wasn't hostile; rather he appeared to be shy or inept at this greeting thing, as his nervous gaze and limp handshake seemed to indicate.

"I . . . I was supposed to talk to Cooper Stanley," was all I could think to say.

"If you would rather, I could go get him . . . ," Steinman said, looking relieved to have been offered a way out.

"No, no! This is fine . . . it's good . . . great in fact."

"Then come with me, please."

We walked side by side through these giant rooms filled with sleek desks and huge monitors. Beating my peripheral vision to death, I watched him as we walked. Maybe 5-9, slender, dressed in preppy casual, he did not give off any sense of celebrity that seems to emanate from people who are stars in the public world. I saw Kenny Rogers once at Sak's in New York. He had that aura which always made me wonder if he actually generated it or we all just conferred it on him because he was famous. But the fact was, everyone in Josh's wake had an almost glassy-eyed look as we walked by.

His office wasn't much of anything, maybe twelve by fifteen feet.

Just enough room for a desk, a couch, and a couple of chairs. It was indistinguishable from the few other offices around it which I found sort of endearing for a guy that was worth—personally—about twenty-five billion dollars. It wasn't the oaken baronial splendour of the past, but nor was it the self-consciously trendy new way some tech CEOs had of sharing offices or not even having one.

I asked him the same question I had put to the Reeds, about his rationale for agreeing to see an insignificant old guy from Canada.

"The thesis your partner sent us was . . . interesting. That is why I am taking Cooper's appointment with you. It occurred to me that you might be onto something important. Plus, we knew of your connection to MacNeil and also that you had seen the Reed brothers, so that too was interesting."

"What?"

"I speak regularly with Alexandra Simpson; she mentioned it. Said you were smart and intense. It was the main reason I agreed to see you."

Note to self: offer profuse thanks to that woman.

I asked him about Ulti/ME's end game.

"We are going to change everything," he said.

"Everything in technology? That's pretty ambitious."

"No. *Everything* everything."

"Excuse me?"

"I want you—I want everyone—to understand that we are not fooling around. We, as a race, need a fundamental change in direction."

"Don't tell me: the ol' paradigm shift."

"No," he said patiently. "More like a paradigm reversal. 180 degrees from the way we are going. Otherwise, we are well and truly finished as a civilization, perhaps as a species."

"And you're going to accomplish this how?"

"By creating the largest cascade of technology the world has ever seen."

Now you'd think that kind of statement would come off pompous or just plain full of shit. Instead, Steinman sounded like he was commenting on the weather. He did not have the messianic zeal I was expecting. He actually was charming, in an awkward sort of way, not by being unctuous or syrupy but casually confident. He just rattled on, in his highly formal speech pattern, without a trace of hype or bullshit, not hoping he was right, but knowing he was.

"And you do this how?" I asked.

"You start this cascade by dealing with the greatest single unnecessary expense in the developed world."

"Starbucks?"

"No. Health care," he said. "We waste billions every year. Billions. For no reason I can see other than we have always done so. Meanwhile, so-called developing countries will never develop because their people are still suffering from things they do not have to suffer from. And what little money their governments do have goes to problems that should not even exist."

Watching Steinman, I could see that he was getting amped up, warming to the subject that probably kept him up at night and gave him a reason to get out of bed in the morning. Sure, there was the practiced pitch that he'd use with shareholders and the media but, just as obviously, there was an underlying passion that went light years beyond making money.

"There are about 350 million diabetics in the world right now," he continued, "and twice as many by 2030. There are at least that many people on the planet with manageable heart disease. That represents about 10% of the planet's population right there. Sooner or later, *all* of them are, theoretically, going to be candidates for what we're offering.

"And, simultaneously, do you not think somebody somewhere is going to come up with a way to simply manage Parkinson's or cancer or lupus or most of the other illnesses in the world?

"And 90% of those patients—maybe more—will have smart phones. So why not let machines far more complex and fail-safed than the rockets and clunky computers that put a man on the moon, be in charge?"

Steinman was on a roll; I was taking notes as fast as I could.

Suddenly he stopped talking. He sighed and his shoulders heaved.

"We squander life so needlessly," he said in a soft voice. "So . . . so wantonly. Why should a baby die because her mother has no way of getting at the clean water lying thirty feet below her hut? Or because she cannot get a dollar's worth of vitamins or anti-diarrhea pills?

"And spare me the tsk-tsking about poor third-world countries.

Automobile deaths in the US: 30,000. Another 30,000 by guns. Smoking: 400,000. Did you know that in the US alone there are 45,000 deaths a year through unintended misuse of prescription drugs, another 200,000 accidental deaths in hospitals? 10,000 die because 9-1-1 can't locate them from their cell phone. Add that up. Almost three quarters of a million people— that is the equivalent of wiping out metropolitan Charleston. Every year. This has to be stopped. I—we—can do that.

"Did you also know that far less than half of ER visits are even warranted? And if you are admitted, you get a barrage of tests, most of which are just expensive ways of hospitals covering their legal liabilities. That too must end."

"Can't see doctors and hospitals and HMOs being keen on that," I said.

"You mean doctors, hospitals, and HMOs *here*. You are Canadian, correct?"

"True north, strong and free."

"Does it make any sense to you that America will not provide free health care when every other developed country does?"

"None whatsoever."

"Does it make any sense to you that, by law, the government cannot bargain with pharmaceutical companies when every other developed country can?"

"Nope again."

"This exceptionalism of ours is killing us. We represent less than 5% of the world's population. We have to start acting more humble and less convinced that we must either call the shots or reject anything we did not invent."

"Like soccer?"

"Like soccer."

"That would be a monumental change—although I'm good with soccer staying on the fringe here."

"But change has to come; change *is* coming because people are starting to wake up. Fire departments used to be privately-owned. Did you know that?"

"I actually did. *Gangs of New York*. Boss Tweed and all that."

"Exactly. Well, soon it was decided that government should take over. Reduce the incidents of fire departments setting fires then charging to put them out. This is no different."

"But isn't Ulti/ME just one huge, privately-owned fire department?"

"Right now it is. But soon I will be able to give the technology away to every country that wants it. We will keep the processing fees."

"And you think it's just a matter of coming up with the technology?" I asked. "I mean, I'm not doubting you can, but there will be huge legal and ethical problems, and that means lawyers will have to get involved."

"Sure, there will be challenges and, at some point, I expect we will have more lawyers on the pay roll than software engineers. But these challenges will be overcome. Remember: it was once illegal and largely unthinkable for women to vote."

"And you're not worried about death panels and all such crap?"

"Algorithms do not have morals or ethics or absurd political opinions. Think of it as a giant DMV."

"Hopefully a little better managed. But how can you possibly believe that this massive system—a system with what? A billion people using it—"

"—probably more."

"A system with more than a billion users can be secure?"

"It will be our biggest expense, for sure. But it is doable."

"Doable? Are you kidding me? It's going be a hacker's wet dream."

"The bad guys are pretty smart but they are reaching the end of their road."

"Meaning?"

"Meaning that we are getting to the point where we can find just anybody. Anywhere."

"And when you do?"

"Governments, somebody, will have to put boots on the ground and go get them. Pure and simple, what these hackers are doing is nothing short of threatening national security. So how about an automatic ten years in jail for stealing health records? Fifteen for taking money. Maybe some countries will make it a capital offense. Who knows? Governments would be crazy not to make sure this happened. In fact, we are betting they will eventually pay us billions to save many, many more billions. And, if you will pardon the expression, you do not have to make a killing on the devices. You practically could give them away."

"And you get a piece of everything, right? Half a penny per transaction, advertisers, drug companies and on and on."

"Yes, I guess we do. We are at the junction, the congruence."

"Like Noriega in Panama?"

"Excuse me?"

"Getting paid by everybody. A slice here, a kickback there."

Steinman went quiet.

"I think I do not want to do this anymore," he said, almost in a whisper.

"Run Ulti/ME?"

"No. Talk to you. Everybody says I should talk more to people. Shareholders like it when I do. Media like it. But I do not."

Steinman wasn't quite looking at me while he spoke. Up a bit and to the right, over my shoulder, so that he *almost* appeared to be making eye contact, sort of like the awkward way we look at people with one good eye.

It suddenly occurred to me that I was very familiar with this thousand-yard stare. I had seen it in my mirror a million times.

"Asperger's?" I asked.

He actually smiled for the first time.

"We should have a secret handshake or something," I said. "We could skip a whole lot of bullshit."

I can't say he warmed up to me, but I wasn't expecting him to. At best, he was a tad more forthcoming.

"So Bio-Watch matters that much to all this?" I asked.

"For the moment. The technology they own is a very important stepping stone. Like everything else, something better will come along. But we are ready to go right now."

"What's your deal with them?"

"It is not done yet, so technically we do not have one. But I expect we will soon."

"What about competitors?"

"We have none."

"That's pretty much what they all say, isn't it?"

"Sometimes it happens to be true."

"And WesCor?"

"Pffft!" was Steinman's initial assessment. "They are not serious about Concord Medical Systems. They have no brand, no infrastructure. They *might* become suppliers, nothing more. I believe they want Bio-Watch's battery technology for all their other divisions and subsidiaries. And that is playing small ball. Now look at us. Right now we have the capacity to collect real-time information of about a million gigabytes of data for the average person. They have nothing like that. The IRS has nothing like that."

"Pardon my bluntness," I said, "but Ulti/ME is basically just a website. All virtual, make-believe. Health is about broken bones and tumours, and microbes and bedpans and CAT scans. Real stuff."

"None of that changes. The bricks and mortar will remain, and we will always need doctors, nurses, and so on. Just less of them attending to the conditions Ulti/ME can manage or help to eliminate."

"What about the ol' X factor?"

"Excuse me?"

"Humans. They tend to mess things up."

"That is the great thing about data mining now. It lets us go beyond the obvious. You go to The Home Depot website looking for patio furniture and next time you log on to *any* site with advertising, poof, a Home Depot patio furniture ad appears. Accomplishing that is simple. I am not talking about that. Go further; think harder about accounting for all the vagaries, the "X" factor as you say. How many people in Des Moines or Delhi just will not take their meds on time? We can find out. We know who they are, where they are, and we have a little sub-routine just for them. We can send them notices. Notices that they will listen to."

I had been writing furiously, suddenly as persuaded as he was that this was all going to happen.

"I have absolutely no doubt that we will become the largest company in the world," he said.

"Do you see anything standing in your way?" I asked, as he stared out his window, apparently mesmerized by the gushing fountain in the middle of the reflecting pool.

He half-turned to me, the mid-morning sun on his flat blue eyes.

"Nothing. I cannot . . . I *will* not let anything or anyone stop this."

He abruptly stood up.

"Now, if you will excuse me . . . "

As we shook hands, I asked if I could see Nigel Hayward. The hand-shaking stopped.

"Why?" he asked.

"Old times. I used to work with him."

The slightest of pauses.

"Of course, you did. My assistant will take you to him."

Ol' Nige actually looked pleased to see me. Same hearty handshake, same cheery and booming greeting.

We shot the shit for a while, nothing too serious. Although I couldn't help but mention that his joining Ulti/ME had been awfully low-key.

"For now, that's the way Josh wants it."

I asked him how he was enjoying California.

"It's brilliant! I haven't been this enthused in a great long while. My life's work is finally going to be used. MacNeil didn't know what to do with it. The Reed brothers didn't know what to do with it. Steinman's a bloody genius; he can move more units in a month than the Reeds could in a decade. The point of the whole exercise is to get a thing out there. Used by as many people as possible. Right now. Because people are dying every day who simply don't have to."

I knew what he meant. On a much, much smaller and less deadly scale, I'm glad I wrote a novel and all but, once it was done, the real point, the *only* point, was having it read.

"I know the monitor works and I know it's the base for doing more useful things," Nigel continued.

"Such as?"

"A completely automatic pump that injects whatever pharmaceuticals you need to make you right. Not just insulin. Every drug you can possibly liquefy."

"Same kind of thing that WesCor's got?"

"So, you are aware of it. Then you should also know that it is a piece of shite!" he said, getting animated. "They took development of it away from me, gave the project to Robert Howe. That man is an utter twat. They are doomed."

"Alright, so not them," I said. "A lot of people are working on the same thing but, by all accounts, it's years away."

"Probably for them but almost despite themselves, Bio-Watch's power system is the real deal. We need them because we're a few *months* away, at worst. Maybe it's only weeks. We've got thousands of people working on this."

"Like the Manhattan Project?"

"Only rather more important, wouldn't you say? And all that horse-power gives us a tremendous infrastructure to build the apps, to collect the files, to lobby governments. Nobody can touch us there."

"And you're square with WesCor and Bio-Watch?"

He stopped.

"Yes, this device is completely different and I share the patent with Josh. But why on earth would you mention that?"

"So it sounds like you'd be crazy to sue Steinman," I joked.

Nigel didn't look as though he found my attempt at humour even remotely amusing. I stumbled on.

"Well . . . you've been, you know . . . active on the legal front," I added.

He seemed genuinely taken aback. His demeanour had changed.

"Now how would you know about that?" he asked.

"No big deal, Nigel. Just came upon it while I was researching the book."

He looked at his Rolex.

"Good lord, I'm running awfully late now."

In short order, after our perfunctory fare-thee-wells, I found myself in the Ulti/ME parking lot, alternately cursing my failed comedy and puzzling over why Nigel had grown so touchy.

True, it wasn't the funniest thing I'd ever said but it deserved some kind of comeback. He and I used to swap insults all the time during my stint at Bio-Watch. And I had done the same thing with all the Brit teachers when I worked in the Bahamas. "Taking the piss outta some-one" was what they had called it, explaining to me that it was a time-worn English custom, like warm beer, shitty cooking, and attempts at world domination.

<CHAPTER THIRTY>

I'd seen enough of the sunny, nameless cities oozing around Highway 101 and, instead, took the 280 which runs up the spine of San Francisco Peninsula, intending to ride it right into the city and Embarcadero where I planned to get a hotel room and then just wander around.

On a pleasant day like this with the State park on my left offering nothing but green to look at it, I whipped along, cheating up to 65 mph.

Suddenly, the car started to veer. I mean suddenly and I mean veer. I tromped on the brakes. Nothing. And at that moment, the engine surged, the steering wheel jerked and I slammed into the median guardrail at a 45-degree angle and kept bulldozing against it for about a hundred feet, the metal shrieking in protest. Then the brakes kicked in, the car pivoted against the rail, and spun around 180, so that the passenger side slammed broadside into the rail.

I finally reacted and shut the car off and sat there staring at the oncoming traffic, my heart pounding and my hands and arms aching from being uselessly locked onto the steering wheel.

My jaw hurt from clenching my teeth.

<CHAPTER THIRTY-ONE>

C alifornia Highway Patrol was on the scene in minutes.
    The young officer who stuck his head through my shattered
window was earnest and efficient.

"Are you OK, sir?"

"Fine. I'm fine. Couldn't be better."

"Have you been drinking, sir?"

"No, officer."

I could actually answer honestly but his skepticism was obvious.

"Can you exit the car, sir?"

I heaved against the door, stepped out of the car, the hinges creaking
from the collapsed metal.

"Will you please blow into this, sir?"

"This is a complete waste of time," I said, as I exhaled into the
breathalyzer.

He read the thing, looked up from it, and got very serious.

"OK, sir, you'll have to come with me."

"I'd rather not. I told you, I haven't been drinking. The car fucked
up! Fucking air bags didn't even deploy."

"There's no need for that kind of language, sir," I was told.

"Offhand, I can't fucking think of a better fucking time for this fucking kind of fucking language!"

For such a shiny, pleasant young man, he was remarkably adept at
slamming me over the hood of his cruiser, my shoulder and elbow joint
screaming in additional pain.

After this second ride in a cop car in less than a month, the whole
procedure had begun to lose its charm. At the Highway Patrol station, I
was hustled into a chair beside a desk in the booking department.

I sat there silent and handcuffed while the patrolman told his story to a duty officer. They hooked me up to another machine and told me to blow. Happy to comply, I exhaled a gust of sober air.

"Point 1-3."

"He blew 1-4 on the road."

"I haven't been drinking, goddamnit!" I insisted. "You blow! Go ahead: blow."

After hesitating, the patrolman did.

"Point 1-4," the sergeant read out.

"That's funny, officer," I said. "You don't seem shit-faced. How about the sergeant here?"

"Point 1-3," he announced after blowing.

"So, can we all agree you've got a busted machine?"

"Two of them? That's pretty long odds."

"Are they somehow networked?" I asked.

"I dunno."

"Well, let's bet they are and let's further wager that a tech weenie better get here real quick."

After a pile of apologies, they drove to me to the garage that had received my wrecked rental. I walked in and waited until the cop car left, grabbed my trusty bowling bag, and then skedaddled the hell out of there.

Lenny Briscoe didn't ever believe in coincidences and neither did I. First, the car, then the two breathalyzers. Machines acting up on their own. Like the brooms in *The Sorcerer's Apprentice*. No sense and intended shitty consequence.

And the biggest coincidence of all: less than half an hour after leaving Ulti/ME, I was pulling myself out of a wrecked rogue car.

At a phone booth down the block, I called my credit card company, reported it stolen and ordered a new one. Let the rental company chase a dead card. It had to be the way I had been tracked. Then I called a cab.

Now, there are people all over the world who spend every waking moment—and probably most of their sleeping moments—fully aware that someone wants to kill them. Political dissidents in shithole countries, soldiers in Mexican drug gangs, they have to live their lives like chipmunks—all twitchy and nervous, always watching, always on the move before that cat or that owl shows up, as the cat or the owl always do.

I wasn't one of those people.

I have to admit I was shaking standing inside the phone booth and wondering what to do next. If Steinman and his gang had my credit card info then they'd also know where I was staying, what flight I was booked on, when and where I'd use an ATM, right down to where and what I'd eaten. Christ, even how big a tipper I was!

For the first time, the views of San Francisco couldn't distract me. I tried looking at them but I was sure the cabbie was eyeing me in his rear-view mirror. I wanted to use the burner phone Jason had given me, but I couldn't do that either because the son of a bitch driver was listening too.

For no reason other than I needed a place to think, a place I knew, I had the taxi drop me in Chinatown, paid cash, and gave him an extra twenty to not log the trip.

Instantly, I was back where I felt comfortable. If I had to get lost in a big city, this was the place. The yellow and red pennants and the tasselled lanterns strung across Grant Avenue. The chickens and ducks hanging in the vendor windows, boxes of odd-looking fruits and vegetables that were still a mystery to me. The impenetrable characters on the banners dominating the streets, English a mere subtext. And people, everywhere people teeming as they should be in this busy stew. About the only thing different from twenty years ago—other than the toned-down hairstyles of the tourists—was the business signage that now sported website addresses. Oh, and there seemed to be a few more karaoke bars—curse you, *American Idol* and *The Voice*.

I blended in, looking like all the other stunned-looking foreigners because that's what we were here. Foreigners. And stunned-looking.

Although I doubted that many of my fellow gawkers had just survived a murder attempt.

<CHAPTER THIRTY-TWO>

As per usual, I tired pretty quickly with the jostling and crowded streets. I found a small park, a mini-oasis from the hustle and flow, took out my burner phone, and called Jason.

After we got by the awkward suspicious who's calling and who's answering phase, I said, "I'm being tracked, Jason."

I told him about the unfortunate demise of my rental car and my fortunate survival.

"Holy shit!"

"I think Ulti/ME's behind it," I added.

"Double holy shit!"

"My reaction exactly. We have to go public with this."

"What?"

"Look up Steve Golding at the *Sun*. Get him one of your pre-paid phones, and then call me with the number."

"No offense, Mr. Lydon, but you don't know how to do this."

"None taken. And it's Jake . . . We have to go to the cops or the media."

"OK . . . And say exactly what?"

That stopped me. The kid had a point. A darn good one. There was no evidence about anything. Realizing that, and the fact that Jason was the only person who knew what was going on, had plainly limited my options to just one.

"So I don't have much choice except to listen to you, do I?" I said.

"No, you don't."

"OK, I'm listening."

"For starters, you can't get stopped by the cops. For anything. Jaywalking, spitting on the sidewalk. Nothing. Alright?"

"Straight and narrow. I swear."

Just to let him know I wasn't a complete moron, I told Jason about the nudge, nudge, wink, wink, twenty bucks I had given the cabbie not to record his trip.

"How long ago?"

"Maybe forty-five minutes ago. An hour at most."

"Where are you right now? *Exactly.*"

"A park on . . . on . . . Powell and . . . John," I said, looking around for a street sign.

"You have to get out of there right now! We can talk while you walk."

"But—"

"—Do it!"

He was practically yelling.

Suppressing my natural inclination to resist a direct order, I got up and started walking. I almost snorted out loud as I saw I'd joined the legion of cell phone walkers and talkers I always used to laugh at.

Jason explained the joys of GPS systems that were installed in all cabs and how if *they* knew the garage where my newly-minted rent-a-wreck had wound up, they could track any cab dispatched to it. And then make the perfectly logical assumption that it was likely me going to Chinatown.

"Fuckin' cabbie took my money anyway," I grumbled.

"And speaking of. Use cash only from now on. Don't even let a hotel swipe your credit card. How much money do you have?"

"Not enough for anything really. Maybe a hundred bucks."

"You need more."

"Well, unless you send me a big bag of it, I'm pretty well fucked."

I had already determined that SF was a likely a better place than most in which to be a street person—except for all hills that made pushing the shopping cart with the wobbly wheel less than fun, regardless of how beneficial it might be for upper arm and calf muscle development.

"I can get you a couple of grand," Jason said. "Anything more might set off alarm bells."

"Perfect. I'm good for it, son."

"I know."

Another pause and I heard the keypad frenzy.

"There's a Citibank on Grant. You have ID?"

"Passport."

"The bank's closed now. You can pick up the money tomorrow. Then you've got about half an hour to get the hell out of San Francisco."

"Why?"

"Why? Because you have to identify yourself to get the money, that's why; and the bank has to record it. *They* knew you were coming to the city, right now *they* know you're somewhere in Chinatown. And *they* probably have people on the way there."

"This is nuts!"

"No. This is the way things are. Now, where are you going?"

"What's this? A pop quiz?"

"Where?" he demanded.

"I don't know. Back to my place at the lake?" I guessed in that hopeless voice kids use in class when they haven't been listening but want to say something, anything when called upon.

"No. No you're not. I'll tell you when it's clear."

"Well then, can I get back to Canada?"

There was a pause. I wondered if I should have said "Mother, may I?" before I asked.

"Jason?"

"I'm thinking . . . Maybe . . . Yeah."

"Maybe, yeah? What the hell is maybe, yeah?"

"I mean yes. But no planes. You can take a bus into Canada."

"I hate buses! Any other way?"

"You can walk."

"Seriously?"

"That was a joke. You can buy a cheap bike or car. But there can't be any paperwork."

"OK."

"Oh, and start a beard and get a ball cap and sunglasses. And keep your head down."

"What? I hate ball caps. Why?"

"Because there are cameras everywhere," he sighed, as if he was patiently explaining things to a child—which, of course, he was. "Toll booths, 7-11s, street corners—they've all got eyes now. Whoever's doing this is probably using facial recognition software. It doesn't work as magically as it does in the movies but, eventually it will. And at customs, they swipe your passport so it's only a matter of time until they'd know when and where you entered the country. And call me before you cross the border. OK?"

"Yes, sir."

"Now get off the streets."

"And go where?"

Another pause, another flurry of audible keyboard strokes.

"The Astoria Hotel. Bush and Grant. About four blocks from you."

"I know where that is."

"Sixty bucks a night."

"I can talk him down."

"No. You can't draw attention to—"

"—now *that* was a joke . . . and Jason . . . "

"Yeah?"

"Thanks, son. I really mean that."

"Forget it, Jake. It's Chinatown."

"OK, that's a better joke."

I found the Astoria attached to the Dragon Gates at the southern border of Chinatown. In normal times, I'd stop to marvel at the gate's colour, its intricate fish and dragons and its two ferocious lion statues. But these were not normal times.

The hotel didn't in any way resemble its New York namesake. The San Fran version was a non-descript seven-story block that made me miss the Quality Inn in Sunnyvale. On the plus side, it was the very definition of anonymous.

The desk clerk wasn't all that interested in credit cards, but the cash made an instant impression.

"Sign in?" I asked.

"Sign in not necessary," he grinned.

"Dear Guest. This elevator is maximum for 3 people only" read the hand-printed sign taped inside. The official California state elevator certificate—which had expired two and half years earlier—indicated the contraption was meant to hold ten.

It was hard to imagine if the hotel had ever had glory days but it was clean and utilitarian as hell with its unrecognizably-branded Gold Star colour TV *sans* remote, bare beige walls, and grey ceramic lamps bolted to the chipped veneer furniture. I thought the paper band across the toilet—with a matching paper bath mat—was a nice touch.

A few blocks over and a couple of decades earlier, I was accustomed to staying at the Ritz Carlton or the Mark Hopkins. At that moment, I missed all their quiet luxury and Masters-of-the-Universe kind of panoramic view of the city, with the Golden Gate and Alcatraz all swaddled in mist.

And down the bay coast, was the hi-tech heart of modern civilization. It was also the location of its current crown prince who, in his spare time, was trying to get me killed.

It was more than disappointing. For a brief moment, I had thought that our common mental classification gave us something like a bond.

I keep making the mistake that everybody makes about other people with similar tendencies. I always thought that southpaws were cooler than righties. Smokers are neater than non-smokers. All Aquarians are the cat's pyjamas, Oakland Raider fans are all swell. That sort of thing. In my head, I know it doesn't work that way—well, except maybe for Raidah fans.

But the fact is, assholes are assholes no matter what their habits. I should know.

My immediate situation was not encouraging. I was going to be in this crappy hotel for some undetermined amount of time after which I would be trying to reach some undetermined place.

With night falling, I thought of Leonard Cohen. "That's right; it's come to this. And wasn't it a long way down?"

All I needed was a flickering neon sign and some slow sax accompaniment to complete the clichéd ideal of the urban forlorn.

Time to end the self-pity party I soon decided. Maybe clinically thinking about death—specifically mine—might distract me.

I considered the distinct possibility—no, the probability—of Steinman succeeding with his fucked-up plan to have me dead. I wasn't really afraid of my own mortality *before* all this shit happened. Theoretically at least, I didn't really have a problem with dying. I hadn't done much and I didn't have much. But chief among my possessions were no regrets. I had had a great wife, a life of relative ease and more laughs than most people seem to get. I did have a great kid, a great friend or two, and a pretty good book that, in some form or other, would last a while. Plus, I had seen the Stones—twice. If we're talking math, compared to almost everyone else who's *ever* lived on the planet, I reckon that put me in the uppermost one percent—top five, for sure.

And if that's not existential comfort, I don't know what is.

I slept like the dead, unaffected by the car horns and music and smells of the city.

But I woke up remembering I had dreamt of Alexandra.

‹CHAPTER THIRTY-THREE›

Funny thing about daylight. Perspectives often change. My *que sera-ism* had gotten me through the black night but I woke up determined—well, as determined as I can ever be—to not die, not just yet anyway. Halley wanted me to be alright. I think Steve and Jason wanted me to be alright. Probably Alex did too. And Carl. OK, bad example. I had no idea what Carl wanted except I had to believe he needed me around to gloat over whenever his fucking Cowboys won.

Sum total: I was pissed off enough to want to make it as hard as possible for Steinman to whack me. And that energized me.

Things to do, things to do.

At the top of the list was getting the hell out of Dodge.

As I was checking out, I asked the clerk if there were any used car lots nearby. Not the big manufacturers, I told him but a small family-owned place. He sent me to a business ten blocks away which most certainly belonged to a family—maybe his.

In gumshoe parlance, I was casing the joint. It fit the bill. One of those cheesy tributes to entrepreneurship, it featured a small lot ringed by faded pennants and containing about thirteen cars, none of which had been manufactured after Obama took office.

In a coincidence of Dickensian order, I found a Pontiac Vibe. 2003 or 2004 judging by the dark grey side mouldings they put on every car regardless of colour. It was a mess. Dented, rust all down the door handles as if from a faulty window air conditioner. A passenger window was cracked and one of its cheap plastic hubcaps was missing. Compared to the previous owner of this car, I had been one of those an anal retentive detailing guys with my Vibe. The only thing that was remotely clean about this vehicle was the big yellow star reading $1500 plastered on the windshield.

Before I could be set upon by a salesman, I beetled out of there and I made my way to the bank, exactly a nine-minute walk, my cell phone informed me. I shut it off before it could tell me how many calories I had expended.

Standing in line, I realized I was as sweaty as if I were a first-time bank robber. Nervously, I turned over my passport as though it were a stick-up note, cashed the 2K transfer, and beat it out of there. I made it back to the lot as quickly as I could without looking like I was fleeing a crime scene. I stood by the car for about a minute, enough time to bring a pushy sales guy/predator out of the dinky hut below the A-I Used Cars sign.

"Good choice, buddy! She's a beaut," he enthused.

"I can give you a thousand dollars. Cash. Right now."

"Deal."

"But there can't be any paper."

He smiled.

"Did I say a grand? I meant fifteen hundred."

Our negotiating done, I took the keys, and, for the first time in what seemed like a long while, I felt comfortable. Sitting behind the familiar steering wheel and dashboard, I noticed the driver's cloth seat even had a couple of cigarette burns like mine did.

It started fine but it felt like I had time to have a smoke during the period between when I pulled the gearshift into "D" and when—with a loud clunk—it actually engaged.

If I was going into business, I always figured opening a brake and transmission shop in San Francisco was the thing to try. Besides what they do to smokers, all those asphalt hills really kick the shit of cars too.

I took stock of my resources. After the car purchase, I had 576 bucks. And 28 cents. US.

I also had no direction but, I comforted myself, no tether either. And, from a different viewpoint, I was loaded. With a little perspective readjustment, I reminded myself that I had once hitchhiked from Toronto to Vancouver with thirty bucks in my jeans. Sure, sure, it was forty-two years ago but, even with inflation, I was at least a little better off now.

Plus, I had boss wheels.

At a gas station, I dusted off and bought a paper map of the western US and plotted a route back to Canada. Deciding the more remote the border crossing, the less likelihood of trouble, I settled on Saskatchewan, home province of Joni Mitchell, Gordie Howe and potash and the punch line of late-night talk show jokes.

I had one number to remember: 80. If things went right, Highway 80 would take me across California, Nevada, and most of Utah.

If things went right.

<CHAPTER THIRTY-FOUR>

After the giant paved spaghetti bowl of Sacramento, I started up into the Sierra Nevada and for the next few of hours spent whole stretches in low gear as the fatigued engine revved its ass off. Then I became continentally divided and started downhill. At times, I was just free-wheeling it, hoping like hell the brakes worked but imagining I was going to soon be screaming past all that grand mountain scenery and into Reno at about 200 miles an hour.

With Reno's electric blanket of neon lights behind me, I plunged into the middle of a mile after mile of nothing, puzzling over what had started out as a mere shemozzle that had then progressively turned into a kerfuffle and was now threatening to descend into a full-blown brouhaha.

It was a spreading stain of incidents, all somehow connected, and all—improbably—with me being pinned to Ground Zero.

I realized I had spent all my time over the last couple of days involved with safely fleeing, grappling with the logistics of survival, thinking about who was trying to get at me and how and when. What I had stopped considering is the "why"?

Why would anybody even bother with me? I fervently believed that the only person I had ever been a threat to was me. And I could live—or not—with that.

Which brought me back to Lenny Briscoe. Break it down the way Lenny would, I told myself. Motive, means, and opportunity. Every week, Lenny had all three down cold within 22 minutes.

So who had all three?

Listen: it might first be handy to figure out what had actually happened.

Well, first off, Alistair was murdered.

Maybe.

Probably. What else?

I was being set up and it was elaborate.

That's for sure, buddy.

That meant there had to be people running all this technology that, most recently, had resulted in the monkeying around with my car.

Back up now. Somebody had to know where I was and when. Beyond the credit card watching. They knew I actually got on that plane; they had to know I picked up that specific rental car.

Back up more. Someone wrote a fake blog under my name. So what's that tell you?

A bunch of systems were being hacked.

Yeah, but maybe all this intrusion technology is pretty simple now. Maybe one smart person could operate it all. Like I knew anything—I mean *anything*—about how all this can or can't be done.

And then there's the break-in.

Nothing hi-tech about that. Two good old-fashioned armed thugs ransacking my hovel. People like that don't just turn up. They have to be hired and paid—do they get benefits packages, I wonder. What about holidays, severance pay?

Snap the fuck out of it! Focus! Go back to the why.

So who stood to gain?

Well, idiot, that all depends on the motive, doesn't it?

Just two that I know of. Love and love of money.

In the sane world, maybe. Where was the money or love for Jeffrey Daumer?

So you can't rule out just batshit crazy.

Or how about revenge?

What'd I ever do to anybody that needs avenging?

According to Jason, it was something in my research.

But everything I'd found so far was available to everyone on the planet.

Who knew about the research?

For sure Jason . . . and Steve.

Stop right there. What about Steve?

Him I know.

Think again. Your daily dealings with him are almost twenty-years-old. Shit happens in twenty years. Two decades ago, he was sort of a friend, sort of a media enemy.

And think about it: he *was* the one who had started me on this book jaunt to begin with. He sent me to Boston, to San Francisco. Why me?

Why? Because, according to him, you're the greatest goddamned writer nobody ever heard of. The better question now, is why *not* him? Why didn't the actual reporter in your dynamic duo go out and do some fucking reporting?

Because he has a fear of flying.

That sounds like convenient bullshit, doesn't it?

And then there's Jason.

Good kid.

Jason? What do you *really* know about him?

That he drove two hours to warn me that something wasn't right.

Why? Because of a twenty-year-old stuffed animal? In whose world does anybody do that? What else ya got?

I don't know.

Well, for openers, try this on: he's the only hacker you personally know.

But he sent me money; he got me out of San Francisco!

Any chance that he and his Anonymous-type buddies just wanted to see if they could pull it off? Break into a bunch of systems at once? Move you around like a dumb little meat puppet.

Maybe.

That's all I'm saying. Maybe.

If you think about it—and you better get a whole lot more serious about the thinking part—Nigel Hayward seemed to be the common factor. He had a lawsuit against Alistair. A lawsuit against the Reeds. Maybe I was screwing up a lawsuit he had planned against Steinman.

Yeah, but . . .

But what?

He's a surgeon, and a medical devices guy. He's not a computer guy. And tell me: didn't he look surprised when you let it slip that you knew about the lawsuits?

Maybe he's a good actor.

Why single him out? Why can't anyone else be a good actor? Why can't Mike or Sarah or Steve be good actors?

I'd know.

Gimme a break! You'd know? Really? The guy who's spent that last fifteen years as a fucking recluse?

Steinman. Steinman can't be acting. He's got what I've got. It makes you a shitty pretender.

First off, how do you know he's got Asperger's? You're only going on what he *seemed* to imply.

I saw it in his eyes.

OK, so say he does, what else did he tell you?

Lots of things.

Think harder!

He said that he would not let anything stop his plans.

Just "anything"?

Or anyone. He said "or anyone."

Gee, do you think protecting a global plan worth tens of billions of dollars might qualify as a motive?

At heart, he's basically a geek so he's got the means.

But technology isn't just the means, is it? It also gives him the opportunity because, with what he knows, he could bring the hammer down on you any ol' time!

So we're back to Josh Steinman.

Except . . .

Except what?

Why am I only thinking about individuals?

Exactly! You can get that great brain of yours to look up the definition of conspiracy, couldn't you?

So why not combinations of people working together? I mean, what the fuck do you know about any of them? You're a goddamned hermit.

I can guess at combinations. Nigel and Mike could have a side deal, despite Mike's claim that he wanted WesCor. Or Steinman directing Nigel. Or Sarah, for that matter.

Let's not forget the Reed brothers. With or without Mike. Or maybe it was both of them.

Why would Mike and Sarah do this?

Christ, I worry about you. Why? For the fattest motive of all.

Money.

Because Mike said he wanted Alistair to sell to the Reeds for a lot more money. But Sarah wanted Ulti/ME; god knows why.

Maybe she's smarter than the bunch of you; maybe she can see a lot more coin in the future.

Yeah, but neither of them could kill Alistair; they wouldn't know how.

So why not bring Jason in on it? Bet he knows how.

His own father?

How shook up did he seem to you?

So what about Jason and somebody else?

What about Alexandra?

Don't tell me that. Not Alexandra.

Well, she knows both the Reeds and Steinman. And she also knew Alistair, so she knows Mike Coulson. Remember now, she's become an idealist. People do crazy things sometimes with strong beliefs on their side. Plus, she knows everybody who's anybody in tech.

No, Jake! Not her. It can't be her.

Why not, Jake? Because you slept with her? Try thinking with your big boy head.

The more I considered individuals, the more combinations presented themselves.

Hey, shit-for-brains, how about maybe you're looking down the wrong end of the telescope? Maybe all this has absolutely nothing to do with any of the people in your tiny universe.

Don't even start down that road. The idea that it's somebody else, some other company or government or hacker ring that randomly picked me is just absurd.

So, you're telling me nothing random *ever* happens? Think about your crisis scenarios.

Despite all the details I have amassed, I'm not much closer to figuring out just what the Christ is going on.

Go back, Jake. Go back and start with the people you *can* eliminate.

About the only person I could clear was Carl—and even then I had no idea about his back story.

And Halley. I wasn't *that* shitty a father. I know that.

Oh, and Alistair. But mostly because he's dead.

Paranoia strikes deep, as they say—well, as Stephen Stills says.

Watch enough crime TV and movies and you just know that somewhere in the drug dealer's handbook is a set of rules. And chief among them, the mother of all the criminal commandments, has to be this one:

Trust no one.

Aaaargh!

I tromp on the brakes, actually fearing I may snap the pedal. Mercifully, for all its faults, the old Vibe has good alignment. With minimal fishtailing the car comes to an abrupt halt amid a shower of gravel on the side of the deserted highway.

The dust settles.

Maybe it's him? *Perhaps* her? *Possibly* this is why? Here's what *might* have happened?

The wishy-washy list of mine is whole lot more confusing than clarifying.

I actually speak out loud.

"Jake, this on 'one hand but on the other' routine of yours is fuckin' nuts."

You have to pick someone. Even if you're not completely sure. If it's 51 to 49, you've got to play it like a hundred to nuthin'!

I'm playing eenie-meeny-minie-moe with my life?

Pick, goddamnit!

Jason. I'll bank on Jason.

Against who?

Steinman . . . in the computer room . . . with the rogue hackers.

As I pull back onto the highway, I realize there is one thing I know for sure: so far, I have been nothing but lucky to be alive.

So far.

PART TWO

HERE AND NOW

<**CHAPTER ONE**>

My attempt at putting a stake in the ground or drawing a line in the sand or whatever the fuck else you could call it, hasn't changed anything. All that's left after my think-think-thinking is a feeling that it's maybe, quite possibly, and perhaps likely that Josh Steinman is actively trying to snuff out my brief candle.

Right here, right now, I'm getting close to Utah and not too much else.

In the past, I have always claimed to like this state. Not Utah, but the state of being completely on my own. That is, of course, more self-delusional horseshit of the sort I routinely shovel on myself. There have always been people around—people I liked or even loved. People who indulged me. People who were kind to me.

People I trusted.

Right now, I'm not near to any of them.

All that's left is a smothering sense of true aloneness where I'm more than disconnected, almost disembodied. Hurtling along Highway 80, encased in a silver Vibe, with no one on the entire planet knowing where I am or where I'm going.

It's dark now and after ten hours of driving I'm tired and stiff and hungry. Just before Salt Lake City, I find a welcoming yellow beacon in the form of an illuminated Denny's sign. All eggs all the time is just hunky-dory with me.

I look no better or worse than any of the few other customers who frequent a roadside fast food place at midnight. There's this dance of the gazes as everybody checks out everybody else, breaking eye contact a nanosecond before, I imagine, comes the "What are you lookin' at? You lookin' at me?" line of questioning.

Stuffed and needing to escape the bright lights, I find a dirt service road running perpendicular to the highway and take it, past the "Authorized Personnel Only" sign until the road ends at four concrete pylons. Headlights off, I am in utter blackness. A faint acrid stench seeps into the car but I barely notice it as I fall asleep.

I wake up disoriented to muffled pounding on my side window.

Through narrowed and startled eyes, I'm staring at a sizeable green-uniformed belly, a shiny black leather belt, and a meaty hand resting on the butt of a holstered gun.

"You can't be here, buddy. Move along, will ya?" the representative of Ames Security tells me, not unkindly.

Apologizing through the glass, I straighten up and look around. The morning light is white and harsh and filled with the shriek of gulls. Turns out, I'm parked on the shores of Great Salt Lake, its bright blue stretching to the horizon.

The James Dickey look-alike trails me as I head back to the highway. So convinced am I that he's somehow running my plate even though he's a rent-a-cop that I head east until the next interchange where I double back.

After a return engagement to Denny's for coffee where—of course—the Ames Security guy and I exchange hellos, I'm on my way again, blowing through Salt Lake City before the morning rush. Its intertwining asphalt is an annoyance, but I'm relieved to hook onto the 15 heading due north towards Canada.

Soon even the towns dotting the highway landscape start to irritate me and I feel good again on the open road I share primarily with tractor trailers and Winnebagos which exist only to slow me down until I get into the rhythm of not giving a shit how fast I am travelling.

By the time I skirt the west side of Yellowstone and start across Montana, I think I have begun to understand long-distance truckers and the Zen monotony of cruising through nothingness. Damned if I don't begin to feel one with the steering wheel and the road. I even stop looking nervously in my rear-view mirror for the tail I'm sure has been dispatched.

Unhooked. That's what I am. As a kid, I didn't know what hooked was. I could stand for hours on highway ramps or street corners with my thumb out and nary a deliberate thought passing between my ears. I sometimes miss those hours of blankness, for they have been replaced by a near-constant blizzard of random musings, images, and worries, and fantasies.

When I do stop for gas and eats at places called Gas & Eats, I think it is somehow reassuring to be among people who couldn't seem to care less about what they or I look like, how they sound or what they say.

An added bonus: it doesn't appear as though any of them wants to kill me.

The only time I offend local sensibilities is in a diner off Route 94 when I order a Diet-Pepsi. The waitress (sorry, *server*) snorts as if I'm trying to introduce Communism to the Great Plains.

But outside Billings, I stop "being in the moment" as pretentious actors say and start to get the heebie-jeebies when I think ahead. That happens all the time when I think ahead because I usually imagine bad being the only outcome.

This cumulative attack of the willies has me imagining that my flight from San Fran towards freedom (in long stretches on the Lincoln Highway no less) is all an illusion, that really my path is known and I am being watched the entire time from some great height. I feel like an ant (but without that insect's strength, speed or sense of purpose) being briefly studied under a magnifying glass by a kid in a playground before the malicious little shit, with gritted teeth, gleefully watches the sun's rays focus and fry the fucker.

"Christ," I remark, "this is a dingy way to die." I almost feel bad for stealing this observation from *Under the Volcano* but, nevertheless, the Counsel's final thought about his life on the planet sort of fit. And it angers me to go out this way.

Which is to say, I'm not going to go down, either quietly or alone. Not possessing such things or having a working knowledge of semi-automatic weapons, I know this will be no Rambo last stand. The only weapon I'm passingly familiar with is the media. A little press can always shine a light, put things on the record, get people thinking of alternate theories.

Which is to further say: I call Steve. If he is somehow involved, I've got the edge because he doesn't know I suspect him. And if he's clean, he could raise a little hell.

It is a bit of a leap but after the pleasantries, I quasi-casually note that someone is trying to kill me.

"Where are you?"

I don't know why, but I'm taken aback by this being the first question out of his mouth.

"The less you know, the better it is for you," I tell him.

"Jesus, you're . . . my partner. Where are you?"

I think for second.

"Chris Whitley."

"Wha—oh, you're in—"

"—Shut it!"

"Alright. Now, why are you there and what the fuck are you talking about?"

I give him the condensed version of all the weird stuff that has happened and conclude with "So now, you gotta write about this."

He pauses, I hope because he's framing the structure for his exposé.

"Are you serious?" he asks instead. "Write about exactly what?"

"That there's . . . there's this conspiracy to take over computer systems. I think Ulti/ME is behind it. It's perfect for that series you're supposed to be working on."

"Jake, let me get this straight: you want me to write a story about how the current giant tech darling is actually a modern-day Dr. Evil who, for completely improbable reasons, has a hard-on for a drunk, recently-accused killer and Peterborough-area recluse retiree? Is that about right? OK, here's a headline: 'The paranoids are out to get me!' Whaddya think?"

"Go fuck yourself. You know me, Steve."

"I do. I also know that you can get all wrapped up in—what do you call them?—your scenarios."

"Go fuck yourself, Steve."

I mean it and hang up.

Instantly, I feel pretty badly about elevating Steve to if not #1 then certainly Top 5 on my shit list.

I have all sorts of open highway to think about our conversation. He is right, of course. No facts to bear out my claim of what has happened, a wild accusation that not even *The National Enquirer* would touch.

But still. His side of the conversation has done nothing to calm me down.

It's pitch-dark now. My headlights make a feeble gash at the wall of blackness around me. Up ahead—wait for it, wait for it—in the distance, I see a bluish dome over dots of white light.

As I had been instructed in San Francisco by Jason—a man who is almost young enough to be my grandson—I call him before the border, at a place called Fortuna, North Dakota, a dusty sort of town about twenty miles south of the 49th parallel.

"Where are you?" he, like Steve, asks right away.

"It's not important."

"Of course it is. Where are you?"

"Near the border, OK?"

I tell him about my call to Steve.

"That was a big mistake."

"I thought I could trust the guy."

"Well that's just great. Do you also trust the science of wiretapping? Do you not fucking think that fucking people who want to fucking find you might consider tapping the fucking phones of your fucking friends?

"I didn't fucking tell him where I fucking am," I offer in my defence.

He has me recount the conversation word for word.

"It's a rookie mistake," he concludes. "But it's done. Now, you have to get rid of the car before you cross the border.

"Why?"

"You've got California plates, I assume, and a Canadian passport. Border guy asks you for license, insurance and registration and then what?"

"Where do I ditch it?"

"How would I know? Just get rid of it. And call me again when you cross. We have to get you back here."

"Who's 'we'?"

"Me and the computer, OK?"

Desperately needing a beer and some prospective car shoppers, I stop at the Border Tavern in Fortuna which isn't near the aforementioned border—maybe ten miles from it.

My Vibe 2.0 is one of the few cars in the packed parking lot. Pick-ups and semi tractors make up the rest.

I don't exactly bring the country music, laughter, and general merriment to a screeching halt when I walk in but my presence is noted. I take a seat at the bar among altogether too much plaid.

"Nice shirt," the bearded hulk beside me notes, examining my little red number covered with hula dancers who, for some reason or other, sport eye patches.

"It is, isn't it?"

"Canuck?"

"Seriously? You could tell that fast?"

"Yup."

"You or any of your friends interested in a car?"

"Like you mean not a truck?"

A lad a couple of sets of plaid down the line says he is.

"Need something for the old lady."

"It's got California plates and I don't have any paperwork," I say, instantly telling myself that I should probably work on my salesmanship.

"Shit, all the better. I can scare up some plates."

Out in the parking lot, the raucous bar noise behind us, we begin the timeless negotiating dance as we both walk around the car.

Actually, it's over pretty quickly.

"She's been awfully good to me," I say.

"How long you owned it?"

"Almost two days."

"How much?"

"A thousand bucks."

"I'll give you five hundred."

"Seven fifty."

"I tell you what: I'll give you six and not call the state police."

"You drive a hard bargain but OK."

Despite the fact the car's depreciation in forty-eight hours seems a little steep, we both are smiling as we shake hands, pleased and amused with our little shtick.

He takes a roll of bills from his jeans and peels off the hundreds.

"One last request. You mind if I sleep in her one last time?" I ask.

"Gimme the keys and you got a deal."

Except for the noise of all the pick-ups fish-tailing out of the gravel parking lot at closing time, I get a good night's sleep.

The next morning, I wander into the small town looking for someone to sell me a cup of coffee. I leave the only gas station with about a 5-gallon cup of the worst coffee I've ever had and, on the kind of whim I can never explain, I go to the public library and log on to the one computer in that great institution after being warned by the elderly librarian not to go looking for those "dirty pitchers."

To once again underline the adage that old habits die hard, I then perform my newspaper routine. Sun Media chain first to get an idea of what had happened in the world while I was sleeping, then the bigger papers, then the Weather Network, then Google news.

After I learn about the latest and maybe dumbest trade the Leafs have ever made, I want to get a clear idea of exactly where I'm going. Sort of my own advance man, I think. I Google map where I am. Originally, I had thought that crossing into Canada on the 85 was my best bet. But the street view of the highway shows that well into Saskatchewan I'd be in the middle of fucking nowhere with all sorts of flat empty space to have bad things happen in.

So instead, I decide to head east towards Noonan which promised a straight shot across the border into Estevan and some civilization.

Back on the highway, I stick my thumb out and I actually feel good, instantly reminded of the hopefulness and boredom accompanying the thousands of miles I had hitchhiked as a teenager. But then I bring myself up-to-date and realize I'm completely pathetic.

Old guys should simply not do certain things. Mogul skiing, for example. And skateboarding—well, nobody should skateboard. Or listening to rap—OK, nobody should do that either. But hitchhiking, for sure; old guys shouldn't hitchhike.

So here I am, just this geezer by the side of the road, who might as well be wearing a sign saying "sexual predator' or "hopeless bum."

Against if not all odds certainly a lot of them, me and my trusty bowling bag get rides. No girl in a flat-bed Ford but a succession of nice people who aren't really interested in talking but are intent on being kind.

Especially kind to me is Dwayne "Bud" Willis, the Mid-Western Regional Sales Director for Klamath Farm Machinery, who not only gives me a ride but vouches for me at the Canadian border.

"Bud" doesn't have to do this and most people wouldn't. He is bald-face lying when, on the spot, he tells the suspicious-looking customs guy examining my passport that he is bringing his lazy, shiftless brother-in-law (me) back to face the music from his long-suffering sister (my wife) in Estevan who against better judgement (hers) has agreed to take me back provided there were going to be some changes around here, mister, starting with burning my Hawaiian shirts and cutting my hair when I next pass out drunk which I would no doubt do in the very near future but what else is a good Christian woman, one who respects her marriage vows and who gave up a promising career as a concert cellist to slave away as a dental hygienist to support me, the big city hotshot, who was going to be Mr. Smarty Pants on the stock market but who, instead, is drinking away his future and all their money, supposed to do?

Out of, I suspect, boredom rather than sympathy, the guard waves us through.

"Cellist? Nice touch," I note.

Bud grins.

"I can spin a pretty good story. Have to in my line of work."

I tell myself I'm lucky that Bud hadn't wanted to sell me a John Deere combine. If he had, I'd be the proud owner of a John Deere combine.

When we hit Estevan, Bud offers to buy me lunch. I'm overwhelmed by his generosity and say I would treat. He declines and lets me out in town, advising me that I'd better take care of his sister or I'd have him to deal with.

Wanting to keep a routine with him, I check in with Jason.

"I'm back in Canada."

"How was Fortuna?" he asks.

"What?"

"How . . . was . . . Fortuna?"

"How did—?"

"—it took me about ten minutes. I got it from your conversation with that reporter. Looked up Chris Whitely and his biggest hit told me you were originally in *Big Sky* country. So I guessed your likely route from there. But then you logged onto a computer at a public library in North Dakota and started reading Canadian newspapers. The way you always do."

"You know about that?"

"I do now. My computer's known for quite some time. It's no big deal. It's a pattern. Everybody has habits. And you *really* have habits. Just algorithms. Let me see: *Calgary Sun* then *Winnipeg Sun* then Toronto then Ottawa, then the *Globe, Post*, the Weather Network, then Google News. That sound about the right order?"

"Yes," I say, somewhat humiliated to see my clever scheme to avoid buying any on-line subscription had been unveiled and knowing that I had been reduced to a formula.

"Now, Jake, how many people in Fortuna, North Dakota—population: 249—do you think have that same routine?"

"Hundreds?"

"And did you stop to think that just maybe the computer camera was on while you were reading about the fucking Maple Leafs."

"Alright, alright."

"And if I know, they know."

"But . . . but, they were going to know anyway, right? As soon as I crossed the border."

"Now you've given them a head start."

"Like you said, it's done and here we all are. So now what?"

"What kind of ball cap do you have?" he asks, apparently out of nowhere.

"Stanford Cardinals. Why?"

"Jake, you have to start thinking about things, OK? You have to fly under the radar. Get rid of the hat; it's probably not a big seller in Saskatchewan. You buy a Roughrider hat before you get on the bus."

"Again with the bus?"

"Yup. I assume you got rid of the car."

"Got six hundred. US."

"So public transit is the only way. Unless you want to spend the rest of your life in where? Estevan, I'm guessing. No? OK, you take a bus to Regina and then your choice—bus or train—to Toronto."

"The world's my oyster?"

"Like I said, bus or train but no plane. Wait . . . Now that I think of it, stay away from the train. Hard to stop one if you need to."

"Well, in that case, maybe I'll just hitchhike."

"Maybe you won't, unless you like the idea of being a sitting duck. By bus, you'll be in Toronto in . . . in . . . 40 hours. 39 hours and 54 minutes to be exact."

"Jason . . . you're almost enjoying this, aren't you?"

" . . . I guess I sorta am. Want to know what avatar I'm using to track you?"

"Any chance it's a bunny?"

"Yup . . . with a Hawaiian shirt. By the way, if you're wearing one, get rid of that too."

"You're doing all this because of a stuffed animal?"

There is a pause.

" . . . No. It's way past that now," he says. "There's something evil happening out there. Not just against you."

"How do you know?"

"I think I used to work for them."

"What?"

"Look, I can't explain it all right now. I'll see you in two days. Call when you get in. And Jake . . . stay safe."

I approach two large young men in the bus station. They look like prairie farm boys heading off to be dazzled by Toronto. I swap my

Hawaiian shirt straight up for a black Jack Daniels T-shirt, size fat, with the smaller of them. He seems pretty darned pleased with the deal—as well he should be. Red Hawaiian shirts decorated with one-eyed hula dancers aren't as common as you'd think.

I buy a ticket, a shitty sandwich, a couple of garishly-covered detective novels and a Saskatchewan Roughrider ball cap, sum total of which has left me pretty much broke. I settle into a window seat for my trip back to the self-acknowledged centre of the universe. It seems as though my recent bartering has created a bond as the guy with one of my best goddamned Hawaiian shirts sits beside me, his travelling buddy across the aisle.

It's a little crowded, what with my behemoth of a seat mate and my trusty bowling bag on my lap as I can't take the chance of losing it and being without my meds. But, that's OK; I plan to be asleep for at least half of the next forty hours.

As it turns, I don't get that sleep and, as it turns out, Jason's instruction that I stay safe wasn't a viable option.

CHAPTER THREE

Jason has made it onto my very short Trustworthy List on pretty slender evidence. He told me to get rid of my shirt and the Stanford hat. If he wanted me to stand out as a target, I reason, he wouldn't have done that.

At this point, that's good enough for me.

I shoot the shit with my new friend for a while. As I had guessed, he and his pal were off the farm, heading to Toronto. But I am properly self-chastised when I learn the lads are University of Toronto students—he in pre-law, his friend in chemical engineering—and both varsity football players. I am deservedly humbled further when he draws out a dog-eared copy of *Mother Night* while I try to hide my shiny new "thriller."

Boring as hell Prairie turns into great pine or spruce or whatever the fuck forests near the Ontario border. I stare out the window at the chiselled and blasted red rock walls rising on either side of the two-lane Trans Canada Highway. For long stretches, the winding road hugs the coastline of Lake Superior. It brings back memories of camping along those shores as a kid with my parents, of wading into the glittering and goddamned cold, testicle-retracting waters, and years later, of hitchhiking, standing near there for hours, aware of the weight of my outstretched arm and my backpack and the absolute irrelevancy of time.

No place to be, no one to see, as free as I have ever been.

Now, here I am, regarding my bus mates with suspicion, carefully watching who boards and who gets off at the string of stations my chauffeur-driven, really-stretch limo stops in.

The towns sprinkled across the pre-historic landscape are distractions but also places for a smoke as I time the intervals between nicotine hits the way all us tobacco junkies do.

At the best of times, as you might guess, I'm not one of those gregarious John Candy-in-*Planes, Trains and Automobiles*-type users of mass transit. No sing-along to *The Flintstones* theme song ever issued from these lips. Instead, here I am, wary, imagining an outrage in the eyes of everyone walking down the narrow aisle.

After a time—I'd say about five or six stops—I have figured the manner in which people join our band of Gypsies. Rising out of the stairwell, they quickly glance at the whole bus interior, then check their ticket then narrow their focus to the seat numbers as they sidle along. Check the ticket again as they stand over their intended seat and begin shedding whatever carry-ons they have.

There's a small asterisk attached to pretty women who don't ever gaze around much when they board a bus—or train or plane—likely for fear of meeting the hopeful eyes of every solo male passenger who just feels better when beauty accompanies them.

This pattern, like the mystery novel I skimmed, is so predictable.

Until it isn't.

That's in Sault Ste. Marie, a town perched on the Michigan border at the neck of wolf's head-shaped Lake Superior.

I finish my lung dart, re-board, and wriggle into my window seat, just as this guy gets on who isn't like the any of the other new passengers I had been watching. For one thing, he is pretty well-dressed and that makes him stand out from the rest of us who would never be mistaken for a busload of fashion models off to a glamour shoot.

For another thing, after his perfunctory scan, there is a slight hesitation when he seems to recognize one of his fellow travelers.

Me.

<CHAPTER FOUR>

He quickly averts his gaze and seems to look anywhere else but at me as he makes his way past me and takes a seat four or so rows behind mine.

I don't know what this guy could do on a crowded bus—jam a needle in my neck, pop me while I'm in the can, just shoot everybody—but I'm not in the mood to find out. I need to have this handled right now, before the bus leaves the station.

My next door neighbour, who is now proudly sporting one of my best goddamned Hawaiian shirts, is a big lad and his friend is even bigger. I lean over and whisper.

"Hey, bud, there's a guy a few rows back. Don't look. Black sports coat. Maybe it's nuthin' but I think I saw a gun."

I let that sink in.

"We can fuckin' take him," he says, his blue eyes steady on me in complete confidence.

"I know you can. Easier than I could. In a little while, you head back to the can, stand just past him, while your friend gets up to follow you. I'll get the cops. Make sense?"

He nods agreement, doesn't look the least bit frightened. He whispers across the aisle to his buddy who likewise shows no hesitation.

They get up and then I get up and head to the front.

"There's a problem back there," I tell the driver. "Just stay here, don't panic. I'm going for the cops."

This said just as my aisle mates pounce on the guy and all hell breaks loose. Someone yells "Gun!" People start screaming and my last look back sees my stalker struggling like crazy in a half-nelson courtesy of a very large farm boy/offensive lineman.

I run into the station, find a security guy, and tell him what's going on. Jack Snap, he's on his radio to the cops as he runs towards the departure bays. I run the other way.

I figure my stalker will be tied up by the police for hours, probably days, which gives me some time to get the hell out of there. I also reckon that his unnamed master wouldn't hear about it for a long time, enough time to get me long gone.

It'd be logical to assume that I would take the most direct route—turn south at Sudbury and down the Trans Canada through Barrie to Toronto. If they send somebody else, that's where they'd look first, I think.

Hoping that Albee is right and that "Sometimes you have to go a long way out of your way to come back a short distance correctly", I choose a different route. I pass through Sudbury heading east in the cab of a pick-up with 747-sized tires and get off at North Bay, intent on taking the 11 which pretty well runs parallel to the Trans Canada but is a whole lot less travelled. Now let's see if ol' Bobby Frost had nailed it.

A long-distance semi chuffs to a stop past me, its air brakes ripping the air.

As I haul myself up, I see the driver is a wiry little guy who doesn't appear strong enough to manage the giant steering wheel or shift the great gear sticks. He is close to my age, I reckon, and has armfuls of ancient tattoos whose colours have run together over the years until his arms look like skinny Rorschach tests.

He seems way nervous about picking me up, nervous enough that he immediately has to tell me about the barroom fights he'd won over the years. I know that kind of man. He probably *had* won his share because guys like that have no quit in them, just buzz-saw terriers. I decline to swap my boxing stories with him as that would likely put him more on edge than the uppers I assume he is popping.

He is bound for Toronto and so am I; at this moment, that's all that matters. Why risk being put out at the side of the highway? Thus, the age-old commerce of the road is conducted. After hearing about his brawling prowess, conversation is pretty well limited to the weather (which the fuckin' Russians were manipulating with their fuckin' sputniks) and, of course, the fuckin' Leafs.

His name is Fred but he prefers to be called Duke.

"After John Wayne?" I ask.

"Nope. These," he says holding up his balled fists.

While not exactly flush, I spring for dinner at a roadhouse near Huntsville. It is the least I could do to repay the kindness of strangers. Besides, I'm starting to like the guy. I like him a whole lot more when he tries to decline my meal offer after he sees the small wad of crumpled bills I pull from my jeans.

"Down on your luck, are ya?" he notes.

"I guess you could say that."

"Been there myself a few times."

Our meal lasts for quite some time. Well, his does, because he takes the face-to-face opportunity to tell me just about everything he can think to tell me about his life. He isn't unburdening, I think, only breaking his hours of silence behind the wheel.

After dinner, I call Jason.

Apparently neither of us is in the mood to chat. I tell him about the bus incident.

"I already know. I've been watching the news sites; it was obviously your bus."

"Who is he?"

"Police don't know or aren't saying. Jailhouse leak says the asshole didn't have an ID and he isn't co-operating."

"What do I do now?"

"There isn't much you can do about it now, is there? There's no other choice but to continue on your way and hope that they've got no more bad guys to throw at you."

He did not seem at all surprised to hear about me careening from one potential disaster to another. He gives me his address in Toronto and hangs up.

Despite my protests that it isn't fair for him to go so far out of his way, the Dukester guides his rig right up to Jason's address. He playfully punches me on the shoulder before I dismount the cab. Damned if it doesn't hurt.

Jason's lair is one of those shitty "units" in a shitty little industrial park in north-east Toronto. Anonymous, one-story cement block, likely with a huge garage door bay out the back, identical style of signage in front. I find Leone Technical Services (Jason had told me about the thing he has for Tia).

Jason is waiting for me in the small, cheaply-panelled reception area. He seems at least as relieved to see me as I am to see him. We hug. Awkwardly. He doesn't seem to want to let go. Or maybe it's me.

"How long have you been sitting here?" I ask.

"I haven't. We've got the parking lot wired so I saw you pull in. Sweet ride, by the way."

He punches a code into the keypad beside a steel door and we enter a cavernous dark room. The only light is the glow from maybe twenty giant monitors clustered together at workstations in groups of four or five. I reckon the set-up is somewhere between an air traffic control centre and a Mars-bound spaceship.

"You run this by yourself?" I ask.

"Well, no."

A head pops up over a set of monitors.

"Jake, that's Connor. And that's Dylan just getting his nocturnal ass out of bed."

Jason points up to an open mezzanine at the top of a spiral steel staircase.

"Where'd you get all this stuff?" I ask. "It's gotta be worth a fortune."

"I bought it. And this place."

"With your old man's dough?"

"No! With mine," he says emphatically. "For the last four years or so, I've been making . . . some pretty good money."

I get the quick tour and am struck by the way the place is decorated. While it had that modern industrial vibe of black, brushed silver and dominating red walls, all the accessories are a throwback. To World War II and, specifically, to the air war. Paintings, prints of bombers—Lancasters, I think—adorn the walls. The ceiling fans look like propeller blades and there's even an authentic and mercifully unexploded bomb standing on its fins. My hand rests on its cool metal nose.

"My mom's dad flew Lancs during the war," Jason says by way of explanation.

He points to a black and white blow-up photo of an air crew.

"That's grandpa—second from the right—the navigator," he says, as I study the seven impossibly young and smiling faces of the men striding away from the hulking plane.

"Whenever I think I have it rough," he continues, "I look at that picture. He was 19-years-old. He and his crew made it back. More than half didn't."

At the rear the office space is a stage. Various guitars, amps, mic stands, and speakers litter it and there is a full drum kit against the back wall.

"Me and the boys like to fuck around after a hard day on the Net," Jason says.

He picks up a battered acoustic from a stand, strums a bit, and then launches into a soft and intricate flamenco sort of thing, a few seconds of gentle excellence. I am humbled and happy to hear all this talent and taste.

"You play?" he asks.

"I can't sing Happy Birthday."

He seems a little disappointed as he gently replaces the guitar on its stand.

"Jake, follow me."

We climb the staircase to what looks like a college dorm. Narrow hallway, open doors revealing small rooms with mattresses on the floor, clothes strewn everywhere; a Canadian flag with a dope leaf instead of the maple variety adorns a window. I couldn't help but notice that there was no evidence of brick and board bookshelves. Or lava lamps, for that matter.

We pass Dylan in his underwear, skinny, dishevelled, yawning, and scratching his nuts as he stumbles to the bathroom. He could've been Jason's slovenly younger brother.

"What are you? The Lost Boys?" I ask.

"The Lost Boys?" Jason repeats. "I like that. We've been looking for a name. Anonymous is taken."

He leads me to a small, windowless, and thoroughly depressing room. It's completely empty except for a mattress on the floor.

"Your suite, monsieur," he says with a flourish.

"I really like what you've done to the place."

Despite my austere surroundings, I am thrilled to be horizontal again and don't mind at all that I'm lying on a legless bed, something I hadn't done since my drunken university days when it just made good safety sense.

I feel safe in this hi-tech womb, safer than I'd felt in a long time, and fall asleep immediately.

I awake to very loud music. I've been refreshed and am absolutely clueless about what time it might be.

Peering down from the mezzanine railing, I see—and really hear—the boys ripping through a more than credible version of *Tales of Brave Ulysses*. I am content to watch and listen as they then launch into *All Along the Watchtower*. As impressive as Jason's guitar work is, I am struck by one line he sings:

"There must be some kind of way out of here, said the joker to the thief."

The song disassembles near its end as Dylan on drums fucks up the beat and boys grind and crash to a halt, laughing.

I clap.

"So this is why I can't reach room service!" I yell.

They stomp their way through *Cinnamon Girl* while I make coffee in the kitchen.

The concert ends and they join me, all sweaty and happy. But soon Jason becomes quiet and serious.

"I've been thinking about this, Jake," he finally says. "You have to disappear."

"But I just got here."

"No, I mean drop entirely out of sight, until this gets cleared up—*if* it gets cleared up."

"How?"

"Basically, you've got two choices. You can go all Montana off the grid. Which, as you know, is primitive and which, sooner or later, *has* to come to an end. Or you can just become someone else—with a new identity, new papers, new everything—someone who can walk among us completely anonymously."

"Like all that zombie shit you kids like so much?"

"Kids?" Dylan says.

"Settle down, son. At my age, anyone under forty is a kid. Can you really just hide in plain sight?"

"I've been doing it for years," Jason says. "It's not all that easy to set up. You have to create a flawless trail. But after that, everybody just relies on the paperwork, the magnetic chips, whatever. If their computers say you're OK, then you're OK. All you really have to remember is to stay away from cameras as much as possible. And you have to build a good story for yourself. It takes some imagination and practice, costs some money and . . . "

"And?"

"And it costs you your old life."

"It's not much but I kinda like my old life."

"Time's past for nostalgia, Jake. Think of it as witness protection."

"But I didn't witness anything. I don't know anything!"

"Well, why didn't you say so? Give me the number and I'll call whoever's trying to kill you and explain everything."

I have to admit that's a fairly impressive piece of sarcasm.

"Come and see what I'm talking about," he says.

We go back upstairs to a door at the end of the hallway. We enter a large neat room, I don't mean neat compared to the others, I mean spotless and organized, with tasteful art and classic movie posters on one wall—*Casablanca, Deliverance, Bull Durham, Deer Hunter.* On another, hangs a large bulletin board.

"I was not expecting this," I say, looking around.

"I guess I picked up a few things from my father."

"Like hospital corners on your bed. I bet your dad was big on hospital corners."

"Yeah, like that. And the value of shell companies and setting up offshore accounts. And, in a way, he was responsible for starting me out on this path of mine."

"How?"

"In school, I found out that I was just a punk with a real talent for software engineering. I soon realized there was a market for what I could do. Particularly after my father hired me."

"For what?"

"He had me design a security system for Bio-Watch. I must say, it was pretty elegant, virtually bulletproof. It still stands up just fine today."

"That'd be worth millions."

"Not to me. My father waved the contract I'd signed at me. It said that he owned all the products of my work for him."

"He fucked over his own son?"

"Said it was a valuable lesson for me to learn. In a bunch of ways, he was right. Legally, of course, I didn't have a leg to stand on."

Not too surprisingly, it was obvious that Jason—the master of logic and good sense—was starting to get emotional. He was rubbing his thighs more fiercely and I thought I could see his eyes getting watery.

"What happened?" I ask.

"I was pissed. I made up my mind to not play a normal game and started getting deeper and deeper into the 'Net. The more time I spent on Tor—"

"What's Tor?"

Christ, I came to regret asking that question! Jason takes a deep breath and starts explaining the story of the darknet. I was happy to let him ramble on, if for no other reason than to take his mind off his old man.

You want irony? Tor was invented by the US government to hide its people, letting agents and spies and such stay in touch and report and not have to worry about a knock on the door in whatever shithole country they were operating. And it let the US agencies—DARPA and Naval Intelligence, the CIA and a bunch of others—do the things they want to do. All these guys in the shadows still kick in half the money to keep it going. But—surprise, surprise—it didn't take long for crooks to figure out it's a handy-dandy tool for selling and buying anything you might want to sell or buy. Billions of dollars worth of Kalashnikovs and heroin and kiddie porn—the entire gamut of illicit and dangerous stuff. All from the comfort of your computer keyboard and all completely anonymous.

"It's also become home," Jason continues, "for all the hackers on the planet and most political dissidents because they can't be traced—at least, in theory they can't be traced—because of all the servers they use to send their encrypted messages back and forth."

"In theory?"

He tells me of a big takedown. The FBI's Operation Shrouded Horizon had nailed 70 people all over the world who were using a site called Darkode for fraud and money laundering.

"If you had told me this bust was coming a month before it happened," he said, "I would've told you that you were full of shit. The game is changing and the US feds are getting better and better. They got Silk Road, now Darkode, so the bad guys have to sink farther into the darknet to set up their marketplaces."

"How do they ever get paid on these sites?"

"Bitcoin."

I am passingly familiar with the Internet currency but, like so many things in my life, have no true understanding of it. Nevertheless, hoping to evade another lecture, I tell Jason to skip the details.

"You should learn about it," he says. "It's going to be big."

"I'll be long dead before that happens."

We pause, both, I think, contemplating the possibility that my current situation might get me killed way before slow suicide by cigarette does.

"Fact is, Jake, I'm with you. Call me old school but fuck Bitcoin. I work in US dollars," he says, in some kind of attempt to cheer me up. "It's also why I'm a big fan of just changing identities rather than trying to hide deeper and deeper in the darknet rabbit hole. This is what I mean," he says, pointing to the bulletin board. It's divided up into columns with different names heading each one and index cards pinned under each.

"What's this?" I ask.

"Me. Five different versions of me actually."

I glance at the cards.

"I really like Donald Blair the best," he says pointing to one column. "He made me all the money as a programmer for hire."

I scan the column. 25-years-old, from Mississauga, single child of deceased parents, mythical diploma from Leaside High school, mythical BA from Western, mythical social insurance number, driver's license, and health card.

Jason tells me he created the fiction more than five years ago.

"And I'm still at large."

He also tells me that for the last four years, he's worked for a single company, using that false ID.

"Who?"

"I don't know. In the early days, I thought I could find them. They sent paper cheques, always on time, always paid in full from bank accounts in the Caymans or Belgium. The company that actually pays me is called Oakmont Holdings which, I'm pretty sure, is just a PO Box somewhere in the Caribbean. The envelopes were postmarked Indianapolis. Or Bruges. Or Mexico City. They're all fake but, then again, so am I. But the money's real."

"If you don't know who you're working for, how'd you get a job there?"

"They found me. I guess they shadowed me for a while, liked what I was doing."

Jason describes his time in the belly of the techno-beast. What struck me as he tells of jobs parcelled out to whiz-bang programmers around the world is the scale of the operation and its secrecy. The overlord apparently uses a carrot and stick thing with his employees (although truth be told, I'd rather be beaten with a stick than voluntarily eat a carrot) whereby his employer e-spoke of possible promotion to The Golden Garden, nerd heaven, the central command centre where all these piecemeal jobs were assembled. And, if you failed to produce, the jobs—and the money—just stopped coming.

The more he talks, I notice, the more he nervously rubs the worn denim on his thighs.

"Golden Garden? Does that mean anything to you?" I ask.

"Nope. Us geeks like a bit of mythology or some medieval shit."

"Where is it?"

"Zero idea. It's probably not a real location, more likely a virtual place."

"Did you ever try to find out who you were actually working for?"

"They told us not to try so, of course, I did. But I gave up. These guys—whoever they are—are very good. They have to have hundreds, maybe thousands of servers all over the world. Maybe their own, maybe hijacked ones. And, of course, they found out I was looking. There was a strong suggestion I not do that again."

"Or what?"

"It came with the threat of action because they knew I had done . . . things."

"What things?"

"Illegal things. Like getting into pharmaceutical company bank accounts. A zero here, a zero there. Most of the guys would break in just to say they did it. Then they'd brag. And then they'd get caught. Believe it or not, at twenty-seven, I'm now an old hand at this hacking thing; there aren't many of us left from those days."

"Why'd you do it, if it wasn't for the fame?"

"I just wanted the money."

"So you're a thief."

"I was. Not anymore. I hack now for the right reason. For good things."

"Like?"

"Like a kid . . . a fourteen-year-old kid gets drugged at a party . . . some animals rape her and take pictures and pass them around. They should be outed. Or a politician running on those good old family values turns into a chicken hawk at night. Or a mining company in South America hires thugs to beat the shit out of its own workers trying to organize. I can tell people about this."

"Have you repaid the money you stole?" I want to know.

"Yes." And he is very emphatic about what might be a first in the world of cyber punkdom.

"What changed for you?"

"I finally saw that there were consequences. The unintended ones are bad enough but you don't truly know about them until after they've happened. It is the intended consequences that got me. It's just wrong. I'm small potatoes. There are some big things going on. None of them good."

"Could it be a government pulling these shenanigans?"

"Naw, not ours, not the US either. They like to watch but I've never seen them intervene or do things like fuck up bank accounts."

"The Russians?"

"Don't think so. There's no political end game that I can see."

"So who?"

"I'm pretty sure it's the outfit I was working for."

"*Was* working for?"

"The jobs just ended a couple of days before I went to see you but after I had pretty well figured out you were being followed. That's too much of a coincidence, don't you think?"

"Yup."

"And . . . "

"What?"

"And I recognized the program, part of it anyway, that they were using to track you."

"You designed it."

"I designed it."

"Well, ain't that a kick in the onions with a frozen boot."

"Sorry," he says sheepishly.

"So because of you, I'm hiding out? You bastard!"

I look around the place. I try to imagine spending years of my life cloistered in this monastery. I then envision repeatedly smashing my forehead into the corner of a metal desk. I think I'd prefer that.

"You like it here?" I ask.

"Not really. But I have . . . responsibilities."

I realize he is talking about Dylan and Connor, as he more furiously rubs his thighs.

"But you've got the false identities. You can be anywhere you want."

Jason pauses. There's something in his eyes that is the very opposite of the confidence and matter-of-factness when he was describing his perfectly-defended life.

Fear.

"You know that running bit in *Butch Cassidy,*" he finally says, "when Butch and the Kid are being trailed by a posse they can't shake?"

"You mean "Who are those guys?""

"Yeah. Well, I think I'm getting close to asking that question."

"Scared?"

"I wouldn't call it scared," he says. "We'll need a new plan soon. But for now, for better or worse, this is our life. In some form or other, this will always be our life. And this is our home. This is your home."

"Jesus, I need a walk, get some fresh air."

"Don't go too far."

Behind the industrial park is a railway spur line. Thoroughly depressed, I walk along it. Jason's prediction—"This will always be our life"—keeps recurring to me. Now maybe my plans for the rest of my days hadn't been all that exciting—I had ruled out running with the Pamplona bulls and co-founding the Stones quite some time ago, discarded the hope of being a walk-on for the Leafs and never entertained the idea of climbing much more than a flight of stairs let alone Kilimanjaro—but the picture I had of me playing out the string was perfectly enjoyable, perfectly pleasant.

And now it is gone. Replaced by months, years, hell, maybe decades of playing global hide n' seek. Only instead of "Found ya!" I get two behind the ear. And there didn't seem to be a fucking thing I could do about it.

It's being helpless that gets to me. Maybe I always was helpless but I didn't *think* I was. Now the matter is settled beyond doubt and, worse, I know it.

Think-think-thinking, I realize Jason is right. Steve had been right. There is no story, no proof of anything. Alistair had probably been murdered somehow and there had been an apparently connected break-in/murder at my cottage—as yet unsolved—but that was it. I couldn't prove any of the fucking around with computers. So tell the cops or the media exactly what? I could rant all I want and join the legion of on-line wingnut conspiracy theorists and get cancelled out in the paranoid noise.

The more helpless I feel, the angrier I become.

I return to the lair, determined to announce my presence with authority.

"I need a new passport," I say.

"Why?" Jason asks.

"I go south every year."

"Not this year, you don't."

"Fuck that! Do you think anybody gives a shit about who I am in Las Terrenas, Dominican Republic? I just got to get into the country and then disappear for six months. Christ, that town is full of ex-pats running from something."

"Staying in Canada would be a whole lot simpler."

"Not gonna do it. Just not."

Jason thinks for a bit.

"25K. All in. That's the price for re-inventing yourself."

"I'm good for it."

"Don't worry about it; it's on me. I can't help thinking I somehow brought this down on you. Besides, you can't go anywhere near your own money right now."

When I get told I can't do something, I always react in a perfectly reasonable, measured way: I pout.

"But—"

"—there is no 'but', Jake. You have to learn that you can't argue your way out of this."

I fall quiet, the very picture of resignation.

I'm not going to tell Jason that Las Terrenas won't be my first trip out of the country.

<CHAPTER SIX>

Oh, and I need to see my daughter," I say.

"You can't."

"What are you going to do? Shoot me?"

"Jake, you're going to fuck everything up."

"No, I won't. I swear. You've managed to teach this old dog a new trick or two."

"It won't be enough. At least wait until you get a new identity."

"Fine. Let's get this done. I've picked my new name."

"Whatever it is, forget it."

"Why?"

"Conscious or not there'll be a pattern. Something that ties it to you. Look, I'll prove it. What's the name you came up with?"

"Mark Lambert."

"Have you ever said on-line or in an e-mail that you liked someone named Mark?"

I thought and thought. Some years ago, I had joined Facebook because I had been led to believe—completely wrongly as it turned out—that such cyber socializing would be essential to selling my novel. At the time, I had noted that Mark Twain was a hero of mine.

"Yes," I have to answer.

"What about Lambert?"

I have to acknowledge that perhaps the legendary Steeler linebacker had been mentioned in one of my blogs.

"OK, OK. You've made your point," I say. "I'll pull it all down."

"It's too late for that. It's there. For all time. And if you try to erase it now they'll be able to trace the IP address. *This* IP address."

"So who am I?"

"I don't know yet. Gimme a second while I generate a name."

Watching Jason's fingers fly over a keyboard, I couldn't help but be impressed with his symphony of click-click-clicking, a fast and light touch, something like Hendrix on a solo, all casual and unerring lightning but without the feedback. Me who has all the manual dexterity of a sloth wearing hockey gloves. He hit the final key with a flourish.

"Glen Johnson," he announces.

"That's it?"

"That's it. I'll get the basic counterfeiting started. I know a guy who knows a guy. You go away and think up Glen's story. As much as you can imagine. But keep it bland. There's an air-gapped PC over there."

"A what?"

"Not networked. Now go!"

After a couple hours of fiction-writing, I print out the results and bring it to him with the same expectation I used to have when I'd show my mother the shitty artwork I'd done in grade 2 and she'd coo and tack it to the fridge door.

He flips through it, shaking his head the whole time. Finally, he tears it up and feeds the scraps into a shredder.

"Why did you do that?" I ask of his harsh editing job.

"Number 2 scorer for your high school football team? Valedictorian at McMaster University? Marketing Director for Molson? Jake, do you not think someone might remember who gave the commencement address at Mac, or that just maybe your high school keeps sports records? Or that there should be newspaper clippings for a senior guy at a giant beer company? You have to have zero achievements."

"But I've already had a life like that."

"OK then, less than zero achievements. Absolutely nothing memorable or traceable."

"Like the "photo unavailable" guy in high school yearbooks?"

"Exactly," he says. "Let's save some time. I'll do it but you *have* to go along with it."

"Why do I even need a back story? I'll have the fake papers."

"Think about it. Glen Johnson just can't appear one day. What's the screen say when they run your passport at the border? When did you get that passport? Where else have you been? When? What about your Social

Insurance Number? When was that assigned? Or your driver's license? Health card? The way it is, we have to go back and alter records, little tweaks here and there. It's not just the government shit. And believe me, that takes time. On top of that, the people looking for you are a lot keener on finding you than any government will ever be.

"And that means dropping your name into class rolls, manufacturing report cards, university transcripts, staggering dates when you got different licenses, being the guy that people vaguely remember but not really. You need tax records, bank records, addresses where you've lived. Christ, we even have to photoshop your ID photos just enough to confuse the recognition software. We have to come up with answers to security questions like 'What's your mother's maiden name?' And on and on. And in your case, add another 'on' because you insist on traveling. And don't forget, making up a 20-year-old's history is a lot easier than what? A sixty-five-year-old's?"

"Sixty. But thanks."

"They can meta scan millions or billions of records. In seconds. Untouched by human hands. Always winnowing down to a shorter and shorter list according to the parameters they set. For example: find all the people in Ontario associated with Mark and/or Lambert who worked at Montrose and who is sixty-years-old. That'd be a list of one in .04 seconds. And it all comes from what you've said or did on-line."

"So I'm fucked."

"No. You just have to throw their scanners off the scent right at the start. For example, we could make you fifty-eight and, if they used fifty-nine to sixty-one as a parameter, instantly you're off their first list."

"Until they re-set the parameter."

"That's why we have to do this right, Jake. If we do, you're in the clear. Forever. Unless . . . "

"Unless what?"

"Unless they put boots on the ground. As long as they stick to computer records, you are who the machines say you are. But if they use humans to investigate, they'll know you're bogus in no time. All they have to do is find two or three high school teachers who have no recollection. Or visit your phoney business and talk to your phoney co-workers or your phoney landlord. It'd be over in a matter of hours, days at the most."

"But they'd only know for sure that Glen Johnson is fake. Not who he really is."

"Then they'd start tracking Glen Johnson exactly the same way they're tracking Jake Lydon."

"So, like I said, I'm fucked."

"You're less fucked if we put some real thought into this."

Until my new identity is constructed and the counterfeit paper and plastic arrives, the simplest act of being normal, of seeing people, doing things in public, even going on-line becomes an ordeal. Going out for pizza with The Lost Boys is an undercover operation.

After only a couple of days, I become stir-crazy. For me, Jason's sanctuary has been transformed into a darkened pit of high tech hell. My roommates are decent kids but, well . . . they're kids.

Jason tells me about how he recruited them. Beyond his general criterion that he needed a decent bass player and drummer, he went looking for two smart guys who were local, essentially unattached and who shared his desire—and his talent—for doing complicated things on the Internet.

"Both these guys are light years ahead of where I was at their age," Jason says. "They just needed a bit of direction."

A high school drop-out with a restless mind and lousy grades, Dylan left home when he was 17. He spent two years couch-surfing around Toronto and spending every available moment on-line, gaming, messing around with other people's sites until Jason found him, gave him purpose and projects.

On the other hand, Connor had been an academic star and was half-way towards a BSc at Ryerson when he just quit, a burn-out at 19. Connor is at large. He lives at home with his parents and shows up for "work" every day, sometimes on weekends when his fictional job as a car stereo installer has overwhelmed him. By being the outside man, he can bring us things, make personal contacts, and do errands that require flesh.

It hadn't taken the trio long to coalesce as a hacking force. Jason allowed that music—particularly 70s rock—had served perhaps more than anything as their great unifier. I saw no squabbling, no extended

instructions from Jason; they worked as single entity, intuitively contrib-
uting their pieces to the whole with a minimum of conversation or
debate.

And when Connor, Dylan, and Jason start tech-yakking I get lost.

Every generation and every sub-set of every generation have their
own language, a lexicon that sounds, at best, laughable when anyone else
attempts to use it and, at worst, as unintelligible as the Canada Tax code
or Eddie Murphy's career choices.

I've been in Mexican street markets where I understood more than
what the boys are talking about.

"Of course you need HTTPS to the car to encrypt."

"Yeah, but with most of them, an 8-bit XOR'll crack it."

"That is so ROT13!"

"For SSL or Wi-fi, it's gotta be AES-256 or nothing!"

Jason translates, telling me they're talking about how easy it was to
take over my rental car. He offers to explain the terminology. I decline.

The lads are clearly amused at my technical illiteracy.

As near as I can tell, they have to spend a lot of time just managing their fake lives. Which means a lot of time fucking around in other
computer systems.

They also have a project they call The Douchebag Patrol. They pick
up a news item, some bit of public chicanery or shady behaviour or
they'd dig into statements made on the dozens of chat rooms they monitor. Everything from politicians taking bribes to child pornographers to
star athletes with a habit of beating up on their women. A kind of kanga-
roo court is convened where they'd discuss the merits of intervening in
the story.

They'd go over the evidence, build a case, discuss the ethics of things
and, if it was unanimous, they would set to work unmasking the shit-
heel.

I'm allowed to watch these star chambers. I even kick in what small
amount of reasonableness I have to slow down whatever fatwah they're
on the verge of issuing. In particular, I try most frequently to rein in
Dylan who, younger and hotter of head than Jason, is invariably keen on
bringing to justice the alleged douchebag du jour. He doesn't quite state
it that way. Somewhat euphemistically, he indicates his vote for action by

saying: "Let's burn this fucker down!"

In the main, however, there is a deftness to what they do, driven by Jason's even-handedness. He shows me some of their past "insertions" as he calls them. Stories I had heard about where bad guys and girls had been unmasked. They weren't big on any loud "*J'accuse!*" moments where they'd claim credit. They'd just set the news cycle on spin, making ripples in the ether pond that got picked up and amplified, the story unfolding over days, weeks, sometimes months. They may have made a rush to judgement to get the ol' ball rolling, but you couldn't find their fingerprints on it and they were never even identified as the proverbial "unknown hackers."

"Ever been wrong?" I ask.

"No."

"Ever have doubts about being judge and jury?"

"We're neither. We let someone else do that."

"Oh come on. Back in the 70s, we used to call that a cop-out. You already know what the public reaction will be; you're counting on it."

"Maybe. All I do is ask myself one question: is the world a little better or a little worse after we get a story out?"

"If you want to change the world, why do you piss around with these small cases? Why not make a big splash by revealing all sorts of government secrets, or going after all those stock fraudsters?"

"Unintended consequences. You can't predict the fall-out. People got all righteous about that Ashley Madison adultery site being cracked, like 'it serves all those cheaters right' but no one knows the story of each one. And a couple of guys—maybe more—probably killed themselves after being outed. Just so people can yell their outrage or get some laughs on-line for a few days? That's worth it? Not to me, it isn't.

"Don't get me wrong. I've got no beef with what Snowden did. I'm sure some people got hurt and that is truly unfortunate but how else do you check a government's power if you don't tell the truth about what's actually going on?"

"And yet he's living in Russia."

"That's the part I don't understand. Other than scale, can you possibly tell me the difference between Snowden and Daniel Ellsberg? Ellsberg took paper from the Pentagon in the 70s; Snowden took storage devices.

Ellsberg's still a folk hero who was never convicted of anything and Snowden's a traitor and an international criminal? How's that happen?"

"I don't know. Context, I guess. Different times."

"That's just bullshit, Jake! And you know it. Wrong is wrong. And all this secret surveillance is wrong. And it's getting worse."

"But if you've got nothing to hide . . . "

"For fuck's sake, Jake, would you be OK with knowing that every piece of mail you ever got had been steamed open and read by the Post Office? Every phone call listened to? Or that some government department has the complete list of every website, every store you ever visited? And are you OK with some low-level government bureaucrat interpreting that information and deciding you're a threat or a bad guy? I'm not."

Jason is angry and I don't blame him. I'm pissed off at myself for offering up arguments that I know are beyond lame; call them wheelchair-bound.

I tell him so and we dial down the rhetoric and call a truce.

One element of Jason's crusade intrigues me. The price he has paid for his isolation.

"Most days, I don't think about it," he tells me. "I'm too busy doing things I believe have to be done."

"And on the other days?"

"It's sad, in a way, if I use 'normal' as a measuring stick. No girlfriend, no freedom of movement, no real relationship with my sisters, my mom. Dad . . . well . . . "

"You said you were worried about your mother. Why? She in trouble?"

"Maybe. I know she's . . . involved with someone. It's none of my business but I know."

"Who?"

"It's *really* none of your business."

"Got it. But you're keeping tabs on her. Is she in danger?"

"There's always danger in relationships."

"Well, that's a little precious, doncha think?"

"Alright, alright. She also had me move some money for her out of a Swiss bank account."

"Lemme guess. About a hundred and twenty-two million?"

Jason is startled at my inside knowledge but composes himself.

"With my father gone, it's hers anyway."

"Interesting but not quite legal way to skip probate."

A few days later, my new identity package arrives. Connor tosses me a bulky manila envelope. I open it like a Christmas present. And just like almost every Christmas present I ever got from my financially-limited parents/Santa, I am disappointed.

Disappointed not only with the mug shots on my new passport, driver's license and health card, but in the very essence of my new persona.

Boy, was Glen Johnson ever boring. After a thoroughly undistinguished academic career at York University, ol' Glen had been a pay roll clerk for the last 36 years with Iron Gate, a middlin'-sized insurance broker. Lived in the same apartment for 25 years. Owned a 15-year-old Volvo wagon, insured by the same company he worked for. Been to Cuba once. Upper New York State, but years ago. Never married, no kids.

Jason explains that fewer records need to be altered this way.

But at least he has gone to the effort of duplicating my diabetes meds prescriptions. There's also an ATM card and a Visa which pick me up a bit. Being essentially indigent since San Francisco has not been very uplifting for me.

"What's ol' Glen's Visa limit?"

"Thinking of buying a Lambo, are you?"

"Seriously? A fucking Volvo wagon?"

"Deal with it."

He also cautions me to carry this ID package with me at all times.

"Why?"

"It's just part of the protocols we've instituted, enhanced security procedures designed for detection avoidance or mitigation."

"Cut the bullshit, will ya?" I say.

"Fine . . . Carry it with you because . . . you never know when you'll have to run."

Jason has me rehearse my new story, such as it is. Whenever I stray or start to embellish he comes down hard on me, just like the way the nuns used to crack my knuckles with a steel-edged ruler when I insisted on writing with my left hand. He drills me over and over again until he's satisfied I've got it down.

"OK, Jake, now you're ready for the big bad world. Call your daughter."

I punch in her number using the burner.

"Dad, where are you?" Halley asks. "I've been calling."

"I can't tell you."

"Are you in trouble?"

"Yup. But nothing I can't handle."

"What's going on, dad?"

"What are you, a cop?"

"Cut the bullshit, old man."

"I need to see you, Hal."

We arrange to meet. Even that takes considerable thought. If my house at the lake is being watched, if everything is being tapped and traced, why not the police too?

I tell her that.

"You don't think we might know we're being bugged?" she asks.

"Just in case . . . "

"OK, I'll play along. Where?"

"Fern Hollow. Now don't say anything!"

I had given her the name of a children's picture book series that I used to read to her at the public library near our place. I have always been fond of the gorgeously-illustrated, wise-ass British woodland creatures featured in them.

"In an hour?" I suggest.

"Fine."

"Now, you might be followed. You have to get out of there clean."

"That's not a problem. Squad cars coming and going all the time out of the garage. *They* can't tail them all."

"And pardon the cliché, but come alone."

"Why?"

"Because people will probably die if you don't, that's why!"

She hangs up.

Despite his misgivings, Jason turns over the keys to the company car and I head for the door.

"Forget something, Jake?"

I wheel and sheepishly retrieve my identity package.

"Ah, they grow up so fast," he remarks. "Be careful," he adds, and now he's not joking.

I drive to the Brookbanks library, a pleasant low building serving the 'burbs.

Here I am, this old guy prowling the stacks looking like an unshaven, ball-capped but apparently literate pedophile. I have to admit I'm a little pleased my own daughter doesn't recognize me when I approach her.

"Oh, dad," she says when she knows it's me.

The look of pity on her face breaks my heart.

"Honey, I have to go away for a while," I say. "But I'll be back as soon as I can. I need to tell you some things first. And you have to believe that whatever I tell you is the truth."

I tell her what I think I know about the cyber criminals fucking with my life. To get it on the record, in case . . . in case I don't know what.

I don't begrudge her the disbelief she's registering. As I unspool the story of the last few weeks, *I* almost don't believe what has happened.

She asks me some questions—most of which I can't answer. I can see her queries are not intended to find out more, but rather to point out the absurdity of what I'm telling her, much the same way I do when I'm engaged in my occasional on-line battles with fundamentalist preachers or nutbars claiming the Jews are lying about the Holocaust.

"Dad . . . maybe you should see someone."

"You're right, sweetie. I plan to."

"Promise?"

"I swear."

Suddenly, there doesn't seem to be much else to say.

"The ol' library hasn't changed much, has it?" I ask and we look around. "Some pretty swell memories, huh, kiddo?"

"Do you know, I still have the library card you got me?"

I can see we were both on verge of getting misty-eyed. So, of course, I piss on the moment.

"Hope you don't try to use it today. I think there are a couple of twenty-year overdue books on that card."

Halley instantly composes herself and shuts down her reverie.

"See somebody, dad. Soon. You need help."

And she walks away.

I watch her go, want to call out, to stop her and tell her that I may not see her again for a while, perhaps a long while.

I want to tell her I love her.

But I don't.

I can't stomach the idea of returning to my new and thoroughly depressing home right away. I've got a car, my new identity package, access to untraceable cash, and a get-out-of-hi-tech-jail card. I am tempted to just say "Fuck it" and take off. Out of Toronto, out of Ontario, out of Canada. Pass through the US and down to Mexico, reasoning that there must be a bunch of Pacific coast towns where I could disappear.

I give in to the temptation and start driving, west along the 401 that used to be on the northern border of Toronto and now seems about the middle of it. What's more, solid urban-ness now lines the freeway hugging the eastern tip of Lake Ontario such that, to me, there is no way of telling Oakville, Burlington and Hamilton apart.

It takes me more than two hours to reach Niagara Falls. I approach the Rainbow Bridge to the US and it is only then I come to my senses. The proverbial jig would be up if I got nabbed at Customs with my undocumented car. And then what?

Besides, Newtonian Law has kicked in again and I fully understand that I cannot yet—or perhaps ever—abandon the inertia of my old life, discard the people and places that populate it. As sparse as it may be, it is the only landscape I have.

At the last exit before the border, I turn off, head into town, and park near the larger Canadian version of the Falls. As I walk to the railing at the abyss, I can feel the ground reverberating, am deafened by the billions of gallons of water thunderously plunging into the gorge, disappearing into the ever-present thick clouds of mist.

Alone and with my family, I have visited the Falls many times. And every one of those times, I have had only one over-arching sentiment.

Boy, are we humans ever fuck-all in the face of this kind of nature.

Leaning on the railing today overlooking the frothing abyss, I think that once more. But then I remember the professional daredevils and garden-variety lunatics who have attempted to go over the falls in everything from barrels to big rubber balls to only the clothes on their backs.

Some lived; most died.

But some lived.

And there is no why this is so. Just 'tis. I understand this passes for hope.

I head back to Toronto to arrive just in time for afternoon gridlock. For once, I am possessed by a Buddha-like calm, unconcerned by our collective snail's pace, impervious to honking horns, and almost oblivious to my fellow travellers' universal lack of understanding about the concept behind the Merge sign.

Thank you, Niagara Falls. Thank you, Doris Day.

The trip back to Jason's place takes about the same time as a flight to Miami.

From some distance I see a plume of dark smoke rising over the skyline. A dread washes over me as a drive towards the smoke. Finally at the industrial park, I see my fears confirmed. Jason's end of the plaza has collapsed into a blackened heap.

Firefighters are pouring jets of water on the charred remains. Red trucks and white cop cars and ambulances surround the scene. The responders are milling around but no one is showing much urgency. The fire is out.

"What happened?" I yell at a fireman.

"Don't know yet. A couple of kids. They didn't make it," he says, gesturing towards two shrouded gurneys being loaded into ambulances.

<CHAPTER EIGHT>

A cop has overheard me. He comes over to me, wants to know my interest in fire.

"I saw the smoke," I manage to say. "Just curious. That's all."

I turn and walk away. I wipe the tears off my face lest they bring further attention to me. In that cowardly act, I feel as though I have denied them, somehow betrayed them with my silence.

In the car, I stare blankly out the windshield. Seconds, minutes pass without thought, a great ball of emotion, of emptiness spreading in my chest.

At least Connor wasn't there, I think, but it is small, small consolation.

I have a car that isn't mine. And a now single-minded urge to end this thing—one way or the other. I drive to Pearson airport, scan the departures board, and buy a ticket.

"Glen Johnson" is shitting bricks in the pre-clearance line-up at US Customs. I mean I would've pulled me into an interrogation room, that's how guilty I must look.

But there is no problem at customs, or at the gate check-in after a cursory glance of my passport. I feel almost giddy as I thump down the boarding tunnel. Invisible. That's what I think I've become.

Once on board, the reality of what has happened expands. Two kids, one of whom saved my life, are dead. Two young humans not breathing, not anything. Denied every event, every emotion, every laugh, every connection that a full life would have granted.

How did that fucker Steinman describe it? Life wantonly squandered.

The plane starts its descent, breaks through the clouds and there is the San Francisco Bay area.

I know, I know. It doesn't make a ton o' good sense to return to the place of the first attempt on my life and confront the guy who had ordered the hit, but here's what I think: There is no way in the world I can outrun Steinman if he's putting his considerable mind and resources to rubbing me out. So if I'm fucked anyway, why not get up in his grill and force him to do something? And hopefully in public.

I take the airport shuttle to Los Gatos, sticking out like the sorest of thumbs from my seatmates who are all hip and brash and well-dressed. And very young. Staring at them, I admire their confidence, their certainty that the universe—now starring them—is unfolding exactly as it should. When they're not scrolling through their phones, they have an excited way of talking over each other and the word "like" figures way too prominently.

In return, they look at me with something like pity and/or contempt, as if I'm a confused old rummy on the wrong bus. Which is not too far off the mark.

The time I had invested in being pleasant to the Ulti/ME receptionist on my last visit pays off. She recognizes me and calls.

Once again, it is Steinman himself who comes out. I see the blank look on his face and I am enraged.

"Mr. Lydon, I did not expect to see you here."

"No, I bet you didn't!"

Instantly, he sees I am, shall we say, a bit agitated.

"What is wrong?"

"The dead guy in my living room for starters and now two harmless dead kids in Toronto! Your boots on the ground fucked up big time!"

I can see my loud accusation has caused some concern in the waiting area. If he notices it too, he doesn't show it.

"I have absolutely no idea what you are talking about," he says.

"You killed them! And you tried to kill me!"

I mean, how else would you word it?

"No, I did not," he quietly states. "I might not, as a rule, get along with people but it does not necessarily follow that I want to murder them."

"Well, it looks like you made a few fucking exceptions!"

"Perhaps you might calm down and tell me what I am supposed to have done?"

He isn't being smarmily solicitous in that fake way some people have when they're found out. Nor is he loud with a protesting deny-deny-deny defence that still others will use. He just looks like he wants to correct a mistake, as if it were a typo.

There is only intrigued interest in his eyes and nothing like guilt or malice. I don't claim to be an expert, but his expression is not the look of an unmasked murderer.

I feel just like a fool.

Steinman can see that I've stopped being an excitable boy.

"We have to get going," he says, after glancing at his watch. "Sunset is at 8:22. Tell me more on the way."

"Where are we going?"

"My place. Carmel . . . if that is acceptable to you."

He doesn't wait for an answer and I follow his quick steps as best I can.

I know, I know. It doesn't make a whole lot of sense to accompany a man who I had just then, on the spot, sort of decided isn't trying to kill me.

We stand outside, not saying a word. A black Escalade pulls up to the curb.

"Bit of a rapper cliché, don't you think?" I finally say.

"No. Bit of good old Detroit metal."

We both get in the back. Steinman sinks into the leather.

"Jake, this is Darryl. Darryl, Jake,"

In a coincidence that would make Dickens proud, it turns out I sort of know the chauffer.

"Darryl Korig? Tight end? Oakland Raiders, 1993-94?" I ask.

"94-95. It was the *LA* Raiders," Darryl says. "And I was just a back-up."

"Of course! You gotta tell me: what's Howie—"

My question dangles there as the smoked glass window between us hums closed.

Steinman hasn't touched any buttons that I can see. I realize that I'd let my tendency towards star-fucking get the better of me. Darryl had raised the glass to shut out my question about his famous team-mate during his two-year stint in the NFL, a brief and unremarkable dip into the spotlight. Frankly, I only remember Darryl because he had the longest hair of anyone on the team, in the league really, and I thought that was pretty cool.

I feel like shit for having offended him.

"Hit the window, will you?" I ask Steinman.

"Why?"

"I insulted him."

"So? He can be real touchy sometimes; I'll deal with him."

"Please."

The window slides down.

"Darryl, I'm sorry for pissing you off. You were one of fifty or so people in the whole goddamned country who could play that position in the pros. None of my business, but that's fucking incredible."

" . . . Thanks," he says.

Steinman abruptly closes the window again.

"You don't mind if I take Highway One?" he asks me.

"Prefer it, actually," I say, remembering the spectacular vistas that startled me years ago. "How long's it take?"

"On a good day, an hour and a bit. I actually have to check to see if they're filming yet another car commercial on the 1 so I can avoid it and take the Salinas highway."

"You must lose a lot of time commuting."

"It doesn't really matter whether I'm in the car or my office. I talk to the same number of people. Once you're connected, you're connected."

"But you're different outside the office," I note.

"Different how?"

"You just used seven contractions."

"Fuck, you *do* have Asperger's."

"And you just swore."

For the first hour or so of the drive, I stare out the window while he talks on the phone. Mostly "yes" and "no" answers so it's pretty hard to figure what he's discussing. Finally, he just says "Stop now," and hangs up.

I haven't been listening much anyway. I'm too busy having my gob smacked by the sheer cliffs we skirt, the pounding surf, and the bays and points of land jutting into the sea, canopied by the darkening sky.

His house is on 17 Mile Drive, sandwiched between Cypress Point and Pebble Beach. I had driven this road years earlier with Beth as part of a pilgrimage to the Hog's Breath Inn when Clint owned it and you could order a mighty tasty Sudden Impact sandwich.

I remember being panicked that our rented Sunfire would be stopped and impounded by the Good Taste Police for even daring to be on this stretch of expensive pavement.

Dusk is falling as we pull into a driveway. Before us, massive black gates open, creating a temporary gap in the 12-foot high, rust-coloured concrete walls running for hundreds of yards through the cypress and pine trees and whatever the fuck at the edge of the road.

I'm surprised that the place isn't grander. Don't get me wrong; it's stunning. Post and beam, sort of post-Frank Lloyd Wright. Magnificent grounds shown to full effect by tasteful lighting.

Inside, the house is cavernous, sparsely-populated with minimalist furniture. There is no art on the walls, but a two-story stone fireplace dominates the great room. Across from it, a wall of 30-foot floor-to-ceiling glass overlooks a huge infinity pool that blends into the Pacific in the distance. I have momentarily stopped to admire the view, but Steinman hasn't broken his stride as he continues to and through a sliding door leading to the patio. He moves with the purpose of someone late for his bus.

We walk to the edge of the angel-stone patio and gaze down at the green smudge of the golf course blemished by its white sand traps, all encircled by the deep blue ocean now darkening.

"Play a lot?" I ask.

"I tried it once. Hate it."

"Me too. No patience."

"I play the game like polo without the horse."

"Me too. Do you hang with Clint?"

"He used to live a few doors down. I ran in to him once when I was jogging. Nice guy."

"You saw him once?"

"No. I went jogging once. That's even more boring than golf."

"I like the cut of your jib, sir."

Our chatter is now diminished, cheapened by the panoramic sunset playing out over the Pacific. Just the right amount of clouds purpling up the celestial joint, the fiery oranges, reds and yellows roil over the ocean, under a vast roof of darkly-shaded blues.

We both fall silent as the sun winks out. I feel I should clap. Steinman does.

We turn and go back to the house. Unseen, as in a movie theatre, soft, recessed lighting begins to glow as the sky darkens; the gas fireplace flicks on. Steinman hasn't moved or pressed a button. A single flamenco guitar starts playing.

Out of nowhere, he says: "What if I could change everything?"

"Even the nature of hubris?"

"This, I swear, isn't hubris. It's doable. It's just math. We have to change the math."

"I was never very good at math."

"Look, we spend 1.2 trillion dollars a year on education in America. Almost 3 trillion in health care. When Ulti/ME succeeds in health care, the government could move, I don't know, a trillion, trillion and a half over to education *every* year. Think about that. Hire more teachers, pay them more than the security guards manning the metal detectors at their schools. Cut tuition, forgive student loans. And what if you could do something like that in every country?"

"So you make a lot more poor people a lot smarter."

"Smart people don't stay poor. You bring the skill level way up and good things have to happen."

"Like?"

"First off, people everywhere might stop believing in dumb shit. Not just religions that hobble so many, but all the pointless, trivial things that occupy our minds. Pop quiz: how many PhDs do you think follow the Kardashians' every move?"

"That's going to be real ugly because the old guard isn't going to willingly surrender their power."

"Agreed, but you make them. Pass laws that, say, 75% of health savings have to go to education, otherwise they don't get the technology. And once it starts, it can't be stopped. You can't unring the bell. It won't take longer than a generation, *maybe* two. And when that happens, maybe we stop getting involved in wars about dumb shit and then everybody stops getting involved in wars about dumb shit. So then defence budgets—mainly ours—start plummeting and you've got billions more with which to do some good."

"But war is big business and it keeps a lot of people busy."

"Get 'em busy doing something else! Apply all that brainpower to figuring out other things. Like getting off oil once and for all. That'd be a good thing, right? How about we beat cancer? That'd be a good thing too. Or revolutionize farming so we can feed everybody. Or saving bees or the Great Barrier Reef or making sure everybody gets clean water.

"And apply the muscle power that's pointlessly sitting around in a sand bunker or a jungle or a USO somewhere to building things. Another Hoover Dam or laying cement floors in third-world huts so families don't get sick from living in dirt."

"What about all the kings and presidents for life all over the world, all the military juntas?" I ask. "They'd just grab the extra cash."

"There are lots of ways to bring them down. Most of them not legal, but with the Internet and surveillance technology and everybody on smart phones, it's absolutely easy to broadcast all the bad crap these dictators are doing to their people."

"Pardon my skepticism but I find it real hard to believe that Alistair was the key to all this."

"Not *the* key, but he certainly held a key. That battery system Bio-Watch owns is a real breakthrough. But Alistair was holding out for a better deal; that was as far ahead as he was looking. Don't get me wrong; he is—was—a very smart guy. I did enjoy talking to him."

I imagine *Colossus: the Forbin Project* and those American and Soviet supercomputers yakking back and forth until they decided that it made a whole lot of more sense for them to run the world rather than we pesky humans.

"What about WestCor or anybody else who has the same kind of idea?" I ask.

"This is one of those cases where being first means winning. And there can only be one winner. For the same reason you don't have two different air traffic control systems at an airport. But there's enough money to go around."

"I don't think the Reeds believe that."

"Their mistake. They're on the wrong side of history."

"Isn't this really like Carnegie and Rockefeller?" I ask, recalling the legendary dick-flopping contest about who was richer than whom. Their contest had made life miserable for hundreds of thousands of shittily-treated workers, but it had also created all the stuff that has made life easier for everybody since.

"Apparently, they think so," Steinman says. "But it takes two to play. And I really couldn't give a shit."

"And yet you went after them when Howe joined Concord."

"Robert Howe stole from me."

"The cops didn't think so."

"The cops were wrong."

"Why don't you just buy all the outstanding shares in Concord and shut it down?"

"Whether I—and I presume you—think appearances are irrelevant doesn't much matter right now. There are a lot of people who do care. So how would it look if 40-billion dollar-a-year Ulti/ME tried to crush little bitty Concord? That's not our brand. We have to play nice. I have to play nice."

"That's why you didn't sue Concord; they'd have to discuss it in their SEC filings."

"Yes. And we don't, because it's not considered material. And besides, I know the Reeds engineered the whole thing."

"How?"

"Want something to eat?" he suddenly asks.

What the hell, I think.

"Lobster?" I suggest, expecting him to summon a cook.

"How about Sidekicks?"

"Whatta you got?"

"Cheddar Chipotle."

"OK, now you're just pandering."

"No. I *love* Sidekicks."

"Do you cut wieners into it?"

"Who doesn't?"

So we bang and crash around the designer kitchen for a while and it's pleasant. He gives me shit for cutting the wieners too thin; I hassle him for overcooking the pasta shells.

Back in the living room, we eat in silence, our plates balancing on our knees. After I finish, I get up to go outside for a post-dinner smoke. He stops me, motions that I sit back down, and presses a button on a remote. The slight hum of a powerful overhead exhaust fan starts.

"I got a crate of Cubans from Castro. I fire one up every once in a while."

"I could get used to this," I say, watching my cigarette smoke drift to the fan. "Need a roomie?"

He instantly stiffens up. And just as instantly I know why. I have asked him for something.

"Dude. I'm kidding," I say. "You like living alone. I get that."

"Just Darryl and me. And I never see him until I need him. He lives near the gate. He drives and offers . . . a little protection. He also does most of the gardening."

"Ever tempted to move? I'm betting you can afford it. Or at least be able to float a loan."

"I like it here. It's . . . "

"Splendid isolation?"

"Exactly! You'd be surprised at the number of people who want something from me. Media, inventors with the next big thing, bankers, real estate developers. But this place, it's . . . easily defended."

Steinman goes quiet, turning all wistful.

"Actually, I'm hardly ever here," he says. "I'm hardly anywhere for very long."

"That's a big company you have to run."

"You know what? I'm not in control of anything. And I don't really have all that much useful to do anymore. At some point, you pass from being a creator to just being the maintenance man."

"Like gardening?"

"Sooner or later, you've planted all you can plant."

"But you can't be sure about what's going on with Ulti/ME every minute."

"No, I can't. And yet somehow we're getting to where we want to go."

I thought of Carnegie fucking off to Scotland to let his #1 thug, Frick, handle the Homestead steel mill strike by hiring a private Pinkerton army to whale on the workers. Then I make a note to self: stop being such a dick; this is a good guy.

"So now, all you've got to do is give all your money away," I say.

"Already have. Most of it anyway."

"I hadn't heard."

"No. And with a bit of luck, you won't."

"Why not make a big splash? Embarrass a bunch of other rich guys."

"Do you honestly think a guy who's devoted his whole life to amassing wealth is suddenly going to say "You know what? That Steinman fella's made me feel really bad; I better get rid of my money.""

"Are you having anything that looks like a good time?" I wonder.

"It's all a good time . . . or at least an OK time . . . "

"But not a great time?"

"My party phase lasted about six months in the early days—and even then, it was five months too long. When you can see ahead to the end you reach it quicker. The parties, the women, the drugs, and the flying around to all those glamorous events. Simple fact: nothing's a treat when you can have scampi morning, noon and night.

"As you can see, I've got no entourage, mostly because I don't have any high school friends. And I'll be in litigation with my few college friends for the next decade or so."

"What about a wife, a family?"

"Sounds strange but it's really hard to meet women. And I don't go out much anymore. I don't know. I'm bored. That's what it is. Bored because there's no anticipation, no surprise."

"Always been this way?"

"Mostly. There have been times when I appreciated it. When I started to make a few bucks, I rented a big house on the beach in San Pancho, a little town north of Puerto Vallarta. I could barely afford it and I could barely find enough people to go with me. Oddly, there is a polo field in the town and one Sunday morning I'm having this awesomely great Mexican brunch, pounding back the mimosas, listening to a flamenco duo and watching polo. Warm, sunny day and I'm thinking to myself: Fuck, I wish I was rich! That was the best. Right at that exact moment. It's been pretty much all downhill from there."

For one of the few times since the evening started, our eyes meet.

"What next for you?" he asks.

"Now that I'm almost sure you're not going to kill me?"

"Actually, I haven't quite decided."

Maybe because it's rare, but he has a pretty genuine smile.

"To answer your question," I say, "I really don't know what's next."

"If I were you, I'd be heading to Massachusetts. Concord, to be specific."

"Guessing or do you know it's the Reeds?"

"I know."

"How?"

"Trade secret. I'd have to kill you and then you'd get all pissed off again."

"Boston, it is. Care to help out?"

"I can't get anywhere near that. It'll just look like I'm trying to sabotage a possible competitor and, like I said, my brand would be done. I would be done. You must know that."

"I do."

"But you can take my plane."

"Really? What's that going to set you back?"

"No idea."

"Can I smoke?"

"Why would I possibly care?"

"Call airport," he says to no one and a phone rings somewhere.

"It's me," he says. "How soon can we be wheels up?"

"An hour, sir."

"Make it 45 minutes. Going to Boston. One passenger. Jake Lydon."

I shake my head.

"Glen Johnson," I say.

"Got that? Glen Johnson."

"Yes, sir."

"End call."

A click and he says: "Call Darryl."

A phone rings again.

"Yes, sir?"

"Bring the car around."

"But I was just sitting down to—"

"—Now . . . End call," he says, turning to me. "Glen Johnson?"

"Oh let's call it my nom de plume."

He rises from his chair, his arm extended.

"I think I'm supposed to say good luck but I don't use those words. It's never about luck," he says.

"Some day, after all this is done, I want to sit down with you and prove that it's *all* about luck."

We shake hands, I grab my trusty bowling bag, and leave him sitting in his great room, the flamenco music now grown louder.

Within minutes, the Escalade draws up to the house. Darryl looks a little dishevelled, as if he had dressed in a hurry.

"You mind if I sit up front?" I ask.

He hesitates.

"Why?" he wants to know.

I don't think it will really matter to him if I explain that, for completely unknown reasons, I feel guilty in the back seat while I'm being driven somewhere. Even in a taxi, for god's sake.

"Better view," I say. "And no mention of the Raiders, I swear."

He smiles.

After I compliment him on his gardening, we have a perfectly delightful chat during the short drive to the Monterrey Regional Airport. Mostly about the challenges of the 10a plant hardiness zone. It's obvious that he knows a shitload and just as obvious that he loves the subject.

At curbside, he starts to get out of the car to open my door. I stop him.

His expression changes, getting briefly serious.

"Just so you know: Howie Long is a goddamned prince," he blurts out.

"Thank you, Darryl. I figured as much."

"Have a good flight, he says, but, oddly, he seems saddened to see me go.

I gotta tell you, it's beyond nice to be sitting by myself in leather-wrapped comfort as I cross the United States at 40,000 feet. I also gotta tell you, they've made great strides in private jet comfort since my life on the fringes of the rich twenty years earlier.

But the five-hour flight seems to take a whole lot longer even though this winged baby can honk. You can appreciate beige calfskin and burled wood grain and plush chairs for so long. I learn my limit's about thirty seconds.

My attention turns to where I'm going and what I'm going to do when I get there.

First off, I know I'm a pretty shaky crusader. Basically, all I have to go on is Steinman's say-so that WesCor is the root of this particular evil. Why not a completely different outfit—one in Korea or Krakow or Cleveland? OK, maybe not Cleveland.

I figure my GPS-less phone is pretty safe, so I check my phone messages at home. As per usual, there aren't many. A bunch of calls from Halley. Dr. Don's office calling to set up an appointment; I'm sure I'm not due but, then again, time has been getting away on me lately. Next is yet another robocall happily informing me I'd just won a Caribbean cruise and then this:

"Hawaiian shirt bunny. 416 543-2250."

My hand is shaking as I punch in the Toronto number.

Jason sounds like shit. I want to hug him across the miles.

"How did—" I begin.

"—Dumb luck. When Connor showed up, I went out to get a hair-cut. When I came back, the whole place was burning . . . I just panicked and split . . . I left them in there."

"There was nothing you could've done."

"They were my friends."

"I'm so sorry about Connor and Dylan. I can't possibly tell you how awful I feel."

"You're not the bad guy here."

"I feel like one," I say. "They were after me."

"What are you talking about?"

"It wasn't an accident."

"I realize that. I also know that there's a bunch of people and companies and governments pissed at me."

"It wasn't any of them. It was the same people who . . . who killed your dad."

There is silence.

"Did you hear me, Jason? I know who did this."

Still no response so I plough on. I recount everything I think I'd found out, ending with the obvious conclusion—to Steinman at least—that the Reeds had engineered the whole thing.

"I'm on my way to Boston right now," I say.

"To do what?"

"I don't have a fuckin' clue."

"Good plan."

"Any suggestions for my next move?"

"No idea. I've honestly got nuthin.'"

"C'mon, Jason. What do you always say: you have to think harder?"

"I'm tired, Jake."

"So, why'd you call then? And why'd you call my number at the lake?"

"I forgot the burner number and . . . I wanted to see if you were alright, I guess."

There is a silence.

"I'm done," he finally says.

"Done?"

"Done with everything. Done with fucking computers, with fucking douchebag patrols, with fucking Golden Garden, and all their threats. Everything."

"And instead, do what?"

"I've got enough money; I've got fake IDs."

"The world's your oyster."

"I'm thinkin' Thailand. In any event, somewhere warm."

"You know, I understand that. Any last hints before you go?"

He thinks for a bit.

"With or without me, you aren't going to beat these guys with technology," he says.

We disconnect, perhaps for good. Although I've only known Jason for a couple of months, I suddenly feel a huge void.

Then it hits me. Something Jason has said has connected the dots for me, caused the creaking tumblers in my wee brain to click to a stop.

It is a tiny thing, but it has proven to me beyond a shadow of a doubt that the Reeds are behind this fiasco.

I'm double jet-lagged after crossing the continent again. Unable to sleep on the plane, I'm actually woozy as I rent a car at Logan. Tempting as it is, I pass on the idea of crashing at Alexandra's. It's just after 9 AM Eastern so she'd be at work anyway. And I truly can't stand the thought of involving her if I don't have to.

I figure I need to be looking and feeling my best for the coming confrontation, so I pull off the 93 and into a Denny's parking lot. Despite the advertised two-hour parking limit, nobody bothers me for five straight hours of blissful sleep.

On the drive to Concord, I stop at a Best Buy to get the only thing I could think that might help: a tape recorder, one of those small jobbies that sports reporters jam in athletes' faces while they mostly glower. And electrical tape. It must be a ridiculous sight watching me in the parking lot fuck around with trying to tape the recorder to my shirtless chest.

So girded for battle, I don't have the slightest shred of confidence as I pull up to WesCor. I sit there for a while trying to imagine any other course of action than the one I'm on right now. Nothing comes to me.

All I can think is that, on the whole, I'd rather be in Framingham . . . with Alexandra.

"Show time," I say out loud.

Chock full of fear and outrage, I more or less demand to see one or both of the Reeds. The receptionist at the security post quite understandably regards me as a lunatic.

A glance from her to an armed guard settles me down. As calmly as I can, I explain that I'm working on a secret project for Cortland and I'm sure he would see me.

"Name?"

"Jake Lydon."

"ID?"

I turn over my passport, too late realizing that the Glen Johnson named on it probably won't convince her that I'm Jake Lydon.

"Shit!" I say by way of explanation.

"Mr. Johnson," she reads aloud and eyes the security guard again.

"See? That's how secret the project is!" I blurt out. "Look! Same Hawaiian shirt in the photo!"

But by that time the security guard is on his way towards me.

"Call Gillian!" I say.

The receptionist wavers; the guard relaxes.

"Please!" I add.

She does and they speak for a while.

"Have a seat, Mr. Lydon," she says to me after she hangs up.

Eventually, Gillian comes to retrieve me and, boy, does she look pissed.

"I really need to talk to the Reeds," I say.

"I believe they were very specific about you only dealing with me."

"OK, OK. I've got a bunch of questions maybe you can help me with."

"I prefer e-mail."

"Oh, c'mon! I'm right here. It'll only take a few minutes."

She sighs and relents, gets me all signed-in, badged-up, and metal-detected. When the machine beeps, she has me hand over my car keys. But the Wicked Witch of West doesn't finish her wand waving over me and the tape recorder escapes notice.

"You'll get the keys back when you leave," she tells me.

I follow her as she quickly marches towards what I assume would be her office. I wish I had a pocketful of bread crumbs to mark our path. Down hallways, up an elevator, down another hallway. The lay-out finally starts to look familiar from my last visit. In yer smarter companies, the PR sluts are stabled in or near the executive offices.

As we reach the doorway of her tasteful lair I see, according to the name plate, her last name is Brewster.

"So, do you have millions?"

"What are you talking about?"

"John Candy, Richard Pryor? *Brewster's Millions?* Mid-1980s. Pretty funny movie."

She sighs.

"Mind if I use a bathroom before we start?" I ask.

Another heavy sigh. She may have severe asthma, I think. I'm worried for her.

"Down the hall on the right."

I perform what I think is a pretty serviceable imitation of Steve Martin in *Dirty Rotten Scoundrels.*

"Thaaannnk youuuu."

After a few moments in the can—long enough to have the mirror prove to me that I look like shit—I creep out and then make a beeline for the executive suite. There is a little broken-field jogging around desks and furniture, until I spy Wesley Reed's office, fling open the door, and march in.

Wesley and Cortland are sitting across from each other.

"Welcome, Mr. Lydon," Cortland says, with a little too much warmth for my liking.

"Thank you, Gillian," Wesley says.

I turn to see Gillian behind me. She has a big smile on her face. Her hitherto unseen shit-eating grin really unnerves me. It's like finding out that penguins can do needlepoint.

"We'll take it from here," Cortland says.

"Take what?" I ask.

"We've been expecting you," Wesley says.

"How? Why?"

"We knew you were coming to Boston about a millisecond after Steinman's pilot filed the flight plan."

It dawns on me.

"Darryl?" I ask.

"Darryl."

"Among others."

"How long have you had him in your pocket?" I ask.

"From the moment Steinman hired him."

"As you can guess, we don't play small ball. Steinman popped up on our radar a few years ago as someone worth watching. So we're watching."

"You going to fuck him up?" I ask, all of a sudden protective about my new buddy.

"We won't hurt him, if that's what you mean. We'll probably have to ruin him eventually. But there's no real need yet. He's not doing anything that threatens us besides getting rich."

"But not as rich as us," Cortland feels compelled to add.

"And there's always enough money lying around for people to get rich."

"Now," Cortland says. "Our turn for a question. We need to know what caused you to be so sure that WesCor—that we—are driving this thing."

"Because I know Ulti/ME isn't," I answer.

"That's not terribly precise."

"There are lots of organizations—well, several—who could do this. Why us?" Wesley wants to know.

"What can you expect from a fuckin' Bruins fan?" I say.

"Whatever do you mean, Mr. Lydon?"

"Golden Garden?" I say. "The French word for gold is 'Or'—as in Bobby Orr, and Garden—or rather Ga-den—the Bruins' old arena."

"I told you it was a stupid idea to use that name!" Cortland snaps at Wesley.

Wesley smiles.

"A little decoration. We'll fix it."

"Well done, Mr. Lydon."

"Is Hayward in on all this?" I ask.

"Indirectly. As far as you're concerned, he's the start of all this."

"We were routinely monitoring Alistair since we first became interested in Bio-Watch," says Cortland. "That's when we discovered his conversations with Steinman at Ulti/ME."

"And we knew he had called you. So that set off another little thread. We started looking into you. Again, just routine surveillance."

"But then you found the co-relation between Hayward's lawsuit in Canada and East Anglia's in the States."

Cortland is referring to a tablet device thingy containing, presumably, a summary of my last few weeks.

"Pacer dot gov then canlii dot ca," he reads. "And back again and back again *for hours*. And then you went to our corporate records. Then Bio-Watch's. And then you made the call to that patent lawyer, all in one day and all from your phone and your computer."

"Pretty smart, actually," Wesley says.

"So I gather Hayward's a plant," I say.

"He was welcomed at Ulti/ME like a defecting Cuban shortstop by the Red Sox. We needed him inside to keep an eye on things."

"And to poison the deal if Alistair ever tried to sell to them, not you, by crapping all over the technology," I add.

"Alistair was, we think, going to sell to Steinman because his wife was pushing for it. We couldn't let that happen."

"You know this how?" I ask.

"From Hayward."

"He hasn't been a bundle of useful intelligence, but that fact is important."

"Oh, and he told us you had been to Los Gatos."

"But we knew that already."

"FYI, I predict we'll settle with Hayward next week. It'll cost us a million bucks."

"If I could figure it out," I say, "I'm bettin' others could—like the police. I told them everything."

"By the 'police', you mean your daughter?"

"We don't think she's investigating too diligently," says Wesley. "She seems more preoccupied with your mental health."

"And if she starts being interested . . . well, let's just say that law enforcement is a dangerous profession."

A switch is flipped and I snap.

"You touch her and I'll fucking kill you!" I bellow.

"Mr. Jordan!" a startled Wesley calls out.

The door opens and a very large man with a military-type buzz cut enters and surveys the scene. His presence instantly freezes the tableau. Satisfied, he stands by the doorway, his hands clasped over his crotch as though he's a church usher or a respectful funeral parlor worker which, as I think about it, he kind of is.

With the arrival of thick-necked muscle, my little theoretical discussion with a couple of barking mad geniuses takes a rather sudden turn towards practical menace. I know I'm running out of time and have already run out of any options for escape.

At this point, at this very instant, the only thing I can think of to do is to keep the brothers yakking. Not because I want to buy time while my keen mind devises a MacGyver-type flight scheme, but because, if it's all going to end for me here, I at least want to know what the fuck they're doing and why they're doing it.

"If you guys are so goddamned smart, why didn't you just steal the specs for the Bio-Watch power system instead of fucking around trying to buy the company?" I say to get the ol' conversation ball rolling.

"We tried; believe me, we tried," Wesley answers.

"There's a really smart computer guy amongst those engineers in Toronto. Their systems were impenetrable," Cortland notes.

I had to smile. I knew Jason was good but not this good.

"And no one who actually knew something about the battery system would take a bribe. We tried that too."

"But Alistair had a unit shipped to you, didn't he?"

"Alistair was quite the trickster. We took it apart, discovered he'd sent us a much earlier version with an inferior battery."

"It was still better than ours but not by much. When that idiot Robert Howe asked for the current model, Alistair knew we'd tried to copy it, and the price went through the roof."

"But we were willing to pay it because we needed that power system."

"With all these big league plans why would you even bother with me?" I ask. "You killed a guy to frame me and get me arrested," I say, warily eyeing the well-dressed goon eyeing me.

"That was a bit of bad improvisation," Cortland says. "A back-up plan. We know you're a dinosaur; you even brag about writing longhand in your blog. Once we knew about your digging into us, we had to see what else you had lying around that dump you live in."

"We sent two men to look around. They found all your bits of paper and pads but couldn't make sense of them. So then we had a change in plans."

"Change in plans?" I say. "That's what you call it? You had one guy kill the other, for Christ sakes!"

"Actually, we didn't. Those two contractors of ours didn't get along. They had a dispute. Gunplay ensued, as they say. When one phoned in, he said the other wanted to torch the place just to be sure. We didn't want that, so he had done the right thing."

"Humans," Cortland sighs. "So volatile. So unpredictable."

"But we have to have them," Wesley says. "We actually prefer private contractors rather than employees. They're the way of the future. Imagine: there were 250,000 of them in Iraq and Afghanistan."

"Judging by most of the material you read on-line, you're a student of history," Cortland says.

"Yeah, I guess," I answer.

"One word. Darien."

"What the fuck does Balboa have to do with this?" I ask.

"Later than Balboa."

"You mean the settlement that bankrupted Scotland?"

"That's right." Wesley says. "The English forbid their Caribbean colonies from trading with them. Doomed them. Over three thousand dead. And it brought Scotland to its financial knees."

"Now why do you suppose the English cut them off?" Wesley asks.

"Do you want my answer in the form of a question?" I ask. "OK, Alex. What is the East India Trading Company leaning on the King?" I say.

"Right again."

"Don't you see, Lydon? You need to rise above the moral outrage. We're not doing anything unusual here, nothing that hasn't been done for centuries."

"It's about scale. That's all," Cortland adds.

"But the scale *is* the thing, dipshit," I point out. "You steal a buck from a pile of million dollar bills or you steal 999,999. See any difference?"

They ignore my question.

"By the way, you can give us your tape recorder now," Wesley says.

"What recorder?"

Mr. Jordan leans over to me and rips open one of my favourite goddamned Hawaiian shirts. I remember most of the wooden buttons clattering on the desk. He then tears off the microphone. I wince as most of my few chest hairs go along with the duct tape, rather than remain with the corpse-in-waiting.

"*Of course* we couldn't imagine you would try that."

"Now give us your shirt."

"What?"

"Give us your shirt or Mr. Jordan will take it from you."

Thoroughly puzzled, I undo the couple of remaining buttons and hand it over to Jordan who heads for the door. He opens it and passes the shirt off to someone.

"I could tell you where I bought it," I call after him. "Beach vendor in Puerto Plata. You could get one of your own."

There's something weird about sitting around bare-chested in a swank office. With all the other shit going on, I'm off balance over this peculiar feeling.

"You look like you need a drink," Wesley says.

"Fine idea," I say. "Might as well get something outta this."

"Over there," Cortland says, pointing across the office at a side table in front of the window overlooking the river.

Among the well-stocked bar, I spot a bottle of Cazadores Reposada. I stand there, my back to the Reeds. I am torn between seizing the bottle and seizing the opportunity to take my chances by flinging myself through the window and plunging into the river below.

"Shatter-proof glass," Wesley calls out, making the decision for me.

I sit down with the bottle and a glass. I take my time pouring a healthy shot and then really take my time sipping (as you're goddamned well supposed to!). The Reeds watch my intently but say nothing as I finish what I assume has a very good chance of being my last drink.

"Now, where were we?" I ask.

"You were temporarily smart when you disappeared in San Francisco," Cortland says, staring at his tablet again. "We lost you after you picked up the cash in Chinatown. But then you popped up in North Dakota when we had bet you'd go straight up the West Coast and cross into British Columbia. So we had to scramble a bit."

"Where did you spot me?"

"Fortuna. Through your rather odd newspaper habit."

"But once again, you showed some initiative by changing the obvious crossing point into Canada."

"I'll admit: you're a little bit idiosyncratic."

"Although ultimately you're predictable."

"So it was a little like herding a slightly willful sheep."

"Gee, thanks," I say.

"There's no point now in letting you labour under the illusion that you had much of a say in what happened."

"There's any number of things we could've done. We could've just emptied your bank account. Or we could've magically put you on the no-fly list or we even could've brought down the plane."

"Too bad you never travel with a device. That would've made it a lot easier. Load it with kiddie porn, the plans for the Pentagon, bomb-building instructions, that sort of thing."

"Each one of those actions can be accomplished rather easily on its own. What isn't simple is joining them all together in a kind of instantaneous shadow network. Then managing the details in real-time so that we mesh a variety of systems that every individual touches, as he touches it."

"Like having you pulled out of line at Canadian customs after we first met you."

"Or your blog. Your car in San Jose. The breathalyzers. The bank in Chinatown. Customs in Saskatchewan. Oh, and your liquor store receipts in . . . in Buckhorn. You see how many systems we had to get into?"

"Don't you fuckers have anything better to do?" I ask.

"Right now, no," Wesley says. "We are just putting the finishing touches on what we've been planning for years."

"You see, Alistair and now you are part of the shakedown cruise. One man: brilliant, plugged-in, high profile and the other, disconnected, anonymous. One man dangerous because he's smart. The other—"

"—that would be you—"

"—dangerous because you don't know what you know."

"So bottom line, I'm just a beta test?" I say.

"Pretty much."

"If it's any consolation, you actually put up more of a fight than Alistair did. You taught us quite a bit about accounting for—what did you call it?—the "X" factor."

"How did you kill Alistair?" I ask. "There wasn't enough insulin in the syringe."

Wesley chuckles.

"He was a good test. He is—or was—inordinately intelligent, as you know. We needed to see if he would ignore the way he was actually feeling and believe the machine, and not override it. Over a few weeks, we increased his insulin intake even though he didn't need it. He'd tingle a bit but likely not call a doctor because his monitor attached to the pump said he didn't have to. So his levels were already dangerously high when we instructed the pump to inject two full syringes within three hours. We just made sure that he never received any alarms after that."

"It was a simple matter to alter the paper logs after."

"And it's getting simpler every day because there are fewer and fewer paper records and more and more people completely relying on what a computer screen says."

"How did you fuck with the particular car I rented?"

"The VIN number of that car gets forever tied to you on the day you rented it through your credit card. As soon as the clerk at Alamo logged it in, we knew we had you. That gave us access to the GPS, and, through Bluetooth, to the sensors that control steering, brakes, and acceleration. Not a big deal at all."

"Controlled from Boston, just the way those drones bombing the hell out of suspected terrorists in Yemen are guided from a bunker in Nevada."

"Most people—and that includes you—think locally. So we decided to mess with the car in Steinman's backyard, figuring you'd immediately blame him because he was near to where it happened."

"And you did."

"I could've died in that crash!" I say, pretty darned proud of myself for noting the obvious flaw in their little plan. "Then where would your little experiment be?"

"It would be over," Cortland says simply.

"And we'd find someone else to test."

CHAPTER FOURTEEN

C ome see what else we're working on," Cortland says.

With some strong arming from Mr. Jordan, I am led to a huge room with a forest of colourful monitors. It's a lot like Jason's set-up, only on steroids.

"These are our hunters and gatherers," Wesley says, sweeping his arm over about twenty multi-screen workstations. "Once you have all the data, it's easy to make the little decisions that add up, and then take the actions that on their own don't get noticed."

"Over here," Cortland motions. "See your shrine."

He leads me to a smaller workstation in the corner of the room where two hipster-nerd types are studying a pair of monitors

"Any news of Mr. Lydon?" Wesley asks one of them.

"No, sir. He's still in Toronto. Hasn't moved."

Cortland smacks him across the back of his head.

"Then who the fuck is standing right behind you, idiot?"

"In another room like this, in Raleigh," Wesley says, "we have the doers. They make things happen, code the algorithms, take the actions we tell them to."

"One group never meets the other. No one has the big picture."

"And no one tries to find out?" I ask.

"Some poke around; we shut them down."

Surveying the forty or so droogs watching and clicking away, I couldn't help but notice that the average age of the bunch appeared to me to be about twelve, maybe thirteen. OK, OK, early to mid-twenties.

"They're all just kids!" I say.

"Very, very smart kids," Cortland says.

"But more important than their brains, do you actually think they're concerned about consequences? Look. Watch them. It's a video game to them."

I gaze over the bunch, listen to their low chatter, see the fist pumps, the "We're #1" finger waves, the pantomime mic drops, that erupt from time to time, signifying some big e-stalking dealie. I think I throw up a bit in my mouth.

"Did you know," Cortland asks, "that an air traffic controller is pretty well finished when he starts thinking about the hundreds of human beings encased in a metal tube hurtling through the air five miles from the ground instead of just playing around with a lime green target coming into or leaving his radar screen?"

"Actually, I *did* know that."

"And look at all the good it did you."

"None of these kids care. They're not evil; they just don't care."

"And we pay them enough to care even less."

"Every one of them?" I ask.

"Clever. There will always be loose ends."

I thought of Connor and Dylan in Toronto.

"Loose ends? Those kids in Toronto were loose ends?"

"That, Mr. Lydon, was *your* fault."

"What?!"

"You led us to them."

"After that incident on the bus in . . . in Sault Ste. Marie," Cortland says, again referring to the tablet screen apparently spot-welded to his hand.

"It's Soo Ste. Marie, not *Salt* Saint Marie, ya dumbass!" I say to his mispronunciation.

"Whatever," Cortland says. "We were able to follow you pretty easily."

"How?"

"Ever hear of Bentley Tactics?"

"Your defense contractor?"

"What do you suppose they make?"

"No fuckin' idea. Defense-y things?"

"Drones."

"Once we had you in *Soooooo* Ste. Marie, we followed you down

Highway . . . Highway 11 all the way to that industrial park," Cortland says.

"We had already identified that location as a source of some troublesome hacking. When you showed up there, we just moved them up on our 'to do' list."

"The drone then followed you to that library and for your little jaunt to Niagara Falls. So we knew you were going to be gone for quite some time."

"After that . . . boots on the ground."

I take a swing at Wesley, clip him on the side of the head—a glancing blow as they say—and in return take a solid punch on the jaw from Mr. Jordan that drops me to the floor.

"Restrain him will you?"

Jack Snap, I have those plastic ties cinched tightly around my wrists.

My little altercation has drawn some attention from the junior cyber criminals. Jordan hauls me to my feet and hustles me out of there. I manage to make a double "We're #1" gesture with my index fingers that gets a few whistles and claps.

The brothers do not seem amused as we return to Wesley's office. I can't help but notice the tequila bottle is gone, as we take our seats again.

"Why do you insist on this juvenile behaviour?" Cortland asks, although he seems more rhetorical than interested.

"It keeps me young," I reply. "Fuck off."

Wesley has been staring at me. There's a growing nastiness in his eyes.

"You're not completely stupid," he observes. "Did you not wonder why you always seemed to be out of the room, as it were, when something big happened? Going through your place at Mississauga Lake? The fire in Toronto."

"That's the key element of what we're doing," Cortland says. "Making changes, decisions on the fly."

"Just the way Bobby Orr used to control a game by himself," Wesley adds.

"So, on the fly, you decided to sink your own company?" I ask.

"No. We planned to do that."

"It wasn't just your incompetence? You deliberately murdered those people in the field trials."

"Collateral damage," Cortland says.

"Late stages of the disease," Wesley says. "They were going to die anyway. And rather horribly."

"We had to see if we could actually produce the results we wanted whenever we wanted."

"But we knew Concord would be hit hard once the news got out that the device was apparently faulty."

"The way it looks now—thanks to Ms. Simpson's report—Concord was an idea that just ran its course, couldn't keep up with technology, etcetera, etcetera. And the investors would tear up their racing slips and find another horse to bet on."

"Actually, we did alright by shorting the stock."

"And, of course, with Alistair dead and Mile Coulson on board, we've got the inside track on Bio-Watch again. I predict that Concord will spectacularly rise from the ashes."

"Led by the prodigal Dr. Hayward."

"Any chance I get to buy in early?" I wonder.

"That's a little too much long-term planning for your purposes, I'm afraid," Wesley says.

"So now what?" I ask.

"For you?"

"Yeah, for me."

"Oh, I'm fairly certain you can guess," Wesley says.

<CHAPTER FIFTEEN>

They'll find the rental car and your body miles from here," Cortland says. "Just off the Mass Turnpike heading west to Buffalo and then to Toronto where you were going to drop off the rental."

"And how do we know this, you ask?"

"Because we've already changed your car reservation to say that's what you were going to do."

"The GPS onboard doesn't know who's driving when the drunken crash happened."

"I'm not drunk."

"You will be."

On cue, Mr. Jordan produces a syringe.

I take the tiniest comfort knowing that there had to be a toll booth camera somewhere which the cops would surely check that would undo these bastards.

"And don't think the toll booth camera at the Weston interchange will help," Cortland says, horning in on my thoughts. "We could just crash it for a few minutes but even that's a little too coincidental. Time for some old tech."

"Ah, Mr. Binks, you're back," Wesley says to the man entering his office.

I vaguely recognize him. But then he directs a shadow box right jab at me. It's the son of a bitch who'd thumped me at the Peterborough gym. He smirks again.

Binks takes a rubbery blob from his jacket pocket and pulls the mask over his head. Instantly, he is me.

"Not bad, huh?" says Cortland, indicating my doppelganger.

"We grabbed your photo from that shitty little novel you wrote.

Then imaging to latex. A bit crude but good enough for our own security cameras and the toll booth."

"While we were chatting, Mr. Binks, your rental car, and your Hawaiian shirt have been out for a little spin. Down the 95 and then west on the 90 past the toll booth and the camera there."

"A bit elaborate, all this?"

"You're right," Cortland admits. "We could've just gone old school. Shot you, loaded you into a trunk and dumped you in a marsh somewhere."

"So, really, you should be proud," Wesley says. "You see, you're still part of the experiment."

"We have to get every detail just right. For what we want to do, we have to think of everything."

"The footage will also show "you" leaving this building about forty-five minutes ago."

"In daylight," Cortland adds.

"The video will be on both the toll both camera and our own security footage that we'll happily turn over to police investigating the death of a Canadian . . . "

"A Canadian . . . what?" Cortland asks. "Journalist? Tourist? A nutbar with a false identity threatening us? But who cares what you call yourself? I doubt either our or your authorities will."

"But people saw me arrive here," I point out.

"People who have gone home for the day."

"And then you'll just disappear. The police will find no video of you at the next toll booth. They'll surmise you stopped at the Park and Ride in between to sober up before you went to say good-bye to your new girlfriend in Framingham—"

"—Jesus Christ! You even know about that!"

"Let's see, Visa receipt from the Colonial Tavern, GPS on your car rental," says Cortland studying his goddamned tablet.

"But because you were so drunk," Wesley says, picking up the less-than-fun narrative, "You became disoriented and wound up on that road where they found you."

"That just won't wash with my daughter," I say. "My *cop* daughter."

"Which daughter? Do you mean the one who, judging from the

phone call she made to your doctor, thinks you're a paranoid schizo-phrenic?"

"You shouldn't feel too badly. We've got years and hundreds of millions of dollars invested in this. The wheel can't be stopped now. Certainly not by you."

"And if it isn't us, it'd be somebody else . . . maybe the Chinese or North Koreans or the Russians. If it's any consolation, we actually are going to cripple them. It's starting now. They're smart too, and ruthless about controlling information."

"But, all modesty aside, we're better."

"Actually," Cortland says, "that's what got me—us—thinking about all this. My daughter—she's about the same age as your Halley—found that out when she was teaching in China some years ago. After three days browsing the *New York Times*, she was denied access for a week, maybe ten days. And instantly cut off if she tried to get into the archives."

"Algorithms," Wesley says. "Just algorithms. It's pretty labour-inten-sive, but once they're set up, they work until someone tells them not to."

"Forget armies, forget the mega-rich. The people who will win will be the people who control the algorithms."

"You think we're alone? What's Al Qaeda or ISIS doing? Uploading recruitment videos, all sorts of jihadist rants. The servers are here and in Canada and all over the world. Pull down the website, it switches over to another server and another. It takes minutes, sometimes seconds."

"Meanwhile, they're using smart phones with mobile apps that are more powerful than the computers that put man on the moon."

"They must be stopped," says Cortland. "And they will be stopped."

"That's the kind of scale we're dealing with."

At this point, I'm getting a tad bored with their zealous recitation in stereo.

"I'll admit I'm a pretty shitty copy," I say, "but this is the part where Bond asks the villain why?"

The brothers look at each other, as if to confirm their mutual disbe-lief at the idiocy of my question.

"It's the money, stupid."

"That's it! That's all?" I say.

"Let's set the parameters, shall we? Would I kill you for ten dollars?

Probably not. How about for ten billion?"

"You douches may find this hard to believe but some people still wouldn't do it," I say.

"Sure, there's the big stuff," says Cortland, ignoring me. "As I said, we actually can bring down a plane. We can crash a power grid in the middle of winter. We can launch missiles or destroy the New York Stock Exchange. But we're not interested in chaos. Quite the opposite."

"And we're not so arrogant as to think that the cyber weight of the US government wouldn't catch on within hours or days."

"The trick is to be incremental. A tweak here, a tweak there."

"As you already know, we can disrupt GPS systems. Put up a false map to an ambulance driver. Re-route it so a guy we're interested in doesn't receive the help he needs. Just have his pacemaker go haywire."

"Or an insulin pump."

"Do you have any idea how many WesCor employees—out of about 85,000 in total—depend on those devices?"

"Gee, lots maybe?" I guess.

"And do you know how many of them have insurance policies paid for by us and naming us as co-beneficiaries?"

"All of them?"

"That's right. Standard WesCor employment practice."

"Can I tell you something funny, Mr. Lydon?"

"Christ, I could use a good chuckle right about now."

"The fact is, you were dead right in our first meeting."

"I was? I mean, *of course* I was. Remind me again."

"Our business model is, in fact, dying."

"Any idea what our private subsidiaries generated in the way of sales last year?"

"Nope."

"295 billion dollars."

"And do you know what our total profit is?"

"Nope, again."

"Nothing."

"Zero, Zilch. Nada. Overall, we lost money."

"All the technology we paid billions to develop, spent years researching, it's all just a commodity now. Designs are stolen or copied. Made somewhere else for pennies on the dollar."

"And meanwhile, we're spending obscene amounts on lawyers trying to protect the rights to our own inventions."

"So some time ago, we understood that we needed what you could call alternate revenue streams."

"At first, we became pretty adept at raiding offshore bank havens. We'd trace where the money was coming from and then make some assumptions based on where it was going. If a big wire transfer originated in Tijuana or Moscow or Shanghai going to the Caymans, it's a pretty good bet the owner wouldn't be complaining too loudly to anybody when it went missing."

"You think they can protect all this? You think a bank wants to admit they got ripped off? You think their security company wants to admit they let them get ripped off?"

"Yeah, but if you pricks can do it," I say, "What's stopping someone from doing the same thing to you, just cleaning you out?"

The brothers smiled at each other, identical smug, shit-eating grins of self-satisfaction.

"Shall we, Mr. Reed?"

"Indubitably, Mr. Reed."

"After you."

"No, I insist, after you."

With their somewhat amusing Chip n' Dale routine over, a button is pushed and a beige brick wall rumbles away to reveal a floor-to-ceiling safe.

"Cash is king."

"Or gold."

"Always has been, always will be."

"When is enough enough for you bastards?" I want to know.

Wesley thinks for a while.

"You don't understand, do you?" he says. "It's not exactly the money by itself, but how it flows and to whom."

"Pardon the cliché, but it really *is* a global village. And all we're doing is eliminating the village idiots."

"Besides, ruining a Mexican drug lord or a Russian mobster or religious crazies intent on taking the world back to the 9th century is a good thing, isn't it? Even getting those cheap un-American bastards who won't pay their taxes."

"But you didn't stop there, did you?" I note.

"It didn't take us long to realize that, even though the money was good, we could accomplish a lot more than just robbing thugs, mobsters, and white-collar thieves."

"We turned our attention to a whole new criminal class—all those other parasites who were getting rich by doing absolutely nothing of value."

"Hedge funds, investment houses, all those assholes who believe they're blessed with superior intelligence and an astonishing work ethic and the sense they personally are absolutely entitled to hundreds of millions a year because they put themselves in the middle of deals and push a few buttons. The very same assholes that almost fucked the world in back in 2008."

Ol' Cortland is getting pretty worked up.

"You may not believe this—and we of course don't care whether you do or not—but we actually like the system we have. Unfortunately, it's on the verge of spinning out of control. There's no sense to it. Everybody just grabs as much as they can as fast as they can."

"It's lost its equilibrium. And the government's not going to do anything to regulate it. So we knew we had the capability—"

"—almost the obligation—"

"—to right the ship."

"Gotta Kleenex? I'm getting all misty-eyed at your altruism," I say.

"Like I said, we could not care less if you believe us or not."

"We pick some winners and some losers to help finance our little operation. So a fair trade coffee company makes a killing financing some poor bastards in Ecuador. So exactly what?"

"And so what if we make some money by acting on merger and acquisition info we can get beforehand?

"Ah, the unconscionable conscience of a 1 per center," I say. "The 1 per centers used to be Hell's Angels. It's right there on their patches. But now, it's you rich pricks rigging the game."

"As it turns out, we can rig it better than most."

"No matter who you have to kill?" I ask.

"If you put it like that," Cortland says, with a cold finality, "No matter who we have to kill."

"What Cortland means," Wesley adds, "is that's how important all this is. We can and we will make lives better for lots of people whether they know it or not. When all this is up and fully operational, we can do things like prevent a 1929-type crash or the 2008 meltdown. We can avoid bloodshed that populist uprisings around the world would cause. Put terrorists out of business. And on and on. There's just too much at stake."

"And meanwhile you get to jerk yourselves off with money and power," I say.

"Spare me the egalitarian crap, will you? There is a thin layer on top, always has been, always will be, and then this massive amount of humans below who go through life completely powerless and unaware."

"And expendable," Cortland adds.

"Hark ye the big lower layer," I say.

"What?"

"Just fuckin' around with a line from *Billy Budd*," I say. "Written by a guy named Melville, used to live around here. You might've heard of him."

"Surely you must understand," says Wesley, "that we simply can't let you or anyone like you upset the . . . the . . . "

" . . . natural order of things," Cortland concludes.

"And surely, you must understand," I counter, "That you guys are completely and utterly batshit crazy."

"Time's up, Mr. Lydon," Cortland announces, glancing at his cheap watch. "You are becoming tiresome."

"I get that a lot. But, hey, just so's we're clear here: you guys are starting to bore the piss out of me."

"Mr. Binks will escort you. Mr. Jordan will follow."

"Say good night, Jake."

Binks leads me out, pushes me into a windowless meeting room that feels like a meat locker. The air conditioning is blasting away.

"Seriously?" I ask. "You really need to freeze my nuts off first?"

He smirks, just as he had in the Peterborough gym.

"Time of death. We need a cooler body," he says, as he straps me to a chair that's anchored to a marble conference table. "See you in an hour or so."

The door slams and I'm alone, shivering in the dark.

They had, I realize, covered all their bases, dotted all their proverbial "I's, crossed their "T's. Everything I could think of, every option gone, every possibility shut down. And this from the guy who believes—until the final buzzer—that the Leafs can overcome a 3-0 deficit.

I've felt this way just once before in my life. The day Beth died, the day it hit me that hope had vanished. In its place, nothing but a vacuum, nothing but a wave of powerlessness and a kind of inertia that felt like my chest had been filled with concrete.

Here I am, playing in one game, focused on that, thinking *that* was the big deal. But in hard cold reality, it was just a minor play on a massive field in an utterly different sport from the one the Reeds had suited up for.

My involvement has been insignificant.

And now about to end.

My final contribution, the only thing I could think to do is rub my wrists against the hard edges of my plastic cuffs. Over and over again, until my flesh turns raw. Maybe it would be noticed by some cop at the crash site who'd say "Lucy, joo got some 'splainin' to do."

Maybe.

<**CHAPTER SIXTEEN**>

I'm inching towards hypothermia when Binks and Jordan retrieve me from cold storage. Shivering like a son of a bitch makes forcing me back into my shirt a little complicated but they manage.

They walk/carry me out a fire exit to my car rental in a darkened laneway. I'm installed behind the wheel where I sit listening to the sound of what I assume is an empty tequila bottle being tossed on the floor in the backseat and a bit of conversation between my escorts.

"Gimme fifteen minutes," Binks tells Jordan. "Boss says your car can't be anywhere near us."

It's pretty weird talking to myself sitting beside me as I drive. Maybe it's just for shits and giggles, but Binks has donned his mask of me. He's a real fucking psycho comedian, that boy.

Binks' right hand is held crosswise across his stomach, the gun pointed at me, as we leave the compound.

"No screwing around, no speeding, no cops or I'll kill you right now," he warns, as he hands me the keys.

"You'll die too," I point out.

"I *might* die," he says, wiggling his gun. "You will for sure. Like those odds?"

I drive on into the night, heading south on the 95 for a while then, as directed, west but not on the 90. We are in darkness, the road hemmed in by tall, dark pine or spruce or whatever the fuck. No oncoming traffic, no lights in the rear-view mirror.

I'm still shivering, but at least I'm a little more comfortable after they returned my shirt.

"I'm betting there's a north-south interstate coming up," I say. "Hang a right and in a few more hours, we'll be in Canada. I'll buy ya a *real* beer.

Whaddya say?"

"You're getting off well before that. Ever been to the Assabet River Wildlife Refuge?"

"Can't say as I have."

"It's real pretty. Although this time of night, it's not much of a tourist attraction," he says with a chuckle.

"What happens when we get there?" I ask, almost amused that right to the end I hate surprises.

"We stop, I stick you, you pass out real quick, I get out, call the boss man and the techies take over the car. Didja know this baby can get up to a sixty in no time?" he says, patting the dashboard.

Minutes pass in silence. It just doesn't feel like a time for idle chit-chat, until Binks speaks.

"You're a pretty funny guy, you know," he says.

"How so?"

"You had a few good lines back there with the Reeds."

"Thanks."

"Also, and this kills me—"

"—given that you're going to kill me—"

"See? That's a pretty good line too. Anyway, I find it funny that you bothered to do your seat belt up."

"What can I tell you? I'm Canadian. We buckle up."

We pass the occasional house on the curvy road. I get the feeling that, despite the bends in the road, we're generally heading west.

"Mind if I smoke?" I ask.

"Yes, I do. I'm trying to quit."

"Good for you, but c'mon, buddy. Guy in front of a firing squad and all that?"

He grunts what I take to be agreement but I'm already reaching over to the centre of the dashboard.

"Shit! Nobody puts lighters in cars anymore!" I complain. "You got a light?"

With his free hand, he reaches for his breast pocket the way he likely had a thousand times before when asked the question all smokers are asked. Instinctively.

That's when I punch him in the side of his head as hard as I possibly can. A right-handed jab, full arm extension that slams his head into the side window.

At that instant, a bunch of things happen: the gun goes off, there's a burning sensation in my gut, I wrench the wheel, first right onto the gravel shoulder then left, the car skids off the road and plunges sideways down a very steep ditch, rolling once before slamming into a tree on the passenger side.

And I don't give a fuck.

I had guessed right; the unbuckled Mr. Binks hasn't counted on a suicide move. What's the line? "Live fast die young and leave a good-looking corpse." At the very worst, they could say I lived a slow life, died in late middle-age, and left a messy corpse, with a bullet hole in either the car or me that the cops had to investigate. That might start the ball rolling.

And, at best, I might actually survive.

This all sounds deliberate but, of course, it isn't really. Maybe somewhere in the recesses of my wee brain is the reaction I always have when I'd watch a movie or TV show where the bad guys improbably get the good guys to dig their own graves. I know my last act on earth is never going to be unnecessary physical exertion.

I'm banged around a bit. But, judging from the blood oozing out of his head and the absence of anything resembling voluntary motion, ol' Binky is banged around a lot. The car is on fire as I quickly bale. I actually try to pull him out but the intense heat keeps me away. My last look at the wreck is through the passenger window at the latex mask of me shrivelling up.

The bullet has ploughed through my beer-assisted paunch. It hurts like hell.

"Just a flesh wound" I think, as I consider my blind dumb luck—like there's any other kind.

Mr. Jordan in the trailing car is bound to come along soon so, rather than climb back up to the roadway, I stumble further into the thick underbrush without a fucking clue where I'm going. The flaming wreck would eventually attract good Samaritans and rubber-neckers with cell phones and the cops, so Jordan probably isn't going to be sticking around the scene.

My bet: he would check out the wreck, see I'd fucked off, and decide, out of a strong sense of either fear or company loyalty, to finish the job.

But first, he has to find me. And I'm fine with that. Gun or no gun, let him try. I have a good head start. And thanks to Carl and our drunken night ops, I have a pretty high level of comfort in the bush at night.

For the first time in a long time, I'm starting to like my odds.

In the darkness, a familiar feeling washes over me. This is wilderness that I know. Black. Not like movie woods at night backlit by a bluish light from a dubious source. Here in this blackness, I just know what direction I'm going in and how to keep a straight line as I grope and stumble away from the crash scene.

Maybe twenty minutes pass and the sounds of what I take to be Mr. Jordan thrashing around in the brush grow fainter. As my breathing finally slows, the miraculous adrenalin rush that told me to both fight and flee is ebbing. Various bruises compete with each other for my brain's attention. My hand is wet and warm from the surprising amount of blood seeping through one of my best goddamned buttonless Hawaiian shirts.

I emerge from the forest to find myself in the back yard of a modest bungalow. The automatic yard lights come on as I cross the dew-slick lawn. I hope that someone is home and that that someone is a light sleeper.

My knees buckle and I collapse on the deck, with the distant sound of sirens trying to keep me conscious.

The sirens lose. I black out. My last thought as night falls in my brain is something of a question. OK, two questions.

Will I wake up to see the sun pasted in the sky like a red wafer?

Will I wake up at all?

I come to with the distinct feeling of floating.

Goddamn it! What a piss-off to have been so wrong!

There *is* an afterlife! And I'm being borne towards it. Quite loudly, may I add and with no idea if harps or heat await me.

It takes a few more seconds to realize that rather than celestial transport, I'm inside a helicopter, strapped to a gurney. The medic sitting beside me is trying to comfort me while explaining just what the fuck is going on. Apparently, all the blood soaking through one of my best goddamned buttonless Hawaiian shirts had convinced the local GP roused to tend me that my condition was beyond his skills. He'd patched me up, doped me up, and called for a medivac chopper to airlift me to Boston.

I wander in and out of consciousness, faintly aware of the bright lights, big city, then our bumpy touchdown, followed by Mr. Toad's wild gurney ride into the ER of Boston General.

While my belly is being sewn up, the doctor attempts to reassure me by pointing out that, despite all the blood, I'm lucky the bullet has passed through mostly fat.

I've got nothing broken, just a wanging headache—of the sort I'm quite familiar with—along with the standard-issue bruises, aches and stiffness such accidents tend to produce.

A cop sitting outside my door all night, oh and some heavy-duty pain killers combine to give me the best sleep I've had in a while.

I suppose I could call some people back in Canada but nobody, except Jason, even knows where I am. And I figure Jason has somehow already found out what's gone on.

So why bother anybody else just yet?

I spend the next morning watching TV, reading papers and very much enjoying breakfast in bed even though the bed is metal not mahogany and the runny eggs arrive on a sectioned piece of plastic.

Although Glen Johnson's traffic mishap doesn't rate much of a media story, the arrest of the Reed brothers creates quite the sensation, even if every story—print or electronic—is devoid of anything resembling a true fact.

The cop assigned to me is a sweetheart as he quizzes me. Actually, Detective Pulaski tells me more than I tell him. I want to think the raving declarations that I had spouted during the ambulance ride about the Reeds' murderous plans for me had convinced the authorities to go after them but, according to Pulaski, they found more persuasive evidence to act on.

Turns out, it didn't take long for the police to figure out that the scene was no simple traffic accident. First, the bullet hole in the door kinda tipped them off, as did the melted remains of Mr. Binks and his death mask. Then they found the armed Mr. Jordan wandering around in the bush at about the same time the paramedics and cops were collecting my unconscious ass from the back deck of the startled homeowner who had phoned it in.

Most compelling were the immediate and lengthy statements from Mr. Jordan, who had conclusively proved—once again—that one ought to consider the human character.

Apparently, my police buddy says, Jordan claimed that as part of a personal services contract with the Reeds, he'd been promised a million bucks to shut the fuck up if he was ever arrested. Just as apparently, Jordan had correctly guessed that he wouldn't have much opportunity to spend his bonus during a thirty-year stretch in prison. So he spilled in the hopes of some clemency.

His true confessions convinced the cops to go after the brothers grim who, it turns out, didn't have much of an exit strategy. I suppose they had become so accustomed to getting away with shit for years that they laboured under the illusion they were safe and protected and above it all. They were picked up "without incident" at a private airfield where they had attempted to bribe their pilot not to file a flight plan to Asuncion, Paraguay. Amongst their luggage, Pulaski tells me, were two duffel bags crammed with cash and bonds.

Detective Pulaski tells me I'm not getting out of Dodge anytime soon as the authorities have all the time and incentive in the world to listen to the tale I've only hinted at. They offer to put me up at the Westin Copley Place. I accept. I love that hotel.

My only condition: that they keep me out of it for as long as they can hold off the media hounds. They agree.

Mercifully, my counterfeit credit card bestows upon the equally fake Glen Johnson enough insurance coverage to handle the $17,450.63 hospital bill.

For a moment, I'm reluctant to turn the card over, understanding that someone somewhere could find where I am and what I had been up to as soon as I use it. Then I realize that I'm not Glen Johnson, even though everybody in Boston, of course, keeps calling me by that name.

I am at a loss as to how and when I should unmask myself, especially now that I'm surrounded by cops. I can't imagine just blurting out: "Oh, by the way, guys. I'm a complete fraud. Did I forget to mention that? My bad."

It gets a little more absurd when Detective Pulaski tells me that I'm being checked into the Copley under a pseudonym. Charles Chelsea.

Know-it-all fucktard that I am, I can't resist pointing out that my fake hotel guest name—after two rivers running through Boston—would be pretty easy to hack if someone really wanted to find me.

"That's the problem with most aliases," I add.

Maybe it's just my imagination but this smartass observation gives hitherto sweet-dispositioned Pulaski a pause. A little later, he excuses himself, tells me he'll be back in the morning. He also tells me that they can't allow any phone calls in or out, which is fine by me.

As enchanting as it is, the 12th story view of Back Bay at night does not prevent me from wondering if the ol' jig is up.

<CHAPTER NINETEEN>

The next morning, Pulaski is back to his cheery self as he knocks and enters my room, just as I'm about to tear into some delicious-looking eggs Benedict from room service.

"Glen Johnson!" he booms, as if he's just found a dear old friend. "Glenny! Glen Fiddich! The Glenster! Mind if I call you Glenny-poops?!"

"No, not at all," I say, waiting for a big fucking shoe to drop.

"How about Jake Mitchell Lydon? How about I call you that?" he asks, turning all serious and pissed.

"I was going to tell you. I swear. How did—"

"—The RCMP was real co-operative," he says. "Did you know they've digitized all their old fingerprint files—even the ones dating back to when you were a teenager assaulting people?"

"Those records were supposed to be expunged!"

"Really? Seriously? That's all you've got to say about the shitstorm you're facing?"

"What shitstorm?" I innocently ask.

"Fraud. Illegal entry for openers. I'm betting there is a boatload of more charges the feds, state and local police can come up with."

"So what happens now?"

"You call a lawyer."

I stare out the window for a bit, then down at my congealing hollandaise sauce.

"I've got another idea," I say. "Why don't I save the phone call and tell you what any lawyer would tell me."

"Which is . . . ?"

"That I should shut the fuck up now."

It's his turn to think.

"Or?" he asks.

"Or you drop all the charges, get me immunity for everything, fix it with Canada too, and I'll give you a story that will make you a crime-fighting legend."

"Just so we're real clear here: the publicity matters squat to me."

"Fine. But I bet you getting at the truth, the whole truth and nothing but, so help you god, does matter to you."

"Gimme a hint."

"What do you have the Reed brothers on?" I ask.

"Attempted murder, lots of unexplained cash, FAA violations."

"I'll see you that, and raise you at least seven actual murders, massive stock fraud, corporate espionage, cyber theft of maybe billions, international money laundering."

I get my assurances jack snap and I spend the next several days yakking away to an appreciative audience made up of federal and local cops from two countries.

My anonymity isn't going to last forever; the waters had been chummed and the press needed some answers and, sooner not later, at least one of the fourth or fifth estate brethren and sistern would piece the thing together as they investigate the curious case of the Reed brothers.

I do manage to keep Jason out of it. He is invisible and wants to stay that way. It's the least I could do, given the tragedy I had brought down on him and his friends.

But, sure enough, just as Jason had predicted a while ago, ol' computer-generated Glen gets unmasked fairly soon.

Word had leaked out that a guy from Toronto named Glen Johnson was being interrogated about the Reed brothers by senior cops from two countries. That led to a bit of in-person human inquiry by a *National Post* reporter who eventually found the Iron Gate Insurance company in Toronto. Yes, according to their records, they apparently had an employee by that name but, no, not a soul could recall knowing him. I see Steve's been on the job as he has sleuthed out Glen's bogus landlord at the home address listed on his employment form and also established that Glen's student number at York University was fake.

That touches off another round of media speculation, this about the identity of the Mystery Canuck. Within a half a day, that little riddle is solved as a "usually reliable source in law enforcement speaking on the condition of anonymity" drops my real name to the *Boston Globe*. Hours later, it's all out there, including attempted interviews with Halley and Steve who both aren't talking. I can picture Steve's anger at becoming part of the story instead of the story teller.

The media does get to Carl. There he is on CNN and Fox—courtesy of CHEX Peterborough—being his usual laconic self, offering up the same answer to a range of questions about me.

"Not surprised by any of this," he says, looking straight into the camera. "That guy is such an arsehole."

Even though they bleep it out, it's obvious what he's said. And I laugh out loud for the first time in a long time.

I feel a little ashamed that Glen/me gets a shitload of credit in the media for being clever and resourceful when Jason had been the master puppeteer.

Besides escorting me outside for a street-level smoke, the authorities give me an hour a day on the Internet and another hour to make calls.

I call Halley.

"See. I'm not crazy after all," I say.

"This actually doesn't prove it, dad."

"You little witch!"

She offers to come down and escort me back. I'm touched but I decline. I also say no to Steve's kind offer to drive to Boston and pick me up. Like I need to be yelled at by either of them for ten hours or so.

Alexandra comes to see me which is sweet. I show her the embroidery work on my Buddha belly. How could I not? Guys always think chicks dig scars. Of course, guys are wrong. She is pained. While she dons a brave smile, there are tears in her eyes as she kisses me. So I mist up too.

That's my last strong memory of Boston. A bittersweet one, but with the hope of turning into something, I don't know what.

Halley is at the airport. Although neither of us is all that prone to physical affection with each other, we damn near crush ourselves. We are surrounded by reporters and film crews whose papers and stations couldn't afford to send them to Boston. That makes it kinda awkward. But Halley has scared up several uniformed troops and the big lads form a pretty impressive blue wall.

"Welcome home, you fucking moron," says Steve, once he gets inside the cop enclosure.

Steve volunteers his place as a hide-out. We are actually tailed by a couple of TV vans and other such media vehicles all the way downtown from the airport.

"Dude, I've got my own fuckin' paparazzi!"

Steve's doorman/security guy earns every penny he makes fending off all the people who want to talk to either Steve or me.

"Where's Kendra?" I ask when we're finally up in his condo.

"Things didn't work out. We just have different priorities, you know, different perspectives on life."

"In other words, she dumped your aging ass."

"Like a wet bag of sand."

"Gee, that's a shame. Especially with you about to sign a book deal."

"What book deal?" he asks.

As perhaps has been glaringly evident, I've done—and continue to do—a lot of stupid things in my life. But ducking all the interview requests and passing on the offers for book rights and movie deals isn't one of them. Whatever exclusive I had, I give to Steve, telling him he might be able to make something of himself. A handshake and an understanding that he would give me whatever he thought is fair are good enough for me.

I trust the guy.

He is grateful; that much is obvious. Also plain to see, his brain is already on the job, starting to form the thing in his mind.

Ever the skeptic, he asks: "I get to write this the way I want to?"

"Completely. As long as you get the facts right, which, in itself, will be something new for you."

"What about the book we were working on?"

"Instead of this story? In the words of John McEnroe: "You cannot be serious!" On one hand, piss-on-a-plate boring technology. On the other, bullets and careening cars and mega-villains. Fuck, even I'm looking forward to reading it. Plus, the tech shitstorm will still be a shitstorm a year from now. Probably worse. So how's about we get this out of the way first?"

My first night back in Canada is not a restful one. I know there's a chess game about to start between us and that scares the hell out of me. In the past, my favourite move had always been left knee to corner of board when I realized I had failed to look ahead and was about to be mated.

The upcoming days or weeks being interviewed by my friend would be tricky. I have determined that he doesn't—and in fact nobody—needs to know about Josh Steinman's less than legal business espionage. I really am not one of those relativist ends-justifies-the-means-type of guys, but Ulti/ME's grand plans to refocus the world actually have a shot at succeeding. Linking Steinman to dirty tricks would not help those plans.

Time to construct a crisis communications scenario.

I knew I could do nothing to stop the discovery of my/Glen Johnson's flight to Boston from Monterrey aboard Steinman's jet. How'd that happen? To explain that to Steve I'd have to talk about my second trip to San Francisco. Simple, I decide. Because nobody—that's Steve and my own daughter, for Christ's sake—believed me in the first place, I went to confront him and cleared him.

And that got me to Boston how?

Why, I mentioned my plan to go to Boston to him and, coincidentally, Steinman said he was sending his plane there to pick up a mystery big wig from an unnamed country. Unnamed because it's proprietary info which is why nobody was listed on a passenger manifest for the return trip. Sorry, FAA, I'll pay the fine.

So what happens if and when they interview the pilot about his passengers?

That's easy.

Both Steinman and I will be so fucked.

CHAPTER TWENTY-ONE

A pparently, it took them about a day and a half to read all the charges in the Boston courtroom. I don't know; I'm not there. But I imagine the legal team the Reeds could, for the moment, afford. I picture ten, maybe fifteen of them, conferring in serious whispers, acting like they're actually doing something. For some reason, I recall what happens when you flip one of those black spiny sea urchins onto its spikes. Out of aquatic nowhere, there's this tiny frenzy of little fish descending on the animal to get while the getting's good inside.

But, from the Reeds' perspective, their school of legal fishies is worth at least some of the millions they were doubtless being paid as it looks like there might be some kind of plea deal. Which would be swell because then I wouldn't have to go back to testify. I just can't imagine what that deal might be. 98 years instead of 128?

Then, for completely indecipherable reasons, I remember that all four states mentioned in Alex's report on the Concord Medical fatalities have the death penalty. The brothers must be angling to not die at the hands of the state(s).

I hope they lose, but I know I don't need anything like closure. What I need is to stick my head in a bucket of Dominican beer.

Unravelling the mess the Reed brothers have made will take years and be filled with billions of dollars of lawsuits and fines, millions of words of speculation, reporting, and investigation. Unwinding all the "tweaks" they had administered to various systems, stocks, and lives will take a legion of forensic techies and accountants and cops. And after all that, Canada would want a crack at them.

But then it will fade, as every big story since the beginning of time has faded. Probably more quickly now because the public these days doesn't forget so much as want to be distracted by another feast of calamity and intrigue. A lot like teenagers grazing interminably with the fridge door open.

After a couple of days at Steve's, we reckon the coast is clear and I skedaddle, retrieving my trusty Vibe from the parking lot, where, surprise, surprise, it shows no signs of molestation.

Odd to say the least to be back—finally—at my hovel by the lake. I realize why it seems strange to be on a laneway I've driven up hundreds of times. I'm alone.

The mid-September sun is just setting. As it sinks, the sun is nibbling at the tree line across the lake that has gone to full glitter, broken only by the black, mini-Viking ship silhouettes of a pair of loons bob-bob-bobbing in the bay. From time to time, they let out a piercing, thrilling laugh (or a cry, depending on your mood).

I let the near-silence wash over me. It takes me about thirty seconds to get used to it. Ah, wilderness.

But then Carl comes by. He's obviously been spying on me, because he shows up, casually wielding a case of twenty-four Ex. He asks if "Mr. Big Shot" would consider a pint or two. I am overjoyed to see him and he seems marginally pleased to see me which is about as excited as he ever gets.

Over the course of the evening, he doesn't ask one single question about how Mr. Big Shot spent his summer vacation. I love him for that.

I congratulate him on being media savvy in front of the cameras.

"Momma always said: just tell the truth. Arsehole."

We have a lot of catching up to do—mostly about the NFL season opener two weeks away. He has the schedule pretty well memorized and I don't, which should have put me at a distinct disadvantage. But because I never let facts get in the way of a good argument, I am pretty vocal as usual about the obvious truth that the Niners have the toughest slog to Super Bowl. And as usual, Carl thinks I'm full of shit.

He leaves and I finally can sleep in my own bed, comforted and thrilled by the loons whooping it up on the lake 'til all hours.

The next morning, a little fuzzy of mind, I fire up my shitty computer and watch in amazement as my In-box starts piling up all my new e-mails in bold. And scores more in my Junk folder. Most of them offer to do my story "justice" in books, movies, TV interviews.

I read a few all the way through and confess to having visions of sugar plum fairies loaded with dough.

But then I give my head a shake and start deleting.

And I buy an airline ticket to Las Terrenas.

My plan—as if anything I had ever done followed a plan—is to spend the remaining six weeks before my southern migration fixing the place up, busying myself with cutting and pruning and weeding and watering in monastic silence and industry, punctuated by drinking and shooting-the-shit sessions with Carl.

Of course it doesn't work out that way.

For one thing, reporters and such turn up at the place from time to time. I hire Carl's Rent-a-Cops because when Carl, shotgun in hand, shoos you, you stay shoo-ed.

Early one evening—having finished up a pretty exhausting day as a yard ape—I plunk myself and a beer down—sweating and grimy—in an Adirondack chair on the deck. I hear a voice behind me.

Quick mental note to self: reprimand Carl for being drunk on the job again.

"Geez," the voice says, "why didn't you look like that when you escaped San Francisco? Nobody would have recognized you."

"Jason!"

Despite my damp filth, we hug.

"I thought you had pulled a Gauguin," I say.

"I will."

"Well, grab a beer, grab a chair!"

We sit in silence for a bit as the sun plunges into the thick forest across the lake gone once more to full glitter.

"Are you really going to unplug?" I ask.

"We'll see. I understand Fiji has pretty solid Internet. And a man's gotta eat."

"Straight and narrow, son?" I ask, aware that I have no real moral high ground to stand on and that I'm sounding more like *Uncle Buck* than *Father Knows Best*.

"Yup."

"Swear?"

"Swear. My talents might be appreciated by some of the outfits I broke into. I mean, mathematically, do you really think that out of seven billion people on the planet, the Reeds were the only two who tried to fuck things up? Maybe not as ambitious as the Reeds, but there's a lot of douchebags out there. I know; I used to be one."

"You realize there's a book coming out?"

"Yes."

"You know I probably have to drop a dime on you?"

"I'm surprised it hasn't come out yet. Thanks for that."

"A lot of people are going to be looking for you."

"Know that too. Let 'em look. Jason MacNeil is gone. I'm Donald Blair full-time now. Promise me that name will stay between us?"

"Promise."

"And give me a couple of week's head start before you tell anyone?"

"Of course."

It bothered me not a bit to hide from Steve or anyone else the fact that the son of a wealthy murder victim had played the crucial role in breaking the even-wealthier Reeds. Oh, and he had saved my life in the bargain.

"You square with your mom?" I ask.

"Yup. We talked. She sounded happy. And busy. The timing of my disappearance works out well. She and my sisters are moving to California. By the way, she sends her best."

"Jason . . . are you still freaked about being watched? You could've e-mailed a note."

"Naw . . . I just wanted to say good-bye."

I wish him well and offer up my address in the Dominican if he ever needs shelter from the storm.

"It's OK; I already have it," he says smiling as he starts up his motorbike.

"Stay in touch if you can, Ja . . . Donald. Or can I call you Don? How about Donny? Maybe Dandy Don?"

"Don't push it, Jake. Donald's fine, thank you."

The whine of Jason's bike had just subsided as I sit down at my laptop. There is a message in my In-Box, entitled "Things work out."

It isn't a generous offer to supersize my sausage or a kind invitation to help retrieve several million dollars from a Nairobi bank.

It's a note from Josh Steinman.

Not exactly a long letter, it simply reads: "*Dear Sidekick, Glad things worked out. I knew they would. J.S.*"

Fuckin' guy always has to be right, I think.

<CHAPTER TWENTY-TWO>

Halley spends a couple of days at the hovel which is a real treat for me. And for Carl. I even meet her one Draconian condition: no Sidekicks. She insists on cooking and cleaning and I let her and am grateful. Over shoe boxes full of pictures of her, Beth and me cavorting in or by the lake, we laugh and cry and laugh about it all again. That was a highlight.

So too is the second week of October, when Alexandra shows up and stays for a week which if I'm keeping score—and I always do— is the best consecutive seven days of my year. Our lovemaking is absolutely swell, as are our incessant arguments over her inexplicable defence of Jane Austen. And Christ, that woman is handy with an ax, splitting dried maple for a fire to ward off the fall chill coming on when we sit outside all bundled up to stare at the sunset.

Carl doesn't seem to mind her presence—actually appears to like her—as the three of us watch an NFL Sunday doubleheader on my ridiculously large TV. She cements the deal with him by leading a cogent discussion on the faddishness of the Read Option.

At her nagging, I even go canoeing which, actually, turns out to be fun after we figure out how to get into a paddling rhythm instead of thrashing around in tipsy circles.

From the lake, the walls of autumn maples separating the cottages and houses are on fire, looking for all the world as though they were plunging into the water to be extinguished while the pine and spruce and whatever the fuck sprinkled among them stand steadfast and green.

Hackneyed maybe, but parting really is sweet sorrow. In that swawvee manner of mine, I suggest she ought to check out the sustainability of the little known rice farms in north-eastern Dominican Republic.

She says she'll look into it and I am thrilled.

I have sworn to myself that I'll keep away from following the Reed brothers' case or anything to do with technology for that matter. And as with every other vow I'd ever made—sobriety, quitting smoking, weight loss—I break it, mainly because Steve arrives with an outline and a couple of early chapters.

I dig up a red pen and have a ball. Actually, it's pretty good, at least as far as characterization goes. Ever the objective reporter, Steve has taken great pains to depict me as a paunchy, dissipated, right place/right time, alcoholic misanthrope on his downside.

In other words, he nails it.

To his credit, Steve pretends to be sensitive about my reaction to his portrayal of me. And, of course, I pretend to not let him off the hook.

"I *had* been thinking Bruce Willis for the movie. You made me look more like Wilford Brimley's evil twin on a bender."

"Wilford Brimley's evil twin? Mind if I use that?"

"Fuck off, Steve."

But really, who *specifically* would give a good goddamn about how I came off? I know I don't.

I cringe a bit when I read the parts where he just doesn't have the facts I do.

It is mostly pleasant having Steve around for a couple of days. Mostly.

First, there is the matter of, oh, let's call it lifestyle differences. He takes one look at the contents of my fridge and cupboards, and flees in horror to the nearest health food store in Peterborough. I tell him if he returns with kale and/or quinoa, he's sleeping on the deck.

Second, there's his predictable but tiresome barrage of picayune questions, many having to do with my escape from San Francisco back to Toronto. How did I get the money to buy the car? What colour was the Vibe I bought? What was the weather like? What was the name of the bar in Fortuna? How about the librarian there? Did she wear glasses? Did they have those chains around them? Why did I head to Estevan instead of going straight north? How big was the gunman on the bus? Are you sure about the date he got busted because I'm going to check? And on and on.

One night, he looks up from the pile of paper in front of him.

"No offence intended, Jake—OK, *some* offence intended—but there isn't a way in the fucking world you could've done all this by yourself."

"Well, that hurts."

"The fake ID, the travelling around, where you stayed when you got back to Toronto, how you had money. It just doesn't sound right. Give."

Here I have to dance, finally admitting that an anonymous hacker had "handled" me for some of the events.

"Who?"

"What did I just say? He's anonymous, goddamnit!"

"So it's a 'he'?"

"I don't know; odds are it's a 'he' because . . . most of hackers are, and because *it* knew that a Stanford Cardinals hat would be rare in Saskatchewan!"

At this point, I'm being all fake-indignant and he can see it.

"I don't buy it, Jake," he says getting all serious and quiet. "You're lying to me."

Springing to mind is a good line from the woefully underappreciated *Tequila Sunrise*. Gun drawn, cop Kurt Russell has his old buddy and reformed drug dealer Mel Gibson cornered on a dock, the water around them ablaze from an ignited oil spill. "I caught you," the Russell character says. "You can't pretend you're not caught."

"Look, Steve. I'm sorry. I really am. But I made a promise."

"Didn't we make a promise to trust each other?"

"Yeah, we did. So promise to trust me for a week. I'll tell you everything then. Swear."

"Alright," he says grudgingly.

"Oh and by the by, I'm fucking off this coming Monday."

"What? I can't finish in three days!"

"Like that's my problem."

"You've got a lot of gaps to fill in."

"They have phones in the DR. Internet, too."

"It's not the same!"

"Look, bud, you can take a train or bus or drive to Miami and then maybe catch some tramp steamer or you could drug yourself and close your eyes for a piddly little four and half hour flight. But me? I got a plane to catch."

Of course, I'm being selfish. And of course, I don't much care. I'm just not going to be loitering around with a central Canadian winter coming on.

I know it goes beyond the approaching shitty weather. Ever the introvert, I have come down with recurring, possibly terminal people-sickness, the human equivalent of store-sickness—which I also suffer from.

Steve gets the hint and leaves, reckoning correctly that he's not getting much more out of me. He tells me to expect a blizzard of questions waiting for me when I get to where I'm going.

I'll deal with them later. Right now, I just want to disappear.

I've done it before.

Late October is the saddest part of the year up here, Excepting for a few tenacious stragglers, all the leaves have dropped off, carpeting the forest floor around their grey trees with a burnt and rotting rust colour. The cold drizzle and dark clouds pervade. There is—to me anyway—a sense of imminent departure, of escape.

Everybody's getting out.

The hummingbirds go first. Those little bastards, besides being endlessly fascinating to watch, impressed the hell out of me when I learned that they winter in the Gulf States. They can flap their tiny wings about 30 times *a second* and can travel 35 miles an hour. So, if one of them's headed to Biloxi from around my place, he can cover the 1,400 miles—assuming it's a non-stop straight shot—in 40 hours, having flapped his little wings about 4,320,000 times, give or take. The way I figure it.

The loons are next. I seem to feel their going most keenly for the lake falls quiet and I'm starkly aware of the silence when I'm lying awake at night listening for them.

And then the geese. In the evenings, flocks of them will arrive to spend the night at my lake. You watch them gliding in, the sun low enough to light up their white bellies. A flurry of splashes and they set down for their proscribed pit stop before rising as one in the morning, almost with an audible whoosh, to continue their ancient circuit.

I picture my plane heading south to Las Terrenas passing over them at 35,000 feet as they make for the Gulf of Mexico where, I imagine, they gleefully spend their winters damaging Canadian-American relations by shitting all over their once-tidy golf courses.

Over three days and nights, Carl and I close up the cottage for the winter in glorious fashion, even polishing off a bottle of cacao whose origin completely mystifies both of us.

Our ritual finished, I am southbound, a little fuzzy-headed and keen to be wandering the empty beaches and sometimes chaotic streets of Las Terrenas.

It's good to see green again as the plane circles over the Samana Peninsula and begins its descent.

The familiar blast of hot air stepping off the plane is the best welcome I can imagine. As I always do, I tell the cabbie to take the old, tortuously-twisted road through Sanchez and up the peninsula's camel-back mountains separating Samana Bay from Las Terrenas on the north shore. Nothing like free-wheeling down a winding steep grade into the beach town to get the ol' juices flowing. I always save the trip along the newer and quite spectacular seaside highway for my return to the airport. One last glorious look back.

The little low-rise condo complex I live in is a heart-warming spectacle. Near the point between two half moon bays—Playas Las Ballenas and Popy—Casa del Mar is lush, meticulously-maintained, and has a huge back-up generator to make up for the town's notoriously vague electricity supply. It also has a great pool and an even greater outdoor bar beside it.

As he routinely does every time he spots me approaching, Alejandro—the world's best bartender™—is already making my large Tanqueray and tonic as I cross the grounds along the cobblestone walkway which winds among the tall, swan-necked palms.

"*Bienvenida de nuevo, Senor Yake!*" he says, as he pushes the chilled tumbler across the counter.

How can anyone's heart not be gladdened by that heat, that drink and by the smiling, ridiculously pleasant man who serves it?

We shoot *la mierda* in our Spanglish about what I have missed over the summer—a couple of bad storms but no hurricanes, another new police chief who apparently is cleaning things up, some protests over the lack of consistent "*luz.*"

He asks me what I had been up to.

"*Nada,*" I say.

I really do want be done with the whole affair so I can return to my indolent lifestyle.

But, yet again, things don't immediately turn out that way.

The first order of business—well, technically, the fourth order of business (after more gin, a slow stroll on a magnificent beach topped off by sharing some coldly-sweating Presidentes at Mojito's Beach Bar with a couple of renewed warm-weather acquaintances)—is helping Steve with his book.

I'm now officially on island time; he is not. The big publishing house that won the auction for the book rights has imposed pretty harsh deadlines for getting the thing onto store shelves before everyone forgets about it. I imagine the rush for topicality has only quickened. Consequently, Steve's is all pushy about getting the pages of his questions answered. Particularly that one question about the identity of my web-based guardian angel.

Figuring that Jason is now as gone as he is ever going to be, I write Steve, telling of Jason MacNeil's role.

I try to picture his face as he reads my revelation. Gobsmacked would have to be pretty close.

The phone rings minutes after I send the e-mail.

"Are you kidding me? Are you fucking kidding me?" he shouts.

"I shit you not."

"How do I get a hold of him?"

"You don't."

"C'mon now."

"You don't get him," I insist.

"But I need him."

"No you don't; ya got me. And, anyway, you'll never find him. I can't. Use some imagination, will ya? Write it like he's a presence out there in cyberspace, just waiting to do something else big. I don't know, call him the Web Avenger."

He grudgingly accepts the situation and I grudgingly return to answering his long list of questions.

Going back and forth by e-mail is ridiculously inefficient, almost as inefficient as the phones. So I just send him my address followed by three initials—AZS—figuring he'd sleuth out that it's the code for El Catey International Airport near Las Terrenas.

Two days later, a little shaky from his trip, he is on my sunny doorstep.

He spends three weeks in Las Terrenas, during which time I try to introduce him to the concepts of adjectives and adverbs as he beavers away on the final draft.

I succeed somewhat with juicing up his writing style but am unable to convince him to start drinking again—and he is unable to convince me to stop—as he piles up the last of his hundred thousand or so words.

Re-living the whole thing is not particularly pleasant. People I knew and people I'd never met had died and for what? Greed, arrogance, entitlement. Hubris.

"You sure you don't want in on this?" Steve asks.

"Positive. Fill yer boots."

"I thought that's what you'd say. So here."

He produces a bank draft and I try to whistle when I read it.

Two hundred thousand dollars. US.

"Ten per cent of the advance," he notes. "And for doing fuck-all really. I gave the same to my agent but she had to work for it."

While I'm thanking him, I try to figure out what that kind of dough translates to in my Dominican beer currency account. I am humbled as I imagine the Great Wall of Presidente cases it represents. But then this fire truck comes screaming into my mind, smashing through the beer palisade. That's where the coin is going, I decide. A used pumper and equipment of the sort that might've saved *Pueblo des Pescadores*, the collection of wooden beachfront fishermen's shanties-turned-restaurants that burned to the sand a few years ago.

This may sound like an uncharacteristically decent thing to do. But there is some enlightened self-interest: I've been known to doze off with a lit cigarette from time to time.

"There's gonna be more from where that came," Steve says. "Netflix deal for a limited series is almost done. Although, sadly, I hear Brimley passed on it."

One morning while Steve is inexplicably doing something called jogging on the beach, I perform my morning sweep of news sites. I find several short articles about how Ulti/ME has acquired the remnants of Concord Medical Systems at fire-sale prices.

Steve returns all sweaty and healthy-looking and I break the news to him that he still has some writing to do.

"Shit!"

"Do I have to drive you every inch of the fucking way?" I ask. "Just make it a one-page postscript. It ties the whole thing up. Ulti/ME picking over Concord's corpse. I'll even do the goddamned research for you, ya big baby."

He wraps it all up in a day and half.

"I want to watch you hit 'send'," I say.

"Can't," he tells me. "Publisher's rules. Hand-delivery only."

He holds up a flash drive.

"Download this onto your lap top as a back-up," he tells me.

"Yay! I don't have to buy the goddamned thing."

"I gotta head back now," he says and there's something depressingly final in his voice.

Despite his mostly clean living, I know I will miss him.

"Seeing how the great silver bird didn't plunge into the ocean coming down here, you might visit again?"

"Ya know, I just might. I'm going to be busy for a while, getting the book ready and then pimping it out. I may even be doing the screenplay. Maybe this time next year."

"Hell, with the filthy lucre you're going to pull in on my back, you could even buy down here."

"Ya know, I just might."

With Steve gone, I can finally and completely unhook. Up north, when I'm not doing yard work, I spend waaaay too much time on the computer, because, well, I just have to find out what's going on, don't I?

Everywhere.

All the time.

As if it mattered.

At all.

In the DR, my torrent of news gathering slows to a trickle. In its stead, I confess to walking a lot more, eating less crap food, playing some tennis, and actually having friends—largely a motley crew of similarly dissipated ex-pats and locals, a regular drunken UN of Americans, Canadians, Dominicans, Swedes, Brits, French, Italians and Germans.

This international gathering would, I believe, like to teach the world to sing, but we forgot the goddamned words. In varying numbers, we convene almost nightly at Big Dave's or, for a change of scenery, Mojito's on the beach.

Our conversations are uniformly warm, insulting, and raucous.

I fill the rest of my time reading real live books, working on my Spanish, teaching some ESL classes at the community centre, and staring blankly at the ocean.

I can honestly say I enjoy every sandwich.

Closet narcissist that I am, I Google me and, amid all the news articles about the Reed case, I find some new reviews for my old novel, mostly positive. So I check in with my publisher. My Account is still active. It informs me that, for a while, sales of the e-book had suddenly picked up—until they just as quickly plummeted. I'm guessing that's because younger e-readers would say it was old-fashioned and boring. But still, over 900 downloads. Enough to buy some books for the community centre and a round of drinks at Big Dave's.

More to my point, it touches off a familiar itch to get writing again. I don't know what I'm going to scribble about, just that the act of it was bound to be a little more productive than, thanks to my beer-drinking, literally pissing away my time.

<CHAPTER TWENTY-FOUR>

A week after Steve leaves, I see that Ulti/ME is once again, in the news. They are paying a shitload for Bio-Watch of Toronto, Canada. The *Globe & Mail* doesn't actually describe the purchase price as a shitload, but you can tell they wanted to.

I have to smile at the headline. "Windfall for Bio Watch." I'm glad Mike has made one last big score and sad but semi-amused for Steve because he couldn't ignore this development and its effect on his project which is fast becoming The Book That Would Not Die.

Chair and CEO Sarah MacNeil did the announcing on their website. This surprises me. Not that long ago, she had been pretty clear about staying away from the business.

She is quoted as saying that "the merger has ideally positioned Bio-Watch for significant growth."

I have to smile again because someone has supplied her with the timeless bullshit PR phrases for business writing that I used to use. Fact: a small company being swallowed by a big one is not a "merger"; it's "your ass is mine" time. Fact: no one on the planet knows what ideally-positioned means and in the history of the self-same planet, no company ever has been.

I switch over to Ulti/ME's website. They see things a little differently. Bio-Watch is going to be absorbed into the new Wellness Division of Ulti/ME. The group is to be co-managed by Sarah MacNeil and Dr. Nigel Hayward.

I wanna say all's wellness that ends wellness, but I just can't as I contemplate the real merger Sarah is happy to be announcing.

Her and Nigel.

Sonofabitch!

It hits me when I recall Sarah's off-hand statement a while back that she was considering moving to California with her daughters. Why California?

"For a change of scenery," she had told me.

Maybe the same kind of scenery change, say, Nigel Hayward must've experienced showing up for no apparent reason in Toronto to be at Alistair's funeral?

For no apparent reason—other than to comfort the Widow MacNeil.

Stupid. Stupid. Stupid, I think. How did I miss that? How did everybody miss that? There it was, firmly planted in the as-plain-as-the-nose-on-your-face category.

I think of Jason who knew exactly what was going on with those two. He had the opportunity to tell me of Hayward's affair with his mother but didn't, even though it would've maybe helped me decipher some things a little earlier. In this age of unthinking and shameless disclosure, I have to admire him for that. He had determined—as he was used to determining—who deserved attention and who did not. Two people in love, he had decided, should be allowed to be two people in love. They might have their intrigues and failures. They might even self-destruct but they would—and should—do so in anonymity.

At the same time, this little revelation has me questioning my alleged talent for figuring out motive. I hate it when I doubt myself, even though there's example after example of why I should do exactly that.

What else did I miss?

Even though the bad guys are in jail and, in some measure, the good guys have money or love or freedom, what else has eluded me?

I spend a good part of the day replaying my less than excellent summer and the people who entered or re-entered my life.

I use Steve's manuscript as a road map. Aside from a few reporter-type embellishments, he has stuck to the facts or—more accurately—what I told him the facts were.

Nothing jumps out at me.

Except one statement. And this has nothing to do with Steve's story. While I read those news items about Ulti/ME, something is bugging me. It's just all too neat. Everything is too neat. The whole escapade had been a giant spaghetti bowl of loose ends. How could it all be tied up?

Above all: how could Josh Steinman, as he claimed in his last e-mail, "really know things would work out"? He couldn't. He knew a lot of things but he couldn't possibly *know* that the situation with me and the Reeds would resolve itself with me remaining above the sod and them in handcuffs. More likely, that part didn't matter to him; because he was sure that, one way or another, the Reeds were going down. I happened to be the blunt instrument at hand.

I dig through my e-mails, write to J.S.

You used me! I type.

Phone#? he writes back.

I e-mail the number and he calls right away.

"Be precise, Jake. I benefitted from something you were going to do anyway," are the first words out of his mouth.

"But I could've died!"

"With or without me."

"Well, did you know that Nigel was working for the Reeds right up to the end?"

"Yes. That was the plan. He was working for me, shall we say, a lot more closely."

"A double agent?"

"You could call him that."

"How long?"

"I met him—through Alistair—when he was at Bio-Watch. When the company stalled—mostly because of Alistair's stubbornness—Nigel and I decided it would be a good idea for him to find employment with the Reeds because, money-wise, WesCor had the inside track."

"Unless he convinced the Reeds that Bio Watch was all smoke and mirrors," I added, "which I'm bettin' he could do, because if the inventor of something says it's a piece of crap, people tend to listen."

"Yes. But also, and you know this about him, Alistair wouldn't deal with someone he thought had tried to fuck him."

"So then why'd you hire him?"

"Time had passed and I think I was able to rehabilitate Nigel in Alistair's eyes. Plus his own wife was pleading Ulti/ME's case. And, I think most persuasively, I could prove that in six short months, with a massive development effort that neither he nor the Reeds could match,

Hayward had produced a new kind of device that far exceeded anything Bio-Watch or Concord had. So all Alistair really owned was the battery system."

"And he'd be smart enough to recognize that. Just a matter of time."

"Yes. The long game is the thing, Jake. Not what's right in front of you but some point in the distance where you want to go. It takes time, but not a lot of time to unfold."

"And so Hayward was how you knew for sure that your ex-guy stole your plans."

"Yup. Robert Howe was quite pleased with himself for screwing me over; when he got to WesCor, he had bragged to Nigel and anyone else who'd listen."

"And Howe was the reason you just bought what's left of Concord. So you could fire him."

"*That* was fun."

"And Hayward was Alexandra's source about the failed field trials?"

"On his way out WesCor's door. Yes."

"Please tell me Alexandra isn't involved in this."

"She isn't. Hayward's eminently coachable. With that British accent and a flair for drama, he's quite good at dropping persuasive hints. Alexandra believed she had conned tidbits out of him."

"And through Sarah, Hayward was also your way into Bio-Watch."

"I didn't put him up to it, if that's what you're thinking. Their affair was years old. And quite real, I understand. What did you call it? The "X" factor. I merely became aware of it and then, once again, benefitted."

"You know they're both going to quit, don't you? They're filthy rich."

"Yes. That's fine. They've played their part."

"Like I did?"

" . . . Yes."

"So you had all the angles covered."

"All of them."

"And you benefitted how with Darryl?"

There is a pause.

"What?" he asks.

"You didn't know the Reeds had Darryl, did you?"

Another pause.

"Josh?"

"No."

"I don't think he hurt you and, anyway, it doesn't matter anymore, does it? Be kinder to him or pay him a little more. Or both."

"He betrayed me."

"Un-betray him. Do it as a favor to me, will ya?"

"Now why would I do that?"

"Welllll . . . for starters, we could let a judge and the media decide if your corporate espionage was nicer that what the Reeds pulled."

"You'd do that? You'd threaten all this over a chauffer's job?"

It was my turn to pause.

"You know what?" I answered. "Fuckin' right I would!"

There's yet another silence.

Then, for the first time, I hear Steinman laughing.

"Deal!" he finally says. "We good?"

"I presume by 'good', you mean eternally silent."

"I do."

"And you'll cover up my free flight to Boston?"

"Already done."

"And we both keep quiet about Nigel and Sarah too?"

"Yes."

"I gotta think about all this."

There is a pause.

"Don't take too long," he says turning all serious; then he hangs up.

What the fuck have I just done? In a nutshell, I've pissed off a multi-billionaire with grand designs and billions more at stake and the technical know-how to make my life either exceedingly unpleasant or short.

And for what? I have to deal with yet another quandary bordering on a moral dilemma. Would I really put a dent in Steinman's laudable global plans over Darryl's job? Am I going to refuse to tell Steve—he on the verge of publication—that I can tie up some loose ends—Nigel, Sarah, and Steinman—and by doing so, blow everything up, including his apparently definitive book?

There's only one thing to do.

Down to the bar I go.

There's a slight breeze blowing in off the ocean. The dry palapa-leaf roof rustles above me. The sky is achingly blue. The white cement around the pool dazzles.

With instant warmth and the minimum of conversation, Alejandro fills my order for a T & T with a beer chaser. He looks concerned and I know why: I usually order one or the other. Such is the evidence the world's best bartender™ works on. I know he knows something's up; it's in our eyes. I can't or won't explain because I've got some think-think-thinking to do.

It's not just Steinman I have to worry about. The Reeds could try to out Nigel as a corporate spy. But being convicted supercriminals and all, it's unlikely anybody would believe them or pursue it. And all Nigel had to do was claim any money he got from them after he left Concord was their settlement of his lawsuit.

Wesley and/or Cortland could also make a case for the authorities going after Ulti/ME for Steinman's shenanigans but, again, even though they'd be right, I can't see anyone charging off to investigate. And if they did, well, my money's on Steinman to cover his tracks. And if they come back on me, how was I supposed to know? Prove that I did.

Everybody else has tons of good reasons to shut the fuck up.

Everybody except me. Although personally, I had no upside to yakking away beyond the satisfaction of knowing that the whole truth would be out there and letting the proverbial chips fall where they may.

But, that's not exactly accurate, is it? I wasn't turning in Jason—or rather Donald Blair—no matter what. That goes to my grave.

So, really, Jake, what's the big deal about keeping a few more secrets? Precisely who benefits from you opening your gaping, slack-jawed pie-hole?

"*Lo siento, senor* Yake," Alejandro says, showing his obvious concern for that which apparently troubles me. "Maybe you go walk, jes? *Playa es muy bien* today."

Alejandro is right of course, although it didn't require much meteorological analysis on his part; the beach is lovely every day, even rainy ones.

Today it's sunny and hot and I start shedding as I stand staring at the huge, sandy crescent bay and its fringe of tall palms. Flip-flops come off first and it's good to feel the warm, sugary sand on my feet, then my

T-shirt with the bright Hawaiian floral print.

It's early December and the main flock of snowbirds hasn't arrived yet. The beach is almost deserted. Well-fed strays play doggie games in the sand, some local Bautistas-in-the-making have a ragged baseball game going on, and there are a few expats striding the strand. Europeans, I guess, for the men are uniformly slim, old, burnt to a dark mahogany colour, and wear Speedo banana hammocks for bathing suits.

I'm over-dressed in sturdy khaki shorts outfitted with at least thirty clever pockets all Velcro-ed shut. As I walk, I can feel a lump in one. I tear it open and find a cell phone, the last burner Jason had given me.

I've got—or I used to have—a pretty good arm. Near as I can count, I get seven skips out of the phone before it skids to a stop in the turquoise water about forty yards from shore. It floats on the surface for a little while then sinks from sight, perhaps to do some good by being the start of a mini-reef.

No more to say, nothing to do, I decide, beyond writing Steinman to tell him that, yes, we be good.

And just like that, I am unattached again.

Well, *almost* unattached.

PART THREE

THE VERY, VERY
NEAR FUTURE

Flightaware.com tells me Alexandra's plane arrives in forty-seven minutes.

<Acknowledgements>

I am grateful to a bunch of people for conspiring with me to produce this thing:

Glenn Torresan (who's still pissed at me for burning down his Hangar 13 studio in the book) for the cover artwork and photography;

Ron Corbett, a buddy and a budding publishing magnate, in addition to being a swell writer;

Sarah Brown for her warm heart for the manuscript and cold, cold eye in editing it;

Magdalene Carson at New leaf Publication Design for her nifty layout;

Stephen J. McGill, my old, old pal who allegedly read the very first draft and whose encouragement right from the get-go kept me at it;

And, as ever, Maggie.

Every mistake in the book is someone else's fault.

<About the Author>

John Owens is the author of two works of historical fiction: *On the Rails*, a cross-Canada Great Depression-era saga and *The Sixth String*, the story of a flamenco guitarist caught up in Hitler's Germany.

He lives with his wife, Maggie, in Morrisburg, Ontario, on the banks of the St. Lawrence River, and Indian Rocks Beach, Florida.

He has not seen snow for many years. But he remembers.